Cthulhu's Heirs

Chaosium Fiction

KING OF SARTAR
CASTLE OF EYES
THE HASTUR CYCLE
ROBERT BLOCH'S MYSTERIES OF THE WORM
CTHULHU'S HEIRS

in preparation

THE SHUB-NIGGURATH CYCLE

CALL OF CTHULHU® FICTION

Cthulhu's Heirs

TALES OF THE MYTHOS FOR THE NEW MILLENNIUM

DF Lewis
Hugh B. Cave
Arthur William Lloyd Breach
t. Winter-Damon
Ramsey Campbell
Robert M. Price
Joe Murphy
Darrell Schweitzer
Jason Van Hollander
Victor Milán
Gregory Nicoll
Charles M. Saplak
Gordon Linzner
David Niall Wilson
Dan Perez
Scott David Aniolowski
Craig Anthony
Crispin Burnham
Cary G. Osborne
Daniel M. Burrello
Michael D. Winkle
Marella Sands

Selected and Edited by Thomas M.K. Stratman
Chapter Decorations by Dreyfus

Chaosium Inc.
1994

D E D I C A T I O N

This anthology is dedicated to Howard Phillips Lovecraft,
for the worlds that he created in tales and the lives he affected in reality.
We humbly thank the Old Man of Providence.

Copyright© 1994 by Thomas M. K. Stratman; all rights reserved.

This edition published by arrangement with Chaosium Inc.

The Franklyn Paragraphs, copyright 1973,1993 by Ramsey Campbell.
From **Cold Print (Complete Edition)**. Reprinted by permission of
the author.

The Death Watch, copyright 1939, by Weird Tales, for **Weird Tales**,
June/July 1939. Reprinted by permission of the author.

The reproduction of material from within this book for the purpose of
personal or corporate profit, by photographic, electronic, or other
methods of retrievel and dissemination is prohibited.

CONTENTS

The Nameless Manuscript

It is a narrow though essential branch of human expression, and will chiefly appeal as always to a limited audience with keen special sensibilities. Whatever universal masterpiece of tomorrow may be wrought from phantasm or terror will owe its acceptance rather to a supreme workmanship than to a sympathetic theme. Yet who shall declare the dark theme a positive handicap? Radiant with beauty, the Cup of the Ptolemies was carven of onyx.

— Howard Phillips Lovecraft, 1890-1937,
"Supernatural Horror in Literature."

WHAT YOU NOW HOLD in your hands was a labor of love. That may appear to be an inappropriate term, when used in conjunction with a horror anthology, but it is the truth. If it were possible to look into the hearts and minds of the many diverse people involved in this project, something truly special would be seen. For they came together primarily to pay homage to one man, which is the ultimate purpose of this anthology.

Every writer who submitted work to this collection endured delays, rewrites, minimum advances, and in most cases (for there were over 120 submissions), the final rejection of his or her efforts. Those people who wrote to me from all over America, England, Canada, the Caribbean Islands, and Australia are ample proof of why I believe Howard Phillips Lovecraft is still a very important part of the genre of supernatural horror and literature in general.

It is well known that H. P. Lovecraft created the fictional mythology of outer beings which we call the 'Cthulhu Mythos', or the 'Yog-Sothoth Myth Cycle'. Tales like "Dagon", "Beyond the Wall of Sleep" and "The Statement of Randolph Carter" have been exciting imaginations since the very first decades of the Twentieth Century. Works such as "The Rats in the Wall", "The Call of Cthulhu" and "The Dunwich Horror" are still recognized by a generation of readers brought up on video games and slasher/gore films. There is no doubt that his works exceeded the norms of stylistic ability and popular duration of most other writers of his

era. The examples are numerous, but my point is this: the creations of
Lovecraft did not die with Lovecraft, nor were they limited only to him
while he lived.

Lovecraft openly encouraged other writers to use and add to his
creations. Writers such as T.E.D. Klein, Robert E. Howard, Stephen
King, August Derleth, J. Ramsey Campbell, Robert Bloch, Clark
Ashton Smith, Hugh B. Cave, David Drake, E. Hoffmann Price, Hazel
Heald, Brian Lumley, Zealia Bishop (I had better stop before I am
accused of leaving someone out) ...at one time or another added their
talents to what is often referred to as 'Lovecraftian' horror. Some added
more than others, but that is not for me to debate in this introduction.
It was through many of these people that H. P. Lovecraft's example of
cooperation among writers continued outward after his death in 1937.

Think of this book as a window and as you throw open the curtains
you shall find more than twenty writers' visions into the landscape of
Lovecraft Country. Through the glass of this window you can witness
areas of hidden truths and places best left unimagined. You can view
that which cannot be described and perhaps glimpse the unnameable
reality of it all.

Or perhaps you will simply enjoy a good read.

The stories within this book span and extend beyond the entire
history of the published 'Mythos'. Craig Anthony presents an old
creation in a new format, that of a scene from a script; while Scott
David Aniolowski introduces a new Mythos entity. Arthur William
Lloyd Breach takes us back to the North Point Light, while Crispin
Burnham leads us to new Mythos lands under Kansas soil and Daniel
M. Burrello brings some 'thing' directly to your own home.

Great masters such as Ramsey Campbell and Hugh B. Cave have
generously added tales of their own creation to this project. Mr.
Campbell's "The Franklyn Paragraphs" has, according to his own
words, only seen limited publication in his own collection Cold Print
(Complete Edition) and Mr. Cave's "The Death Watch" has not been
printed in over fifty years. They are rare and welcome additions to this
diverse work.

Newer voices such as DF Lewis, who shows the Great Old Ones
from a different view in a decidedly different reality and established
names like Gordon Linzner, with his insight into one of Pickman's
paintings, also brought their admired talents to this project. Different
times are also witnessed within this anthology, from Victor Milán's tale
of modern terrorists and dark futures, to Joe Murphy writing of three

inhabitants from the summer of love. Gregory Nicoll and Cary G. Osborne take us from an old cemetery encounter to a fiction convention encounter.

Dan Perez introduces a new medium for the Great Old Ones to pass into reality and Robert M. Price gives a new twist to an older avenue of contact. Marella Sands warns of new gates through new technologies while Charles M. Saplak writes of the dangers in an old written work.

Darrell Schweitzer and Jason Van Hollander show new dimensions and resolutions to an established Mythos problem in their cooperative work and David Niall Wilson gives us a new communication from an established Mythos location. Michael D. Winkle shows a new problem concerning the modern recording of information, while t. Winter-Damon gives us a work in the ancient form of poetry.

While reading this anthology you will be exposed to the vast variety of storytelling styles that have kept the art of H.P. Lovecraft alive for more than fifty years after his death. Some people are not going to like all of these tales (although I hope that to be a very small number), but I expected that such a diversity of styles will find some critics. So be it. I believe, that for every story which has someone who feels it to be 'unLovecraftian' there will be another who can quote paragraph and word as justification of the interpretation. And folks, it really does not matter. Every writer in this anthology had to go through the editor, so final judgment on the merits of each tale fell to me. I fully accept this because I know that I did my honest best to secure the tales that best entertained, frightened, or caused me to think some new thoughts (the three terms were not mutually exclusive).

If you are already a reader of H. P. Lovecraft's works, whether a casual "read a couple" or a "quote his personal letters" type, I believe you will find something in here for your tastes. If you have never read or heard of Mr. Lovecraft, well hold onto your sanity for you have just opened a personal gate to the world of fantastic weird fiction that hopefully will have you searching your local bookstore for his latest editions. As Shakespeare has said, "Present fears are less than horrible imaginings."

— Thomas M. K. Stratman

Watch the Whiskers Sprout

by

DF LEWIS

THE STREET, far from here and now, was little more than a space between lean-to slums and steaming piles of horse traffic. The beggars mooched. The one-room families slouched and skulked. And the cat's meat man, by the name of Blasphemy Fitzworth, exercised his trade.

There was one small girl who often traipsed behind Blasphemy's creaking cart, to hear the tales he had not yet told. Her name was Chelly. One day, as he momentarily ceased his rhythmic call for custom—"Spout cat! Gout cat! Watch their whiskers sprout, cat!"—he pointed to a nearby warehouse wall. Clumsily affixed there were pieces of discarded lumber forming the letters "RM".

"You know, liddle girl, that reminds me of a time when I was starting out in trade."

Whilst gathering his thoughts, a down in the mouth lady offered a tuppence pit for a slab of seething melts, which Blasphemy shoveled from an inner sanctum of his cart. She left, grinning widely, for that night her loved ones would have a stew which crusted thicker.

Blasphemy perched himself on an overturned washtub and continued: "Did I ever tell you I once worked in a hospice?"

"Nope—but what's a hos-piss, Feemy Fitzworth?"

"Don't rightly know, liddle girl, but it had a sign outside—said the words of a prayer, or something like it. Looked a bit like a pub. They needed someone to be a cellar-man and bar-polisher, so I fitted the bill, right well."

"How old was I then, Feemy Fitzworth?"

"Ho! You weren't even a twinkling star in your old Mum's sky—that be a fact."

"How old were you?" wheedled Chelly.

"I was as old as the years and as young as the grave, that'll do for your curee-ossity, liddle girl. Anyway, the customers died in the nights and I had to cart them off. Too much of the drink. Too much of the late nights and the hearty backslap. The bar was full of them till the wee wee hours—a harking, a joking, a hugging and, at the dead of night, a heaving in their last throes of life. The panic set in from the skies above the hospice. The moon was at first whiter even than your poppy-pretty face, then gradually grew darker and darker and darker, till it were darker than the night sky around it...."

"Were it the angles coming in for their prize, Feemy Fitzworth?"

"No...they were more than angles, or less than."

"Were it the devils, then?"

"Sort of...I think. The hospice keeper mentioned the olden critters of Yog Sothoth, or something. He had scuttled out of sight, anyway and stiffened his moustache with grease, curled his hair with bent nails, fuzzed his ears with corpse-cloth, turnstiled his private parts 'gainst night piss...and drifted off into his usual dreamless slumber. He did not want to know about the doings of the opposite side of day...."

Chelly hopped up and down with her hoop. "Were it really those critters, Feemy, Feemy, were it, were it?"

"Yup...they were Great Old Ones with hanging dewlaps that scraped across the slates. I heard them clambering over the skylights, around the chimney-corners and scumming the gutters for food.... But the food they wanted best, that they needed to take back to their mother in the sky, was corpse fodder, you know, me dear. And we sure had plenty there. From the smoking, the croaking, the filling of the bellies, the voiding of the bowels, and the pitiful groans of those who were stoppered. Death from those causes, my dear, is very ugly indeed and we tended them, made it as much good for them as was possible, through the long nights of desperate, dire pain. Then we carted them off to the cobble yards and watched the shapes hover down in bellied ranks, watched them gnaw and knacker the dripping flesh, pink and pecker the stripped bones, blend and blanch the crazy weaving of the tripe...."

"You left the hoss-piss, then, to come here?"

"Well, they wouldn't keep me, after I tried to wake the hospice-keeper from his slumber. He just didn't want to know...and his sleep could not be broken...as if he were socket to socket with the mothering of the black black moon. I came away with bits of them any way. I didn't let the Great Old Ones have all the rumps and hams...I got slivers of them belching in my cat's meat pans, even today. I also cut a slice or two from the critters' wattles...."

Blasphemy Fitzworth suddenly ceased his memories of the hospice, for he realized that he had left the point. Chelly had slipped off, bored and hungry, she too forgetting about the "RM".

The echoes lasted for a good while.

"Spout cat! Gout cat! Watch their whiskers sprout, cat!"

* * *

Another day, the cat's meat pan brimmed wide with ever burgeoning folds of melded offal. Blasphemy sold such stuff to the poor as well as to cats, but often sensed instinctively that he was touring a Victorian mock-up called London. His rounded face full fed and rubicund indicated that he did not really belong to that place nor even to that time. He was merely sought some clue or other to the whereabouts of Yog Sothoth and the Great Old Ones, for such had shaken a loose tail as far as the nineteen nineties were concerned. So, he traced them from point to point, to see if a picture emerged of their formulations.

From behind the cat's meat cart, he suddenly spotted a sign that made the melts boil over.

"I won't be placing bets that they're not here," he said to his knickerbockered giggle of Victorian girl groupies.

Arranged in rude wooden slats across the frontage of an inn that would be a protected property come another century, were again the letters "RM", fixed with rusty nails, from each joint slowly dripping goo.

"They been around here, no fear nor favour," he said, pointing to the telltale sign. The roofs were showing gutters from beneath their skirts, heavy with the inarticulated wastings of those Great Old Ones, who had evidently spent the previous night perching, preening and unbundling themselves across the ridge-trees of the would-be buildings.

But gutters would only win a proper reality, later, in fact. So Feemy Fitzworth soon smelt a rat, as the meat in his pans softened to a consistency more akin to water than flesh.

* * *

As the little girl Chelly plaintively gazed out at the darkening rim of night sweeping like the tide, the hunger literally ate into her. But, then she heard the distant call of her friend Feemy the cat's meat man: "Gout cat! Spout cat! Watch their whiskers sprout, cat!" But it was only his sad leftover ghost. Then, she heard a rogue Old One flap in, to roost and brood just above her head on the camouflaged roof. She extended her head from the mock window and , turning her face to the sky, opened her tiny mouth to catch the droppings from the Old One's hindquarters. Pitiful to report, the false gutter caught it all.

* * *

Whether Blasphemy Fitzworth really believed that he traveled between the fixed berths of time, disguised as a cat's meat man, commissioned by his pub pals to seek out the Great Old Ones, only time will tell. What was certain, however, such critters were rumoured to roost on the night side of twentieth century roofs and, so, it was left to tipplers a little the worse for wear to read the signs. This was because, upon leaving pubs, after hours, they would shiver in the chill wind coming in off the back end of the last world war...and, with their hands shading their eyes against the night sky, they were the only ones capable of spotting the tell-tale bunches of shapes perching on the ridge-trees of the city.

They were always cheered by he sight of the Old Ones who kept nightly vigil against the possibility of other more insidious cosmic forces settling their irreducible terrors upon the beds of man. And now Feemy Fitzworth trod time, as if he knew no tomorrows, gradually widening out his catchment area...as the meat in his pans gradually turned to slugtracks.

He had reached that part of a lesser known universe currently under the jurisdiction of a one-time London barrow-boy called Asa Thoth. This creature was squatting in a time-hole, his skin hunched and runnelled with tidal eternities, pretty sure he was protecting the interests of the Great Old Ones. Blasphemy wanted to interrogate him.

Seeing Asa Thoth flaked out, Fitzworth spooned into his mouth a smidgen of his now legendary cat's meat medicine which, at first, ran down the scalings of Asa's corrugated chest towards his coiled arrangements down below. But, a sip was enough; Asa awoke from a dream that he had not yet dreamt: and the self-same Old Ones that had or were about to brood on Earth's roofs were, at this leading edge of time, still young. And the Old Ones flapped in around Asa's huge head like Goyesque figments of a frightening Victorian dream.

Gathering his wits like soggy speech bubbles, Fitzworth shot back along the back-doubles of time and space to the pals in the pub; to tell them where the Old Ones could be found but his pals were too drunk to care.

Meanwhile, another version of the same cat's meat man wheeled his cart through the Victorian slumways, humming and, basically, minding his own business. He kept the half-extruded lumps of offal on the boil by means of a coal fire in the bowels of his cart. His customary call rang out: "Gout cat! Spout cat! Watch their whiskers sprout, cat!"

The Victorians mostly ignored this familiar figure of their times. They little suspected that he was an infiltrator from another time. Who had ever heard of a spy who shouted attention to himself?

He called his wares and soon forgot indeed what he was supposed to be spying upon. He was satisfied by his role of cat's meat vendor in a Victorian London that seemed to fit in with how history had described it. He was now simply the cat's meat man and nothing else.

But he never saw even one cat rummaging around those (God)forsaken alleys. Meantime, his pals, a universe and a bit away, as it were, welcomed back one who looked like Blasphemy Fitzworth. Well, he looked very much like the original but decidedly peculiar with pieces of give-away cat's brains still hanging from his head like hair ribbons. This must be someone masquerading as someone else.

* * *

There were so many little girls in pinafore frocks who traipsed in the wake of Blasphemy Fitzworth, he lost track both of their identity and significance in the scheme of things.

One day, a small pudding-faced child, whom he had indeed met before but had forgotten that he had, who was not much older than ten, in a red run-up, came up to him again when he had begun to sell cat's meat from pub to pub as bar food. She skipped up and asked: "What have you got in your cart, today, Feemy Fitzworth?"

"I've got fat pipings of meat scraped from my old Mum's innards," he half-joked.

She giggled a "Ooooh!" but, not really seeing why it was funny, questioned him again: "How much it cost, eh, Feemy? I've got a pretty shiny farthing in my pinny—is that enough for a tasty chewy bit?"

"Less of your questions, young missy. And what is your name?"

"Chelly. You know I'm Chelly."

"Chelly Mildeyes, I guess, looking into your deep wells of sight."

"No," she screeched, in uncontrollable mirth. "I've not got an after name. We're too poor for anything but a Christian one."

Her face was as round as an apple pie, with a spammy forehead and eyes like large brown meatballs in lashings of milk, and he began to sweeten towards this moon-calf, despite her cheek. He wanted to pull her leg. "Who cut yer hair like that, Pansy Pie—your dentist? After he set out yet milk teeth like broken fence-posts, no doubt."

She did not laugh. "Don't call me Pansy Pie. It's bad luck to call anybody but by their proper name."

She then proceeded to dip her hand into the bottom of the cart and pulled out a particularly stringy clutch of valves from his ancient mother's lower endings. She also picked carefully into his tray of gnawing-bones and positioning them painstakingly amid the already pulsing mess in her hand, she held it all across he face.

"Is this any better? Am I prettier now?" she asked quite seriously.

A tear welled at the corner of Feemy's eye, for the pity of it all. He scuttled off to the next pub on his roster. But she followed him, that little scare-flesh, through the encroaching murk of an early dusk.

His eyes flowed with something he could not explain. He turned round and looked at the dear Medusa of his heart—and realized that with no doubt he had fallen deeply in love with her meat-dripping mask. A love that was worse than a pain.

The landlady shook his hand as he arrived at the Jackass Penguin pub.

"Hi, Blasphemy!" she bellowed. "How's things? Got some juicy meatings for my hungry microwave? It's jawing on a wadge of used pork scratchings at the moment. It needs a lump of your choice cuts to suck."

Feemy put a hand into his seeping canvas bag and pulled out the tenderest, pinkest steaklets. She whistled between her teeth and paid him a wow of a gratuity, which he immediately swapped for a pint of best and a medium shovelful of scratchings. He then sat in the corner and slowly sipped at his drink. But when he happened to look into the surface of the liquid, he did not see the reflection of his own face but the imploring face of his lamented mother. And when he looked up at the pub's see-through oven door, he caught a fleeting glimpse of something he did not know was Cthulhu. Then inside the oven appeared the wide, white poppy face of sweet Chelly, somehow desperately trying to tell him something with her mild haunting eyes.

Indeed, Chelly once used to follow him, in her pinafore, along with a troop of other girls and, shame to say, they used to mock him and run their filthy hands through the sticky strands of his merchandise. But, he always had a supply of smiles for the likes of them. He sometimes called her Pansy of Lettuce. She did not know with whom he got her muddled.

Well, come the Jubilee, he had been a regular feature of her life for most of it. But no cry of spouts and cats and whiskers sprouting came that morning. At first, lying in her truckle bed, she did not notice the absence. She just felt beyond herself that something somewhere was awry. Tales had gone on amongst the girls in Feemy's flock that he was not really a human being at all, that he was a traveler of all times and worlds but, in those days, nobody had heard of time travel. Only monsters.

She just stroked her cat Ulthar, for whom she was meant to buy Feemy's wares, but her Mum and Dad usually got hold of the stuff first and dressed it up for the family's supper. Her mother had both hips dislocated and her father was always off "slaying dragons", or so he said, with his "trusty spear". So not much money came their way, only the bits and bobs that Feemy gave Chelly in loose change.

Therefore, she felt some responsibility for the welfare of the cat's meat man and, knowing he was always complaining about his liver, she feared that this organ, the nature of which she then did not understand, had at last given up the ghost. Her innocent girlish concern was understandable.

She grabbed Ulthar and hugged him to her empty chest, kissed him goodbye; and he gave a dry lick to her thighs as she pulled on her knickerbockers: he always did that to see if he could lap up her moles.

She trudged through new-fallen snow, early this year; her father had evidently been down the alleyway already for she saw his footprints leading in the same direction as her's. She had never been to Feemy's abode before, but she knew from his various tales, that it was called Mowsle Barton, somewhere toward Inner Hackney. She was a boisterous little kid most of the time, but that morning there was something impending which seemed to staunch her natural joy. As she approached the tall chimneys that were once the property of a large house, with several wings, but were now fast becoming just another factory complex, she realized that she was utterly lost.

She had long since overtaken her father whom she had seen showing off in front of some of his cronies, pretending he was a horse and whipping his own backside with a small branch, as if he was the steed about to take him towards the brave crusades of which he had always bragged. The cronies laughed out loud when Chelly passed, but their grins were nothing but missing teeth as if she were the denture fairy of their dreams.

She wished she had brought Ulthar with her; he would have been able to sniff out Feemy's socks.

She managed to get home, sad that she had not been able to locate her Feemy. But her father did not return; and her mother was so caught up with her ailments she forgot to notice either Chelly's presence or the husband's absence; Ulthar had disappeared too, which made Chelly even sadder for she feared she would never see him again. All she could do was sleep.

She then had a dream, which is still going on.

She found Mowsle Barton, which was indeed the large house before it had become a factory. She heard the resonant cry from within just like an opera-singer practicing: "Gout cat! Spout cat! Watch their whiskers sprout, cat!" She managed to get in through a groundlight and wound herself through gridwork corridors before she reached the source of the singing. There was her old friend Feemy Fitzworth, seemingly years younger, propped up in a four-poster, mending his cat's meat as if he were knitting. Ulthar was there too, with a cat smile so human Chelly thought it must be herself, but it wasn't; Chelly was standing by the door, watching Ulthar nibbling at Feemy's cat's cradle of curded meat; she laughed out loud for it meant the knitting would never get any longer however long Feemy clacked his bone needles....

It was as if she had prepared what she had to say. Feemy looked up at the sound of girlish laughter and, seeing his dear face, she said:

"I'm your fairy God-daughter."

Immediately, she felt her hips widen, her privities sprout whiskers, her chest grow a pair of proper breasts so perfect in their symmetry she needed to fondle them herself.

And with a decency, she left others to imagine the rest of her dream.

There was a night, too, when and old lady first heard the call of the cat's meat man, she had already taken stock of her life and, in the seeping light of a log fire which had also been used as a depository for the snotrags from her running nose, she settled upon the creaking wooden bed and hoped to die. But why she hoped to die is a story in itself but suffice it to say that she was both a loser in love and money. She couldn't even remember her own name. Lettuce? Pansy? Rachel? Tonight seemed the culmination of the ages that constituted history, having traveled here in tides of darkness across the plains of time, baling the hay of laughter and dropping stacks of sadness behind.

Victorian London became the old lady's final haunt, a time and place that seemed to bind bad and good with the cement of honest truth. She hoped to honour it with her death. She felt she had been born in the times of Jesus, cleft to man in the realms of the Sun King, studied the courses of the stars under the skies of the Pharaohs, buried the fruit of her loins in the trenches of the wars of the twentieth century, and wrote out notes for dreams whilst upon the New Horoscope Starships. It was only fitting that she should search out Charles Dickens to turn those notes into the sentences that she was too clumsy to forge.

Of course, Dickens wrote only what he wrote. History could not allow her to find him. In fact, she found only vagrants in gutters of the city each of whom said he was the real Dickens.

"I tell yer, I be the chap who wrote those fine words. I tell yer straight, I'm a literarree man," each would vouch. Some even spoke darkly of Old Ones who inhabited their brains. And could they *all* be wrong?

So, having listened to the echoing calls of the street, night on night, she suddenly came face to face with one who sold death:

"I'll sell you age in this vat of thin blood,
See it pickled like a lump of brown mud."

The deathseller was offering it to those who could pay and even the smallest children in those days bought from him with their silver farthings. The cat's meat man told her that the deathseller was on the same beat as himself.

"Oi! I wouldn't be worried about you selling death to people, if it weren't for the fact that they and their pets eat my cat's meat." Feemy Fitzworth shouted this heart-felt complaint at the deathseller from the top of each straight terraced road as the other turned into its bottom.

Now, in the darkness, the old lady had become another deathseller, but only having herself with whom to barter.

"Gout cat! Spout cat! Watch their whiskers sprout, cat!" echoed the call of the cat's meat man, as he trundled his steaming, burping cart along the ever-darkening alley-ways.

She hung from the window and emptied her chamberpot followed by her own writings into the deep seething pans of the kitty-cart below, the handwords to be stained indecipherable by the seeping blood of Feemy's scrag ends—whilst his words crested the ranks of reek:

"Come and buy, Ulthar, Howard and Dickens,
The meat's over-ripe, but the gravy nicely thickens."

Such sales calls of the cat's meat man echoed on through the centuries... batted back and forth between the dark enveloping wings of a greater writer than Chelly, the ball of time, the endless game of life. She hoped to die of old age before she died of cold and hunger.

* * *

And, now, we must begin our story proper. Churles Fitzworth had made a lifetime's study of the family trees, particularly his own. Being still alive, he was one of those fruitless individuals who feature at the bottom of such dynastic algorithms, hanging about at a loose end, as it were. However, Churles preferred to consider himself more as a root than a branch, with trees always being that way up.

He was surveying the trappings of the Country House which his parents had left him, he being the only child. The rooms were far too big for him, so he filled them up with servants to make them seem more lived in. Not that he expected them to do much work, merely to keep him company with endless doodles of small talk and do an odd bit of ewbanking, light dusting, cooking for his bird's appetite, dashing away with the smoothing iron, laying the fires in every room and so forth.

He retained a minimum of furniture; he could see no joy in polishing for its own sake. There was a special place in his heart, however, for the oil paintings that depicted the previous members of the Fitzworth family. These queued up the stairways in order of seniority, ending outside the master bedroom with the founder, Pious Fitzworth, who had originally made a fortune from the slave trade. If it were not for these "crystallisations of demeanour" (as his bookish Maiden Aunt had always called them), the people on the Family Tree would only have remained as what they were: Names, mere words on fancy documents, bloodstained notes on the flyleaf of the gold-tooled bible.

Churles was convinced there was a name missing from the Tree. Otherwise, it did not make sense—the flow of births, marriages, miscegenations, wrong blankets, right sheets, precocious girls, young shavers, the whole gamut of generational flux and counterflux had one basic flaw, which years of poring over the complex angles had not yet revealed, let alone reconciled. At first, he had tested the water of historical logic, even extending the diagrammatic cycles into an extrapolated future. He was often interrupted by the little old lady who'd been hired as the live-in cataloger of the Fitzworth family library, who tried to convince Churles of her own version of the alphabet. Yet, after much study, he had come to the inevitable (but illogical) conclusion that Pious the originator (the family's First Mover, as it were) had a legitimate half-brother (a half-twin, if such a concept exists) by the name of Blasphemy who had, of all things, sold cat's meat to down-and-outs in distant Victorian London!

The next obvious source of investigation was the paintings themselves ....

"Excuse me, sir, I recommend that 'The Great Old Ones of Cthulhu' by Asa Thoth should be filed under Fiction rather than Fact," intervened the little old lady, as she brushed away Churles' pencil shavings into an old fashioned dustpan.

Rather than argue with her that the book in question was neither Fact *nor* Fiction, he gave assent to her wild ramblings (not caring for the way the wrinkles on her face visibly multiplied even as he watched them)—because he was close to cracking the Mystery of the Tree. He could not brook such side issues. He was ruling triangles all over a copy of the Tree to see if such devices threw any light on the interface between otherwise unconnectable generations. He had even once hung nameplates from the larch in the garden, sometimes breaking branches off and forming them into letters. It was said such strange practices once went on in Victorian London. And indeed such signs pointed to a figure called Blasphemy Fitzworth, no getting away from it. .

The cat's meat salecry of cats and whiskers often sounded in Churles' dream like a cipher. He seemed to be viewing events from the camera of someone else's head: trundling a cartful of steaming, belching pans, in which faces of stew grinned and slobbered. Girlish urchins in five piece frocks dabbed their fingers in to taste—only to screech with pain at the piping heat. He always woke amid a pool of gravy, more akin to congealed blood than sweat. One of the many servants would be by his bedside mopping up his brow. Hired for the purpose.

One night, as Churles walked unsteadily up the wooden hills towards his bed (which, by rights, was the four-poster in the master bedroom), he counted off the faces on the sloping walls. The banisters made bars across these windows into the past, more prisoners of their own self-imposed Fate than Death could ever invoke. Curse it, how could he not have noticed it before? The faces were one too many. The Tree was one too less. But which the culprit face? Churles' own likeness was at the foot of the stairs, glowering out at him, a mockery of life. It was a good resemblance, no mistake, even more real than the real. He even scowled back at it. "Damned be your features!" he intoned. But a busybody servant told him not to tempt Fate; so he shrugged and proceeded up toward the even deeper uncertainties of sleep.

One painting was indeed more haunting than the rest put together. It depicted a face that Churles likened to a plate of school dinner. When passing this meticulously daubed artifact, the whispers would come ... casting doubt on Churles' own legitimacy, let alone his sanity. How could he be dreaming, even before he had reached the bed? He would hesitate upon this particular landing, listening to the faint crackling of all the fires that had been laid. Burning to the very roots of his Tree.

Another Sunday, Churles Fitzworth sat and stared at the diagram. The servants had gathered to listen to the final reckoning, like masters used to deliver sermons from the Family Bible to the whole household of women, children and servants. It was as if Churles realized that they should have delivered them instead from a bible-black Necronomicon. The Fitzworth clan had come to its double-deadended cul de sac, as many of the rumourmongers had indicated. On the other hand, a few of the rumours pointed to an extension, that the very last in the Fitzworth line (Churles himself) was indeed growing big with child. A bladder child. The Kidney Kid. Something was surely swelling his belly so.

"Friends, may I call you friends? You ceased to be servants the day you entered my house. So be not afraid, you're hearing an equal, *not* your master. History is fast proceeding into the future—far be it from me to put a spanner in the works, but this diagram of branches I've finally finished proves...."

"Sir, sir," interrupted the little old lady, red-faced from slaving in the library, "I've just discovered a double-stacked book which says that *none* of the Fitzworths deserve the slightest whit of what Fate's granted them. They're mere fictions created by a Victorian lady writer...."

It was akin to hearing the wrinkled family Solicitor intoning the last will and testament—with absolutely none of the hopeful inheritors being given a brass farthing (let alone a shiny silver one).

The little old lady signed off with her initials—RM—for Rachel Mildeyes. She preferred being called Chelly, but had forgotten. With this sad flourish of her pen, she filed the story in the fiction section of a dubious library. The peaceful hospice was the next stop for the likes of Rachel, who was soon to forget everything, including handsome Blasphemy Fitzworth and the liddle girl with no luxury of an after name.

"Gout cat! Spout cat! Watch their whiskers sprout, cat!" The call echoed on for a tandem of eternities—whilst the idiot god, Azathoth, that amorphous blight of nethermost confusion, blasphemed and bubbled at the centre of infinity as well as in the meatcart.

The Death Watch

by

HUGH B. CAVE

IN A WAY it was my fault. But I had known Elaine Ingram for years, and when she asked me for the details of her brother's passing I could not force myself to tell her the truth.

When she said to me that night, right after the funeral, "Did he ask for me before he went, Harry?"—I lied to her. I had to.

"Yes," I said, "he kept asking for you. He kept saying how much he loved you."

"Did he say he would come back?" Elaine whispered.

"Yes," I told her; "he said he'd come back."

She and her husband, Peter Ingram, took over the old house out there at the edge of the swamp. Peter was a writer; he could make a living anywhere. And Elaine insisted on moving in because, she said, Mark would be coming back sometime and he would surely return to the house in which he had died.

For six months they lived in that house, and I got to be pretty good friends with Peter. He'd come over to the radio station every now and then and sit with me while I was on watch. Sometimes on the mid-watch, which is usually dull around four in the morning, he'd poke about, asking questions, and I'd tell him what I knew about being a radio man.

He had a natural aptitude for that sort of thing and before long he could have sat there at the bug and worked a shift without much trouble, if I'd dared to let him.

One night he was sitting there, watching me, and when a lull came and I leaned back to light a cigarette, he said suddenly: "Harry, I'm worried about Elaine."

I knew what the trouble was. Elaine was convinced, you see, that her dead brother would come back to her.

"She just sits there in the living-room," Peter said, "and never says a word. Old Yago sits there with her. Harry, I've got to do something about it. It's driving me insane."

I said: "Why don't you get rid of Yago?"

"Elaine likes him."

This Yago had lived in various shacks around town for as long as I could remember.

He claimed to be a Seminole Indian. He drank a lot, and folks said he was queer. Whatever he was, Elaine had taken a fancy to him and hired him to work around the place; and now he was living there.

"Harry," Peter said, "I've got to convince her that she's wrong, that the dead don't come back. But she won't talk to me anymore. If I sent Yago away, she'd just go deeper into those damned books of hers."

I thought it over for a few days, and one day I said to him: "Why don't *you* read up on spiritualism? You can't expect to argue with Elaine unless you can talk her language. Study the stuff for a while and you'll be able to pick holes in it."

He had been fooling with an old amplifier which had been lying on my desk. He looked up at me, stared a moment, then nodded. I didn't see him again for two weeks.

* * *

Bill Macy said to me one day: "What the devil is Ingram up to? I was in the post office this morning and there were half a dozen boxes of equipment from the Beacon Radio Company, addressed to him. I thought he was a writer."

"The poor guy's got to have a hobby of some kind," I said. "He's lonely."

But that night, to satisfy my curiosity, I figured out an excuse for calling on him, and drove over there about nine o'clock.

It was a black night, and when the nights get black in Florida they're like ink. I drove slowly because the road was bad, and I could hear the frogs grunting in the swamp all around me, and after a while I saw the lighted windows of the house.

You can't imagine a house in a place like that unless you've lived in Florida and seen some of the left-overs from the boom. This place was enormous. It had about twelve rooms and looked like a small hotel, very ornate and elaborate, and yet it was the only house for miles around.

As I remember, some wealthy chap from New York figured the town would grow out that far, and sank a small fortune in the house and then realized his mistake. He put it in the hands of an agent, who couldn't sell it—because who would want to live miles from civilization on the edge of a swamp filled with snakes and 'gators and bugs?

So the agent rented the place to Elaine and Mark and their mother—this was before Elaine married Peter Ingram—and I think they paid twenty a month for it. Then the mother died and Elaine was married, and Mark stayed on alone.

He was a radio man and a good one, but that house did something to him. We at the station noticed the change in him and begged him to move into town, but he bought a lot of books and told us to mind our own business.

He gave up his job in August. Bill Macy relieved him one morning at eight, and he said to Bill: "Tell Crandall I'm though." Just like that. When I heard it, I went out to the house and begged him to reconsider. I told him it was unfair of him to quit like that, without giving me a chance to get a man to replace him.

He stared at me, and there was a queer, dull light in his eyes, and his eyes never blinked. "I'm sorry," he said, "but I have work to do."

For a month I didn't see him. Then the rumor spread around that he was sick, and I went there to find out.

He was sick all right. That queer, dull light in his eyes had become a wild glare that scared me. He looked half starved and had a raging fever.

I drove back to town and got Doc Wendell. And that night, while Doc and I watched over him, Mark died.

Now Elaine and Peter and old Yago had the place, and when I climbed out of my car that night, Yago opened the door to me.

"Hello," I said. "Is Mister Ingram at home?"

Yago nodded and I followed him inside to the living-room. It was an enormous room, with a big fireplace and a lot of musty furniture, and Elaine was sitting there, reading. Yago limped over to a chair near the fireplace, and paid no more attention to me, and Elaine looked up and said:

"Hello, Harry."

"I've got a swell story for Peter," I said. "Is he around?"

"He's upstairs."

She didn't get up to go after him, but just sat there, staring at me. She was a good-looking girl, Elaine, a little bit on the short side but slim and trim, with very even features. She seemed tired, though, and I could see that she hadn't bothered much about her looks lately. Careless, I suppose, because they didn't have many visitors and she seldom went anywhere except to the village.

"I'll go talk to him," I said, but she shook her head.

"He's working. I'm afraid he won't want to be disturbed."

Well, there was something queer in the air, and I didn't exactly know what to do. I could have laughed it off and gone up to Peter's workroom anyway, but something in the way Elaine was looking at me gave me the creeps.

"It *is* pretty late," I mumbled. "Maybe I'd better come around some other time."

But just then I heard a door open upstairs, and Peter called down: "Is that you, Harry?"

When I went up, I saw right away that he was in bad shape. He was wearing slacks and slippers and no shirt, and needed a shave, and looked all in. He couldn't have looked any worse after a week's drunk.

"Been a long time since I've seen you, Mister," I said.

He nodded, and kept on nodding for a moment while he stared at me. He seemed to be making up his mind to do something, and then rather abruptly he gripped my arm and said: "Want to show you something."

His workroom was at the end of the hall and he didn't release my arm until we were inside with the door closed. "Even my wife hasn't been in this room for the past two weeks," he said. "Look."

I looked, and my mouth sagged open.

It was a big room and reeked of stale cigarette smoke. The shades were down. I guessed that they'd been down, and the windows, too, for a long time. And the whole back end of the room was piled with radio junk!

"What the devil," I demanded, "are you doing? Building a broad-casting station?"

"Look it over," he said quietly.

I looked it over. He had some ultra-short-wave apparatus that was unlike any "ultra-freq" stuff I had ever seen. The receiver apparently was still in the experimental stage, with loose wires and disconnected condensers sprawled in a mess, but the transmitter was what made me suck in my breath.

I knew what this "ultra" stuff was all about, but the weird-looking amplifiers Peter had hooked to his transmitter stumped me.

He saw me squinting with disbelief.

"Don't worry," he said. "It'll work. I'm throwing the ultra high-fre-quencies clear out of the spectrum with that amplification hook-up."

"About all you'll do," I said, "is drive the boys at the station mad, interfering with our reception. What's more, you haven't a license."

"For what I'm doing I don't need a license. Besides, it's far from finished. I'll be a month working on it yet before I'm ready."

I walked over to his desk, and he had a stack of radio books there that would have tested the learning of an advanced electrical engineer. I started to look them over but he said gently: "Never mind those, Harry."

He pulled open a drawer. There were more books in the drawer — books of a different sort.

"Some of these were in the house when we came here," he said. "Mark must have been studying them. Others I obtained by mail, from a collector."

I skimmed through a couple of them, but it was all Greek to me. Stuff about the Black Mass and Bethmoora and the black lakes of Hali. Stuff about voodoo and the dark arts.

"Hell," I said, "only a nut would bother wading through this junk. What's eating you, anyway?"

"She reads it," he said.

"Who? Elaine?"

"Yes."

"You mean she takes this junk seriously?"

He nodded. I didn't like the way he stared at me, or the way he handled those books when he replaced them in the drawer. He seemed to resent my disbelief, and he touched the books the way some folks touch a Bible. Reverently, sort of.

Then suddenly he said: "Elaine mustn't know about this. You understand? She thinks I'm working on a novel."

"That's what I thought, too," I said.

"Well, you know better now. But you mustn't tell Elaine."

I told him I wouldn't tell Elaine. I told him he could stand some sleep, too, and if he didn't ease up a little he'd find himself in bed with a nervous breakdown.

His answer to that was a crazy kind of laugh, and the same sort of laughter kept coming in little gusts from way down inside him as he walked with me along the hall.

"I'll be over to see you soon," he promised, and held my hand for a minute; and I felt his eyes on me as I went down the stairs.

I turned, said, "So long," and walked into the living-room to say good-night to Elaine. Evidently I didn't make much noise. Elaine didn't hear me coming.

She was on her knees there in the shadows, and in front of he was a table on which stood a photograph of Mark. Her hands gripped the edge of the table and her gaze was glued to the photograph. I thought she was praying.

Naturally I took a step backward and would have faded into the hall again without disturbing her. But then I heard the words that were whispering from her lips.

"Hear me, O Mighty Nyarlathotep!" she was incanting. "You who walk in the farthest shadows by the black lakes of Hali, listen to me, I entreat you! And you, O Hastur, O Prince of Evil! Send him back to me, for my own god has failed me. Give him to me as he promised to return...."

I stood there, chewing my lips and gaping at her. It didn't make sense. It was a mumbo-jumbo that scared me, and I felt little shivers crawling over me.

Then, while Elaine went on repeating those same words, I saw Yago, the Seminole. He was sitting on the other side of the room, staring straight at me. It was dark over there, and his eyes were like red coals in the darkness, and I suddenly had the feeling that if IO intruded, those coals would burn me.

I'd had enough. I tiptoed out of there and closed the front door behind me as softly as I could. I got into my car and turned it around and drove back out of the swamp.

That night I stood the mid-watch, and jumped at every slightest sound. My nerves were as tight as fiddle-strings. Even the shrill cackle of code couldn't make me feel at ease, and once, while I was working the *S. S. Exhibitor*, a big housewife spider came slowly through the open door into the operating-room, and I went over backward with a shriek.

I didn't go near Peter Ingram's house for three long weeks. I wanted to forget what I'd seen there. But then one night....

Macy was supposed to relieve me at midnight. At eleven, his wife phoned to say he was sick, so I called George Latham's home, to get George out. His wife answered. George was at the fights. When he came in, she said, she'd hustle him over to the station.

At one o'clock I'd been on duty for nine hours, and was all in, and suddenly everything went wrong. A Norwegian freighter was calling with important business, and a mad clatter of meaningless dots and dashes came out of nowhere to drown him out and tear my ears off.

For half an hour it continued unabated. When George arrived, I was a mental wreck and was cursing my head off.

"Listen to it!" I said.

And suddenly there was something else for us to listen to!

It was the voice of Peter Ingram! For a while it slurred up and down the scale, the way a phonograph sounds if you press a finger against the turntable, slowing it, then letting it speed up, then slowing it again. We couldn't distinguish words right away, because of the crazy variations in tone. But finally the tone leveled out, and Ingram's voice roared through the operating-room.

George Latham and I stared at each other, and neither spoke. I don't know what he was thinking, but my thoughts were back in the shadowed living-room of that big house on the edge of the swamp. I was standing there with Yago's glittering eyes on me, and I was watching Elaine—because the words that came roaring though the phones were almost the same words I had heard Elaine whispering, on that other occasion.

Something about the black lakes of Hali...about Nyarlathotep and Hastur and the Prince of Evil...and Mark, Elaine's brother, who was dead and who had promised to come back.

It went on and on, on and on, and we listened to it. An S.O.S. couldn't have silenced the air-lanes any more completely. Both George and I knew that every operator within listening distance was doing exactly what we were — forgetting his job and concentrating on that weird, crazy babble of words from Peter Ingram.

Finally George said explosively: "I've been telling you for weeks that guy is goofy! Listen to him!"

I was listening. "Harken to me O Mighty Nyarlathotep! You who rule the midnight forests by the shores of Hali, hear me...."

"I'm going over there," I said.

For Peter's sake, I had to. For our own, too. The crazy fool was interfering with all kinds of important business. If he kept it up, he'd have the law down on his neck, and then maybe it would get back to us—we'd been criticized for having let him monkey around the station.

I didn't want to lose my job. I didn't want Peter to get into any trouble either, because, in spite of what I'd seen and heard, I still thought the world of Elaine.

So George Latham took over, and I backed my car out of the station garage and drove over to that house on the edge of the swamp. It was raining a little, and the road was black and dangerous, and there was light in Peter's workroom, but the rest of the house was in darkness.

I stepped into a pool of water at the foot of the steps and began cursing. The door was locked; I had to knock, and then had to stand there for what seemed like an hour, waiting for someone to answer my pounding.

Old Yago opened up. I said, "I want to see Peter; it's important," and I pushed past him. He turned to stare at me as I strode to the stairs. I could feel his eyes eating into my back. Not until I was halfway up the staircase did he close the door; and while I was hiking along the hall to Peter's workroom I heard the Indian climbing after me.

Peter's door was shut. I banged on it. A chair scraped inside, and there was a queer, heavy silence for about ten seconds — which seemed a long time — and Peter said: "I'm not ready for you yet. Go back to bed."

"It's Harry Crandall," I said.

"Who?"

"Harry Crandall. And I've got to talk to you!"

The chair scraped again, and I heard footsteps. I should have been prepared, I suppose. I should have remembered how thin and emaciated he'd been on my last visit. But the door opened, and I took one look at the man and stepped back, cold all over. He was like a ghost.

"Come in," he said. "I thought you were my wife."

I kept staring at him. His face was dead-white, and his eyes were like holes burned in a sheet. He hadn't slept, hadn't eaten, for days; I was sure of it. His hands shook, and a bulging little muscle at the side of his mouth kept twitching, and his breathing was hoarse and fast, as if the effort hurt him.

He closed the door, put a claw-like hand on my arm and pulled me toward the desk on the other side of the room. The desk was a radio table now — of a sort. It was cluttered with wires and paraphernalia, and in the midst of the chaos hung a microphone.

"I'm working on ultra high-frequency waves," Ingram said. "This outfit here"—and he pointed to the transmitter—"is a special apparatus for throwing the signal outside the known spectrum."

I put my legs wide apart and jammed my hands against my hips and glared at him. "You weren't working the high-frequency waves a while ago," I growled. "You raised hell with everything on the Atlantic coast!"

"I was experimenting then. Probably had some parasitics. That's ironed out. Now I'm ready to begin."

I glanced over his apparatus. I'm no Marconi, but I know enough about radio to know that ultra high-frequency stuff is all in the experimental stage, and damned deep. Evidently he'd been doing a lot of reading.

But the book that lay open beside the microphone was not a radio book. It was one of those tomes from the desk drawer and was full of stuff I wouldn't want to read unless I were good and drunk in broad daylight. Queer formulæ, queer names, rituals...all that stuff. Necromancy, I guess you'd call it. And some of those formulæ, if I know my languages, were in Arabic.

"This," I said, "is what you were sending out over the air?"

He nodded. His hand was pawing my arm again, pulling me aside, and there was an odd expression on his face—a queer twist of unholy anticipation —as he lowered himself into the chair. The hand that closed over that microphone was as thin and bony as the fist of a corpse.

"Listen," he muttered. "I'll show you!"

"But—"

"Don't worry. I'll not interfere with the station. What I have to say will go out where no human words have ever gone before. I've worked for weeks to reach out into the void. Tonight, just before you came, I had an answer."

"An answer from what?" I said, frowning.

"I don't know yet. But now—"

Well, I stood there and listened to him, and before many minutes passed I was cold as ice, And afraid. I'm a sober man; I've stood many a mid-watch alone, with wind rattling the windows and rain hammering a dirge on the station-house roof...but the words that whispered from Peter Ingram's quivering lips scared me.

It was the same old stuff at first, but the ghastly eagerness in Ingram's half-mad face made it different. The guy actually believed he was talking to someone. You could tell by his eyes, by the way he glued his mouth to the mike.

He mumbled Arabic, then went back to English. "Listen to me, O Nyarlathotep, O ruler of the darkest dwelling-places of the far departed. Hear me, in the name of the twisted ones who crawl through the halls of Hell! Hear me, in the name of her who suckles the legless children of the vast Lake of Hali. The Mass is midnight black, and crimson blood flows from the wounds of the gods I have denounced. Take me to thine own scaly bosom and hear my prayer....

"I was an unbeliever, O Mighty One, I sought thee first with ridicule for my wife who believes in thee. I would have proven to her that there was no life after death, no hope, no return for the departed. Now I would bring the dead back to her, and this is the night. This is the night I have awaited, O Prince of the Darkest Dark! He died when the wind wailed as it does tonight, and when the storm gathered. Tonight the way is open...."

Peter Ingram wasn't talking for my benefit. He didn't even know I was standing there watching him, listening to him. When his voice trailed off he still sat there, gripping the mike, and his hands were shaking, and beads of sweat dripped from his wasted face and splashed on the open book in front of him.

The room was still as a tomb. The rain whipping against the windows seemed to make no sound, and wind whining around the house had no voice. Not for me. My heart was sledging, and I was cold, and scared.

Something here was all wrong. In a kind of daze, I realized that. Weeks ago, Peter Ingram had dug his teeth into the study of this stuff in order to prove to Elaine that she was wrong in her beliefs. He'd been determined then to convince her that her dead brother never would or could come back. And now he believed all that she believed, and more!

The man was mad!

"Listen," I mumbled. "For God's sake, stop this business. Forget it."

But he was whispering into the microphone again, paying no attention to me.

"Send him back to her, O Mighty One," he pleaded. "It was on a night like this that he died, and on his lips was a promise to return. Grant him that dying wish this night! Let him return!"

Suddenly he stiffened, sat there with his eyes closed and began to tremble from head to foot. I took a step backward, staring at him.

"Listen!" he shouted. "Listen, Elaine! An answer! I swore to you I'd get an answer, and I have! I am!"

Well, I didn't hear anything. I told them later, at the police station, that I did not hear anything, and I repeat it here, so help me God, *I didn't hear anything!* Peter Ingram sat there, sucking breath and gasping it out again, and I stared at him, and that was all.

For about one minute—one endless, horrible minute—that was all. Then I did hear something downstairs.

A door opened. The wind hurled it shut again, and glass broke—so I knew it was the front door. Then I heard footsteps.

They weren't the king of footsteps you'd have made or I'd have made. They were heavy, house-jarring thuds that rattled the walls and shook the floor on which I was standing. They were slow plodding steps.

Someone down there had come in by the front door—which was locked —and was walking along the hall. Someone huge, heavy. My mind flashed to a picture of Frankenstein's monster, striding in out of the storm....

Peter Ingram swung around in his chair and stared at the door. The door was closed. I think now that Peter expected the thing downstairs to come up and open the door—to come up in answer to the words he had mumbled over the mike. But Elaine's room was downstairs, and the thing strode along the hall down there, and I heard a door clatter open, and then—and then a woman was screaming.

God, that scream!

The sound came wailing up to us, shrill as the zero-shriek of a hurricane. It ripped and slashed its way through the whole house, drowning out the yammer of the rain, the voices of the storm outside. For one long, ghastly minute it continued unabated, and then it became a hideous gurgling sound, and I heard something else mixed up in it.

I heard a guttural, snarling voice, and a sound of human bodies thrashing about in a death-struggle. The voice was a man's.

"Damn you!" it bellowed. "You left me alone! You left me here to rot! Damn you!" And then the voice became a grisly peal of mad, maniacal laughter, and the woman's screams were silent.

About that time, I reached the door of Peter Ingram's workroom, and got the door open, and went stumbling down the hall toward the stairs. And the voice was still hurling out bursts of triumphant mirth.

It was dark down there. I think I yelled out: "Elaine, I'm coming! I'm coming!" but I'm not sure of that—or of certain other things, either. I do know that a scurrying shape was whimpering and sobbing like a frightened animal, and it rushed to the front door, which was open, and it vanished into the night. It was Yago, the Indian.

I do know, too, that Peter Ingram stood there at the head of the staircase and kept shouting: "They answered me, Elaine! They answered me!"

But Ingram was crazy. The doctors said he was crazy.

Anyway, I got to the bottom of those stairs and found a light-switch and went stumbling along the lower hall to Elaine's room. The door was open, and I would have rushed in if the light hadn't shown me what awaited me.

The room was a shambles. Chairs were overturned, and the bed-clothes were all over the floor, and the floor was red. Red with blood. Elaine lay in a crumpled, twisted heap against the legs of a dressing-table.

I didn't have to go any closer to know that I couldn't be of any help. I could see her face, her throat. Something with unbelievably powerful hands had torn her....

I backed out over the threshold. I turned on all the lights and staggered to the foot of the stairs and stared up at Ingram, who was still up there, waiting.

"Come down," I mumbled. "For God's sake, Peter, come down here!" But he just stood there, gripping the wall with one hand, the bannister-post with the other, and he kept shouting: "I've had an answer! Tell Elaine to hurry! I've had an answer!"

I left him there. I staggered out of the house and got into my car and drove to town. When the police went there, about half an hour later, they found Ingram pacing back and forth along the upstairs corridor, enraged because his wife would not go up to him. And they found Elaine in her room downstairs, as I'd left her.

Later they listened to me, and I told them exactly what I've told you, and they stared at me and exchanged glances and said firmly: "Yago is the man we want. We'll find him."

They didn't find Yago. They haven't yet. He was a Seminole Indian, and the Seminoles know every inch of the Everglades, every hiding-place of the great swamp.

Yago will never be found, and perhaps that's best. Because if they caught him, he might tell them the truth—or what I think is the truth—and he might make them believe it. And then they would question me again, and *I* might tell the whole truth.

I think about it when I'm alone on the mid-watch. I hear the wind wailing out of the swamp, and hear the frogs grunting...and I think of the night Elaine's brother died. Because in the very beginning I should have told Elaine and Peter *how* he died, instead of lying to them.

I should have told them that Mark was a raving maniac when Doc Wendell and I sat beside his bed that night. I should have told them that he not only promised to come back, but *swore* to come back— swore in a mad outburst of rage to return and destroy his sister for having deserted him.

The hours of the mid-watch are long and black...and more than once, on my knees, I've prayed for daylight....

The Return of the White Ship: The Quest for Cathuria

by

ARTHUR WILLIAM LLOYD BREACH

I AM NATHANIEL ELTON, Keeper of the North Point Light which my father, grandfather and generations before them have kept. Here, for untold ages, have waters from all the world passed in silence or violent fury before the grey lighthouse which my ancestors have served so well.

On many nights, under the glow of a full moon when the stars themselves shined as distant beacons, did I, in the times of my youth stand upon the jutting, craggy rocks and looked out into the great expanse of that watery world. There I would stand and wonder about what secrets were locked in her unfathomable depths.

For years, the sea yielded none of her secrets. For the wisdom brought about by long hours of solitude had not yet hardened upon me and the ways of the depths are not easily understood. Many, who were unwary enough ventured too far into strange waters have gone mad by the visions of things great Neptune did send. But I had seen, and truly are those wonders as vastly different from each other as they are curious each to behold. With a desire greater than any normal passion, did I seek to learn the ways of the ocean depths.

I can recall the times when I heard from fine, weathered salts tales of distant golden shores of incomparable beauty. They weaved many a fancy yarn of sweetly perfumed lands whose breezes were carried to passing ships by gently rolling, foamy waves. I yearned to travel to those distant lands to dwell amidst the splendor of stately, shimmering cities and quench my thirst by the banks of cool, musical streams.

* * *

During the final years of my grandfather's life a great sadness had befallen him and without his spoken word, I knew the cause of his unrest. It was my longing for those distant shores which had caused a dark shadow to extinguish the glow in his eyes. Sadly one night, when the moon hung full and high in the heavens, he told me the tale of the

White Ship and how it came to him on a similar night long ago when he was still young. He warned me repeatedly of Cathuria and the Basalt Pillars of the West. He told me how once he had rejected the beauty of Sona-nyl and never again would be permitted to behold its splendor. He bade me abandon my yearnings for the distant shores I had heard of in song and tale. I could not promise this, so I remained silent. He knew where my heart would lead and soon died grieving the lost Sona-Nyl and beauty which might have been.

* * *

For years unremembered in the minds of men have I been the guardian to the secrets of the subaqueous worlds. The key to the realm of wonder was surrendered unto me one night when the White Ship returned in the season of Uthlos from the land of Zar. That distant place wherein dwell all dreams and thoughts of beauty which come to the minds of men but once and are then forgotten. To distant Zar have many voyaged but none returned; for it has been told that he who treads the sloping meadows of Zar may nevermore return to his native shore. For it is the land of the Forgotten and the Unremembered. The gods are greater than man and *they* have conquered...but are also forgotten. The White Ship never returned to my grandfather. But there came a season of wonder to the land of Zar when the gods did forget the secrets of the ancient land. And that season was known as Uthlos...when the unremembered return to dwell amongst mortal men once more for a time.

Gliding silently out of the South did the White Ship sail as it once came to my grandfather in his youth. The moon, on that fateful night hung full in the sky like a radiant jewel. A curious, phosphorescent mist rolled in from the sea; and it was not long thereafter that I espied it out on the horizon. Her spectral masts, tall and mighty, were clearly defined at the junction where the sea met the sky. Swiftly it moved towards the shore and me. As the ship drew nigh my location, I could discern the figure of a man waving excitedly to me. The oars which propelled the vessel onward seemed almost to dance in rhythmic fashion—and lo! The White Ship sailed not upon the crest of the ocean waves—*but above them!*

Was this the White Ship from the South of fabled legend? *Yes!* I was certain of it. It moved with great speed until at last the ship was just beyond the jagged rocks of the lighthouse station. Then, on a bridge of moonbeams spread across the calm waters, the grey-bearded captain walked and stood before me. He spoke in an unremembered tongue but, strangely I understood.

"The gods are great, but time has prevailed upon their senses. Their thoughts as their memories have grown lethargic, for they have sipped the waters from the river Ages where breed the wild flowers of forgetfulness. And once again have I returned to share the secrets of the seas."

At that time the captain, whose eyes seemed filled with the infinite knowledge of the unknown, gave me a key most magnificently wrought in precious ore and fashioned with rare gems from distant lands. The key in all its splendor gleamed with the promise of new horizons. He spoke again.

"This is the key to the Gates of Wonder wherein lie all the lands of fancy and mystery. Therein may be found all hopes and dreams of man and the secrets which dwell beneath the waters."

I took the key. Then we both walked out over the waves upon the bridge of moonbeams and sailed off into the starry night.

For many days and nights did we sail and we were never in want of provisions; all were filled to contentment. The hours were passed in leisure with the happy songs of the oarsmen and the tales I heard were more splendid than those my grandfather had told me long ago.

Then one day, when the seascape was bathed in the soft orange glow of late afternoon, did I see off the starboard bow a land which inspired within me such a sense of wonderment that scarcely could I contain myself. Mighty mountains majestic in their impressive grandeur rose into the clouds so that none might behold even their uppermost reaches. As we drew nigh those magnificent peaks, I could discern their lush, green, gently rolling slopes with such clarity that I longed to tread them to the highest reaches to learn what no other man had ever glimpsed. I bade the ancient captain tell me what this land was. He told me thus in a soft voice:

"This is Ennon; the Land of Music and Poetry wherein resides the dreamers and poets who have gone into the world to share their visions but were rejected by those whose hearts knew not song. *Here*, the days are filled with lyrics and merriment, and at night, under dancing starlight, can be heard the ancient music which once had a place in the souls of men but later fled as age fell upon the world and wonder went out the minds of men."

What the bearded captain spoke of I knew to be true. For carried gently to my ears from some point upon those *remarkable* peaks did I hear songs long since forgotten; and the voices which sang them were remembered to a younger world. On the shore I beheld a young poet whose hair shimmered in the setting sunlight, who played gaily upon the lute with such sweetness that tears swelled in my eyes. As he plucked at the instrument; so also was a remote chord in my heart touched. I heard many a fantastic tale being weaved with such eloquence that I was caught up in its spell. I heard tell of a gypsy from a strange and distant time speeding through the shadow of a million years upon the eternity road. As he played he wept for treasures sought in vain and the truth which gently fell with the rain. In the sincerity of his voice I learned of the storms upon the ocean of life we must rise above and the dismal things without form awaiting our arrival upon the other side of life. At once I knew this to be Jin H'yard, the mystic poet and dreamer out of Eglind whom I knew of from the days of my early youth. Such was the time filled with song and poetry till the sun turned flight to the encroaching night when the moon once more shone full in the starry heavens.

Again, I cast excited eyes toward the mountains which had first captivated my interest and I could see that they were now bathed in a soft blue, ethereal mist. "And of those haunting peaks?" did I ask the captain of the mysterious White Ship in eager anticipation.

"They are the mist-shrouded mountains of Ayell-Tzarthica, the place of Deep Mystery," he replied evenly. "For who knows what lies concealed within the veils of blue-litten mist where few have dared to tread? It is told that the poets who have glimpsed through the mists have told of wondrous things beyond the stars. Even to the poet, as to the dreamer, madness awaits those who reach its summit. They know only of the soft, iridescent slopes they sing and weave fancy tales of. Not since the days when the great city of Gafn stood tall and mighty have minstrels journeyed through the lofty summits of those mountains and returned to tell of it."

Once more did the moon, in ways unfathomable, shine forth, and, upon that gleaming bridge of silver moonbeams did we disembark the White Ship to shores of flowering beauty. There did we dwell for many aeons in the land of ancient melodies. All throughout this land of Ennon, the hills rose wild and curious. But none more curious than the mist-shrouded mountains which held firm my wistful longings of the unknown. Time and time again my eyes strayed toward those unconquerable peaks and each time I recalled the words of warning the ancient captain told me...*madness awaits those who reach its summit.* I therefore wandered blissfully about the gentler, verdant slopes of Ayell-Tzarthica. Upon many a blossoming slope did the dreamers and poets inscribe upon parchment the accumulated knowledge of their years. At great length did I sit with them in the shade of the great Upas trees which grew in abundance about their steepled towns nestled in lovely valleys of lush, perfumed greenery.

The change was subtle which one day came to Ennon. A breeze blew out of the north carrying with it a strangeness which beckoned. The first stirring of unrest tugged at my sense of curiosity and I went in the direction of the blowing wind to explore new territory, leaving behind the stately, shimmering cities and the pensive minds which dwelt there. Over hills of multi-hued flowers and across cool, musical streams did I drift lazily carried on by the strange breeze which blew through Ennon. For days I passed over breath-taking sights ever so lovely and never before beheld by mere mortal men.

Then came the time when I was left sleeping upon a green shore fragrant with lotus blossoms. Upon my awakening I still knew this to be Ennon, for in the distance, the lofty summits of Ayell-Tzarthica still rose eerily. No sooner had I risen when a sickly youth came to me bearing in his possession a lamp most unusual in its appearance.

He held out the object to me as he approached as if somehow seeking approval. A sad smile played about the corners of his thin lips and his eyes were dulled and saddened, though, simultaneously, they were filled with a burning desire. A desire which had since perhaps been long fulfilled or left ravaged and abandoned upon the callous roads of a flickering life. His voice reflected a profound sadness fringed with the pain of wisdom. "You came, good. I've been awaiting your arrival."

"Have you, indeed? And whom might you be?" I asked in amazement.

To which he replied, "I am Ward Phillips; the Keeper of the Lamp. I have visions more splendid than those you have seen on your voyages. Come, I'll show you. I know of remote Cathuria and the route which will permit you safe passage through the Basalt Pillars of the West to the Land of Hope wherein shine with unblemished brilliance the perfect ideals of all that men know elsewhere to be true. Hope is eternal there and is not a thing of yesteryear as it is in the world from whence you came."

This was the legend of Cathuria. Instantly I bore to recollection the words of my ancient grandfather as he warned me of Cathuria, the unobtainable Land of Hope. Despite all warnings, the obsession to behold the abode of the gods themselves filled me with such a sense of paramount importance that soon all else seemed secondary.

The lamp was then lit. Instantly a flame leaped to the sky in a display of vibrant colour. A door opened on to alien vistas unbound in their beauty. Instantly I knew that indeed Phillips had spoken true. By the mystic glow of his lamp I beheld that land known as Cathuria. Never, would I have conceived that *such indescribable beauty* could have ever existed.

By the passing of many moons, nestled in a canopy of stars, did I listen intently to the amazing tales of Cathuria and the legends which abound of it whilst the scenic landscapes shifted before my bedazzled eyes. I returned to the grey-bearded captain filled with the wonder of these new horizons revealed. The beauty that was Ennon waned in its loveliness in contrast to that of Cathuria. I spoke fervently of all that I had learned. The captain remained silent while watching me intently as I revealed to him the mysteries I had discovered.

"The way to Cathuria, the Land of Hope is known to me. Once we were denied entrance to this great land and at the hands of wrathful gods did we suffer. The gods have forgotten and the secrets of the ancient lands once jealously guarded have since been yielded unto me."

"On the morrow, then, we shall weigh anchor and set sail at the next full moon for Cathuria," I informed the captain. He nodded in agreement but spoke no word to indicate his feelings. Where before there had been infinite knowledge mirrored deep in his eyes, a shadow of uncertainty now appeared.

As the night we had made port in Ennon many aeons ago, the moon cast a silvery beams over the waves and we walked on this bridge of moonlight across the placid harbor of melodious Ennon to the White Ship. We sailed for many days and nights over calm seas headed towards an uncertain fate. Though in silence we sailed, I could detect the fear which the captain carried from the painful memory of long ago. As we drew closer to our destination, I could see the horror of a suppressed memory as it rose in his eyes. Heedless of these warnings, we proceeded on our journey.

After many more nights we came at last to the Basalt Pillars of the West. The words of my grandfather paled to insignificance by what lay before us. Words failed all description as to the awe-inspiring sight which humbled before it both me and the tiny vessel upon which we sailed. These truly were the gates to the lands of the gods!

The captain told me how once he had been greeted most deceptively by the sweet songs of many lutanists upon his first voyage there with my grandfather. But for us, this was not the case, songs sounding our praises were not to be heard. Only the sound of the swiftly rushing sea was there to greet us. Through the fine, misty ocean spray we sailed passing betwixt the Basalt Pillars. As the mist lifted we beheld not remote Cathuria but a raging, violent sea. My first thoughts were those of disbelief. *But how? How?* In silent horror I gaped at the maddening monstrous whirlpool which sucked down into abysmal nothingness the waters of the world and all else which had drifted beyond those guard posts. A deafening roar of thunderous crashing waters filled our ears as we waited for inevitable doom. In utter despair, the captain turned to me, with a wild look about him, screaming above the onslaught of the sea. "Again have we been denied the beauty of fabled Cathuria! All hope is now lost!"

But no sooner had those words escaped him when there appeared before us, directly above that whirling chasm, a hole in space emanating a brilliant light which seized the White Ship and bore us all through that nightmare to a new and utterly alien world.

As we were carried through that hole in space, I felt compelled to peer into that yawning chasm beneath us, but that light through which we passed was blinding and I caught only a squinting glimpse of what reposed in those depths. Had I peered wholly at the abomination which I saw rise out of that unnatural darkness to seize us, every vestige of sanity would have been stripped off my brain. Though in darkness it remained, I discerned a blur of tentacles with wings and hundreds of greedy mouths which fell back into blackness once we passed safely through the bright opening. As that opening closed behind us, I fancied I heard insane screeching from hundreds of mouths which were not human.

A great burden had been lifted. Safe passage we had been granted, but I was perplexed. For the visions I beheld through Phillips' lamp were not related to our passage. But what was actually wrong eluded me, so I set those thoughts aside. Relief washed over the grey-bearded captain's face and the transformation in him was a marvel to behold. But the sensation of relief which touched him did not linger, it fluttered away and concern came to rest upon his features. He did not communicate his concern to me, it was not necessary.

There before me was a new world. A world which my grandfather had sought to obtain but failed. I filled my mind with the wonder before me. We had at last reached Cathuria, the Land of Hope!

It was everything I had so imagined and more. The waters over which we glided were bluer than the deepest azure sky throughout the known lands; be they from Ennon to Sona-Nyl. Gaudy were the fish which I saw there. The waters of the sacred Narg emptied into a sea without known bounds and it was beside this place we made port and disembarked the White Ship under the soft glow of a full, enchanting moon. That night, we happily slept upon lily-lined shores by the babbling waters of the Narg which soothed us into delightful slumber.

At first light we languidly rose and strolled through the fragrant forests of aloe and sandalwood. High above us, in the tree tops fluttered sweet song birds with plumage of the like no man had ever before beheld. Lovelier than the loveliest meadows of delicate beauty were those slopes. Lush and green were the groves and pastures which we crossed through while the wind whistled pleasantly about us. Not long thereafter did we come to the first city of Cathuria whose name was unknown to me. Its radiant beauty was apparent. The crystalline spires of their buildings reached to the heavens reflecting light in prismatic colour schemes not of the known world. Their pavements, as the walls of their city, were forged in gold and also reflected light bright enough to sting the naked eye. As we went deeper into this fair city, music fell upon our ears, but I could neither discern its origin or source of instrumentation for it was a sound totally alien to anything I had heard before. The music which accompanied us seemed to hint of unmarred beauty and splendor in a world which had never known the horror of suffering.

Somehow I felt that our presence there would destroy that tranquil order. I *knew* that man, as a race, had not yet evolved enough to relish the purity of Cathuria, the Land of Hope. Once before we had been denied Hope. This time would be different, we would be *expelled* from paradise having glimpsed Hope but denied its final obtainment. The good in life, like a candle, flickers and soon dies leaving in deep pools of darkness lurking shadows which mock our steps in which we must stumble about the rest of our lives.

For a time I lamented over not only this, but of the other truisms man had far too long denied. And though I saw man as a weak, frail thing filled with chatter of great self-importance, from this I could not divorce myself, for I too, was a sad part of that disgracefully myopic scheme. Man, over the course of his evolution, had not evolved far from a dark, hulking, savage, superstitious primitive; he still sought the bliss of darkness and hid from the light in his world of fears. But every great now and then, through the mist of doubt, which blankets the very existence of man, a ray of hope shines into the world briefly piercing the dense cloud cover which hangs over the world as a pendulum of doom. To those who will see it, there awaits upon their weary sojourn a belief in something greater beyond the waking world. I was blessed, for I was such a person.

To those who can not see the promise of hope, we must be their eyes and open the way for the rest who stumble about in the darkness. In that instant, I realized the reason why we were granted a privileged glimpse of Cathuria.

No sooner had this realization dawned upon me when there appeared before us a beam of light shot as a bolt from the heavens above. Subtly it shape altered and there stood before us a most radiant being more dazzling than the glow of the city itself. So brilliant was the visage of the creature before us, that we had to divert our stare to ward off the blinding effect it cast. Though gazing at the being before us was impossible, the well modulated voice with which it spoke was velvety and hypnotic. And as it spoke, a profound sadness struck my heart, for what was said confirmed what I knew in my heart to be true.

"I am Ariel, The Truth Bearer. Into remote Cathuria you have been granted safe passage. Though you know another way into our world, we, have seen fit to guide you here to show you the ways of Hope. Without hope man has stagnated and has ceased to grow. As a flower in the garden of life you once displayed promise. But since then, the garden has become noxious with rank growth, and the beauty once there has been overrun by foul weeds."

In that instant I understood desolation, the desolation man had imposed upon his own dreary, little existence. And in it, for the first time I saw the tragic *waste* of so many innumerable years gone by as leaves in the autumn wind.

"We have sipped the forbidden waters from the river Ages and returned to a time of innocence when we walked amongst mortal men in the days before beauty fled the elder world. But as all things must come to pass, so to has this. Never again shall we permit man in his primitive state to encounter the enchanted Land of Hope. For it is only after man finds belief in something greater than his own shadow that the shackles of greed and pride shall be severed thus permitting him the freedom to grow wise and evolve into higher consciousness. But this shall never be. The beast which guards the gateway to Cathuria grows stronger with the passing days. Soon it will have gained sufficient strength to breach the barriers, and the daemon given life by man's desires and blood lust shall then destroy Cathuria utterly. Hope will be vanquished and man will be forever lost. Age after countless age of despair and darkness shall plague man till he too, is no more. Destroy the beast within —lest it destroys you. Now leave. You have been warned."

Suddenly a smear of images whirled about us. Everything became as one. Light, sound, images and shadows blended together in a symphony of insane streams. We moved, though I felt no movement. Strangely, moments later, I was aware that we were on the White Ship leaving the ever beautiful Cathuria. The spaces opened and once more we passed through. I turned to take one final glimpse at the world I would never again see, but the portal had already closed. There remained only a twinkle which gleamed briefly and then vanished. Through the Basalt Pillars we passed, leaving behind the raging sea and the sounds made vocal in the throats of things not human.

We sailed to my own native shore. In the aeons since I had left, I had come to know much. I held the key to the Gates of Wonder and pondered if ever again the White Ship would take me to new and distant shores. The gods which once forgot now remembered. If never again the White Ship would return, I would still cherish the memories of long ago. For there came a season of wonder to the Land of Zar when the gods did forget the secrets of the ancient land. And that season was known as Uthlos, when the unremembered returned to dwell amongst mortal men once more for a time.

KADATH / The Vision and the Journey

by t. Winter-Damon

Long I sought—
for Kadath,
in the high, cold waste,
possessed by promises,
dream-glimpsed,
in red-lit visions of Ngranek's face.

To seize the madness
of this Dreamer's
Unknown Quest;
to grasp for secrets
better left...
unguessed.

Whispers (who can swear the truth?),
that the last
who sought this thing:
now the rumored, ivory-fragile jewel—
cursed cameo— bold Zenig's polished skull,
is mounted in
            some Titanic Master's ring

Long I sought—
for Kadath,
in the high, cold waste;
to know the darkness's fevered kiss
and the nightmares
of an Elder Race.

From the Gates of the Waking World,
down Lighter Slumber's steps
my echoing footsteps came,
to beg the sooth of bearded priests,
Nasht and Kaman-Thah,
in their chamber of the pillared flame:

"Seek not the Great Ones' onyx keep,
or the death of your soul
we see!"
Beyond all reasoning my descent,
winding the seven hundred final stairs,
my ears deaf to their plea.

Long I sought—
for Kadath,
in the high, cold waste;
to reach that fabled Bastion of the Gods,
gladly,
a thousand perils I embraced.

The Gate of Deeper Slumber passed,
reckless, I plunged
through tangled tunnels of Enchanted Woods,
followed ever through the phosphorescent gloom
by fluttering speech
of furtive zoogs.

Past fungus grotesques, ancient oaks
and moss-cloaked stone circle thrusting for the stars,
aeon-haunted by the half-heard chants amid the dell,
of dancing and the sacrifice.
Shun the clearing— its stony slab! its massive, rusted ring!
For beneath it squirming evil dwell!

Long I sought—
for Kadath,
in the high, cold waste,
beyond the realms of Mortal Dream,
beyond the chains
of Time and Space...

(As Melmoth) a wanderer I trod
the wild, plunging banks of the laughing Skai—
where down from Lerion it rushes, bubbling in icy mirth.
(*Known it has the drunken rhythms as the Young Gods dance!*)
Through sloping farmlands, chimney-dotted,
like hearth-warmed, half-remembered dreams of Earth.

On through Nir, the one-street hamlet,
cross Skai Bridge... (*muse not its flesh-sealed centerstone!*),
down Ulthar's quaintly twisting, cobbled ways,
where fur flows in tides— of tiger, cream, white, and calico...
Where black shadows prowl along peaked roofs.
Where the friendly purring chorus warms the nights and warms the days.

Long I sought—
for Kadath,
in the high, cold waste.
Of all my lodgings,
one only I have missed
— *this place!*

Hushed gossip drew me...to that tower of ivied stone,
Temple of the Elder Ones, and He, *the survivor*,
who had known Barzai the Wise.
Atal had scaled Hatheg-Kla's summit, there to glimpse
in the moonlight Earth's Gods as the danced.
(Barzai Impious! screaming! sucked into the skies!)

In the obsession of my vision, there I did this wicked thing!—
my host's staid tongue I loosened,
plying him with mad moon-wine!
Seduced the secret of Ngranek on the far-off isle
of Oriab; there, too, I learned
of Randalph Carter, and of his Quest akin to mine...

Long I sought—
for Kadath,
in the high, cold waste.
So, down from Ulthar led my road,
through violet lanes, a sea of gable peaks,
awash with sunset's mystic grace.

Catching the breeze-borne jingle of caravanners' bells of silver,
stepping lightly through the meadows, swarming
with butterflies— like Cathay's fantastic rainbow kites.
Wading waist-deep through gently swaying emerald blades.
On. On. Past thatched farmsteads, 'neath arcing spans across the Skai.
Then, *at last!* On horizon's black spires I set my sights—

Quays of basalt lapped by sapphire tides. Trade winds heady
with strange incense. Dark, brooding taverns fevered with smoke
of thagweed and the sweat of Lotus Eaters' waking nightmares...
"*Beware!*" the drunken sailors whispered,
"*Beware the sinister black galleys, that oft-times dock in Dylath-Leen!*
Trade not with turbaned ruby merchants—
                                   By the Gods! Avoid their snares!"

Long I sought—
for Kadath,
in the high, cold waste.
"*Sample not their reeling, giddy liquor!*
drawn from flasks of carved ruby!
slavery and death lie in their taste!"

"*Too brisk the stroke-beat of their three-tiered oar-banks!...*"
"*Uncouth the bicorned fashion of their turbans!...*"
"*Right devilish their mincing walk!...*"
"*Rubies for gold..and..fat, black slaves from Parg—*
purchased by the pound!..."
Can I convey those horrid *implications* hinted in the sailor' talk?

So I lingered as the Moon flowed through her black and crescent cycles,
till (at last!) she rose full-faced—
then came that barque from out Baharna, tricked out with shark-fin sails
of saffron, gaudy as a gypsy's palette;
heavy freighted with her cargo: pottery like eggshell, fragrant resin,
               fetishes and figurines of mountain lava.
"Land Ho! Fair blown the Winds of Fortune!" her greybeard captain hailed.

Long I sought—
for Kadath,
in the high, cold waste.
A nor'wester in our sheets, swift we weighed from port...
like a page torn from *Vathek*, dwindled,
vanished in a molten, purple-crimson haze.

Spume haloed round our decks as she lunged the crests
and pitched between the swells. And she cut a wake like new-tapped ale,
that beneath the waning moon burned green
As witch-fires O'er the autumn fens.
Ten days out was sighted shore— Ngranek's snow-bound cape,
stained pink and gold, the veils of a waking Eastern Queen.

And tier-on-tier Baharna rose, still sleeping in long shadows.
Emerald flies swirled in droning shoals, through the quivering
heat of the market, ere the dust of my zebra's hooves churned grey, as I set
my heels to her flanks.
Two suns rose flaming! Two nights ringing with the Vooniths' howl!
Beneath the resin trees, scales glitter moonlight,
         slithering into the hidden lava tarns by day.

Long I sought—
for Kadath,
in the high, cold waste,
possessed...
by promises, dream-glimpsed,
in red-lit visions of Ngranek's face.

Driven by my private daemons, far up into the star-split heights
I scrambled, clawing upwards past the clouds;
then, struck dizzy by its lofty vastness, my mind reeled at the sight:
fired red as blood by sunset, that jealous aspect of the race of Gods—
eyes like slender almonds; ears, long-lobed and pendulous.
Fingers knotted in the black stone, I clung there through the night!

This had I searched for— *the mark of the Gods, wrapped in the*
         face of men!
For ever were the Old Gods virile! and lusted for the morning
glory-flesh of mortal women, there to sow their seeds of flame!
Yet they strode in guise among men's daughters—
round Kadath where they dwell, their stamp
ill-hid should be, blazing the trail from whence they came.

Long I sought—
for Kadath,
in the high, cold waste.
But now my path shone clear—
for already
I'd descried their trace!

In the tavern billed, "Where Sea Meets Sky"— as is the custom
of the naming in the port of Dylath-Leen—
an onyx trader I had seen, and when I questioned of his kind
was told: *"Seldom do we see his outland breed,*
from out the north, once yearly do their dark, chimeric vessels glide,
to Celephais to trade for brighter things the onyx
         they have mined..."

A rush, a blur of images fragmented, glimpsed as in a
          nightmare sweat,
or in a Lotus Dream, my flight from down Ngranek's heights,
oblivious save for *the Vision*, burning
like white phosphorus within my hapless brain—
(to seize some well-loved child of gods! In ransom for their far off songs,
their queer and lofty thoughts, *forever homeward turning*!

Long I sought—
for Kadath,
in the high, cold waste,
heedless of danger,
hagridden by
the demon, *Haste.*

Sea-lashed, I sensed nothing save *my Quest*,
          Dylath-Leen swirled by uneen...
the River Skai, the bridge by Nir, on through Enchanted Wood—
what labyrinths of briar and oak! What horrid, skulking beasts I slew!—
then following Oukramo's song through golden haze and flowered hills,
Past Kiran, the Jasper City, its terraces, its temple of the River God.
Downriver, treading perfumed meadows— close upon the farther shore
          the dark and ancient forest grew...

Then, like a second sun, new-risen from between the hills—
the thousand golden spires of Thran,
coquettishly exposed amid her veils of ever-changing cloud.
I spoke three dreams beyond belief, before the pilgrim's door;
with sweeping flourishes the red-robed sentry bade me welcome.
I thanked him heartily; his honor, justly, made me proud.

Long I sought—
for Kadath,
in the high, cold waste.
Yet traveling these lands of fable,
one thought ever terrified me—
"*What if I should wake...?*"

Silent in her haughty grandeur, marveling, I traversed that snow-white
          tunnel,
where it pierced Thran's alabaster walls.
I traded tales with strange, bearded sailors, paid homage to her
Dreaming Gods, explored her taverns and her wharves.
There I bought passage on a tall-sterned galleon,
baroquely carved fromfragrant cedar.

Riding the river's gentle, drowsing currents, past scattered shrines,
high upon the right bank, snaking beneath ancient, arching boles
of Jungle Kled— senses reeling with narcotic blossoms'
essence and the magic of the Elder Ones. *The cry of gulls on salt breeze blown.*
The creaking of the ox-wains, hubbub of foreign tongues in barter,
music, clash and clatter, faintly upriver comes...

Long I sought—
for Kadath,
in the high, cold waste.
The nightshade pleasures
of the Gods
to taste!

Hlanith, stolid merchant port— hurdy-gurdy, hustle-bustle,
her thoughts that border Waking Worlds... Cerenerian, the Eastern Sea,
foaming azure, crashing beneath her wharves of oak.
Five days we rode a lively gale, yet our captain held us hard to course.
Aran, snow-capped, like a giant breaker touched the sky.
The land of Ooth-Nargai, and Celephais, City of the Timeless Folk.

Ten thousand years dissolved like smoke outside her polished marble
          walls; within,
the passing of ten thousand hours. Virgin gold, Celephais'
minarets, wine-purple the Tanarians beyond, potent and mystical,
          masking the forbidden ways,
to distant realms of Other-Dream. Here, King Kuranes rules
in lordly splendor, from his rose-crystal Palace of
the Seventy Delights. (He, who was once of Earth, shall rule here till
          The End of Days...)

Long I sought—
for Kadath,
in the high, cold waste.
From quays where painted galleys dance the ageless tidal rhythms,
across the great stone bridge, where Naraxa laughs and babbles,
my weary footsteps, lighter, came.

Unto those vast gates of burnished bronze where, hammered as if in
          breath, Nath-Horthath's twin faces stare:
the face of past, the face of future— half seraphim/half cherubim and daemon.
And up the onyx pavement I strode, into the turquoise temple of the god,
          where chant *the eight*, orchid-wreathed:

"By He Whose Breath is Sea and Sky! Seek not what the Elder Gods have willed
        to hide! Draw not the wrath of The Messenger, and those He serves—
                the Other Gods Outside!"
Yet, unheeded as on ears of bronze (as on the fabled statues of Celephais'
        walls) their ill omens clamored
— within my soul *the Questing* seethed...

Time did not pass but only *waited*, till out of Inquanok, the Twilit Land,
teakwood and ebony, phantasmagoric-carved,
a tall carrack, violet-sheeted, ran swift before the wind—
the ghost of vesper's madness billowed. *Aloof, these sons of gods—*
strange, haunting ballads spinning ever from their lips, like spidersilk,
like echoes of moonlight on a far-flung coast.

Long I sought—
for Kadath,
in the high, cold waste,
to know the darkness' fevered kiss
and the nightmares
of an Elder Race.

As an onyx quarrier I shipped out. Three weeks and three days we sailed.
I spun them dreams they'd never heard and they traded me in kind.
Lower and lower the sun wheel rolled,
each league the mists swirled thicker:
dusk ate day, soon the nights burned brighter— clouds torched by saint
        Elmo's fire, the stars were blackened ashes.
Inquanok— where strange shadows fall, where no cat can endure to dwell,
        where ever rule twilight and cold.

Inquanok fantastic— basalt quays and bulbous domes, sky jagged with
        onyx spires. Inverted icicles of carbon,
thrusting fungal colonies of polished, frozen midnight, writhing with
gold   traceries and intricately chiseled flowers,
carved heads of Gods to guard each frowning gate, encircling squat city walls.
Above all, the central spike on this Hell-Lord's crown— the temple tower
        of the bell,
gonging deep within the air and stone, answering urges of some secret,
        sacred cycle,
chorused by refrain of skirling pipes, stringed shrieks and hallowed calls.

Long I sought—
for Kadath,
in the high, cold waste.
There dwell the Gods—
the Gods that seven lines of priests, black-hooded,
shall offer *vapor-steaming bowls and praise*!

Sixteen the facets of the tower—*fraught with power, fraught with meaning.*
Seven the number of its doors. Seven the number of its onyx causeways.
As I stood entranced, awestruck by this paragon of godly archimagic,
down from on high, upon the broadest cause, the Veiled King, Lord of the
    Mighty, issued forth in golden chariot, yak-drawn.
Flames leapt from the lofty parapet, like bursts of revelation, mirrored in a
    thousand basalt-bottomed pools.
Chanting. Silence. Rhythms of the mystic, warding some dark, lurking
    doom— *impending, tragic...*

Among the crystal music of uncounted fountains, trailing blossoms'
    riotous fragrance,
the voice of iridescent singing birds, up steep stairs of stone
I clambered to the hill summit whereon is raised the clustered palace of
    Veiled King—
its central dome of polished midnight blackness, housing
the fearsome Father of all Shantaks.
*Stare not too long in wonder! To the curious, incautious, weird and terrifying
    dreams he brings!*

Long I sought—
for Kadath,
in the high, cold waste.
North,
Skirting the grey and solemn peaks,
like mammoth tombstones, cloud encased...

Out from the Gate of Caravans. Out, plodding the cobble-studded track,
straight as a well-ploughed furrow. Hoarfrost-white my great bull yak,
    shaggy kilt of fur, ground-dragging,
his brutal horns, lance-sharp and copper shod.
Past domed farmers' cots. Past tilled fields and coppices of lygath.
Past rock-strewn hills and onyx miners' camps. And ever the cliffs reared
    high upon my right
mist writhing phantom-chill the lonely, echoing trail we trod.

Treacherous. Steep cut and slick with rillets, runoff from the
         heaven-piercing crags.
Lung-searing raw, mind-reeling sparse as *wine of edelweiss*, the star-sieved
         draughts of air I, gasping, drank.
Scree— quicksilver shifting, skittering and clattering into the yawning
         gulfs below.
Rope straining as I tugged a struggling horde of darkly rippled beasts
between a rift, near vertical, of glisteningly slivered stone.
Abrupt. The chasm leered like death's-head jaws, lit by an eerie glow.

Long I sought—
for Kadath,
in the high, cold waste.
Beneath me stretched the Quarry of the Gods—
acres gouged, a chasm hewn from bottomless depths of night.
Rooted to the brink I clung... *as in a drunken daze!*

Ravens wheeled and screeched above, swooping, whirling down into the pit,
answered by a weird, spine-freezing cry.
Within its void some nameless, brooding terror shrieked— *urhags,*
         perhaps.... or worse!
Bellowing in primal fear, my yak plunged, wild-eyed, into the gap
         through which we'd inched.
Then, black against the phosphorescent sky, a swarm of monstrous,
         flapping forms descended from the farthest peaks.
No wholesome birds were these! but demons of some nether curse!

Shantaks! They could be no other!—
Larger than elephants they were, horse-headed, winged and scaled...
I drew my blade to harry them. They plummeted. They shrieked and
         gyred.
My scimitar no better than a pin!
Grasped by a giant claw, I struggled: *as if a mouse might thwart an eagle!*
Into the distant North we swept, on mighty pinions never tired..

Long I sought—
for Kadath,
in the high, cold waste,
— beyond the realms of mortal dream,
— beyond the chains of
Time and Space...

Into the distant North we swept. On towards the semi-circled barrier
      range, crouching mastiff-like,
pressing the leprous ceiling of corpse candle clouds.
Guarding the limits of the North and West, carved by no human hand:
vast, onyx statues of the Elder Gods, mitred and twin-headed,
right hands raised in eternal warning to mankind:
"*Enter not this land!*"

Then, wheeling, soaring towards the ultramontane East, past grey clouds,
where the hideous Plateau of Leng, rumored,
is said to lie...
Down we dropped through luminescent shrouds of mist, stiff-limbed and
      crusted with the stellar rime.
Scattered fires like air-starved candles pushed trembling against the night,
      against the denser blackness of the barren plain.
From among squalid huts of stone, insane piping of flutes and rattling as
      of a thousand angry serpents mingled with the Shantak's cry.

Long I sought—
for Kadath,
in the high, cold waste.
Up rushed constricted night— jabbing deadly coal-hard fist,
looming larger. LARGER...
Blurred and strangling our groundward pace.

Twitching shadows leaped and twirled. *Immense. Distortions sinister, dancing
      Unreason's hypnotic tarantella.*
Bonfires licking darkness with impassioned tongues.
Capering, goat-hoofed abominations. Cavorting, horned obscenities—
spawn of that shunned and evil race that barters rubies for fat, sweating
      slaves.
Vision of a wind-ripped instant.
Vanished.

As Shantak wrenches level... planing currents of chill breeze.
      Hunched like a rabid wolf of stone, the monastery, dripping
        terror, circled by its standing slabs.
Above my captors hovered, shrieking in syllables like shattered glass.
To earth. Too numbed with frost to stand erect. Huddled. Kneeling in
      grotesque parody of prayer. Unwilling,
yet goaded forward by those horrid steeds, crawling towards the blackly
      grinning portal of that diabolic fane—
groveling, drawn onwards by some voiceless lemming-call.
Then, distant in corridors unseen, there rose the whisper of seductive,
      bacchanalian trilling...

Long I sought—
for Kadath,
in the high, cold waste.
Down frescoed passageways I stumbled, past images in ancient,
yet still garish pigments: memories of a species damned and hellish, *old
        before the birthing of the moon.*
Nightmares echoed in this maze:

The raising of the Leng-folk's Lethy cities; battles with bloated purple
            spiders of the vales;
star-spanning voyages of conquest as the lunar galleys came to plunder
and   to subjugate—
the amoeboid moon-beast' *loathsome hunger*! *appeased by living sacrifice*!
Sarkomand. The City Older Than All Others. Dead one million years
            before the Rise of Man—
Six gates sphinx-guarded, symbols of enigma. Six broad streets lined with
            columns, *duality, initiation*. The central circle,   wheel of change.
Twin sphinxes, huge and silent, flank the staircase down from
            Dreamland, down into the great abyss.

Into a domed expanse I stumbled: and unholy sanctum choked with coffin
            stench and writhing shadows,
entwined and undulating amidst blasphemous bas-reliefs.
Six blood-stained altars ringed a yawning, stone-lipped pit, that seemed to
            swallow endless, gurgling echoes and the sickly candle-glow.
Five steps led upwards to a dais, mounted by a golden throne—
there squatted the lone high priest, steeped in fabled evil, yellow-robed
            and yellow-masked in silk.
His flute, carved of ivory, spun trilling webs of indecent ecstasy
            — answered from the Vaults of Zin...far below.

Long I sought—
for Kadath,
in the high, cold waste.
Mad-blind with terror beyond death, I fled
down corridors pitch-black,
as though *the Hounds of Tindalos* gave chase.

Down. Down into the charnel bowels of Leng... Scraped raw and livid
sweat searing throbbing wounds. Battered by the cryptal walls.
An eternity of sightless moments flowed like ruptured kegs of tar...
My feet churned air... bounding, bouncing down a steep sloped
            shaft... sensations of endless falling...
I awakened. Ruins sprawled upon a plain, cloud-lit by baleful luminescence.
The sound, the scent, of tide-surge rhythms drifted from afar.

Shattered pave-stones. Shattered pillars. Broken remnants of
     eroded walls.
Pierced by scrub grass and twisted, gangrenous thrusts of shrub.
Basalt cliffs leered behind me, exploding skyward, summit lost
     among the swirling clouds.
Patterns jelled within my brain. An ancient vision flickered:
colonnaded avenues, straight-spoked into a central plaza hub; two
winged lions dominating all; Sarkomand alive and pulsing with
     half-human crowds.

Long I sought—
for Kadath,
in the high, cold waste,
gnawed by Starvation's rat-sharp kiss,
reeling like a broken sot,
staggering— near lame.

A flight of bats swarmed black against the northern phosphorescent glow,
     vigorous and swift they came—
closer, racing down the sky. *No mousy fliers these!*— larger than men. Dark
     as coal!
Flapping sail-like membranes. Horned. Barb-tailed as Hell-spawn. Void
     of identity...nightgaunts...*Slaves of Darkness cast without a face!*
Though I strove to sprint, in sooth, I hobbled; with ease they clasped me
     to their slippery and danksome flesh,
with fingers rubbery they snatched me off into the wind... gyring above
     the necropolis below. Gyring above that eyrie-probing basalt thumb.
Gyring far above the ashen tablelands of Leng, as with the *raiding Unseelie*
     Host, on leather-pinioned wings we rushed beyond this barren place...

North and West we surged, spanning the soaring, ragged peaks— like
     rotting teeth of shattered skulls—
across the chill, twilight steppes of Inquanok. North and West, below the
     goblinfire of cumuli,
across the haunted stillness of sleeping secrets and the indiscretions of the
     Gods in flesh and stone.
Rushing like a nightwing torrent towards those glaring mountains carved
     by no mere mortal hand—
half circle of twin-headed guardians, feet rooted in the shifting desert
     sands, mitres crowned with writhing   mists of pallid flame,
right hands, taller than khufu's slopes, upraised in silent warning: *"This*
     kingdom is the Gods' alone!"

Long I sought—
for Kadath,
in the high, cold waste.
To reach that fabled *Niflgard,*
a thousand terrors I was forced to best,
a thousand obstacles I overcame.

Shantaks spewed shrieking from clefts among the dizzy heights;
swift they closed, then wheeled in panic— nightgaunts they hold inviolate!
for nightgaunts serve not Azathoth, but revere only the Hoary One,
          Nodens, Lord of the Great Abyss!
Unmolested above those peaks we winged; across a sere and dusty sea, ever
          colder, ever dimmer waned the sky,
until, at long last, the world burned black as light within some
          long-sealed tomb!
Undaunted were my nightgaunt carriers— *night is their seed! the blackest*
          crypts their womb! stirred they are by Darkness' kiss!

Through distorted distances we raced, through carbon velvet absolute,
          beyond all Reason's boundaries,
beyond the shackles of the Sane— Obsession was a raging torrent,
          plunging through the nighted gulfs of Time and Space...
where sounds whisper in unknown tinctures of the prism, where perfumes
          swirl in unfathomed shades of resonation.
Suddenly, the stars broke free, unveiled from riven Midnight's misty
          shrouds— vivid with newfound significance, beckoning
all of existence *Northwards*— answering a geometric tyranny of
          inescapable seduction: each curve, each angle, warping, bending
                    to the pattern...
Quickening the vision and the viewer onward to an ultimate convergence,
          somewhere beyond this frozen plane, somewhere beyond dimension...

Long I sought—
for Kadath,
in the high, cold waste.
Northward! Beyond all North! The riptide current streamed...
Northward! The distant, chimeric mountains flowed...
Northward! All energy and matter swayed...

Then, above the fretwork crevices and eastern granite phantasies,
pacing our torrential progress— as some vast pair of mitred heads—
twin crags bobbed, echoing our course. Abrupt, against a rift of stars
          erupted Revelation—

striding in titanic solitude, stalking, unflagging, breathless...
uprooted mountain sentinel, hand lowered as it followed, towering
       grotesque and ogreish —
twin heads staring from a thousand meters elevation.

Backwards I glanced; four more of those carven mountains trailed behind!
Faster, ever faster our slipstream passage gushed—
the nightgaunts' bat-like membranes folded, useless in submissive apathy,
       sucked Northward by the cyclone draught.
on high— a firefly cluster frozen on the rim of Nihil's chalice.
Above all things this pinnacle of onyx vaulted,
Above all things of terrene clime this nightmare palace of the Gods I sought!

Long I sought—
for Kadath,
in the high, cold waste.
Bitter the cold! Bitter the dust I'd stirred along my road of Quest!
But hot and sweet the promise, the addictive vision,
this triumph vinted of dark-dreamed obsession, a supernal poisoned wine,
       this *succus lunariae*, I lusted for its searing taste!

Like fragile autumn leaves we swirled and tumbled, driven
by the whirlwind's blast.
Proportions swelled and warped and curved, as if viewed through
some gigantic reading glass,
drawn closer, ever closer to the eye, while the hapless hands that held the
       glass diminished in perverse inversion,
till, mote-like sentience, through the yawning palace arch we flew!

Impelled by Fate of Force *unseen*, down corridors as canyons vast
the nightgaunts and I rode that hurricane of dark.
Then gloamed a swirling iridescence, mists like a million peacock feathers
       preening.
In the distance, drawing anon closer ever closer, I could hear a music,
          mystic and mesmeric, narcotic as the drifting remembered scent
             of Jungle Kled,
spilling forth a crystal chant, impossible of earthly tongue, wild jingle-
       jangle and the booming thud of countless
bass and tambourines and tabors, the raucous bleat of brazen horns and the in-
toxicating note of silver trumpets keening.

Long I sought—
for Kadath,
in the high, cold waste.
The nightshade pleasures
of the Gods
to taste!

Corridor walls, at long last, opened up like some rare and prismatic orchid
        of Jupiter, titanic blooming,
into a chamber more *sensed* than *seen*, dimensions straining to eclipse the
        sky of night.
The music of unfathomed centuries and spheres bubbled and cascaded,
        torrential sentience of rippling vibration!
Point and counterpoint this celestial symphony of vision and sound;
        dark and glistening the fragrantly oiled skin of that serpentine
                procession—
towering black slaves, iridescent silk their loin cloths, of virgin gold their
        clanking chains and lofty helmet-torches fashioned;
incense smoke, sweet-cloying, billowed in the flickering
        shadow-play of golden lamplight's radiation...

Gentler winds blew, allowing my descent, cradled by an airy hand, my
        bootheels lightly touched the solid pave of onyx stone.
Upright, poised as a conqueror with chin held high I strode, no,
        swaggered (*I must say to be correct!*), burning eager to claim my
                victory, hard-wrested.
My faceless army behind me fluttered like a cloak of darkness woven;
        before my gathered might, the host
of Kadath parted as the sea at Moses' stern command!
Wilder the drums beat! Wilder the echo of the trumpets' blast! Wilder
        the thunderclap of cymbals! High and sweet those throats voiced
                their arcane melody!
Then, looming stately and majestic rose the Lords Who Dwell in the Cold
        Waste— each cautioning with upraised hand! Each cautioning
                my unvoiced boast!

Long I sought—
for Kadath,
in the high, cold waste.
Haloed in blazing aurora-borealis radiance they were,
crowned in jagged spires of ivory and diamond—
the Great Old Gods, *the living image of my Quest*, I faced!

Haughty they were,
hooded in weird, fantastic flights of dream,
fierce, narrow, cruel their eyes, their lips.
Haughty they were,
knife-thin of nose, knife-sharp of chin,
their ears, long-lobed and pendulous...

Silence flowed thick and honey-golden, stuporous as resin, cool and
                tingling scented, oozing from the boles of conifers primordial,
Till all sound, all motion froze, as if trapped in distortions of glistening amber...
For a moment or an age we waited.
Vistas of vibration, at first sensed only as ripplings in subconscious
depths,   cosmic rustling of the spheres,
swelled in trilling harmony as unending strings of silver, brushed and
                caressed by trembling bows—
vibrating as each black-skinned servant raised his chimeara-tipped wand
        of crystal slowly in upward camber, slowly in homage
                to *The Masters and The Fated*...

Long I sought—
for Kadath,
in the high, cold waste;
to reach that fabled Bastion of the Gods,
gladly,
a thousand perils I embraced!

Forward stepped one stately giant from among the gathered throng.
                Taller! More exquisitely aesthetic in perfection! More ancient!
                        More steeped in glorious and wicked wisdom—
in words that whispered and roared like liquid fire he spoke:
"Fool! *Embodiment of Everyman*! Lusting ever for that which has been
        forbidden, that which beckons unattained!
Know you that some fruits are better left untasted! Some races better left
        unrun! Some battles better lost than won!
Gladly would we bid you welcome, *Twice-warned*! But condemned you are,
Fool! who struggled too hard to reach our tabooed heights! They claim
        your soul in tribute for this zenith you have gained!"

Closer the Great Ones and their minions circled, chanting a
        litany in syllables stygian and nigromantic!
Swiftly I pivoted upon my heel, my nightgaunt force to muster—
...*they had vanished*!

Grimly I faced my certain death. Grimly I sought some magic key
          for my escape... "VANISHED!" was *the word*! *The key*!
"You cannot harm me!" I shouted valiantly, "It is *I* who plunged
          into this dream by choice!— and now *I* choose to *wake*!
Then wild my laughter gushed and spiraled— *I had won*!
          My fears were banished!

Long I sought—
for Kadath,
in the high, cold waste.
Now I sought the waking world,
now with my power,
the Vision I erased...!

And the Great Ones cooed
and Warbled sweetly
to the curiosity within the cage—
skull of Ruby, Spiderweb of silver,
and a shadow form therein imprisoned,
shrieking in its voiceless rage!

I awoke upon a bed of fresh-turned sheets, cinches buckled tightly on my
          tailored jacket,
babbling mindlessly and giggling at this *boundless* (pardon!) cosmic jest!
Till at last the Darkness claimed me to the world of slumber— *I awakened*
          with a sobbing scream!
Nevermore the retreat of drowsing golden vistas, but the ebb and flow of
          harshly taunting reason!
So I struggle to pen this narrative as caution to you wild and reckless
          Dreamers, who, too, would dare *The Quest*...
for the Old One, tittering, had whispered in answer—
                              is Madness not a Waking Dream...?

Long I sought—
for Kadath,
in the high, cold waste,
possessed by promises,
dream-glimpsed,
in red-lit visions of Ngranek's face.

Beyond the realms of Mortal Dream.
Beyond the chains
of Time and Space...

To seize the madness
of this Dreamer's
Unknown Quest:
to grasp for secrets
better left—
unguessed.

To know the darkness' fevered kiss
and the nightmares
of an Elder Race...

Long I sought—
for Kadath,
in the high, cold waste.
At last I came to face the fear that had shadowed secretly my every
    footstep through my far-flung travels—
that if all Life is but "A Dream Within a Dream" (was it not Poe who'd
    mused in verse?)
 ...let the Dreamer pray he shall not wake!

Errol Undercliffe *is a Brichester writer whose work has only recently begun to reach a wider public. Apparently a recluse, he often wrote for the Brichester fanzine* Spirited, *whose editors, however, never met him. Rumour has it that he spoke on a literary panel at the Brichester Fantasy Convention in 1965, but a photograph taken of him on that occasion has yet to be traced. In 1967, aged about 30, he disappeared after an attempt at amateur psychical research. His stories, most of them contemporary treatments of traditional macabre themes, have been edited into an omnibus collection,* Photographed by Lightning, *and the Korean film director Harry Chang, an Undercliffe admirer of long standing, has completed a triptych film of his stories,* Red Dreams.

The Franklyn Paragraphs

by

RAMSEY CAMPBELL

THE DISAPPEARANCE OF Errol Undercliffe in 1967 from his
flat in Lower Brichester was not widely reported. The little
speculation provoked by mystery was soon resolved by the belief that
Undercliffe had 'disappeared' in search of publicity. While he has not
reappeared, his public seems still to be waiting for him to produce
himself out of a hat. At the time I hinted in print that I could supply
evidence of something more sinister, but I fear that the general
branding of Undercliffe as a charlatan was sufficiently persuasive to
dissuade me from publishing evidence in case Undercliffe declared
both his absence and his last letter a hoax.

Undercliffe first wrote me in 1965, when my first book had just
become available from Brichester Central Library. Typically, he en-
closed a cutting from the letter-column of the *Brichester Herald*; under
the heading 'Can Ghost Stories be Libelous?' one 'Countryman' had
written: 'I have recently perused a book of ghost stories by a Mr. J.
Ramsey Campbell, mainly located in Brichester. Mr. Campbell seems
to look upon the citizens of our town as either witches, warlocks, or
illiterate "country folks". The advertising for the book makes much
of the fact that the author is still an infant; since this is obvious from
the contents, I would scarcely have thought it necessary to advertise
the fact. I would suggest that before he writes another such book Mr.
Campbell should (1) visit Brichester, where he has clearly never set
foot, and (2) grow up. 'And so on. I could have replied that on the basis
of my several visits to Brichester I didn't consider it the sort of town
where I'd care to spend a night; but I find this kind of letter-column
duel a little childish, and didn't feel disposed to join swords or even
pens. For the record, these days Brichester has an impressive mundane
surface, but I still sense that it may crack. When I and Kirby McCauley
passed through the area in 1965, a month or so before Undercliffe's
first letter, I was disturbed to be unable to find the turn-off to
Severnford and Brichester, and the groups of youths inert in the sun
outside a shack-like cinema in Berkeley (showing, oddly enough, Jerry

Lewis' one horror film) proved less than helpful. Hours later, after dark, we were directed by a roundabout policeman, but without conferring we sneaked around the roundabout—only to find ourselves somehow on the road originally indicated and to stay at an inn whose sign we discovered in the dawn to be that of a goat!

However, I digress. I quote the letter from the *Herald* at length because it seems to me to demonstrate some aspects of Undercliffe's character; not that he wrote it (at least I shouldn't think so), but he did enclose it with his first letter to me, though it is hardly the sort of enclosure most of us would choose when initiating a correspondence. However, Undercliffe's sense of humor was wry—some might call it cynical or cruel. I'm inclined to believe it was the product of a basic insecurity, from what little I know of his life. I never visited him, and his letters were rarely self-revelatory (though the first batch here published is more so than he might have wished). Most of them were first drafts of stories, signed and dated; he kept a copy of every letter he wrote—these were carefully filed in his flat—and several of our correspondence turned up virtually verbatim in his short stories. In particular the description of the disused station in *The Through Train* was lifted bodily from his letter to me of 20 November 1966.

If this says little about the man himself, I can only maintain that for the rest of us Errol Undercliffe was the Mr. Arkadin of the horror-story world. 'Errol Undercliffe' was almost certainly not his christened name. His refusal to provide biographical details was not as notorious as J. D. Salinger's, but it was fully as obsessive. He seems to have been educated in or near Brichester (see the first letter here) but I cannot trace his school, nor the friend whose engagement party he describes. I never saw a photograph of him. Perhaps he thought the aura of mystery with which he surrounded himself carried over to his stories; perhaps, again, he was bent or preserving his own isolation. If so, he served himself ill as far as his final ordeal was concerned; he had nobody to whom he could turn.

When I went down to Undercliffe's flat on hearing that he'd disappeared, I was less surprised than saddened by the experience. The Lower Brichester area, as I've mentioned elsewhere, is the sort of miniature cosmopolis one finds in most major English towns: three-storey houses full of errant lodgers, curtains as varied as flags at a conference but more faded, the occasional smashed pane, the frequent furtive watchers. Somebody was tuning a motorcycle in Pitt Street, and the fumes drifted into Undercliffe's flat through a crack in the pane and clouded the page in his typewriter. The landlady was making ready to dispose of this, together with Undercliffe's books and other possessions, as soon as the rent gave out at the end of the month. I finally persuaded her to let me handle the disposal, after a good deal of wrangling and invocation of August Derleth (who'd never published Undercliffe)' the Arts Council (who'd never heard of him, I imagine) and others. Having ushered her out at last, well aware that she'd prepared to search me before I left the house, I examined the flat. The wardrobe and chest-of-drawers contained two suits, some shirts and so forth, none of which could have looked particularly stylish at an engagement party. The bed commanded a fine view of an arachnidial crack in the ceiling (clearly that crack which 'suddenly, with a horrid lethargy, detached itself from the plaster and fell on Peter's upturned face' in *The Man Who Feared to Sleep*. The wallpaper had a Charlotte Perkins Gilman look; once Undercliffe complained that ' such an absurd story should have used up an inspiration which I could work into one of my best tales'. The window looked out on the fuming motorcycle, now stuck stubbornly in first gear, and its fuming owner; at night I suppose Undercliffe, seated at his typewriter before the window, might have waved to the girl slipping off her slip in the flat across the street, and I carried on his neighborly gesture, though without much success. On the sill outside his window cigarette-stubs had collected like bird-droppings; he tended to cast these into the night, disliking the sight of a brimming ashtray. He'd go through a packet per thousand words, he once told me; he'd tried chewing-gum once, but this drew his fillings, and he was terrified of the dentist (cf. *The Drill*). All this, of course, is trivial, but I needed—still need—distraction. I'd already followed Undercliffe's search through the first three letters printed here, and that page still in the typewriter—a letter to me, probably the last thing he wrote—told of what he found. I removed it, unwillingly enough, and left; the landlady let it go. Later I arranged for transportation of the contents of the flat. The books—which seemed to be Undercliffe's treasured possessions, books of horror stories bought with the profits from his horror stories, a sad and lonely vicious cycle—are now held in trust by the British Science Fiction Association library; the rest is in storage. I wish more than ever that Undercliffe would come forward to claim them.

Undercliffe's first letter to me (15 October 1965) contains a passage which in retrospect seems informed by a macabre irony. 'The implicit theme of your story *The Insects from Shaggai*,' he writes, 'is interesting, but you never come to grips with the true point of the plot: the horror-story author who is skeptical of the supernatural and finally is faced with overwhelming evidence of its reality. What would be his reaction?Certainly not to write of "the lurid glow which shines on the

razor lying on the table before me"!!This is as unlikely as the ending
of *The Yellow Wallpaper*. I'd be interested to hear whether you yourself
believe in what you write. For myself, I think the fact that I take great
pains to check material on the supernatural here in our Central Library
is eloquent enough. By the way, have you come across Roland
Franklyn's *We Pass from View*?The author is a local man who has some
quite arresting theories about reincarnation and the like. '

Which brings us to Franklyn and *We Pass from View*, in themselves
as mysterious as the fate of Undercliffe; but I suspect that the two
mysteries are interdependent, that one explains the other—if indeed
one wishes to probe for explanation. Before discussing Franklyn,
however, I'd like to note some of Undercliffe's work; I feel obliged to
bring it to the notice of a wider public. His favorites of his own work
were *The Drains* (the blood of a bygone murder drips from the cold
tap), *The Carved Desk* (the runes carved on what was once a Druid tree
call up something which claws at the ankles of anyone foolish enough
to sit down to write), and *The Drifting Face* (never published: originally
intended for the ill-fated second issue of *Alien Worlds*, it now cannot
be traced). I favor his more personal, less popular work: *The Windows
in the Fog* (in which the narrator's glimpses of a girl across the street
mount to an obsessive pitch until he accosts her one night and rebuffed,
murders her), *The Steeple on the Hill* (where a writer fond of lonely walks
is followed by the members of a cult, is eventually drawn within their
circle and becomes the incarnation of their god), and *The Man Who
Feared to Sleep*, which lent its title (*Peur de Sommeil* in France) to
Undercliffe's best collection, under the imprint of that excellent
publisher who rediscovered such writers as Pursewarden and Sebastian
Knight and made again available Robert Blake's legendary collection
The Stairs in the Crypt. It is amusing to note that the entire contents of
Undercliffe's collection—including the title story, which is surely a
study of insanity—was listed under 'Supernatural Phenomena' in the
H. W. Wilson *Short Story index* (in an earlier volume than that which
placed my own *Church in High Street* under 'Church Entertainments',
making it sound like a parish farce or a Britten mystery play). Undercliffe was latterly working on a script for Delta Film Productions, but
producer Harry Nadler reports that this was never completed; nor was
his story *Through the Zone of the Colossi*, a metaphysical piece based on
a reference in my *Mine on Yuggoth* coupled with material from *We Pass
from View*.

Which brings me back to the necessity of discussing Franklyn's
book, a duty which I fear I've been avoiding. I've never seen the book,
but I have little desire to do so. I refrained from consulting Brichester

Central Library's copy when I went to Undercliffe's flat; I suppose I could obtain this through the National Central Library, though I suspect that in fact the copy (like all others, apparently) has mysteriously disappeared.

Although, as Undercliffe points out, *We Pass from View* displays marked affinities with the Cthulhu Mythos in certain passages, such Lovecraft scholars as Derleth, Lin Carter, Timothy d'Arch Smith and J. Vernon Shea can supply no information on the book. I understand that it was published in 1964 by the 'True Light Press', Brichester; references in Undercliffe's letters suggest that it was a duplicated publication, originally circulated in card covers but probably bound by libraries taking copies. I have not been able to discover where, if anywhere, it was on sale. An odd rumor reached me recently that almost the entire edition was stolen from the 'True Light Press'—actually the house of Roland Franklyn—and has not been heard of since; perhaps destroyed, but by whom?

Here is the little information I've obtained from various sources. The British National Bibliography gives the following entry:

129. 4—Incarnation and reincarnation
FRANKLYN, Ronald
We pass from View. Brichester, True Light Press,
9/6. Jan 1964. 126 p. 22 cm.

However, the Cumulative Book Index, which lists all books published in English, does not acknowledge the book; at least, neither I nor the staff of Liverpool's Picton Library can trace the reference.

While correlating notes I was surprised to turn up in my commonplace book the following review, which might have been copied from the *Times Literary Supplement*:

PSEUDOPODDITIES
The last few decades have seen the emergence of many disturbing pseudo-philosophies, but *We Pass from View* must rank lowest. The author, Roland Franklyn, has less idea of style than most of his kind; however, the ideas behind the writing are expressed with less ambiguity than one might wish. His basic thesis seems to be that the number of souls in the universe is limited, by some illegitimate application of the conservation of energy principle, and that humanity must therefore acknowledge an infinite number of simultaneous incarnations. The last chapter, *Towards the True Self*, is a sort of reductio ad absurdum of the theory, concluding that the 'true self' is to be found 'outside space', and that each human being is merely a facet of his 'self', which is itself able

to experience all its incarnations simultaneously but unable to control them. There is a suggestion of Beckett here (particularly *L'Innomable*), and Mr. Franklyn has infused enough unconscious humour into many passages to cause hilarity when the book was read aloud at a party. But a book which advocates the use of drugs to achieve fulfillment of black-magic rites is worth attention not so much as humour (and certainly not as it was intended) as a sociological phenomenon.

Laughter at a party, indeed!I still find that remark rather frightening. What copy was being read aloud?The *TLS* review copy, perhaps, but in that case what happened to it?Like so much in this affair, the end fades into mystery. I doubt that many indignant letters replied to the review; those that were written probably weren't printable. In 1966, I heard vaguely of a book called *How I Discovered my Infinite Self* by 'An Initiate', but whether it was ever published I don't know.

Undercliffe quoted several passages from *We Pass from View* which, though I find them faintly distasteful, I had better include. I still have all of Undercliffe's letters; some day I may edit them into a memorial article for *The Arkham Collector*, but it seems in rather bad taste to write a memoir of a man who may still be alive somewhere. The letters printed here are, I think, essential.

In his letter of 2 November 1965 Undercliffe wrote:"Here's a bizarre passage which might set you off on a short story. From the first page of *We Pass from View*: "The novice must remind himself always that the self is infinite and that he is but one part of his Self, not yet aware of his other bodies and lives. REMIND YOURSELF on sleeping. RE-MIND YOURSELF on waking. *Above all, REMIND YOURSELF* when entering the First Stage of Initiation". As for this first stage, I've traced references later in the text, but nothing very lucid. Franklyn keeps mentioning "the aides" which seems to be drugs of some sort, usually taken under supervision of an "initiate" who chants invocations ("Ag'lak Sauron, Daoloth asgu'i, Eihort phul'aag"—that ought to ring a bell with you) and attempts to tap the novices subconscious knowl-edge of his other incarnations. Not that I necessarily believe what Franklyn says, but it certainly gives you that sense of instability which all good horror stories should provide. I can't discover much about Franklyn. He seems in the last year or two to have drawn together a circle of young men who, from what I hear, visit Goatwood, Clotton, Temphill, the island beyond Severnford, and other places in which you're no doubt as interested as I am. I'd like to get in on the act. '

I replied that he surely didn't need drugs for inspiration and that, warnings from Dennis Wheatley aside, I didn't feel it was advisable to become involved in black magic. 'Experience makes the writer,' Undercliffe retorted. Subsequently he avoided direct quotation, but I gathered he had not joined Franklyn's circle; his own decision, I think. Then, in September 1966, when he was writing *The Crawling in the Attic* (I'd just started library work and sent him the manuscript of *The Stocking* to read, which he didn't like—'elaborately pointless'), he quoted the following:

'Today's psychologists are wrong about dreams coming from the subconscious mind. Dreams are the links between us and the experiences of our other incarnations. *We must be receptive to them.* TELL YOURSELF BEFORE YOU SLEEP THAT YOU WILL SEE BEYOND YOUR FACET. The initiate known as Yokh'khim, his name on Tond, came to me describing a dream of long tunnels in which he was pursued but could not see his body. After several sessions, he managed to see himself as a ball of hair rolling through the tunnel away from the Trunks in the Ooze. The ball was known on Tond as Yokh'khim. He has not attained the stage of Black Initiate and spends his time beyond this facet, having set aside all but the minimum of his life on Earth. '

I hadn't much to say to that except to suggest that Franklyn had plagiarized the 'Tond' reference, provoking Undercliffe to reply: 'Surely Franklyn has undermined your complacency enough to make complaints about copyright a little trivial. Anyway, no doubt he'd point that you knew of Tond through your dreams. 'I couldn't decide whether his tongue was in his cheek; I passed over his comment, and our correspondence fell off somewhat.

In February 1967 he quoted a passage which is significant indeed. 'What about a story of a writer who haunts his own books?' he suggested. 'Franklyn has a paragraph on ghosts: "The death of a body does not mean that the soul will leave it. This depends on whether there is an incarnation for it to pass into. If not, the body continues to be inhabited until it is destroyed. The initiate knows that Edgar Allan Poe's fear of premature burial was well-founded. If the death is violent, then it is more difficult than ever for the soul to leave. FOR HIS OWN SAFETY, THE INITIATE MUST INSIST ON CREMATION. Otherwise he will be hopelessly attracted back to Earth, and the burrowers of the core may drag off his body from the grave with him still in it to the feast of Eihort. '

Interesting, I said somewhat wearily. I was rather tired of this sort of verbal delirium. On 5 July 1967 Undercliffe reported that the *Brichester Herald* had noted Franklyn's death. This meant little to me at the time. Then came the final sequence of letters.

7 Pitt Street: Lower Brichester, Glos:
14 July 1967 1. 03 a. m. :
slightly intoxicated

Dear JRC:

Always this point at a party where the beer tastes like vomit. Pretty putrid party, actually. Friend of mine from school who got engaged and sent me
an invite. Can't think why, I'd just about forgotten him myself, but I wanted
to meet him again. Didn't get near. Great fat bluebottle of a woman he got engaged to pawning over him all the evening and wanting to be kissed, messily
at that, whenever he tried to act the host. Good luck say I. So I had to make
my own way round the conversations. I just don't know where he got them
from. All bow ties and 'God, Bernard, surely you realize the novel is absolutely
dead' and banging down tankards of ale which they'd bought to be all boys together, sloshing them over and making little lakes down these trestle tables in
the Co-op Hall (another blow for the old town and the Brichester folks—our
engaged friend kept patting his bluebottle and bellowing 'I had a wonderful
childhood in Brichester, absolutely wonderful, they're fine people', no Palm
Court for *him*). Whole place murky with smoke and some tin band playing in
the fog. Hundreds of ashtrays surrounded by those pieces of ash like dead flies.
Finally our friend fell to his feet to give thanks for 'all the superb presents',
which didn't make me feel any more accepted, since I hadn't known it was
done to bring one. I feel a little

Better. Repartee: the morning after. Beg pardon, I shouldn't have mentioned engagements and fiancees. Still, I'm sure you're better off. Writers
always bloom better with elbow room. I have your letter by me. You're right,
your last argument with your girlfriend in Lime Street Station cafeteria with
the bare tables, balls of cellophane and someone next to you trying not to listen—it'd never come off in print, even though it happened to you they'd be
sure to scream Graham Greene was here first. And then her calling down 'I
love you' through the rain before her mother dragged her back from her window—yes, it's very poignant, but you'll have to rewrite before you can print.
More on our wavelength, what you say about this other girl running out of
your haunted Hornby Library in panic certainly sounds promising. You going
to lock yourself in there overnight?I'd give a lot for a genuine supernatural experience.

There was this idiot at the party wanting to know what I did. Horror stories I said. Should have seen him blanch. 'Why do you write those things?' he
asked as if he'd caught me picking my nose. 'For the money. ' I said. A young
couple sliding down the wall behind us laughed. Great, an audience I thought.
No doubt if I'd said I wasn't joking they'd have laughed harder. 'No, but seriously,' said this poor man's F. R. Leavis (you couldn't write for anything as
base as money, you see) 'would you not agree that the writer is a sort of Christ
figure who suffers in order to cohere his suffering for the reader's benefit?'The
extent of his suffering was his bank manager calling him on his overdraft, I'll
bet. 'And don't you think the horror story coheres (I wasn't cohering myself by
that time) an experience?"Are you telling me you believe in what you write?'

he demanded as if it'd been *Mein Kampf*. 'You don't think I'd write something in which I didn't believe?'I retorted, carefully placing the preposition. The young couple left; the show was over. He stalked off to tell Bernard about me.

At least the streets were clean and empty. Remarkable girl in the flat across the street. You should come down. Anyway, to bed. Tomorrow to work on *Through the Zone of the Colossi* and check the library.

Best,
EU

* * *

Pitt of Hell: Lower Brichester, Glos:
14 July 1967: later!

Dear JRC:

I don't normally write twice in a day. Today's events, however, are too important to let fade. I have had my experience. It will unquestionably form a short story, so forgive me this first draft. I trust you not to use it.

Today, as anticipated, I visited the library. After last night/this morning, I felt somewhat sick, but that's the penance. On the bus I was trying to cohere *Zone of the Colossi*, but they wouldn't let me; you must know how it is. Half the passengers were ducking and screaming beneath the flight of a wasp, and the other half were sitting stoically pouring forth clouds of tobacco-smoke, which curled in the hot air. I sat next to some whistling fool and my thoughts kept getting sidetracked into a search for the lyrics in order to fit them to his tune and be rid of it. Not an auspicious start, but *Zones of the Colossi* was forgotten when I left the library. I couldn't find *We Pass from View* on the shelf in the Religion section; mind you, some cretin in an aged mac was pottering round the shelves and sampling books and replacing them at whatever position he'd pottered to, earning himself glares from the staff. Someone else had erected a fortress of books on one of the tables and behind it was completing his football coupon. He cursed me visibly when I examined his barricade; I've rarely felt so self-conscious as then, his gaze on my canted head. But there it was: *We Pass from View* beneath *The Mass in Slow Motion* and *The Catholic Marriage Manual* and Graham Fisher's *Identity and Awareness*. I pulled out the foundation, but the wall held.

The book was bound in bright blue. The table-top was pastel green. The room was warm and sunny, if a little stifling. At the further end, behind a creamy desk, one of the staff was recounting his adventures in a branch library, how he'd been plagued by old ladies pleading for what he called 'cheap novelettes'; I could tell he looked upon all fiction as the poor relation of non-fiction, like all academic librarians—so much for our writing. You couldn't get further from a Lovecraft setting, but then this was the real thing.

I turned back the cover; it slapped the table-top. Silence fell. A blade of sunlight moved along the floor, intensifying cracks. Then the pages of *We Pass from View* began to turn of their own accord.

At first I thought it must be a draught. When you're sitting in a bright new library among books and people you don't think of the possibility of the supernatural. When the book exhibits traces of its readership (chewing-gum on one page, a dead fly on another) it's difficult to view it as haunted. And yet

I couldn't take my eyes from those moving pages. They turned up the dedica-
tion ('to my faithful friends') and for a second, as though my vision were
failing, I saw lines of some other print waver as if superimposed on the text.
The page turned to the next, a blank leaf. I put out my hand, but I couldn't
quite bring myself to touch the book. As I hesitated, lines of print appeared on
the blank paper.

HELP ME

It stood out starkly on the paper, next to the fingerprint of some unclean
reader. HELP ME. The letters held for several seconds: great black capitals
which seemed to burn my eyeballs as I stared at them. And I was overwhelmed
by the sense of an appeal, of someone trying desperately to contact me. Then
they blurred and faded.

FEEL SOMEONE READING MUST BE

That flashed and disappeared; I read it in a second. The room seemed air-
less; I was sweating, my ribs were closing on my lungs. I could see only the
book open on the table and feel a terrible, tortuous strain, as of a mind in torment trying to communicate its suffering.

SHE HAD ME BURIED HER REVENGE TOLD HER CREMATE
BITCH WOMEN CANT TRUST HELP ME

That HELP ME was molten.

FEEL THEM COMING SLOWLY BURROWING WANT ME TO
SUFFER CANT MOVE GET ME OUT SAVE ME SOMEWHERE IN
BRICHESTER HELP ME

And the page, which had been lifted trembling, fell back. I waited. The
room assembled round me in the merciless sunlight. The page remained blank.
I don't know how long I waited. At last it occurred to me that the setting was
wrong; back in my room I might be able to re-establish contact. I picked up
the book—holding it rather gingerly; somehow I expected to feel it move, struggle between my fingers —and carried it to the desk and back into mundanity.

'I'm afraid this is a reference copy only. ' said the girl at the desk, flashing a smile and her engagement ring at me.

I told her that it seemed to be their only copy and that there were various of my books in the fiction section and that I knew the chief librarian (well,
I'd glimpsed him enthroned in his office as someone bore in his coffee the day
I was invited by his secretary to sign my books). I could have told her that I
felt the book throbbing in my hand. But she replied 'Well, *personally* I know
we can trust you with it and if it were up to me I'd let you have it, but —' and
much more of the I'm-only-doing-my-job speech. I set the book down on the
desk in order to wave my hands about and she handed it to a girl who was replacing books on the shelves, belatedly asking 'You didn't want it again, did
you?'

I saw it carried away on the toppling pile; already the transcendental was
being erased by the mundane; Franklyn would be filed and completely forgotten. And that showed me what I must do. Of course I knew that it was
Franklyn whose paragraphs I had been reading from beyond the grave, indeed,

from the grave. But I didn't know how to find him. The *Brichester Herald* had given neither his address nor where he was buried. 'Do you know anything about Roland Franklyn Himself?' I inquired.

'Yes, he used to come in quite often...' but she obviously didn't want to talk about it. 'Eric, don't let Mary do all the clearing,' she said to her companion at the desk, who was building a house of holiday postcards.

'Franklyn, the little queer in the cloak?' he addressed me. 'You're not a friend of his, are you?Good Job. Used to come in here with a whole crowd of them, the Twelve Disciples we used to call them. One of them came up to the desk one day because we were talking about his master and waved his great emaciated fist at us—you could see the drugs running out of his eyes. Why are you interested in that queer?Can't think what attracted them all, what with that moth-eaten cloak and that huge bald head—he'd probably pulled out the last few hairs to stick on that spidery beard. He had a wife too, I think—must've been before he came to the crossroads. What's the matter, Mary, you want me to rupture myself?'

'Do you know where he lived?' I stayed him.

'Bottom of Mercy Hill. House looked like Satan was in residence. You can't miss it. 'He knocked down the house of cards and walked away, and so, feeling rather adrift, did I.

I suppose I could have tried to find Franklyn today, but I wanted to crystallize the experience, to preserve it before it lost its form. I came home and set this down; I think it needs rewriting. Reality always does; I suppose we have to give it some form, even while paying the price of distortion. I keep thinking of Franklyn in his coffin, aware of something tunneling towards him, unable to move a muscle but still capable of feelings. But it's dark now; I couldn't find him in the dark. Tomorrow, more. Goodbye, girl in the window.

EU

* * *

a fixed point: 15 July 1967

Dear JRC:

Today has been disturbing.

I knew Franklyn lived on Mercy Hill, but the Hill covers a lot of ground; I couldn't search it for his house. Finally I thought of the street directory—odd I didn't think of that before—and called at the library today to check. There was only one R. Franklyn on Mercy Hill. I did return to the Religion section but they couldn't find *We Pass from View*; I suppose they're classifying me as one of their regular cranks.

I caught a bus to Mercy Hill. High sun, slight breeze; a bluebottle was patting its reflection on the window, trying to escape. In the streets couples were taking their ice-creams for a walk; toward the Hill tennis-balls were punctuating their pauses, girls were leaping, bowls were clicking, and from the houses behind a procession was bearing trays of cakes to pavilion. It was one of those days when if anything is to happen you have to make it happen; or for me to complete the next episode of my short story.

I dismounted at the foot of the Hill and climbed the piled terraces. At one corner they were erecting a new school; workmen were sunning themselves on girders. Two levels further up I came into Dee Terrace, and at once saw Franklyn's house.

It was unmistakeable. The personality which gave that house its final form was not the architects. One chimney had been built into a frustum of white stone; an extra room had been added on the left, and its window had been blocked with newer brick; all the curtains, except those of one ground-floor window draped in green, were black. The house looked deserted, the more so for its garden, which could not have been tended in years; grass and weeds grew knee-high. I brushed through, imagining things crawling into my shoes. A bustling cloud of flies rose from something to one side. I reached the front door and saw the green curtain move; a face peered and drew back. I knocked. There was silence for a moment. Then inside a woman's voice screamed: 'Oh, lie down with you!' Before I could ponder on that, the door was open.

The woman was certainly not in mourning—which was encouraging, for I hadn't known quite what approach to make. She wore a red dress, which looked pale against the crimson wallpaper of the hall. She was heavily, if inaccurately, made up, and her hair was rather arbitrarily bleached. She waited.

'Would you be Mrs. Franklyn?'

She looked suspicious, as if I'd intended a threat. 'Roland Franklyn was my husband,' she admitted ungraciously. 'Who are you?'

Who indeed. It didn't seem as though I'd get far by declaring the supernatural nature of my quest. 'I'm a writer,' I compromised. 'I've read your husband's book several times. I was shocked to hear of his death,' I added to get it over with.

'Well, you don't have to be. Come in, anyway,' she said. She looked round the hall and grimaced. 'Look at this. Would you live with this?Not likely. Getting them in the right mood—half of them didn't know what they were being got in the mood for. Nice boys, some of them, to begin with.'She kicked the crimson wall and ushered me into a room on the right.

I wasn't prepared—I couldn't have been. A ground-floor room with wardrobe, dressing-table complete with cob-webbed mirror, a bed beneath the window, piles of women's magazines, some thick with dust, and a cat chained to the leg of a chair in the middle of the floor; it wasn't a sense of evil or fear that choked me, it was a sense of something locked away, forgotten and gone bad. The cat padded up to meet me; its chain gave it freedom of the room, but it couldn't quite reach the door.

'Pussy likes you,' said Mrs Franklyn, closing the door and sinking into a chair amid a haze of dust; her dress drew up her thighs, but she didn't pull it down. 'That could be a good sign, but don't they say only effeminate men can make friends with cats?Why are you looking at me like that?'I hadn't realized I was looking like anything in particular; I was carrying the cat, chain and all, to the chair I took opposite her. 'Don't like the chain, is that it?But me and my cat, we're all we've got—I'm not letting her out so they can carry her off and sacrifice her. They would, you know, on their nights. I take her in the garden, that's all; wouldn't trust them further than that,' I remembered the flies. 'What do you write?' she demanded.

In this context it seemed a little pale to say 'Stories of the supernatural. '

'Stories, eh?Yes, we all like stories,' she mused. 'Anything's better than the real thing. Do you want some tea?I'm afraid that's about all I have to offer. '

'It's all right, thank you,' I refused; I could see cracked cups in the kitchen behind her head. She caught my eye; she was always doing that, damn her.

'Oh, I can't blame you for thinking,' she said. "But it gets you down after a while. After he took the house over—you didn't know that, did you?—yes, he did, he married me and then he encroached on every room, keeping things I wouldn't touch all over the house, until I took this room and the kitchen and I told him if you try anything in my rooms *I'll kill you!*' She thumped the chain-arm and dust flew out.

'But why did you put up with it?' I had to ask.

'Why? *Because I married him!*' The cat fled, knocked over a pile of magazines, sneezed and jumped back; she reeled it in and fondled it. 'Now, pussy's not scared of mummy,' she soothed and put it down. It began to scratch at her shoe. 'Lie down with you, for God's sake,' she hissed. It came to me for comfort.

'When I married him,' she returned to me, 'he promised I'd have all this house to entertain, to do all the things I never could. I believed him. Then I found out how he really was. So I waited. Every day I wished him dead, so I'd have my house, what was left of my life. I haven't spoken to him for years, did you know that?—hardly even seen him. I used to leave his meals outside his room on a tray; if he didn't eat them that was up to him. But when he didn't touch them for three days I went into his room. No, I didn't go in—all those filthy statues and lights and books—but I could see he wasn't there. He was in his stupid little printing press room. He was dead all right. There was a book— he must have been going to copy something— but I didn't read it; the way his face looked was enough. I threw it in the bin. Didn't touch him, though—oh, no, they're not going to say I killed him after all those years I've suffered. '

'But how did you stand it?' Of course the answer was—she didn't.

'Oh, he made me long ago. We met when we were students—I was impressionable then, I thought he was a good man, the best—and later we got married. I ought to have known; there was a rumor he'd been expelled from the University even then, but when he swore he hadn't I trusted him. Then his parents died and left him this house and we got married. My husband —' He face contorted as if she'd put her hand in something foul.' He took me down to Temphill and made me watch those things dancing on the graves. I didn't want to but he said it was for a book he was writing. He held my hand, then. And later we went down the steps below Clotton—oh, you may write, but you'd never dare to write about.... I don't want to think about it. But it hardened me. It made me tough when he began his mummery back here, trying to stop me destroying all his muck... '

That sounded like a cue. 'If you haven't thrown away all his books do you think I could look them over?Purely from a writer's viewpoint,' I tacked on, why I'm not sure.

'But you're a nice young man, you don't want to become another of his,' she said, and sat down on the bed; her dress rose again like a curtain. She began to clear piles of magazines festooned with dust away from the bed; atop one was a vase of dandelions—'Just a touch of color, what's it matter what they are, no-one ever comes,' she explained, though the petals had curled and dulled in the flecked light. 'Did you ever write from experience?How could you, you've never had what I'd had to put up with. The things he's doing even now to hinder me—Only yesterday I picked up one of his books to throw it out and it went sticky and soft things started pushing between my fingers— God!'She wiped her hands down her dress. 'I used to lie awake listening to him going to the bathroom and wishing he was dead—and last night I heard him flopping round his room, beating on the walls. And this morning I woke up early, I thought the sun was coming up—but it was his face floating over the rooftops.... It came to the windows, filled them, it followed me from room to room, mouthing at me— God!You'd never write about it, you'd never write about anything again. But he can't get me down, and he knows it. He was always scared of me. That's why he kept me here, to keep me quiet. But he can't have left many of his little tricks behind him. He knows I'll win. But you don't want to get mixed up with the wrong things. You're a nice young man. ' She swung her legs up and lay back on the pillow, where I could see imprints of hair-dye.

For some time now I'd had the impression that my short story was taking over its own writing; now we seemed to be building to a climax I hadn't foreseen. I had to be direct. 'You husband was buried, wasn't he?' I asked. 'Didn't he want to be cremated?'

She seemed to take an age to sit up; her eyes were on me all the while. 'How did you know that?' she demanded softly.' You gave yourself away there, didn't you?You *are* one of his!I knew it before you got to the door!Yes, he's buried, where you all should be. Go on, go up and be with him, I'm sure he'd like you to be. He must be able to feel them coming by now—I hope he can. Yes, he was always on about his Eihort, but he doesn't like it when they come for him. You go and look after him, you—'

I didn't know what she might be capable of; I retreated hastily, seeing her watching in the mirror and sneering when she caught my eye. Somehow I dislodged a heap of magazines and buried the cat, which fought its way out and tangled my feet in its chain.' Don't you touch my cat!' she screamed.' She's worth a million of you!What is it, darling, come to mummy —' and I escaped, running down the hall, an inflamed intestine, and through the grass, careless of what I might tread in unseen.

Suddenly I was on solid pavement. Down the street an ice-cream van was playing *Greensleeves*. This time the intrusion of mundanity didn't seem so tasteless. I walked home.

By the time I reached my typewriter I'd glimpsed the paradox. Even the supernatural-story writer who believes what he writes (and I'm not saying I don't) isn't prepared for an actual confrontation. Quite the reverse, for every time he fabricates the supernatural in a story (unless based on experience) he clinches his skepticism; he knows such things can't be, because he wrote them. Thus for him a confrontation would be doubly upsetting. It would at least force him to re-think all his works. Is this desirable?From the self-completion angle I suppose it is. At any rate, I'm going.' Go up and be with him' she said—it must be the cemetery on Mercy Hill.

Tomorrow.

EU

* * *

(Undated, Unaddressed)

I don't know what (Foregoing deleted, does not appear on carbon; page apparently withdrawn, carbon attached, reinserted into typewriter) Nonsense. Of course I can write about it. The very fact that I can write proves that I'm still functioning.

I took the bus up Mercy Hill at the height of the day. Few things moved; flies and pedestrians crawled, and the workmen climbed sluggishly on the skeletal school. At the intersection with Dee Terrace I saw the house; it seemed swallowed up by grass, forever isolated from its surroundings.

I wanted to get this over. The caretaker directed me down an avenue, and when I reached—No. Description of graveyard. Why write as if this were my last page?Willows, their branches glowing stippled curves, were spaced carefully toward the Hill out of which the cemetery was carved; in the Hill it-self were catacombs, black behind ivy or railings, and above stood the hospital, a grey reminder of hope or despair. What awful iron juxtaposed hospital and graveyard?The avenues were guarded by broken-nosed angels yearning heaven-ward; one showed a leprous patch where her left eye and cheek had sloughed away. Urns stood here and there like empty glasses at a sick-bed, and a young woman was kneeling with a wreath at a shining memorial; I wonder how long before she shakes him off?And then, toward the catacombs, I saw the new head-stone and its bed of pebbles. They gleamed behind the high sun. I read Franklyn's name and the framing dates, and waited.

It eventually occurred to me that I didn't quite know what I was waiting for; not in that sunlight. Yet the air had hushed. I paced around the grave, and the pebbles shifted. My shadow had moved them. I'm still capable of an anti-climax! My God. I thought: Franklyn is alive down there—or perhaps no longer. Then I saw a possibility. I looked back down the perspective. The young mourner was passing through the gates. I lay down on the grass and put my ear to the pebbles. They ground together, then there was nothing. I felt vilely uncomfortable. Suddenly I realized that I was visible all the way down the avenue to the gates. I went hot all over and scrambled to my feet.

And on the way up I heard something. Something. If only I knew. It'd be better if I had something to confront, anything but this uncertainty which sucks the confidence from me. It could have been the foreman at the school calling over the noise of the riveting. Or it could—yes, must write—it could have been someone imprisoned, paralyzed, summoning a last muscular spasm, screaming thickly for help and beating his fists in the dark as he was dragged downward, downward....

I couldn't run; it was too hot. I walked. When I reached the school the girders were rippling in the heat-haze, as if they were alive. I wish I hadn't seen that. No longer could I trust the surface world. It was as though it had been instantaneously revealed to me that there were countless forces awake in everything, invisible, things lurking in daylight, shifting, planning—What had they built into the school? What would stalk unseen among the children?

I walked. Of course I was visualizing too much, but I could imagine, I could feel the pavement thin as ice, ready to engulf me in a world where life crawled. I sat in the parks. It was no good; I didn't know what watched from the trees; I didn't know how many of the passers-by might be masked, agents not of this world, preparing the way for—*what*? Who had Franklyn left behind? The peril of the writer: he can't stop thinking. He may survive by writing, but he doesn't really survive. Why am I no—mustn't give in—I wandered until dark, found a cafe, I don't remember. I was in a deserted street of shops with one red window lit above a darkened store. I don't know why, it seemed evil. Franklyn's hall, I suppose.

So I came back and typed this. The street is empty; only the shadow of the streetlamp seems to move. The window opposite is dark. What may be there, waiting?

I can't turn round. I stare at the reflection of the room behind me. The reflection—like a framed photograph about to be split open by something climbing forth. When I've written this I shall turn around.

'I don't dare,' I have just said aloud.

Where can I go where I don't sense movement behind the scenes?

(Unsigned)

Behold, I Stand at the Door and Knock

by

ROBERT M. PRICE

SID NEARLY DIDN'T HEAR the knock at the door, what with his favorite CD of Fried Spiders blasting on the box. But whoever it was, he was so bloody persistent that he was still knocking at the pause between songs, and that's when Sid got up out of the lotus position, back aching, to answer the door. He just turned the volume down instead of turning the thing off, since the little gizmo that should have allowed him to locate the cut he wanted after turning the machine back on was broken. He wanted to hear the rest of the album, and he hoped he could get rid of this pest quickly.

As he stuffed his black concert T-shirt into his jeans, he hoped it wasn't another bloody bill-collector. He had them all paid up this time, he thought.

In the doorway stood a man in his 50s, Sid judged, with the look that all door-to-door salesmen have: they had been neat as a pin in the morning, but by the time they got to you, the day's mileage showed in skewed tie, rumpled jacket, dog-bitten pants. How did these blokes make enough to keep themselves in pants?, he wondered with redoubled annoyance now that he saw who, or what, it was.

The man extended a hand, saw it was the wrong one, shifted his sample case to the left, and put out the right for a shake. Sid hated this intrusion of privacy as well as of personal space. He didn't want to shake like a friend with a man he'd as soon kick off the stoop. But he shook, kind of a jellyfish shake, all he could muster at the moment.

"Good day, Mr. Hingley. I wonder if you'd allow me to take a few moments of your time this afternoon. I'm sure you'll find them an investment well spent."

Sid glanced at the huge case, which looked less like a suitcase and more like a foot locker with a handle. Imagine carrying that bloody burden around all day. Poor joker must need the money. Of course Sid needed it too, but it was tough making a paying career out of interests like his. So he read his books, listened to his albums, and stayed in contact with a few other like minds, while by night he washed dishes in a local Brichester pub and by day he passed out leaflets for a Mercy Hill massage parlour. But this he'd never stoop to, God help him.

"Say, how d'you know my name, anyway?"

"Oh, rest assured, you're on the list, Mr. Hingley. Now if you'd just let me show you...."

As the salesman began unsnapping the case, Sid glimpsed the spines of a set of well-bound books.

"I can see you're no stranger to books and reading. That's good," the salesman said, his hand motioning around the tiny room, one of the two Sid could afford in this low-rent block of red brick flats in the worst section of the old town. And books there were in some profusion, scattered here and there in inelegant cinder block and board shelves. There was Colin Wilson's *The Occult*, the book that had started it all for Sid Hingley, plus a Kenneth Grant or two, some Panther reprints of work by Norman Owen and Ronald Shea, even a few odd volumes of a cheaply produced reprint set of *The Equinox*.

"Yeh, that's right, but you can see for yourself I'm no Britannica man, so you're wasting your time. Last time I used it was in school. Cribbed from it for a paper. Failed it—must have used the wrong set. Micropaedia instead of Macro. Not long enough."

"Not so fast, Mr. Hingley; you misjudge me. Shouldn't judge a book by its cover, as they say. I think you may find our product interests you after all. If you'll just take a look."

Bloody record was ending. With visible irritation, Sid grabbed the book and, ignoring the engraving on the spine, he opened to the title page for a quick look. He wouldn't be much more interested in The World's Classics than he would be in a set of encyclopaedias. But the page announced:

THE REVELATIONS OF GLAAKI

Sid's inner gears shifted. Suddenly the man and his books moved from the periphery to the center of things. Sid's irritation vanished. He had heard of this book, or set of books. He'd even tried to get a look at a copy a few years ago.

He'd felt sure the library over at Brichester University would have it, but he was told the set had disappeared. This was back in the days of the local flap about somebody named Franklyn and a secret cult of homosexuals. The University curators suspected the queers of stealing the books, but they never had any proof.

The Revelations purported to have been channeled by the wor-shipers of some God that lived in a lake, one more local Nessie. The contents, as far as Sid knew, were a jumble of strange facts, almost an almanac of occult oddities, written in fragments by different members of the group. It was almost as if a bunch of people had gone into a library at random and each copied odd passages out of totally different books. Or that was the rumour. He had liked what he'd heard.

So, yes, he was much interested in the salesman's product. He just couldn't believe the books were now mass-published...let's see, by Ultimate Press. Hadn't they become an imprint of Collins or something?

"How many volumes to the whole thing? One, two...."

"I have twelve here, but there are more in the works. It's not exactly a definitive edition, y'see. More of a work in progress."

"Well, it's sure not the Britannica, you're right there. How much would the whole set cost me? I haven't much to spare just now. But I would enjoy having the books, Mr...?"

"Undercliffe, Errol Undercliffe."

"Mr. Undercliffe, I really am interested. But...."

"We offer the books on a subscription plan. Why don't you keep the first one on a trial basis for a week? See how the book suits you. I'll be back then, and we can discuss terms."

Sid shrugged. Sounded more like a drug dealer than a book sales-man. But he had no objection. And in any event, there were always ways of getting some extra money in Lower Brichester.

Undercliffe left him his calling card and retreated down the weed-grown front path. Sid watched him for a moment. The man did not turn down the next walk, nor the next. He rounded the corner and was gone.

He would have liked to examine the book at greater length then and there, but it was nearly time to head downtown to the pub, the Black Goat. He hadn't to dress up much for the job since he entered through the alley to work in the kitchen, but he fixed himself up a bit just the same, because there was that new bar-maid, Jill, who had paid him some attention last week. So he was off.

As it happened, he wished he'd called in sick. The first sight he caught of Jill was of her coming on to one of the Rugby men from the University team. Bitch. How did that cheap tart get in with them? He turned to his dishes and mugs, and he began to think about the book.

He felt he might be on to something, finally. Not just paperback Necronomicons from Corgi Press this time (though he hadn't been above trying one or two of the spells given there for love and money).

He remembered how his dad had thrown him out of the house a year ago when he'd seen Sid ready to board the Underground wearing his O.T.O. robe and carrying his ceremonial blade for the Gnostic Mass. "Oh, for Christ's sake, Sid, you're not going out in public with a bloody knife...!" And when the old man snooped into it more, he'd accused him of going just so he could see the naked girl they used for an altar. "Be like normal people, Sid, go to a f—in' peep show or something!" It was only a month later he was told to leave, his mother blinking back tears on the doorstep as she watched him sullenly leave the nest.

Suppose he was on to something. Suppose the Revelations really had something. That would go a long way to vindicating him. Yes, it was worth a try.

That evening he set the Spiders to spinning again, and a bit of pot didn't hurt either, though after a while he found it hard to keep his mind on the confusing text before him. Next noon he would find it impossible to tell at just what point he had dozed off. But somewhere during his reading, he began having visions.

He received an engraved invitation. Who gave it to him? Someone at the door, as if it were a telegram. Was it Mr. Undercliffe? He couldn't be sure. But it was inviting him to something called the Feast of Eihort. In the dream he had gone to his closet to don a tuxedo, as if he'd own one. Once he had taken it off the hanger he saw that hanging there it had concealed a trapdoor in the closet floor that he had not known was there. Storage space?

Once the tux was on him, he stooped down and managed to claw the wooden plywood panel upward. Dimly lit below was a decline of many yards. He knew his path lay here if he was to go to the feast. A few unpainted plank-steps soon gave out, as did all but the faintest radiance coming from somewhere in the distance, and he had to feel his way onward through a squirming tunnel-surface of wet mold and fungi, punctuated by the occasional salamander or insect.

After a vague period of this blind trudging, he reached an opening into a large dining hall. And now it seemed that the entrance through which he stepped was at the end of a long and elegantly appointed foyer, like a huge restaurant. Looking down at his pants, which he felt must be caked with revolting filth, he was surprised to find them as crisp and clean as they has been in his closet.

A soft-spoken maitre d' took his elbow and guided the nonplused Sid to a dining room specially reserved away from the general clamour of the dining throng. He accompanied his guide through several winding hallways and through a medieval-looking oaken door. Inside there was a great company of feasters. On a second look, these figures threw a start into him, for each was a duplicate of the other, all swathed in blue-black robes and cowls.

Their baggy clothing seemed to bulge and bend in unaccustomed places, but Sid scarcely noticed this as he took his designated seat. He fumbled with his napkin, feeling uncomfortable in his tuxedo. For though he had never been in less danger of under-dressing for an occasion (something his parents always berated him for), he felt positively out of place without a robe like theirs.

He looked around at his silent dining companions, whose occasional expansive gestures and pats on the back implied merriment, but whose voices he could not hear at all.

In all the confusion it took him a moment to notice just what constituted the main course for the evening. There was a huge meat platter on the large banqueting board, and some great beast had been laid out, cooked, upon it. With a start, and a bit of nausea, he saw that it was a plump human shape, though by now an arm and the best part of two legs were missing. But the light was dim, the fickle product of bracketed tapers set into the great stone-block walls.

It was only once the chef emerged from what might have been the kitchen door and served Sid the head on a platter, with an apple in its mouth, that Sid saw plainly that the head was his own.

He awoke, apparently straightway out of the dream, on the floor of the tiny bathroom, heaving into the toilet. Lucky he hadn't puked lying down and choked on his own vomit. He rested the remainder of the afternoon, pondering what he had dreamed. And then it was time to go to the designated corner with his leaflets.

Each leaflet was a little bit of pornography, showing a poor color photograph of two women, neither your top-grade model, not even by industry standards, giving sexual service to the same man. One sucked him, the other squatted on his face. Better to imagine your own face there, he supposed.... Still, his was not to reason why.

He took the stance of the pamphleteer, leaflet at the ready, held out tentatively so as not to seem too pushy, never meeting the eyes of a prospective customer unless he seemed to slow down. He would mumble some inanity, it didn't much matter what. He wasn't particu-

larly eager for anyone he knew to recognize him. It was a pitiful line
of work and paid a pittance. Still it did add to his washer's income and
kept most of his day free for studies and sleep.

And there were the side benefits. One or two of the Asian girls would
give him the five minutes he needed occasionally, especially when he
did favors for them. Their English was not so good. After the way Jill
had spurned him (had he only imagined her initial interest?), he felt
like taking a bit of comfort. So he arranged things with Benazir for
closing time.

At the Goat nothing much was happening. No Jill to be seen. Maybe
she'd married her University man and he'd taken her away from all
this. Time dragged by, and he tried not to give much thought to his
dream. But he couldn't let it go. He didn't know what to make of it
except that it had coincided with reading the Revelations, and it made
him think things were beginning to spark. Time to go. Benazir was
waiting, he hoped.

He hadn't seen her in recent weeks. Arrested in a recent raid, which
was always a danger, though little more than a formality, an occasion
for the Brichester police to get their cut, he guessed. But the girls
would be tested on such occasions, and there was some merit in that.

He entered through the back door of the establishment, wanting
to avoid the tangle of a couple of drunken underaged teenagers being
shown the door by the bouncer in a rare display of scruples. He passed
the bar and went right into Benazir's "dressing room," they called
them. She was wiping herself from another of the teenagers who had
proved too drunk to aim himself properly. He was passed out on the
couch, from which Sid dumped him unceremoniously into the hallway.

"It is good you are here to help me, Sid. I am wanting to be rid of
this bastard."

"Yeah, I'll see they don't let him in again" (sure, as if Sid had any
kind of authority in the matter).

As he unzipped his pants, his erection already making him zip
carefully to one side, he said, "Get the gag, OK? You know how I like
it."

She let him chain her to the bedposts, waiting for it to be over, with
the eternal resignation of the women of the East. She knew there was
nothing to fear, that it was this ritual symbolism of power more than
anything else that was important to men like Sid.

He mounted her and began to ride, feeling himself get stiffer and
longer. His hands rested a moment on her rib cage, his sweat falling
like raindrops on her stomach, collecting like a rain pool in her navel.

He looked at her full breasts and licked his dry lips. He made to grab her and squeeze, but his eager hands went numb as her breasts began to elongate fantastically, forming a pair of squid-like tentacles. These caught him in a cloying embrace. Each was lined with a double row of suckers, but Sid could see, and more to the point, feel that the suckers were shaped and worked like human lips, kissing him everywhere at once.

He began to feel a kind of lust he had never known, a lust for things he had never known were possible. He was almost able for the first time to give a name to urges he could never before identify, much less fulfill.

He was floating in a cloud of heady ecstasy, even though the illusion passed quickly. But now something else seemed to be happening. Was this possible? He seemed to go right on growing, reaching the maximum dimensions of the biggest erection he'd ever had. Benazir could tell the difference, too, as her eyes widened in interest, then, it seemed, in panic. For it kept growing, like a python expanding within her.

The thrill of it was almost too much for Sid, who was now sure it was another of those strange dreams. He was about to faint with the painful pleasure of it. Benazir was flopping like a fish now, desperate to get out of the straps and off the bed, to get Sid out of her. The gag stifled her screams effectively, but the cuffs were cheap stages props, and she soon had shaken one of them off. But before she could go further, she stiffened, back straight.

Sid's back arched, and at first he only heard and did not see the impact against the headboard as his living club of a penis, having penetrated her entrails, ripped resistlessly through her esophagus and tore her head three quarters away from her shoulders. It was the splash of blood which brought him out of it.

There he squatted, astride the mutilated form of a Pakistani whore, the both of them soaked in blood. He stumbled off her, off the bed, and grabbed a towel. A few moments later he tried to listen, then ventured a look out in the hall. The place was deserted. How long had he been at it?

He looked himself over. He seemed physically normal. He would have sworn it was all one of those crazy dreams, but the carcass on the bed gave the lie to that. Unless he was maybe still dreaming. For now he'd best assume it was all real.

He felt no grief; the girl was merely an instrument to him. And with the clarity that emergency lends, Sid went back over things in his mind. Who had seen him go in? He didn't think the bouncer had noticed him. Most patrons had left.

Well, there was no way to clean this up, that was for sure. He just hoped no one would think to suspect him. And from the type and especially the extent of the damage, he wasn't even sure they'd be looking for a single assailant, maybe not even a human one.

So with a surprising air of casual nonchalance, Sid quietly locked the body into what had now become a meat locker, and made for his flat. He had a quiet confidence that in the last analysis no facts could justify, that he would not be caught. He somehow felt that someone or something was watching over him. And he wondered just what would happen next time he felt in the mood.

What followed was a night of lamplight reading of the Revelations. Despite the crudity of the writing in many places, it was something Sid just couldn't put down. Much of it, too, was apparently providing the answers to questions he couldn't even understand. What the f— was the Zone of the Colossi anyway? He was in way over his head. But he'd take it slow, find an entry point somewhere, and then he was sure things would start making more sense. But it was bloody interesting anyway. He suspected that if he did get to understand it better it wouldn't be as interesting. Less of a sense of mystery.

He dreamed again. This time he was in a slaughter house. He stood beside a man wearing a bloodstained apron. He was working over a side of beef. But suddenly the man seemed to be a doctor, and Sid dimly realized he was playing the role of the man's assistant. And the side of beef was now the body of an obese man. It was a relief to see that this time it was not his own.

The doctor/butcher reached down to the side of the slab table on which he was working to hoist up another meaty mass. It was a different color, pale blue-green. And the texture didn't quite match either. Sid looked closely and was surprised to see it was a whole octopus. The doctor handed it to him and, though inert, it was still unwieldy, and he came close to dropping it.

While he held the reeking thing, he watched the doctor neatly saw off the head of the corpse before him. Dropping this heedlessly on the floor, he motioned for Sid to hand him the dead octopus. This he somehow proceeded to sew in position where the man's head had been. He injected some fluid at several points on the hybrid form.

The tentacles began to stir, at first slowly. As they parted, Sid could see the beak of the octopus, but then the feelers parted again, and the beak had been replaced by a set of human lips. And they were forming words. He bent close to hear, his curiosity overcoming his natural repugnance for the nightmare before him. He heard gibberish: Ph'nglui mglw'nafh Cthulhu R'lyeh wgah'nagl fhtagn.... He had no idea what it meant but instantly his heart began to pound, and he awoke. He was shaken. And yet there was a whisper of a desire for more.

And there was more. Two days later he returned to Mercy Massage, and there was Benazir, her cherry lipstick almost purple against her natural swarthiness, just as alive and tawdry as ever. It had been a dream, then. So, just to see what would happen, he got her to let him tie her to the bed frame again—and the same thing happened. And just before she started to scream, or to try to, there seemed to come into her shaded eyes a strange look, as if she knew what was coming, as if she remembered it.

He found himself the next night facing a lonely row of a half-dozen dilapidated houses that leaned crazily in all directions, seeming to support one another like a group of drunks staggering together down the street till they all fall in a heap. It must have been two in the morning, and he didn't know how he had come to be here. The wind whistled off a lake behind him. It chilled him to the bone. Then he noticed he was naked, and that some kabbalistic designs had been painted on his body. Hm, had he done it? He couldn't remember.

He took a few steps closer and looked at one of the houses. Dimly visible through a large front window was a gaunt man, peering, he supposed, at him. He could make out no features except that he was sure that the man had a full beard, which, unless the dusty shadows lied, moved like a nest of serpents. He stepped forward, up onto the rotting porch, and stared straight into the window where the man was.

He couldn't have been more than six inches from the face that he still could not quite see, except for the fact that, yes, those locks of beard—if that's what they were, were moving. There was a thick coating of grimy fingerprints and caked dust. Just couldn't see through the window glass even at this range.

And there was a sudden conviction that he was missing something, like a punch line of a joke that left him feeling stupid, not getting it. He knew in a moment, though he knew not why, that what he must do was to recite the Daoloth formula. He had read it in the Revelations and seemed to know it well, though he didn't recall bothering to memorize it. There was much here unseen, and he wanted to see it. The words came unbidden to mind.

It was pitch black, but a geyser of light now seemed to erupt from behind him in the direction of the lake. And in that light, things were transmogrified. There were no more six crazily leaning houses before him, but rather six huge, high heaps of living stuff. From the top of each waved three primitive eye-stalks, and from the sides emerged a forest of porcupinish spines, giving the things the improbable appearance of titan, living haystacks.

And then Sid flexed one of his eye-stalks and beheld that he no longer faced the houses, or the Colossi, but was instead one of their company, the one on the extreme left.

The visions and hallucinations went on all week. By the middle of the week, he had called in sick at the pub, just stopped showing up at the massage parlour.

The knock came again. This time no CD spun on the player. Sid Hingley lay, naked, in the middle of the floor, dry mouth and bloodshot eyes wide open.

"I see the door's not locked. I trust you are well, Mr. Hingley? I see you've made full use of the book. Remember, it's just the first in the set. Wait till you get to the one I wrote, that's number fifteen. It's at the printer's now, they tell me. Can I sign you up?"

Sid had risen with difficulty to a sitting position. He fingered his crotch with one hand and rubbed his reddened face with the other. "Yeh," he muttered, "it's really great...I didn't suspect. But how much? What price to pay?"

He began to manifest the drunk's belligerence. He rose unsteadily and tried to grasp Mr. Undercliffe's lapel. "Y' bastard! It's too much, ain't it? More than somebody like me could pay in a lifetime, idn' it? Why? Why'd y' torment me wi' it, then?"

Straightening his jacket, Undercliffe tried to reassure his star customer. "You don't understand, Mr. Hingley. We don't want money. We're simply concerned that this important truth be propagated. We'll give you the books. I suppose it's really like winning a sweepstakes. We wanted to see if you were the man for the job. And you've acquitted yourself well. Don't think we haven't been watching the past several days."

"Unh?"

"Let me put it this way, Mr. Hingley. In every age the world has need of a Mighty Messenger. I feel that from your studies that name will mean something to you. Over the years, the centuries, really, special individuals have been chosen to transcend the limits of the mundane and to carry out that special task. It is a path of glory and knowledge untold. You have tasted a sample of it. The rest of the books will fully fit you for that task. I am in the position to offer you this high privilege."

Sid was speechless, but the dimensions of what he was hearing were quickly pulling his mind together. He was beginning to understand what was being offered him.

"Now, I don't want you to tell me anything now. I know it's a big move. A life change. Nothing will ever be the same again. Sleep on it, Mr. Hingley, and I'll call on you again tomorrow. Is this a good time?"

The door shut. Sid dragged his naked form, which he now realized, with acute embarrassment, he had shamelessly displayed in front of the officious Mr. Undercliffe, into the shower. The cold water helped bring him farther along the way to normal waking consciousness. It was really funny, he thought underneath the pressure of a now-blinding headache, how the after-effects of a mystical trance were so similar to those of a drunk.

Coffee helped him even more. In the cold light of early afternoon, by the slanting of declining sunrays against the wall, illuminating his posters of Fried Spiders and the Whisperers, he found himself considering his position. Here in these familiar and, he admitted it, depressing, surroundings, he faced two possible futures.

One was as a worthless ne'er-do-well, bearing the scorn of family and employers, his pretensions of esoteric knowledge and a higher purpose revealed as a pathetic defense against an adult world for which he was unsuited.

The other meant confusion, to be sure, even horror, but that was just the acclamation of the worldly mind to the glories beyond. He had seen enough to know that firsthand. And though it meant the end, really, of human life as he knew it, the end of any hope of a normal existence...what choice did he have? He knew too much.

And to go in one big jump from being one more nothing from Lower Brichester to being the Mighty Messenger, winging across the void bearing forbidden knowledge...visions of Hermes Trismegistus and Thoth, Crowley and his Aiwass, the Word of the Eon. It could be his. He would do it.

* * *

Some weeks later, the Mighty Messenger was hard at the job. But things weren't quite as he had imagined them. For one thing, no matter how much of the Revelations he might read, the wild visionary splendours were a thing of the past. Unless he tried for a day to shirk his duties—then visions came, came with a vengeance! Like the one in which he played the role of supine Benazir strapped to the bed and torn apart in unspeakable ways. Yeah, those visions came easily enough.

Thus muttered the great Revealer, the Mighty Messenger, as he pounded the pavement of Temphill one hot August afternoon, looking for the next address on his list, his neck-tie chafing him, dragging along that bloody suitcase full of books.

1968 RPI

by

JOE MURPHY

"SO WHERE DID you get these?" Nathicana shoves the comic she was reading under the counter. She stares at my books and runs a slender, bell-braceleted hand through Prince Valiant hair.

"Found them in our attic." I smile my best capitalistic smile, follow her eyes down onto the flaking brittleness I placed before her. "My friends and I just moved into a new pad, lotsa books still there."

"*Cult of the Worm* is fairly rare." She traces her finger over crimson stained parchment, stroking each volume with hands and eyes. I can see she'll want them, my mission of mercy might just succeed.

"Certainly it's very establishment of me to ask, but how much will you give for them?"

"Thirty dollars in merchandise." Her best capitalistic smile would fit a shark. I blink, pretend surprise, materialistic bartering is not my thing, man. Yet my mission demands it.

"You're jiving me, sister. Come on show me the true revolutionary spirit—give me cash." I allow the sleeve of my nehru coat to fall across the books, reminding her they're still mine.

"It's no jive, man." Nathicana throws her arms wide. "Check this place out. I'm not Sears. I run a shop, I am the shop. I'm offering a piece of myself in exchange for these rarities. It's the best deal I can make." Her eyes zero in on mine, the deep dark blue of cold empty seas.

"I appreciate that, good shop keeper lady, but my own financial needs and those of my comrades are what I'm all about. Some of them extend past your doorstep."

"Think hard, my man." She touches my hand, fingers hot, stroking mine to explode shivers of a delicious kind. "I've got what everybody needs in here. Look around while I study these a moment." She touches my face with a softer innocent smile. "Just browse, see if you don't agree."

"Alright." Nodding, I pull back from her. I'm no sexist pig, but what a touch, she's using feminine charms against me, melting my hard capitalist backbone. What a way to go. Grinning, I wander through her shop, checking out counters filled with candles, vast piles of underground comics and mags, paraphernalia of mystic and mundane purpose.

I see it then, the perfect gift for comrade Lacy. There on a shelf cluttered with prisms, a silver hummingbird beckons with turquoise eye. Within shining claws it holds a crystal globe, glinting rainbows in the dust streaked light from outside. "This is something worthy of my friend." I take the silver chain which binds the hummingbird, lay it gently on the counter.

"A perfect gift. You can find still more." Nathicana promises, never looking up from my books. A clutter of comics catches my mind. Something I truly appreciate in the same connoisseur's manner which Nathicana regards my own books. Five comics come into my hands, rare issues of anti-establishment wonder and perversity.

"These are for me." I toss them on the counter by the chained bird. Two down, two to go. Here I run aground, nothing fits my friend Eugene, and then there is our mutual need still to be satisfied.

"We do have some things not out for general display to the masses." Again her eyes test mine. Now there's a groovy tinge of cunning understanding glinting across the space between us.

"Something perhaps for the head?" I smile, showing teeth, not a shark but a Cheshire kitty.

"How serious are you about this stuff? Have you read these books?"

"No, we're not into literary studies. We like to absorb information the psychedelic way."

"Wait here then." Nathicana flows around the counter in an ancient renaissance gown, swirling the dusty floor into a faint brown tide. She disappears through a paisley curtain dangling with bells into a back room mystery. That's when I spot Eugene's gift. The comic she was reading when I first came in, now face down, splayed open on the shelf below the cash register. Its up-side-down cover flares with eye smarting day-glo colors. A series of stars and geometric shapes, the up-side-down name "Einstein," that's what catches me. I strike like a true capitalist war-monger. Bending far over the counter, I stretch and catch. Caught up in the craftiness of this wheeling and dealing trip, my karma suffers for my friends. Technically it's stealing, but I'm not the technical sort. I slip out another comic, one I had in my back pocket, covers the same color. Flipping mine open, I switch, put mine where her's was, the new one hides in my pocket just as the bells jingle out of the back.

"If you're serious worshipers of cosmic consciousness I've got just the thing." Nathicana glances around the shop, like the FBI might have staked us out. "Mandrake cubes."

"Something new?" I study her hand, nesting in the palm are tiny pea-sized square-cut shadows.

"The oldest of the old combined with the newest of the new." Nathicana giggles little syllables of pride. "If you're searching for truth on the inside of your skull, this even beats electric kool-aid."

"Deal 'em out. We can do business." I strike my utmost coolest pose, leaning on the counter as she counts out the cubes. Moments later I'm free-birding out the door, a handful of gifts, a pocket full of mind miracles. Mission accomplished, my feet touch ground half a block away.

"Hey, hey you damn hippy." Nathicana's voice follows, chasing me down on the summer breeze. I turn and spot her in front of the shop clutching the switched comic in a totalitarian claw. "You ripped me off."

"Peace!" I make the sign, shift the feet to overdrive. Scooting down along the boulevard, her curses warn me she follows. The freeway looms its ugly concrete head before me, I dance the desperate dodge between traffic, win the freedom of the other side.

"Hippy scum." Her shout is the sound of truck engines and commuter cars, metallic harsh. Nathicana stomps and shakes a gleaming fist on the far concrete shore, the traffic too heavy for her to follow.

"Bye Bye." And I'm gone, down the few blocks to the pad we just rented. It was an old house yesterday, but it's a new home to us. Stained glass and gables make it look like some red brick dragon laying in wait between the neighboring stucco bone piles. Crossing through its double doors, sitar music from Lacy's stereo strokes my ears a welcome. I prepare to impress my comrades.

"Did you have any luck, Cosmo?" Lacy sits cross legged on the meadow green sofa. A fresh from Idaho smile rises over a melancholy sadness, she brushes her corn silk blonde mane back from sunny freckles then puts down her crochet.

That's her thing, crochet, and birds.

"We're groovin." I flop down to her left so I can see the long chain of golden birds dangling from her ear.

"Far out, you got tickets to Monterey?" She hugs my arm, birds flutter in my hair.

"Our karma wasn't that strong." Sorrow enters my voice. All our friends found paths to the famous pop festival, but we three, our finances freshly emptied to get this old house, were left behind. "Still I have managed to save the day."

"I thought it must be you." Eugene comes down the stairs, slide rule in hand. "Heard the doors squeak."

"Just in time." I scoot up against Lacy, make room for him on the sofa. "No tickets to Monterey, but I've booked passage for unknown shores."

"You scored some mind candy?" Lacy's smile fills with August sunshine.

"And more." I pull out the humming bird crystal, suspending it before her berry eyes. "For you."

"Far out." Lacy touches the chain, dangles the bird and strokes its crystal. "It's beautiful, Cosmo."

"And for you, my friend." I turn to Eugene. "Something from your hero." My fingers flash into my jacket, magically produce his carefully ripped off comic.

"Underground art is your bag, not mine." Then he sees the title and grabs it. "Necro Chron, Comparisons of Arcane Magic with Einstein's Relativity Theorems. This is truly far out, dude." Eugene's eyes practically jump out of their sockets, nuzzle his wire rimmed glasses.

"Naturally." I know the perfect gift for a physics major when I see it. "And now the ultimate." Got their full attention, yes sir, my friends truly believe in my love for them. "You've heard of and sampled Electric Kool-aid?"

"Of course." Eugene answers, eyes back in his book.

"You were there." Lacy nods, watching the humming bird dance at her breast.

"This is reputed by experts to be even better." I hold out a handful of little black cubes. "Mandrake."

"This man is a karmic masterpiece." Eugene's eyes leave his gift, study my palm full of night cubed shadow.

"What a friend to have in the Summer of Love." Lacy plucks a cube, rolls it between fingers and pops it on her tongue.

"Great friends, great times, great drugs." I place one in my mouth. It tastes cold, a bit salty, no other flavor, just cold. "What more can a spirit ask for?"

"Only for this to go on forever." Lacy's eyes close, ecstasy already flashing across her face.

"It can." Eugene jumps up, spreads his new book on the coffee table crate. His grin is wild and wide, like some hidden aborigine just initiated into the secret rites of his tribe. He snatches a cube and gulps it down. "Do you realize what you've got here?" He caresses the yellowed open pages, marked with pentagrams and strange glyphs already beginning to waver and writhe in my eyes.

"Einstein comics?" My voice sounds deeper than I remember.

"The key to the infinite hour glass, this is a study of spells which can stop time." Eugene reaches out, takes my hand, grips Lacy's. "We can make the summer last forever."

"Do it." Lacy cries, her voice a high pitched chirp.

"Let's keep the fall and classes far away. Spend eternity in cosmic consciousness."

"Cosmo, clear back the table, I need to draw things on the floor. Lacy, get candles, all the candles we have." Eugene's fingers blur with anxious energy, tracing patterns on paper which won't remain still.

"We obey, master." Lacy giggles as we rush through rubbery air to do his bidding.

"Iä-R'lyeh! Cthulhu fhtagn Chron!" Eugene's words mean nothing to me. He kneels, one hand grasping the book, the other reaching out, beginning a chalk line on time-marred wood. The stereo deepens, sitar music slows to chiming melodious gongs, the first three notes of the next raga begin but never end.

* * *

My fingers leave house's hand, the doorknob, glass facets icy sharp. The world pulls me, grabbing velocity from micro to macro seconds. I move through the years with instantaneous abandon, to a three note heartbeat reverberating with my mission. It's not yet complete, the floor pentagram, it will be.

My palms find the sidewalk, warm and rubbery. Tiny boulders scrape flesh, like my giggle scrapes the air. Hair snakes around my face, the warm spring irradiating my skin, I look at this red brick and hedge trimmed neighborhood. So much has changed here since the Summer of Love, so much has grown and decayed. Frumpy curse-putting cars are bigger and smaller than I remember. The lawns suck up blustery exhaust clouds, green infinite planes of life spanned by wrought iron fences guarding brick cubes. No one sees my physical limp, none witness the up-side-down light bulb egg shape holding my spirit.

"Another House trick, Cosmo," I hear me telling myself, springing to feet, feeling the pistons in my legs bounce in base obeisance to gravity. I haven't been out of the House in a while, crossing the double doors of perception always lands me somewhere new.

"Not in thirty years." Mr Lincoln stares in coppery majesty from the sidewalk, winking today's date in telegraphed living information. Reaching out, my arm extends for miles, down to his circular coinhood. His metallic cry muffles from my pocket.

Walking through two overlapping continua, I toddle/toggle between alternate visions. Thirty years ago this was all Boho clubs. Rock and roll pods housing the new green families, Children of God who blossomed into the revolution. Now heat shimmers from red brick and stucco of the Children Gone to Seed, rebuilding the sins of the establishment with chrome and ticker tape glory. Making my way through the shadows of love-ins, be-ins, chain-ins, wretch-ins, into the blights of BMWs and corporate tentacled conglomerates.

Where these places overlap is where I move, past frozen shadows to Nathicana's Shop. The smooth blonde wood of its walls has thrown off the years like ducks shed water, without effort, secure in its natural state like some great mountain in the center of time. Tides of scents fill me with the ringing of the tiny brass bell above the door. Myrrh, henbane, and ambergris well up, with each dinging echo. Nathicana hovers, cross-legged behind a counter of crystals and sandalwood, absorbed in the lotus, she doesn't remember me.

I move through the wire rack trees of ancient wisdom, bound in paper and glue of our technological age, deep into a forest of squeaking rustling stands with bent metal branches. Upon each branch, secure in antiseptic plastic, are the herbs and suffumigations Nathicana peddles. Her thoughts wash over me as I my mission begins. I feel them like gnats, insect planets in orbit around my mind.

Jamming hands into the pockets of my bell bottoms I play tourista, gawking innocently at the edges of sin. The gnats swarm to the ringing modulations of the telephone. Is it House, coming to my aid, I wonder? Perhaps Eugene or Lacy, my cosmic comrades inferring from divinatory bones of space that I need a distraction? Certainly and of course not.

Nathicana's voice enters the wires, drawing her mind along. I erupt my golden center of gravity, extruding a tentacle from my navel. It snakes, invisible to the tree stands and snatches a black plastic packet, sucks it into my hidden aurora. I float to her counter, where she cradles the phone between shoulder and ear, a urine yellow copy of Zap Comics clutched in my left hand while the right scoops up some milk duds and carob dung.

"Three dollars and twenty cents." She rings up comic and munchies, never looking up, never knowing I ripped her off. The translucent veins beneath her sculptured skin have not changed with the years. Her flagrant ebony page boy cut is the same as it ever was.

"Good by Mr. Lincolns, so long old Georges." I smile in god-like ecstasy and flee. Stepping out of her shop, I'm in the cool caressing shadows that shroud House. Oh, how they stroke the body mind with scents of lilac and crickets as I find the verandah and merge into the stained glass doors. Within, cloaked in timeless dark sputtering of candles that cannot burn beyond their present stubs, the endless three note cycles flux from Lacy's old stereo. Ravi Shankar of course, in time spanning sitar and tabla ragas, but only three notes. We've stopped time here, ground it to a bloody halt, filled with dancing molecular chains.

"Did you get it, Cosmo?" Lacy is just that, a three dimensional shadow of crocheted daisies and pineapples, her blonde mane of beauty rose and trilby. She rises from the bean bag throne, a glowing joint in white thread fingers. Inside, held in a living cage of white silk and yellowed cotton, flicker birds, dancing with her movements. A sparrow peeps through embroidered eyes, a lark's tongue licks her lips.

"We're groovin." I toss the packet onto the ivory carved table, into a brass tray. Laid out like aperitifs for the shiny black shoes of the establishment, among paper tabs of LSD, between green bitter buds of peyote, amid the dark buttons of magic mushrooms, are piled scores of random medicinal condiments we have melded, merged into a single force. We have stopped time!

"Far out." Her soul comes to me, wrapping hairpin doily arms around my tentacles. My lips retreat, showing tombstone teeth stained with betel nuts and peppermint, her tongue flutters in my mouth. "I'll get Eugene."

"Here I am." A thin glowing vermilion ribbon snakes over the mold cities of the sofa, coiling into its familiar indentation by the tray. The ribbon swirls in its own wind, begins to find a mummy's shape, but there was never enough of him to go around. Eugene appears like some figment of Escher's genius, a glowing road to Nirvana wrapped around spaces starless, and bible black. The ribbon parts in pearly white symmetry to smile. "House told me you are here." Living shadows curl cat-like around us. House is here, cradling us, buoying up our vibrations with its own, creating firmament from shadow. House is living, the walls around us concave, convex with each musty breath. Multiple window eyes opening, closing as it peeps into the tray. Far back in the millennium, house was just a structure, home to innumerable hippy dippy art students. Now it's as much a part of the new entity as we, old wooden beams hold back the universe, our bones prop up the sagging timbers.

"Shall I do the honors?" Eugene reaches for the black plastic packet, the final brick in our fledgling universe. "Deal," Lacy fills her round doily shape with albino smoke, passes the joint that can never burn out to my tar smeared tentacle.

"Tonight we ride the gestalt to the end." I suck in the fire itself, pop peyote buds and red caps of scopolamine into my empty eye sockets. The fading Persian rug beneath us falls through the floor, leaving only the tattered strands of the almost pentagram burnt into the wood, burnt with offerings from our hair and finger nails.

"This is the cusp, the final push." Eugene tears the black plastic as he once tore the skin from his face. Licorice colored roots drop from the bag, tiny human shaped vegetation that must seem the be all and end all upon our motionless shoal in time.

"So that's what whole mandrake looks like." Lacy holds up a tiny writhing tuber, watches its mystic motions as the mandrake seeks escape.

"The real thing, sister. Just exactly what we need." Eugene begins pulling them apart, splitting them down the middle in wheedling fits of root screams. "It took us forty days, forty days and forty nights of high powered grokking, ingesting endless quantities of chemical aid, invoking rituals of astonishing antiquity to transform 1968 Urban Drive into 1968 Forever House. Now in this final second of forever, we expand. The mandrake provides the final push, it will coat the earth in sappy sticky love. We turn back the hands of time, and return the planet to the Summer of Love." "The new garden of Eden," I cry out. "Unraveling the cold and blustery strands of corporate Amerika, we weave time to the psychedelic beat throbbing from the mountains of madness."

"We'll meet in endless summer festivals. Grooving. Uniting all life in new patterns of eternal love, new equations of space and matter." A falcon's beak pierces her doily lips, snips the mandrake and swallows.

House nods with darkening shadows and fizzling galaxies of candlelight. It is the collective well, holding spirits of our brothers and sisters who couldn't keep their heads together while their minds expanded, those who succumbed to the big chemical bang.

"Nyarlathotep," Eugene bites into the mandrake, summoning the envoys of those who move through the space between seconds.

"Shoggoth Ka," Whole mandrake is bitter, worse than peyote, but I'm beyond the affect of sensory input, no sensation is too strong.

"Pnakotica," Lacy trills in bird song, her head folded back as House shadows reach in segmented night for its share. "Eryx."

"Ulthar."

"Celephais." Shadows strengthen, rolling like mushroom clouds, the walls around us expand. House flows outward, filling the world. A chalk splinter rises from the table top. A white photographic negative of the mandrake, it moves with our will, climbing to the floor. Squatting on the pentagram our minds begin to guide it.

"Zais,"

"Sarnath,"

"Cydathria," I feel the concrete jungle outside begin to die, strangling in its own carbon monoxide vomit. The streets give way to cool crisp forests and ferns. Steel spans of bridges melt into sweet cedar trestles washing away the grimy excrement of slum building refineries, scenting the air with green sugared growth. Weeping sitars replace FM commercials, trilling three note epiphanies. Monoxious trucks and trains slow to a speeding halt, becoming vast complex iron caves, filled with black shod commuters who haven't yet looked up from the evening paper.

"Iä...." The candles snuff into silence. House shudders, the floor creaking and waving like a wooden ocean of alarm. The shadows pale, burn into white fog.

"Nooo." Eugene drops his mandrake, it runs screaming from the table top, gathering its fellow roots in mathematical regressions.

"Something's uncool." Lacy flows to her feet, needles springing through the lace of her fingertips into searing claws of anger.

"We've a visitor." My tentacles unfurl. Behind us the stereo slows its 1,968 revolutions per infinity, three notes lengthen to four, five, the raga goes on.

"Nathicana!" Eugene points a ribboned finger at the burning doorway.

"She must have followed me." I turn, revolving on my center of gravity. Nathicana's skin is white marble, clothed in alabaster robes, her hair carved from black onyx. The face is a studded mask of iron, red, exuding coppery fumes from nostrils. Eyes of molten metal scowl.

"You ripped me off, hippy scum." Her steps shake House, wooden beams cringe from her wrath. "Meddling fools, undisciplined children of a self inventing god, give to me what is mine." Mandrake roots flee to her, opening mother of pearl portals in her feet and ankles, they tumble in.

"Bad vibes." Lacy snarls, flows above them to grip Nathicana's earth veined sinews. There in the clench they struggle, Lacy magnifying the very movements of atoms and molecules as they swirl in micro orbits. Nathicana's arms crack and fissure in her grasp.

"You have stolen from him you shall worship." Nathicana embraces the swirling lace, steel lips part in sizzling flames, crisping the lace into black strands of cinders that race through Lacy. Her internal birds are fried, our comrade dissolves into dusty motes of ash, sift into the splintered floor boards.

"Bad trippin, man." Eugene coils, snake-like, hissing venomous gobbets of peyote pulp. His ribbon head whips out, whacks Nathicana's neck with the sound of meat frying on a chrome fender. He flicks back as Nathicana's head snaps off.

Fountains of fire billow up from her shoulders. House burns. "Stairs." I wrap a tentacle around Eugene's calculated middle, pull him from the orange tongues before they taste him away. We flow into the basement, our secret stronghold. "It's not fair, we almost had it." Lacy, now a swirling galaxy of fine gray powder weeps as I come to her. Eugene's ribbon flows like Saturn's rings around us, preparing our final defense.

"We'll devour her." I promise, tentacles brace against the rusting furnace and rotting stone walls, others forming mystic angry runes. "She will voyage into the endless summer as our ship."

"I'll be your vessel, filled with sniveling self centered souls." Nathicana's stoned immaculate feet, snap the boards of the stairs as she comes to us. "Open yourselves to me. The endless summer you seek is but a faded shadow of alien renaissance." Her pointed nipples breath like sharp daggers as she opens liquid alabaster arms.

"NO," I throw my tentacles wide. "The Summer of Love is the flame from which all shadows flow. Fall into our green world."

Nathicana tromps forward, intent upon our embrace. I fling the body electric full of harmonious vibrations, tentacles unfurl in virginal flowerings to receive her. Eugene's ribbon shifts, forming razored angles of crimson light, folding into a living pentacle promising nonexistence with its touch.

"Come taste the true meaning of time." Nathicana breathes the scent of poppy and fish. Odors form ripe skin over my tentacles, slowing my movements with physical limitations of matter. Her breath fills with black mandrake shadows, flowing over and through us, darkening Eugene's ribboned glyphs into meaningless ultra violet strands. Nathicana's will moves with webbed fingers, grasping, connecting us all, bridging a giant's synapse.

"A presence beyond her. She's a puppet." Lacy screams for us, infinite vibrations of each ashen molecule, each atom of agony while Nathicana draws us through the wires of night into her mind. We are swallowed up inside her.

We who dwelt in the frozen dreams of House, who thought a mere thirty years of time contained our own galaxy of being and purpose, fall into a true void. So deep is Nathicana our cries of mercy and terror echo into exhaustion never reaching her boundaries.

Visions of timeless cities well up to engulf us. Gardens of hanging flowers, it must be Babylon, anoint us in the scents of rose and persimmon. The endless gray stone of Crete binds us in mazes of infinite complexity. Thule and Phoenicia, blend in whirling flashes of linen and bronze chains, binding us to dimly remembered ancestral homes. "Look with wonder Children of Atom, look with awe at your beginnings." Nathicana's laughter floats on merciless breezes, dark with the astringent reek of henbane and lignum aloes. Even House tumbles among the racial corridors, discovering its kin in the bones of Stonehenge, between the paws of the Sphinx. We flicker in darkness bound, no longer separate entities but single cells of a greater conscious. Riding the vortex of ages back to a pinprick island smack between the pillars of Hercules, down deep beneath the blue salty blood of Poseidon.

"Now you will see the true beginning." Bound in salt rimmed night, mired in protean muds and slime, Nathicana appears before us. Clothed in the shadows we once called House like some ancestral robe which bares her bosoms. Her prayers reform us, draw my comrades to those cold mounds of moonlit glory, we whimper into reflections of our own making. "Welcome to R'lyeh." Nathicana's voice, sifts through the cold muck of ancient oceans in currents dark and eldritch. A dead city rises around us, bleak gardens filled with entities who dwell forever beneath rotting luminescence. To see them is to learn all they teach, living data. Their voices ride the cold plasticity, a sound we know, a sitar sound moaning in tri-note agony.

"Whose visions do we hear?" Lacy and Eugene wail grateful dirges from orbits parallel to mine. An immense entity dwarfs us all. Even Nathicana's infinite insides seem a single molecule, trapped in an ocean of inter dimensional enigmas.

"He who dreams in omegan splendor, who will swallow the world. Your infinity is only a tick-tock mirage. Your trickles into time cannot be allowed to delay his rising." Nathicana swims beside us.

"1968 Forever?" I add my wonder to theirs, whether AD or BC we can no longer know. Still, we flow down, deeper into liquid night, between cyclopean stones until dead dreams bloat us with corpulent eons of strange visions.

"You but tapped a power of sublime magnificence. My master takes it back." Nathicana shrills in sonar pulses. "Time must not stop until Cthulhu rises."

Those of the Air

by

DARRELL SCHWEITZER and JASON VAN HOLLANDER

DECLINE, DECAY, THE STENCH of years closed over me as I drove through Haverbrook Park that colorless wintry afternoon. My old neighborhood had become a hollow place of blackened brick and faded gray clapboard, peopled by phantoms from my past, by vanished friends, by deceased neighbors, by the aging effigies of my parents in their final, precipitous plunge into decrepitude—by everything I thought I had broken free of, the dust I thought I'd stirred for the last time, the chains I thought I'd cast off one evening, ten years before, when I'd screamed "Fuck this goddamn shit!" at the top of my lungs for no immediately apparent reason, packed a hasty bag, and stalked out of the house, informing my startled and but perhaps not entirely sorrowful parents that I wasn't coming back, ever.

I'd made that promise stick for ten years. Now I was coming back, one more time.

Because of an inescapable loose end. Because of Jeffrey, my half-mythic older brother, who wasn't able to leave as I had.

I glanced at the passing scenery: heaps of rubbish on sidewalks, a burned-out building that might have been a private home or a warehouse, but I couldn't remember which; four more stores closed, one of them Kohler's delicatessen where, thirty years ago, my father, then a young parent trying to show off to impress his embarrassed sons, used to pound counters and bellow for corned beef.

Now he wasn't much up to pounding or bellowing for anything, I knew, even before I pulled into the familiar side-street and inched my way behind the brick rowhouses, weaving among trashcans and the occasional tricycle until I came to our own, familiar, unpainted garage door.

He met me at the back door, after ten years no more than a wizened caricature of his younger self.

"Hello, Dad."

"Hello, Son."

I'm sure what he meant to say was more on the order of: Why the Hell did you come back after all this time? I'd hoped you wouldn't have to.

And I wanted to reply: You know perfectly well. It isn't my fault, Dad. Or even yours.

But so many of the important things never manage to get said. Jeffrey is my brother. I can't help that, but he is.

So, overnight bag in hand, I followed him slowly through the tangle of our basement, then upstairs, through the kitchen—it a disaster area, far, far messier than I had ever seen it in my life—and into the still immaculate, plastic-covered living room.

He sat on the plastic-covered sofa, to weary to continue, his very presence a stain on this inviolate shrine of a room.

I remained standing. I tried not to touch anything. An awkward silence followed.

Finally, Father ran a liver-spotted hand over his almost bald head. He sighed.

"You look different, Jerry."

Unthinkingly, I ran my free hand through my own thinning hair.

"Yeah. I guess so."

"Your Mama's dead, Jerry." He hadn't called her Mama since I was very small. I think he was retreating into memories just then. I couldn't blame him. I didn't want to be the one to yank him into the uncomfortable present.

The silence resumed.

Then he said, "It was just a stroke that killed her. Just a simple stroke. Like that." He snapped his fingers. This display was meant to comfort me. No, she didn't suffer from some hideous malformity unknown to science and melt away into putrescent slime. Very neat and tidy. Just a stroke.

I swallowed hard, and was about to say something.

"I'm sorry you missed the funeral," he said.

"I'm sorry too. There was a strike in Buenos Aires. I couldn't get a plane until yesterday afternoon."

And now, an absurdity so agonizing it was a torturer's stroke of genius. The old *Mister Ed* theme went rattling through my brain. It was all I could do not to sing aloud something about people yackettey-yacking and wasting the time of day. But I didn't. Be thankful for small mercies. I wept, just a little. Father doubtless thought the tears were for Mama, and seemed moved.

We can't say the important things. Words fail us.

I sat on one of the plastic-protected chairs. In silence. For a long time. Outside, the sky darkened.

Gradually, very subtly, for all I knew he was still locked in his room in the attic, my brother was there, with us, impatient as always.

I had to say it at last. "How's Jeffrey, Dad?" There, I thought. Did it.

"He's still changing. Like the book said he would. I'm afraid of him, Jerry. I don't think he knows me anymore. I don't think he'll recognize you either."

But I'll have to try, remained unsaid. You know that, Pappa.

* * *

I remembered that it had been on a winter evening much like this one, the year I was thirteen and Jeffrey was seventeen, that the two of us went outside together for what should have been the last time.

He'd shambled into my room, knocking over books, sending my portable record-player to the floor with a screech that guaranteed that my copy of Sgt. Pepper's Lonely Hearts Club Band was going to have to be replaced.

"Let's go out. And play. Please." He smelled particularly bad just then. His tusks gleamed and dripped with drool. He had to squeeze himself sideways to fit through the doorway. Something, probably a new, vestigial limb stirred underneath the extra-extra-large Philadelphia Eagles sweatshirt he always wore.

I picked up, then unplugged the record player and set it on my desk. The record itself was so obviously ruined I could only drop it into the wastebasket.

For just a second, I was angry enough to hit him.

"Want to p-p-play." His eyes, sunken in his mottled face, were still my brother's eyes. I still knew him. Some of him, a little bit, was still that Jeffrey who had walked to school with me as recently as five years earlier, before he was taken out of school and all the kids started beating me up and teasing me, shouting, "You're brother's a retard and you are too!"

No, it wasn't that, of course. For a time, doctors came and said it was some rare and spectacular disease. There even an Englishman from Merck. I didn't know what that meant. For the longest time I thought Merck was a place in England.

Then Mother wouldn't let them come anymore and wouldn't let Jeffrey go out of the house.

But tonight, she and Daddy were off somewhere. It might have been one of their periodic frenzies of church-going. They might have been off asking God to make Jeffrey normal again. Take this cup away from me, as the phrase went.

Even I knew it wasn't a matter of cups, or God's business. Jeffrey knew it too. I think that my parents were just as certain, but they still prayed, so they wouldn't give in to despair.y brother shook his head violently from side to side, banging against the doorframe with his teeth like an angry bull with its horns, gouging chunks out of the wood.

"Okay! Okay! I'm coming." I hurried to put on my hat, coat, and gloves, while he stirred and stamped. A stain spread down the front of his jogging pants and started to pour onto the floor. I'd clean that up later. I reached up and put my arm around his neck, to calm him. One of the huge tusks slid wetly against my cheek, but bristling with sharp edges and points from the endlessly intricate carvings he spent most of his time executing.

("Scrimshaw." He'd read that word in a book. "Scrim! Shaw!" like a football cheer, but sputtered, grunted. "Yes, carvings on the teeth of a whale," Mama said, then added, in one of her frenzied periods, "for you are Leviathan, the Great Beast.")

So we waded out into the still-falling snow, in the evening twilight, me all bundled up with long scarf trailing, a regular boy, and Jeffrey, still in his Eagles sweatshirt and jogging pants, barefoot.... I would never have taken him out in broad daylight, no matter how much he wanted to play. No, I couldn't. But now, there was a certain thrill to it. He was my secret, the vast and potent magic I alone commanded...or so the game went.

We scrambled quickly across the narrow concrete strip that served as a common driveway for all the houses in our row, then I easily mounted the fence—but I had to find an opening for Jeffrey, who was too heavy—and slid, slightly out of control, down the embankment into the comforting security of Haverbrook Park itself, that not-very-large, hilly woodland which seemed endless as the night came on.

He was clumsier than ever before, crashing through the trees and briers, moving on all fours much of the time, but not on his knuckles like an ape, instead with his hands flat on the ground, leaving, huge, perfect handprints in the snow.

He grunted and laughed and even clapped his enormous hands when he came to the stream, and wallowed right in, sitting in the frigid water, splashing. The cold didn't seem to bother him.

Carefully, I tried to cross on a log, but slipped, and found myself standing in water to my knees, my boots filled, the water so cold it burned before my legs went numb.

"Play!" Jeffrey sputtered, like a very small child, happy as he could be, like the mental retard the neighborhood kids always claimed he was.

But I knew better. I had always known better. Jeffrey merely enjoyed his frivolous moments, when he momentarily escaped those cares and fears he could not express by any means other than carving strange figures and letters on his nearly foot-long teeth.

I was glad for him, just then. I waded to the further bank.

"Come on, Jeff," I said. "Let's play."

So we ran and climbed among the rocks and trees, wandering deeper and deeper into the park, as the land rose and the woods shut out the lights and noise of the city that surrounded us. We came, at last, to a series of stone terraces, high above the stream. Some people said they were man-made, that there had once been a forge there, back in the time of the Revolution. Certainly there were a lot of stories about that place.

On this particular night, as it had been some times before, it was our place alone, a secret we two brothers shared. We sat on the highest stones, in the darkness, hidden from the world. I was shivering all over then, clinging to Jeffrey for warmth; but in vain, because he wasn't warm, and felt cold and hard, like living metal beneath his soggy, half-frozen clothes.

"Fairy tale," he sputtered. That was his other truly childlike characteristic. He liked fairy tales, always had, since he was small, and the way to tell him one was to make him part of it, one of the characters.

"Once, long ago, in an old-time kingdom, there was a Beast that lived in the woods. That's you, Jeff. You're the Beast. That's not a bad thing to be, because the Beast is really a prince and he can do magic."

"And...what you?"

I shrugged. "I guess I'm the King's huntsman." I tried to laugh. "You don't want me to be Beauty, do you? I mean, that would be queer, like a girl, you know—"

"Does the huntsman kill the Beast?" For once he didn't sputter. The question was startling. He'd seen right through the tale.

I didn't know what to say. "Um, no. Of course not."

"What's the rest of the story then?"

"I think it's that the King got so angry with his oldest son—the Royal Wrath was something everyone was afraid of—and when the King was in his rage the ground shook, and there was lightning in the sky—and the King was so angry with his son that he put a curse on him, and the kingdom was cursed too, and the trees died, and the rivers dried up, and there was only silence afterward. Everyone went away, and they left the Beast alone, everyone except his brother, the younger prince who was not afraid of him. And—"

I started to cry then, because I was lying, because the story didn't go that way. It wasn't as simple as that. It was so unfair that we couldn't just be brothers and grow up together, like other kids did. I didn't know how the story would end and was afraid that it never would; not because of anything we'd done, or even because of anything Father had done in his Royal Wrath or Mother had in her prayerful frenzies. No, it was nobody's fault that our grandparents and great-grandparents and great-great-grandparents had come from the Whateley family of Dunwich; and that someone had passed on from generation to generation an old book called the *Necronomicon*, and that some of the words Jeffrey carved on his teeth were in that book and Daddy could read them, but would never tell me what they said.

It wasn't fair that sometime back in the 1920s the Whateleys had tried a great Experiment and failed, but, somehow, that Experiment had worked its way down the years and through the bloodlines until it came out again in Jeffrey.

I cried because of all that, because it wasn't fair.

And my brother did the most extraordinary thing. He touched me gently on the back of the neck, almost as if he were stroking me—if anybody else had done it, it would have been queer—and he told me a story, struggling for the words around the impediment of his ungainly tusks. I didn't understand very much of it, but it was about how the Beast was not really a monster after all, but part of a different family, and how "Those of the Air," as Jeffrey put it, would come someday and take him to a better place, maybe another planet. I couldn't make that out. There were a lot of words in the story that were just buzzing and spitting and barking sounds.

"Does the younger prince get to come too?"

"No. Blood of Them in him, but not enough. He can just barely see them."

And we sat for a long time in the darkness after that, and it seemed indeed —I was certain I imagined what I saw, that it was a kind of dream—that the wind circled around us again and again, with a whispered whoosh like a fleet of huge trucks passing, and sometimes I could see shapes among the trees, distorted bodies, and luminous faces floating among the branches. They called out to Jeffrey, and he answered back, in a language I didn't know.

I nearly froze to death. Jeffrey had to carry me back to the house. He smashed in the back door because he couldn't open it. Father was waiting for him, and in his Royal Wrath beat Jeffrey with a shovel, and locked him in the attic room, and never let him out again. I went to the hospital for frostbite and missed some school, and later, I could only talk to my brother through the locked door when I slid his meals in through the slot Father had installed. Jeffrey didn't answer back much, and I never got to tell him any more of the story of the two princes.

* * *

"You go upstairs and rest for a while, Son," my father said. "You've had a long trip up from South America. I'll fix us a little something in the kitchen. Then you come down again."

I don't know how he thought I'd want to rest, or linger here at all, considering what the inevitable outcome must be, but he, I think, wanted to delay it just a bit longer, and I granted him the courtesy of this reprieve. Maybe he just wanted to be a father again, one last time.

So, silently, I went upstairs, into my old bedroom. I flicked on the light and saw that absolutely nothing had changed since the day, when I was twenty-three, I had stormed out of the house. There was still a 1982 newspaper on the floor, under the dust. And a pair of dirty socks.

I sat down on the bed and just stared into the indeterminate distance of the room, which was not a matter of physical space at all: at the bookshelves, even the model airplanes which had dangled from the ceiling since my childhood.

And, irony of ironies: the sleeve for *Sgt. Pepper's Lonely Hearts Club Band* was still on the shelf in front of me. I had never gotten around to replacing the record.

My hand found something on the bed, under the covers, something which had not been there before: a leather-bound photo album. I recognized some of the pictures, from family outings, graduations, and the like. I paged through it with a mixture of dull curiosity, then something almost like anger, then just exhausted sadness. The pictures had been altered, mutilated with a ballpoint pen. My own image had sometimes been made into that of a prince, with crown and flowing robes and a sword, sometimes the huntsman, with a gun or bow-and-arrows and a Robin Hood cap. Once, my eyebrows had been raised and I'd acquired long fingernails and a pigtail— a comic Chinaman. I had no idea why.

Mother's image had been the object of anger, the eyes and sometimes the whole face gouged out. She'd been given ass's ears more than once, and there was even an enormous posterior drawn in the sky over her wedding picture. There she was, a bride, on the church steps, her face scraped away, and it was raining shit.

The final picture in the book was one of father, exhausted, reclining on a plastic-covered sofa. I think it had actually been taken one Christmas, as he snoozed after all the preparations were done. But now there were wires going into his arms and sides, and a carefully-rendered monitor on the wall above him, the line on the screen a zig-zag, flattening out. Father in Intensive Care, dying.

The one truly frightening thing was that I didn't know if this was Jeffrey's work, which it should have been—but how had he known I was coming and how had he gotten out to place the book here for me to find? —or Papa's own.

Above me, something stirred, then hit the upstairs floor hard, again and again, as if stamping its hooves.

God help me, I thought of that stupid TV sitcom theme: A horse is a horse—

And fully, and deeply, I wept, lying there on the bed, amid the dust and papers and old laundry.

* * *

Father and I ate in silence, badly cooked eggs and bacon. He couldn't look me in the eye. He stared at his plate, swirling his fork around in the grease.

I was thinking in cliches. I should have felt that there was so much I had to say to him: that I, his estranged son, truly loved him after all, that I wished our family could be together again, like old times, the whole routine. But there, sitting with him, I couldn't think of anything to say at all. I was empty. I'd cried my last tears on the bedspread upstairs, and that was the end of that.

Two floors above us, the pounding was louder, insistent.

"Come on, Son," he said at last. "We've got to finish this."

So I followed him upstairs that last time. He paused at the first landing, staring into my bedroom, where I'd left the light on and the photo album out on the bed. Then he turned into his own room. I went to follow him. He held me back.

"Wait."

He still had to have his little secret, his final one. All right. He could have it. I waited patiently while he rustled around in the dark. I could only imagine that the bedroom, too, hadn't been touched, that my mother's things were exactly as she'd left them. It sounded like her closet Father was rummaging in.

He came out with something wrapped in a garbage bag. Even before I felt the heavy, iron-bound covers through the plastic, I knew what it was: the ancient *Necronomicon*.

"You'll have to study," was all he said.

That was almost the very last thing he said to me, ever. He flicked on a light. We went up the attic steps in silence. He indicated that I should be the one to remove the heavy, five-pointed stone sigil that leaned against the door of the attic room. By now the smell was almost overpowering, the stench of garbage and excrement and something that almost might have been burning, sulpherous, vile, but ultimately unidentifiable. Why the neighbors didn't have the Board of Health or the police in long ago was beyond me.

There was no sound at all from behind that door, as I dragged the heavy stone away, as Father undid the padlocks and slid the bolts back.

He opened the door, and I took the first step inside, my feet stirring what must have been old steak and pork bones.

"Jeff? You there?"

Father grabbed me from behind with surprising strength, his arm in a choke hold around my neck. He hurled me back, across the tiny landing, against the opposite wall. He held me there with both hands, and for once his eyes met mine and his face was utterly, utterly inscrutable. I could make out the King with his Royal Wrath, and Papa, exhausted beyond words, despairing, wanting only for it all to end, and more. Possibly he wanted to explain it all to me, or ask my forgiveness, or merely wish that things had turned out differently. I don't know. He was angry, sad, firm, and stoically uncaring all at once.

All he said to me was, "No. Wait here. It was supposed to be your mother. Now it has to be me."

"Father, I —?"

He squeezed my hands tight over the *Necronomicon*, then turned from me and went, meekly but unhesitantly, into the dark room. As a final offering. Because Jeffrey was grown up now, and it was time.

In the instant of silence that followed, I found myself plagued with another comic, irrelevant thought, a memory of a Gahan Wilson cartoon showing a puffy-faced young man confronting his seated, frog-faced father in what must have been the great hall of an old English manor. Portraits of frog-faced ancestors lined the walls, and the caption read, "Son, now that you're of age, it's about time I told you about the old family curse."

About time.

In the room, my father was screaming. But I knew he wouldn't want me to come in.

The screaming stopped. Something heavy and wet dropped to the floor. Then I heard a sucking sound, like an electric pump struggling with a clogged drain, and after that a series of snaps, which I knew were bones breaking.

Again, silence. The smell grew even worse.

I knew what I had to do. There was only one possibility left.

"Jeffrey," I said. "It's me. It's Jerry. Come out. I want to tell you a story. Remember?"

And from within the darkness came my brother's voice, "Play?"

"Yes," I said. "Let's go out and play."

Holding the book, I backed down the steps, and he came out onto the landing, whimpering a little as he brushed against the five-pointed stone; for he had grown so huge that he could not help but touch it.

He didn't wear clothes anymore. His whole body, even his tusks, had turned a greenish-black, the color of tarnished metal; but his muscles and numerous limbs I couldn't quite make out seemed more like a huge tangle of ropes come alive. He stumbled and thumped down the stairs, squeezing between the walls, one surprisingly human hand grasping the railing. His head, on top, seemed almost an irrelevancy, like a basketball floating on frothing water. But I could still see his eyes, and they were my brother's eyes.

Of course his passage made complete havoc of Mother's immaculate living room. It was only there, in the better light, that I realized that Jeffrey had an extra mouth where his chest should be, vertical, like an insect's mouth, lined with needle-teeth. Praying-Mantis claws held the remains of our father firmly in place. Jeffrey streaked the living room, and the kitchen, and the back stairs, with slime and blood and the debris of smashed furniture.

Outside, in the darkness, in the swirling snow, I coaxed him through the fence, into the park. We waded through the stream once again, as we had when we were boys, and it was just as cold now, and once again I didn't care. This time I didn't fall, though. I clutched the plastic-wrapped *Necronomicon* tightly under one arm.

"Play," Jeffrey said, clapping his hands. "Play."

Once more we climbed the hillside, in the darkness, Jeffrey shoving the trees aside, making a terrible racket—but no one disturbed us—until we reached the terraces.

And in our secret place, we sat together, and I told him the rest of the story of the Prince and the Beast, how the younger brother released the elder from the castle's dungeon, how the Beast devoured the King, as was only fitting; and the King's guards fled in terror at their approach, and the two of them retreated far, far into the forest, where no huntsman could ever follow, until they reached the secret and eternal land of the beasts, where animals spoke in their own languages, and no human being was ever admitted.

But because the Prince was the Beast's brother, he was allowed to the very threshold of that land. He could see into it through the thick underbrush, just for an instant, as the leaves parted when the Beast and those who had come for him went back inside. The other animals did not kill the Prince, and, knowing that he would not betray them, they allowed him to leave.

"Is that the end of the story?" said Jeffrey.

"I don't know. I don't think so." I should have been sobbing.

That would have been right. But I had run out of tears. As before, when I sat with Father in the kitchen during his last meal, I felt only empty and had nothing more to say.

Then They of the Air finished the story, whispering to Jeffrey in their own language. I saw them, clearly this time, huge, winged, impossible shapes with fiery faces, half like smoke, swirling in the night sky, weaving between the trees, their passage a great whirlwind. Branches flew. Trees creaked and swayed. Jeffrey, wild with excitement, leapt up, doing a kind of dance on the hilltop, howling and hooting, stamping his several enormous feet. I was irrelevant to all this, like a pigeon that's wandered into a parade. I could have been crushed. I scrambled down the hill-side, out of my brother's way, and looked up just once as a particularly brilliant flash of lightning tore the sky apart. My eyes were dazzled. I couldn't be sure. But Jeffrey seemed transformed once more, into something utterly indescribable and powerful, with wings that reached out to touch the horizons. He and the others filled the sky, rising up.

And then there was just me, sitting alone in the cold and the dark on the hillside, still clutching the plastic-wrapped book I didn't know how to read, unable to understand how the story had turned out.

Mr. Skin

by

VICTOR MILÁN

T HE WATTS TRACT HOUSE had already slumped into smoking ruin when I arrived. The gunfire had ceased. Firehoses played over the rubble, hot afternoon sunlight striking incongruously delicate rainbows from their arcing streams.

The crowd melted from my car like mercury before a fingertip. The mostly black faces turned toward me were sullen at the violation of their neighborhood in tear gas and blood and fire. I could not blame them. Yet neither could I blame the police for their handling of the situation. The Sylvanian Freedom Front had shown itself callously willing to kill on numerous occasions.

Standing on a sidewalk on which balloon-headed stick figures had been scrawled in childish chalk, I donned the yellow rainslick with Coroner stenciled on the back which is my robe of office on such occasions. The media turned their cameras on me as I made my way forward. A voice called, "Dr. Ozawa! Is Lynn-Holly inside?"

I ignored the question. I didn't know the answer any more than did the reporter who asked it. But I feared it was inevitable; the charred body of Miss Racer, beautiful blonde daughter of that great lady of the screen Aubrey Racer, must lie within, beside her abductors'.

The living room gaped open to the sky. Studs framing one inner wall still stood, bleeding fitful smoke as a fireman played an extinguisher's white breath on them. The reek of wet ash and burned furniture, the sweet barbecue stench of roasted human meat, surrounded me like mist.

A young SWAT officer who followed me in rushed outside to vomit as the smell hit him. It had no effect on me. Such aromas are as drearily familiar as the carbolic acid of my autopsy room.

Inside I located five bodies. One was of a black male whom I tentatively identified as Reginald Martindale, known to the world as Field Marshal Kabbarega, founder and leader of the SFF. The other four were women, all burned beyond recognition. It would require comparison of dental X-rays to determine whether Lynn-Holly Racer was among them.

To my surprise, only two of the victims, both female, had actually died above ground. The others had chopped through the floor in the bedroom and retreated into the crawlspace beneath the house, continuing the fight as the house literally burned down around them. The last, whose slight build led me to fear she might be Miss Racer, lay with one outflung hand still holding the charred stock of an M2 machine carbine. The other clutched a curious object.

Crouching, knees gracelessly framing my ears, middle-aged thighs cramping with the unwonted strain of trying to keep from touching the still-hot floor joists above and melting my rainslick to my back, I made the standard preliminary examination of the body. Then I detached the object from calcined fingers. It was a small idol, carven in the likeness of the *naga*, the many-headed serpent the SFF used as its symbol, joined to an oddly bulbous body. Its substance was unfamiliar, a lustrous green-veined black, with the glossy feel of soapstone. The heat had not harmed it. I placed it in a plastic evidence bag and continued my grisly task.

As the world now knows, Miss Racer was not among those who died in the house on East Fifty-Fourth that seventeenth of May, 1974. That left two questions which came almost to obsess me: where were Lynn-Holly and her remaining abductors? And what would inspire such children of upper-middle-class privilege as Linda Ann Sperling, whose hands in death held both a weapon and a mysterious talisman, to burn to death rather than surrender?

* * *

I sat at a table in a room the sun never shone, inside Soledad Correctional Facility where. Deathwatch Ray McCandless sat across from me, the uncertain light of a fluorescent bulb overhead jittering on his dark smooth-shaven head, looking every bit as ominous as his name. His wrists and ankles were fastened to a staple in the wall behind him by heavy chains, implying that it had not been given lightly.

"Reggie was just a stone-ignorant nigger," he said in a voice which, while rough and untutored as his appearance, was far from lacking in intelligence. "Where he hear about this Kabbarega and shit?"

Assumed his question to be rhetorical, I did not answer. Presumably the prison library contained historical references to the nineteenth century monarch of what is now part of the unhappy country of Uganda, suffering under the misrule of the madman Idi Amin. Martindale had set the fashion within the SFF of assuming *noms de guerre* based on historical or fanciful figures; Miss Sperling, for example, styled herself "Marshal Aïda."

But McCandless—who resembled a statue carved from mahogany with blows of an axe, serving life without hope of parole for his many crimes of violence, feared by the worst inmate as much as the toughest guard for his strength and utter disregard of safety, his own or others', when provoked—was not a man for idle talk. He cast a single contemptuous glance over his shoulder at the door, outside which a guard stood nervously fingering his nightstick. Then he leaned forward to the fullest extent of his chains.

"I tell you where he learn it, man. Mr. X.."

I nodded.. In the taped ravings he periodically sent the media, Martindale had often adverted to a Mr. X. Despite similarities in their anti-white rhetoric the Black Muslims firmly denied any connection with Kabbarega, and claimed their followers inside Soledad had firm instructions to avoid him as dangerously unstable. Prison authorities likewise disavowed knowledge of the aptly-named X.

"Tell me more about him," I urged.

Before responding McCandless looked furtively left and right, as if afraid someone might have stolen up to overhear. I wondered who this terrible man might find to fear.

"I grew up in the Atchafalaya. There was these Coonasses out on Alligator Bayou, had this funny look to 'em. Some said they got it from brother marryin' sister, that kind of thing, some said from somethin' worse. Sacrificed animals, and people too. Wasn't no *voudoun*. Not Satan worship neither. It was things from the stars —*Old Ones*, they called 'em. Used to own the Earth, they said, and now they fixin' to get it back."

My face must have mirrored my astonishment at this digression, because he glowered. "Easy for you to laugh, man. You never hear the old folks talkin' low 'bout evil sights they seen back in the woods. Never hear them devil-worshipers chanting by night, strange and low out across the black water. Never had your baby sister just up and vanish one evenin' after dinner, and hear your momma late at night, prayin' to God her baby girl was dead and safe with Jesus."

I kept my expression as neutral as I could. Clearly McCandless was in the grip of overwhelming emotion. Though superstitious fancy colored his memories, the tragedy was all too real.

"Laws raided them Coonasses when I was eight-nine. Louisiana State police and St. Martin Parish sheriffs. Said it was 'cause they was moonshinin' in there, but we knowed better. Lotta shooting goin' on, and them they didn't kill the laws hustled off, women and children too. For days afterward them police was in there, settin' off dynamite and sayin' nary a word what they was blasting."

"I'm sure this is all very interesting, Mr. McCandless—" I began.

"We kep' clear them crazy Coonasses," he said, as if I hadn't spoken, "but time to time a boy couldn't help but hear 'em talk. Used to speak of a big black man, come and visit 'em, but only by night. Used to whisper to 'em, secrets, dark things—said if a body listened too much, he might as well fergit about ever sleepin' again. He was a messenger for these Old Ones they worshipped. Eight feet tall he was, and he didn't have no face. Just blackness, like a mask."

I must have fidgeted. That intimidating jaw set beneath the furze of grizzled rusty beard. "You think I jiving you?"

"No, no, of course not. I just don't see—"

"Then wait," he said imperiously. "I celled next to ol' Reggie. We was both by ourselfs. They got me alone 'cause I so mean, they got him alone 'cause he so crazy. And I be lyin' there on my bunk in the middle of the night, an' I hear him *talkin'* to somebody."

I drew a handkerchief from my pocket and wiped my forehead. I tried to conceal my disappointment. I had hoped for some concrete lead, some insight into the founder of the Sylvanian Freedom Front that might explain the grip he held on his followers. Instead McCandless was carrying on about the midnight mutters of the terrorist leader-to-be as if they were anything more than products of a disordered mind. Clearly, I had wasted a trip.

"What tear it, man," McCandless was saying, "is, I hear somebody talk *back*. Low voice, real deep, like it come rumblin' up from the middle of the Earth. And Reggie, he don't talk like that.

"We keep these little mirrors, so we can like see what's goin' down after lockdown. So one night I just sits and waits. 'Long about two, three in the morning I hears them voices. I take my mirror out and slide it out through the bars, easy-like, so's I don't make no noise.

"And I sees my man Reggie, he ain't alone in there. There this other dude with him, blacker than the shadow, talking in that growly old voice."

"Surely that's impossible," I blurted.

He lunged at me. I almost fell over backwards. The chains brought him up short with a ringing clangor. I stood up, steadying the chair with my hand, opening my mouth to summon the guard.

But this hard man, who once killed a fellow inmate with a single blow of a push broom handle after the unfortunate stabbed him in the back, looked into my eyes and said, "Hear me out. *Please.*"

After a moment I nodded, and somewhere found the courage to resume my seat. "Very well."

"I *know* it ain't possible. But it's *true.* There was this other nigger in there talkin' to Reggie. And then, the worst part of it was, when he stood up—"

He drew a quavering breath. "Mr. X, he looked me right in the eye, in my little mirror. He was eight foot tall if he was a inch. And he didn't have a face, man. *He didn't have no face!*"

He slumped back into his chair and covered his face. His breath came in sobs. I stared at him, wondering what I had learned.

Deciding I had nothing to lose, I drew from my coat pocket the object I had taken from Linda Ann Sperling and laid it on the table between us. Light shimmered on the plastic bag.

McCandless lowered his hands and saw the idol. He recoiled as if the sight burned him. "It's her!" he exclaimed.

"I beg your pardon?"

He was kicking his chair back with his heels. The legs made unearthly shrieks on the cement floor, like tortured mice. "Take it away, man. It one of *their* things. For the love of God, *get it away!*"

I covered it with my palm. It seemed warm to the touch. Perhaps my imagination had been fired by the man's tales—incredible though they were, they were told with utmost conviction.

"It seems to resemble the SFF's so-called *naga,*" I said evenly as I could, hoping to soothe him as I might a frightened dog. My research connects their symbol both to Hindu mythology and Yoruba folk magic. Can you tell me anything about this object?"

He had turned his face away, pressing his forehead to the raw cement wall. To my astonishment I saw a trickle of blood run down the wall. "I ain't sayin' no more," he said in a moan. "Only—don't take that thing out in the woods by the dark of the moon, man. Or God have mercy on your soul."

* * *

I confess I enjoy the smell of my pathology lab. When an autopsy is not in progress, there is no smell of corruption there, only the strong astringency of the antiseptics used to scrub down the place. It is much cleaner than the world outside, and ever so much better organized. A calm place. A place I can relax.

I sat in my office next to the autopsy room perusing police reports. My attempts to cast light on the motives and nature of the Sylvanian Freedom Front had brought me only confusion. McCandless' story was fantastic. Yet there was something about the man which made it impossible for me to dismiss him as a lunatic out of hand.

From the files I learned that even after the Racer kidnapping Linda Ann Sperling continued to work as a topless go-go dancer at an establishment called the Tender Trap on Hollywood Boulevard. That seemed a curious occupation for a member of an avowedly feminist revolutionary organization.

Yet Linda Ann had burned rather than desert her leader or her cause. Was it so surprising that she bared her body to the lustful gaze of strangers, and risked discovery and imprisonment to keep providing income for the Front? And still I did not know why.

I knew law-enforcement officers were vigorously pursuing all leads. But I was determined to learn all I could about what had driven her and her comrades. Perhaps I could glean some clue as to the current whereabouts—or future fate—of Lynn-Holly Racer.

The cramped interior of the Tender Trap managed to be at once dim and garish, lit by a myriad of tiny colored lights and a many-mirrored witch ball, such as one might find at a fashionable discothéque. The denizens were surprisingly solicitous of me, especially after I displayed a willingness to pay for whatever they might be able to tell me about their former co-worker. I did not, of course, reveal my identity, and I was thankful that I was of a more retiring nature than my predecessor in office, so that my face was little-known to the general public. I do not know what motives they ascribed to the solitary, middle-aged *Nisei* asking questions about a young strip-tease dancer who had recently died in such a hideous manner. Nor do I care to speculate.

A performer styling herself Bambi informed me that Miss Sperling had engaged in prostitution, an activity she was herself hasty to disavow. I was initially skeptical. However, the assertion was independently confirmed by several of Bambi's associates, all of whom had names which ended in a short "i" sound.

Miss Sperling's pimp, Bambi informed me, was a light-skinned Afro-American male who styled himself *Mr. Skin*.

* * *

It is a truism that nobody walks in LA; and yet of course people do, even in Beverly Hills—when they desire to make an impression. When I first saw Mr. Skin he was strolling before the glittering display windows of Rodeo Drive as if they were his, a small, trim man, whose grace was evident as he walked. He was dressed head-to-foot in white, in an open-necked suit and Panama hat.

Parking was as always at a premium in Beverly Hills. I had to resort to leaving my Buick sedan double-parked with my medical examiner's placard displayed in the windshield and running after the pimp in most undignified fashion.

By the time I caught him up I was grateful that I try always to keep in shape despite the sedentary nature of my occupation. I felt self-conscious shouting the peculiar sobriquet the man had chosen, but he turned at once.

He showed neither surprise nor alarm at seeing me running after him. His features I would describe as being more perfectly regular than handsome. Dark sunglasses, the only non-white item of his apparel, hid his eyes.

"Can I help you, man?" he asked. "If it's diversion you're after, you've caught me a bit outside of office hours." His voice was a well-modulated baritone. He seemed not even to consider the possibility that I might represent the authorities.

"I'd like to talk to you about Linda Ann Sperling," I blurted. "I understand she was one of your, ah, employees."

"One of my whores? Yes." Even through the sunglasses I felt his scrutiny. I determined not to show reaction to his considered crudity, though I felt my fists ball. The demands of my profession have never allowed me to contemplate marriage, but I'm angered whenever I hear someone speak disrespectfully of any woman. I feel as if he is showing disrespect to my late mother, who gave so much for me.

"Quite a waste, what happened to that girl." He cocked his head, studied me a moment. "Business or personal?"

I took a deep breath. He had been close to saying "pleasure," I somehow knew. "You might say both. I am Dr. Richard Ozawa, Chief Medical Examiner for Los Angeles County."

"I know."

That took me briefly aback. "I, I am conducting my own, as yet unofficial, investigation into the Sylvanian Freedom Front. I find myself wondering what could lead young women such as Miss Sperling to do what they did."

"You're looking for the blonde honey? Little Lynn-Holly."

I moistened my lips, nodded.

He stood a moment, then nodded abruptly. "Why not?" And he flashed a smile full of faultless teeth.

* * *

We adjourned to a nearby coffee shop which seemed to have no objection to Mr. Skin's flamboyant pimp garb. Indeed, they looked more askance at me. I did not much resemble the Beautiful People who seemed to comprise their usual custom.

Over cups of espresso I asked if Miss Sperling had ever discussed politics with him.

"All the time," he said. "I just didn't listen."

"But didn't she try to recruit you for the revolution? And didn't she—I mean, the SFF espoused feminism of very a radical stripe."

"As I said, I paid her no mind. When she got too pushy—" a slantwise smile. "—I just went upside her head." And he made a slapping gesture for emphasis.

I felt my face grow warm and forcibly reminded myself that I was not here to reform this creature. I had to admit that, other than in dress, he little conformed to my conception of a pimp. He was well-spoken, cultured almost. Perhaps it was the influence of the clientele to whom he catered.

"Do you have *any* idea what might've motivated her?"

He watched a long-legged woman in hot pants stride by outside the window. "Maybe some of those old books she was always after me to read."

"What books? Marx? Simone de Beauvoir?"

"No, nothing like that. Peculiar stuff—nonsense. *The Golden Bough. Nameless Cults. The Necronomicon.* Superstitious trash."

"Did she ever show you any?"

"No. Said it would 'blast my sanity' unless I was prepared for it. Whatever *that* means." He laughed.

"I don't understand. I thought the Sylvanian Freedom Front was a political movement. You make it sound like a cult."

"All I know is, she was always taking off to go running through the woods with her little friends, worshiping some kind of nature spirit. Forest mama, or some such. I maybe should have kept her on a tighter rein, but hey—she was a reliable income producer. I could afford to be indulgent."

He tipped his head to the side. "I daresay you might have favored her yourself, Doctor. She was quite popular with the older set, and I think she enjoyed them more herself. The daddy thing, you know."

Clearly the interview had gone as far as it profitably could. I gave him my card, thanked him, and left as rapidly as decorum permitted.

* * *

For the few weeks I was unable to pursue my investigation. The CME's office in LA county is, regrettably, always busy.

Two days after my meeting with Mr. Skin an unusual report crossed my desk. Though Soledad lies outside my jurisdiction, the warden there thought I might be interested, in light of my recent visit.

Deathwatch Ray McCandless had been found slashed to death in his cell. There were, of course, no witnesses.

As in most prison killings, the wounds evidenced extreme violence: severe lacerations to face, throat, and upper chest, defensive wounds on the forearms. The only atypical feature was that microscopic examination revealed they were not *cuts*. The skin was torn, as though by the talons of an animal. The coroner who examined the body theorized that some metal implement like a gardener's hand rake had been sharpened to form an artificial claw. The guards were tearing the cell block apart in search of the weapon.

It is not my habit to second-guess my colleagues; the autopsy was competently performed. Yet the ME had overlooked one detail: the tines of a rake are relatively immovable, and would create parallel slashes. The photographs showed signs of spreading, as would be the case, say, with wounds left by an animal's claws. I made a notation to suggest that the guards look for some sort of artificial claws made to slip over a man's fingers. It was possible that such devices might be fabricated in a prison shop, despite the authorities' watchfulness.

It occurred to me to wonder what sort of man might choose to face Deathwatch Ray McCandless with such weapons. Still, it was not my problem. I put the matter from my mind.

* * *

The UCLA librarian regarded me in a most peculiar manner when I asked after the titles Mr. Skin had mentioned. She consulted a mimeographed list from a bottom drawer of her desk, looked at me again, and excused herself. I waited, surrounded by the quiet bustle of students studying for final exams, until she returned with Mrs. Hoskins, the chief librarian, who resembled a pouter pigeon with a silver bouffant. She ushered me straightaway into her obsessively orderly office.

"I am sorry for the commotion, Doctor," she told me. "But, frankly—" She hesitated in evident embarrassment. "Frankly, the Federal Bureau of Investigation has requested notification whenever anyone asks to see the books you named."

I was surprised. Under the Nixon Administration the Justice Department had ordered that such surveillance be kept over certain books, to the displeasure of civil libertarians. But those works dealt mainly with topics which might interest terrorists of the Weatherman ilk, such as the home manufacture of explosives.

"Madam," I said, "Frazer's *The Golden Bough* is a standard anthropological work. I read it myself as a sophomore."

"It's of interest when mentioned in context with those other titles. We do have copies of them, but they're on the restricted list. I'm afraid I can't let you see them."

"Mrs. Hoskins, I am hardly some indigent off the street, thumbing through art books in hopes of finding nude pictures."

"Does this concern an investigation?"

I barely hesitated. "Yes." It wasn't really a lie.

"Very well. Come with me."

She led me to a remote storage area, opened a door to what I at first took for a broom closet. Inside was a small antechamber, musty with disuse, furnished with a reading table and a solitary chair covered in age-cracked leather and a coating of dust. "Wait here," she said, and used a key from her ring to pass through a door in the far wall.

I sat, amused as well as exasperated by the whole rigmarole. This was the Twentieth Century, after all; men had transplanted human hearts and played golf upon the Moon. What had we to fear from *books*?

She came back with several stacks of photocopies, pierced and bound with brads. "The originals are too valuable to handle," she said. "I hope you won't mind."

I told her it made no difference to me. "I have *Nameless Cults* here, and another book from the list, *The Book of Eibon*. We have only a fragmentary copy of the translation of the *Necronomicon* attributed to Dr. John Dee. I'm sorry."

"Dr. Dee? Queen Elizabeth's court astrologer?"

"That's the one." She pushed the sheaf of papers across the table at me as though eager to be out of contact with them. "I've glanced through a couple of them myself, I admit. They are most disturbing."

I nodded and thanked her. She left. I began to read.

Indeed, such works *would* be highly disturbing—to the impressionable. To me they were a farrago, ravings which would be hilarious did they not indicate minds sorely troubled by mental illness. Some of the material did possess a certain manic grandeur. One couplet in particular sticks in my mind:

> *"That is not dead which can eternal lie,*
> *And with strange eons even death may die."*

For the most part, though, the books consisted of disjunct ramblings about some mighty and ancient race of beings—gods or space aliens, it was difficult to discern—who once owned the Earth, but had somehow been dispossessed. They lusted ever to return and bring down our human civilization in fire and horror and woe. They were called the Great Old Ones and had names which sounded like gargling: Tsathoggua, Yig, Ithaqua, and most dreaded of all, Great Cthulhu, a pelagic divinity who, though dead, waits in his sunken city R'lyeh for his human devotees to perform the rituals necessary to revive him.

These horrors were in some allied way to "Outer Gods," who included such collections of vocables as Azathoth, Yog-Sothoth, Nyarlathotep—a sort of demonic Hermes, messenger of the gods, who possessed a thousand forms—and Shub-Niggurath.

This latter was known as "the Black Goat of the Woods with a Thousand Young," which recalled the Forest Mother of whom Linda Ann had spoken to Mr. Skin. However Dee, or rather the "mad Arab Abdul Alhazred" whose work he claimed to be translating, described her Avatars, known as Dark Young, as "a writhing Blackness, like unto a fell Tree in the Branches above and the Trunks below, yet walking, and pierced with a thousand Mouths all agape, and reeking like the Grave"—hardly the image I had in mind.

In the margin by this passage was scrawled a note of obviously recent provenance: *Lovecraft was right!* That brought the whole thing into focus. I had heard vaguely of this Lovecraft, a pulp fabulist of the early part of the century, whose morbid stories were enjoying something of a renascence. I am a believer in a free society, certainly, but I wonder if it is healthy to allow those disturbed enough to find such material entertaining to feed their fantasies.

The similarities between this gibberish and the McCandless' reminiscence did not escape me. Perhaps Mr. Lovecraft had researched the lesser-known folkways of certain people of the bayou country of Louisiana. Or perhaps a forebear of the hapless Acadian cultists had fallen under the influence of Dee's work or some similar confabulation.

After all, such nonsense might prove compelling to the uncritical. The minds of the SFF's members had been open to Field Marshal Kabbarega's inchoate mix of environmentalism, feminism, and social revolution. Who knew but that they might have fallen under the sway of this "mystic lore" as well?

The *Book of Eibon* fragment actually contained a ritual for summoning Shub-Niggurath's Dark Young, her terrestrial manifestations. It required a stone altar in the woods, "well-imbued with gore." *That* sent a shiver down my spine. The Manson case, which had broken while I was still an assistant ME, remained fresh in memory. The hints raised during the investigation, of victims both nameless and numberless, had emphasized what everyone connected with California law enforcement was vaguely aware of already: that there are a great many unexplained disappearances each year—each *day*—in the Golden State. The discovery of victims of apparent ritual murder was a more common event than anyone liked to think.

Might the SFF practice human sacrifice? I was filled, then, with genuine horror—not the counterfeit Lovecraft and other such *poseurs* sought to stimulate, but fear for Lynn-Holly Racer, fear so great I could barely restrain myself from jumping from the chair and racing into the street. It had been assumed that, if the Sylvanians meant to kill her, she would have been dead long since. But what if they were keeping her alive *until a certain propitious time?*

* * *

That night I sat in the recliner in the darkened study of my bungalow in Alhambra, with a snifter of brandy by my hand and my shelves of books a comforting insulation against the traffic noise without. The contents of the manila folders piled beside me confirmed the distressingly high incidence of unexplained disappearances and cult-related events.

One in particular caught my eye. Two years ago, in the ominously named Diablo Range northwest of Los Angeles, rangers from Los Padres National Forest had discovered, not far from State Highway 58, a stone altar covered in a dark, suggestive stain. Samples examined in our then-new Forensic Science Center were found to contain both human and animal blood. Rangers and San Luis Obispo County sheriff's deputies had staked the altar out without result, then blown it up.

I sat back. The case bore an undeniable resemblance to McCandless' account. Here in the dark of night the ravings of mad Abdul and the rest seemed not so ridiculous after all.

From the reading table beside me I took down the talisman I had pried from Sperling's fingers, hefted it in my palm. *Writhing blackness; trunks and branches.* Its blackness baffled the eye, but my fingers felt the way it seemed to separate into tentacles—or branches—at the top, and into a compound trunk, banyan-like, at the bottom.

Through the plastic bag I became aware of a sensation of warmth. Hastily I put the object back on the shelf beside my three-volume *Forensic Medicine.* I could not permit myself the fevered imagination of an addict of the fantastic fiction of a Lovecraft. It would quickly drive a man in my profession mad.

Out in the woods by the dark of the moon the summoning of Shub-Niggurath's avatar was carried out on the New Moon. It was two nights away.

I took out two photographs, one of Linda Sperling from the Whittier College yearbook, the other a glossy of Lynn-Holly Racer. I set them side by side, propped on a sheaf of disappearance reports, and stared at them. No answers came to me.

* * *

The Special Agent in Charge of the FBI's LA field office listened politely to my discoveries, then excused himself and ushered me from his office, all with the air of a man dealing with a mildly deranged relative, like an uncle prone to expose himself to guests. At that, it was more deference than his Bureau often shows local officials. Still, it did not encourage me to try the District Attorney's office. What did I have, after all, except a few hints and a generous helping of horrific surmise?

Clearly I would have to turn up something more concrete.

* * *

"So the Forest Mama rang the cherries," Mr. Skin said as we walked together down Sunset. "She was always on about her. Said she was going to teach women how to do without men altogether."

He snorted a soft laugh. "Always wondered what reason a brother might have for peddling that line of jive. Guess my man Kabbarega was a total turkey."

It was a sultry late afternoon, with the traffic streaming by and the smog thick enough to bring tears to the eyes. This was not the sort of neighborhood I usually think of strolling in myself. But despite his lack of size the man walking beside me had that about him which did not invite anyone to trifle with him.

Mr. Skin's manner belied the common criminal which I knew him in fact to be. I found myself oddly drawn to him, as if I could confide in him. I did not give in to the impulse. At least not entirely.

"You mentioned before that Linda and her SFF comrades were always 'running around in the woods,' " I said. "Did she ever mention where?"

"Don't really remember. I'll have to think about it and get back to you."

I nodded. The swollen red ball of the sun was about to drop through the bottom of a rusty sky. For some reason the imminence of night disturbed me.

"You're looking peaked, man," Skin said. "Why don't you just let this go, let the Feds handle it?"

"I feel as if I've gone too far to turn back."

"It's never too late. Let me fix you up with one of my stable. I'd be doing my girls a favor; you're a handsome man, not to mention clean."

I could not help drawing away from him in repugnance. For all his cultured speech, it really was as if he were an alien being.

* * *

The phone roused me from deep sleep. "Hello?"

"It's Skin. I remembered."

I fumbled for my glasses, irrationally. It's a reflex. "You remembered?"

"About Linda Ann and the woods," he said. "Something she told me about a special place—a holy place, she said. It was up in the Diablos. In the national forest off 58."

* * *

The brisk mountain wind that ruffled my hair should have been a relief after LA's smog. But I felt a sense of oppression. Perhaps it was the way the firs seemed to stand with their lofty heads together, as if sharing dark secrets.

It was late in the afternoon of June 18th—the night of the new moon.

My sedan had made heavy going of the dirt track up the mountain-side toward the site mentioned in the ranger reports. Eventually I had to abandon it and hike up the slope. I have little experience of wilderness, but the woods seemed oddly still. No birds sang, no animals stirred the undergrowth. There was only the wind, making the tree branches rub together like soft insect legs.

It was difficult picking my way up the steep slope, clambering over fallen trees, ducking under branches. My breathing grew labored, drowning out the sound of the wind in the trees. I began to worry that I had misread the map.

And then the firs fell away before me, into a clearing a good hundred yards across. I knew at once I was in the right place—for in the clearing's center stood a waist-high altar of native stone. *Someone* had rebuilt it.

And more than that. Even at this distance I could see it covered in a stain like brown moss.

My heartbeat began to thunder in my ears as I walked forward. I seemed constantly to be passing through invisible membranes, as if forcing my way through half-congealed air.

There was a rusty smell about the altar, and a sweetish stink of decay which I knew too well. I took my handkerchief from a pocket of my windbreaker and pressed it to the stain with trembling fingers.

The stuff that covered the stone was tacky. The handkerchief came away red. I did not need my gleaming lab on Mission Street to tell me that blood had been spilled on the altar within the last twenty-four hours.

I turned and fairly flew down the mountain, crashing through brush, vaulting half-rotted trunks. The forest seemed filled with ominous presence. Limbs plucked at me as if seeking to impede my flight. It was a minor miracle that I made it back to my car without going headlong and breaking my neck.

Ten miles back up 58 there was an outdoor phone booth at a gas station whose sign banged ceaselessly against its standard in the wind. The station was deserted, a casualty of recession and the oil crunch. The Los Padres ranger station didn't answer.

The deputy who picked up the phone at the San Luis Obispo sheriff's office seemed half asleep. My report seemed more to bemuse him than waken him. Even after I satisfied him as to my identity he didn't bother to hide his skepticism. The sheriff was out, he said; he would give him a call on the radio, but even the sheriff would have to clear matters with the Forest Service before he took any action on Federal land.

I had dialed the first five digits of the FBI's LA office before I stopped myself. The SAC already suspected I was unhinged over the Racer case. If I insisted that Lynn-Holly's captors would be sacrificing her at a secret ritual in the Diablo Mountains that very night....

Slowly I replaced the receiver in the cradle. The phone book hung from its cable like a suicide victim, pages fluttering like the last breaths of an exsanguinated woman.

I looked up at the mountains. Up here the dark came early. The sun had already dropped from view, and an edge had come upon the air. I felt a more than physical chill.

I knew what I must do. Perhaps I alone could accomplish nothing. But I had to *know*.

* * *

Night had fallen in earnest by the time I made it back to where I had parked the car before, driving with my lights off, navigating by feel, praying to gods I had not believed in since I was nine to keep me from breaking an axle or stranding myself on a high point. As I drove the last few hundred yards I could see the lights up-slope.

The woods seemed blacker than was natural. I picked my way up through them, fighting the urgency that pulsed in my veins like an amphetamine. I did not wish to make noise to alert whoever was up there.

I might have saved my effort. Before I came in sight of more than the fugitive flicker of bonfire light through underbrush I could hear the ecstatic chanting. My mind seemed to pick the syllables *Shub-Nig-gurath* from the unintelligible flow. I became aware of the obscene statuette in my pocket.

It had grown warm against my hip.

There were at least eight of them, mostly women, more than the number of SFF adherents believed to remain at large. Two stood watching down slope with Soviet-made automatic rifles, no doubt smuggled back from the Vietnam conflict, held ready.

The others danced around the altar and chanted. On the bloody stone lay a young woman, nude. She was slim, and her hair was gold. I could not doubt this was Lynn-Holly Racer.

A glint of flamelight on blade. I looked desperately around for some fallen branch I could use as a club, though I knew the watchful young women with the automatic weapons would cut me down before I crossed half the intervening distance. A figure was thrust forward to stand beside the altar, a long-haired youth in vest and jeans, a derelict or hippie hitchhiker. His hands were bound behind him.

The flourish of a knife, and his lifeblood gushed black over Lynn-Holly's nude form. He dropped to his knees while a pair of captors kept a grip on both biceps. The idol was uncomfortably hot by my hip.

I felt my nails break the skin of my palms.

The chanting reached a crescendo. The captive girl writhed. The youth collapsed after the boneless fashion of the dead, like a suit of empty clothing.

The trees above the clearing began to bend and thrash, as to a gale-force wind. There was no wind. I felt my heart pound in the base of my throat. Tension twisted me like a garrote.

From the woods a looming blackness stepped. A *writhing* blackness, like unto a tree in the branches above and the trunklike legs below. Mouths gaped at random in the ropy black mass of it, drooling ooze. A smell like a corpse left to simmer three days in the May LA heat washed over me.

The Dark Young of Shub-Niggurath danced toward her victim on hell-black hooves. Her image blazed sunlike in my pocket. I smelt the fabric begin to burn.

My mind snapped. That's the only way I can describe it. In gibbering panic I turned and fled, bounding through the woods like a boulder.

But before I fled a vision burned itself everlastingly into my brain: Lynn-Holly Racer rising unfettered from the altar, blood and golden hair streaming down her naked body, and dancing toward the horror from the woods, her pale arms outspread in welcome.

* * *

He was waiting for me in my study when I got home after midnight, sitting in my favorite chair with the footrest up. I was beyond surprise. I was even beyond fear.

He smiled at me with a trace of something like regret. "I tried to tell you, man," he said in a quiet voice. "I warned you not to mess with it. You should have taken me up when I offered you one of my girls. They're the best, you know."

I stood there, knowing I should scream, or flee, or go mad, or something. All I felt was infinite emptiness.

"You helped me," I said at last. "Why?"

"I'm an errand boy," he said, seeming to speak to the air before him. "I don't bear you any animus; I do what I'm told."

He looked at me. I remembered that Alhazred described him as having the sometimes semblance of a handsome Egyptian man. Egyptian—or a light-skinned black.

"Being the Messenger of the Outer Gods is lonely work. I'm the only one remotely human. The others—you couldn't comprehend. Just understand that it's good to have someone congenial to talk to. But you—"

He shook his head, laughed softly, almost sadly. "You insisted on knowing the truth. You thought it would help you rest easier."

He sat silent while the cosmic irony turned my knees to gelatin. I could feel a wild mad shout of laughter rise up my throat like bile, I who would never know rest again. I bit it down.

"So I helped you, Doctor. Why not? There's nothing you can do, you know."

"I'm a respected public official. They'll have to listen to me?"

"Who? The Special Agent in Charge?" He laughed.

"And what are you going to tell them? That you were guided to an invocation of Shub-Niggurath, the Forest Mother, by Nyarlathotep, Messenger of the Outer Gods?"

Laughing, he stood up—and up, and up, till he towered a good two feet taller than had the pimp called Mr. Skin. His skin was black, the shiny smooth blackness of obsidian, not the brown pigmentation we miscall "black." He looked at me without a face.

"The Way has been opened," he said, in a bass that shook the walls like a San Andreas tremor. "You can neither help nor hinder."

And he turned and walked through the wall.

* * *

Eight months later the Oregon hideout where the SFF's last survivors had holed up was raided by the FBI. Lynn-Holly Racer was freed unharmed. She was far advanced in pregnancy—with Kabbarega's child by rape, it was reported.

She was reunited with her mother at a special ceremony at the FBI offices in Los Angeles. The media were invited, as were local law enforcement officials. The FBI can be generous when it has all the credit thoroughly sewn up.

No one questioned my presence. I was still Chief Medical Examiner, after all, though by that time a storm of controversy was breaking around me. I had become mentally unbalanced, the rumors said. No longer fit to discharge the duties of my office.

And they were right.

It was a production worthy of Hollywood—indeed, gossip had it that certain of Aubrey Racer's industry friends had advised the FBI on staging. There in the nova glare of spotlights Lynn-Holly, radiant in a yellow maternity dress, was escorted forth by a pair of unsmiling agents in suits. As flashbulbs flared she flew into her mother's arms. Then she turned to face the phalanx of microphones thrust toward her from the auditorium dark.

I pushed forward through the crowd. For the first time in sleepless months, darkness was my ally. Before anyone paid me any mind I reached the foot of the stage. I removed my right hand from my pocket, extended my arm, and, as deliberately as I could, fired nine shots from a West German-made .22-caliber revolver into the abdominal region of Lynn-Holly Racer.

* * *

A knock on the door. The suspect sat by the table with hands on knees and his head hanging.

The detective lieutenant from LAPD Homicide moved first, while the FBI stenographer was still typing the final words of Dr. Richard Ozawa's confession. The lieutenant had practically had to draw his piece before the FBI would let him into the room. The Fucking Big Idiot had no damned jurisdiction in a homicide; they were making noises about the crime being committed on Federal property, but that was crap.

The lieutenant had no intention of losing control of the situation now. He opened the door.

It was a uniform cop with his hat in his hand. He coughed at the wave of cigarette smoke that rolled out of the interrogation chamber. Trying not to grin too widely at the Feds, the lieutenant grabbed him by the shoulder and steered him out into the hall.

In a moment the lieutenant was back. He walked over to stand above the unmoving assassin. He thrust his hands into his pockets and stared down at Ozawa while the FBI boys fidgeted with their neckties.

"Well, Doctor," he said at length, "we got good news and bad news."

When Ozawa didn't react, the lieutenant continued. "The girl didn't make it. She died on the operating table. You're looking at Murder One—though I bet some fancy-ass lawyer can plea that down. And of course we don't have the death penalty in California any more, you lucky bastard."

"Jesus, Meléndez," an FBI agent said, "what's the *good* news."

"They think the baby's going to make it—no thanks to the Doc, here. They're doing the C-section now."

And Dr. Richard Ozawa began to scream.

Just Say No

by

GREGORY NICOLL

I T WAS SKUNK'S IDEA to park the van on the edge of a sharp curve at the end of the block, where the streetlights were all burned out. Weiner didn't like it and neither did Boneboy, who complained that it was too dangerous because this was Prowl Night for the Plymouth Rockers. But since Skunk was the only girl who would ever go out with either of them, the two guys let her have her way.

It was quiet when Boneboy shut off the ancient Volkswagen's sputtering engine. The night air was quite cool, carrying the scent of tree sap and fresh cut grass, and a light wind rustled through the high branches so that the oaks and the willows seemed to beckon from the other side of the cemetery wall. The three of them got out slowly, the van's front doors creaking as they left its inner sanctum. A Grateful Dead skull decal, with a purple VW emblem branded on its forehead, leered out at them from the vehicle's darkened windows.

"Still don't think it makes sense to park a black van on a dark curve," Weiner grumbled as he walked, his flipflops slapping against the soles of his feet like lukewarm applause. He jostled a bulky green backpack, which clung tentatively to his shoulder by one frayed canvas strap.

"The van's not all black," said Skunk. "There's those stickers. Now come on, let's go."

Boneboy hoisted a six-pack of Narragansett Lager out of the beer cooler, slammed the VW's sliding door, and scrambled to catch up to the other two. "Yeah, like those hot-rodders are really gonna notice my Thrill Kill Kult and Ed Gein's Car decals when they come skidding around that turn," he observed sarcastically.

"Or the one that says, Just Say NO to Drugs," added Weiner.

Skunk laughed. Eager to proceed, she was virtually invisible in the darkness of deep night as she led the way. Her boots, her leather skirt, and her Brando jacket were all as black as her skin; the two boys could see only the bright streak of white in her hair, which gave Skunk her nickname. She seemed like some unearthly spirit, just a small sliver of ivory which bobbed five feet off the ground up ahead of them.

Skunk stopped abruptly, the white streak pausing in mid-bob.

"What is it?" asked Weiner.

"Shhh!" she hissed. "Okay, dudes. Everybody over the wall, now."

Boneboy blinked in the darkness, shifting the uncomfortably cold beer bottles to his other hand. "Why?"

"Because I said so," she answered through clenched teeth, adding, "and because I don't wanna run into your buddies the Rockers right now." In the distance, tires screeched and a Hemi engine thundered, punctuation for Skunk's sentence.

"How did you hear that car before we did?" asked Boneboy, impressed.

"She's got the way," said Weiner. "She always had, and she always will."

"Over," Skunk said firmly. The little streak of white inclined itself in the direction of the cemetery wall.

They fumbled against each other, climbing, boosting, and tugging until all three had made it to the top of the wall—backpack, six-pack, and all. From this vantage point they watched as two supercharged Plymouth Barracudas swept down the wide and dark avenue, engines blasting fire as their stereo speakers competed in a brutal round of Name That Tune. David Byrne's "Psycho Killer" whined from the big blue Plymouth on the right, but it was lost in the heavy metal roar of a Great White cassette from the 'Cuda on the left.

These cars were followed by a Duster sporting a 340 Wedge, and a Roadrunner Superbird brought up the rear. With a final squeal of tires, the column of muscle cars rounded the far corner and swooped away into the night. Then silence returned, broken only by the gentle susurrus of the wind in the trees.

Without a word Skunk tossed the backpack over so that it landed with a dry slap in the new-mown grass of the burial grounds. She jumped after it, leather creaking as her skirt and jacket stretched. She landed on her feet like a cat. "C'mon, boys."

They followed her without question.

The Swan Point Cemetery spread out before them, dim starlight playing over thousands of upright marble gravestones. Overhung by oaks and weeping willows whose boughs swayed spectrally in the breeze, the grounds sprawled for acres in three directions. The caretakers had been busy, for the smell of the fresh-cut grass was chokingly strong. Skunk led the way, Weiner hobbling along behind her with the backpack and Boneboy bringing up the rear with the beer, his trail marked by drips of condensation from the little stubby brown bottles.

They moved among the dead.

All around them lay the late sons and daughters of Rhode Island, the Friendlys and Pages and Williams, the Smedleys and Slaters and Stones, the Gamwells and Scotts and Galpins. Skunk started out quick and eager, almost skipping as she crossed the crowded grounds, but she slowed her pace as the cumulative presence of the dead weighed upon her.

At last the three of them passed a small mausoleum and made their way quietly to a fork in the paved central path, where a family plot was marked by a tall pillar. Here they stopped.

Behind the pillar, in shadow of great oak, stood a modest marble headstone. By now their eyes had adjusted to the darkness, and the moonlight provided a faint glow, but the inscription on this small gravemarker was particularly difficult for them to read. However, although none of them could discern it in the dark, they all knew what it said:

HOWARD PHILLIPS LOVECRAFT
AUGUST 20, 1890—MARCH 15, 1937
I AM PROVIDENCE

For a few minutes the two boys stood watching Skunk as she stood upon the grave, her arms spread like a divining rod. Then Weiner grew impatient and lowered the backpack to the ground. Canvas rustled and crisp paper crumpled dryly as he fumbled in the pack.

Eventually he withdrew a roll of masking tape, a sheet torn from a sketchpad, and a broken red crayon.

Boneboy sat cross-legged on the moist ground and twisted the cap off a bottle of Narragansett. The beer hissed and foamed as he raised it to his lips. Its malty aroma briefly overpowered the scent of the cut grass.

Stepping around Skunk, who was still "divining" over the grave, Weiner knelt down beside H.P. Lovecraft's headstone. With two sharp Velcro-rip sounds, he peeled off a couple strips of masking tape. Smoothing the sketchpad paper over the marble inscription, he fastened the sides down tightly with the tape and began to rub the crayon across the wide flat surface. A rough copy of the marble's inscription began to appear on the paper.

"Hey Skunk," he asked, "do you think Mr. Lovecraft minds me doing this rubbing?"

Skunk shrugged. "He's probably grateful for the attention."

"Did you sense anything?"

She shook her head, the white streak of hair bobbing. "No, but I almost never do on the first try. It's the ouija that usually opens the channel. If I can reach him first with it, then this way should be a lot easier."

Weiner continued his rubbing as Skunk went over to the pack and dug around in it. She came back with the ouija board, which she unfolded and laid directly on the center of the grave. At each corner of the board she placed a tiny metal figure from a role-playing game based on Lovecraft's stories: Great Cthulhu with his rippling mouth of tentacles, a winged and faceless Night-Gaunt, a cone-shaped member of the Great Race, and a subhuman fisherman of Innsmouth.

"What're those for?" asked Weiner curiously.

"To get his attention," she said. "They'll help open the channels of communication."

Boneboy frowned as he looked at the strange, tiny figures. "Did Lovecraft make up those critters himself or did he copy them from old legends?"

"Depends on who you believe," said Skunk, her leather skirt scrunching as she sat down on the far side of the board. "There are folks who say Lovecraft alone knew that these gods and monsters really existed. They say he encountered them in his dreams, and when he wrote about them, he was forced to conceal his revelations as fiction."

"Why? What was the point in disguising them as stories if he knew they were really real?"

"Because otherwise they would've locked him up."

"What? You mean in Arkham Asylum or something?"

Skunk smiled. "Yeah, or something."

"So what do you believe, Skunk?"

She shrugged. "Well," she answered carefully, "I think H.P. Lovecraft was the most creative, awesomely talented dude who ever wrote in the English language. I believe he had a really strong connection to what might have been the spirit world, or what was—I don't know—maybe some other dimension."

"But you don't believe in Cthulhu?" asked Weiner, still buffing the gravestone with the crayon.

"No," said Skunk. "I think Lovecraft made all that up. But that's part of his strength and power as an author—that he wrote it all so well that it still makes so many readers believe in all those weird creations."

Boneboy laughed. "You just say No to Cthulhu, right?"

Skunk laughed. "Yeah, that's it—I just say No to Great Cthulhu!" She shook her head. "But I'll tell you dudes this: I don't want just any old cheapjack outlet-store spirit describing the Other Side to me tonight. Unh-uh. I'm here to get the lowdown on the afterlife from the man who can tell it the best—the master of them all, H.P. Lovecraft himself."

She looked back and forth between her two companions, Weiner with his grave-rubbing project and Boneboy with his beer. "All right then. So which one of you mugs is gonna do this with me?"

Boneboy shook his head. "Not me. This is all a buncha crap."

Skunk frowned. "If you don't believe in this, Bone, just keep quiet. That negative energy of yours could ruin the whole experiment."

"Lovecraft didn't like blacks," Boneboy said. "He'd never answer your call, Skunk."

"He thought we were supernatural," she said coldly. "If he feels me here, he'll seek me as a channel. Did you ever read the description Lovecraft wrote of that prizefighter, the Harlem Smoke, in Herbert West—Reanimator?"

Boneboy finished the last swallow of his Narragansett and tossed the empty into the bushes. The bottle clinked faintly against a rock. "No," he said, "but I saw the movie."

Weiner paused in his grave-rubbing. "Good movie," he interjected. "Loved that Barbara Crampton. In the scene where she was strapped on the table, and the doctor's severed head was starting to—"

"Chill," said Skunk angrily. "I'm not talking about that stupid movie, or that dumb, sexist scene in it. I'm talking about something Lovecraft wrote—something that wasn't even in the movie."

The boys were silent. Wind whispered through the oak branches overhead, rustling the leaves.

"Lovecraft wrote," said Skunk calmly, "that just by looking at this African-American's face, you would get visions of 'unspeakable Congo secrets and tom-tom poundings under an eery moon.' If that doesn't show he thought we were channels to the spirit world, then you just tell me what else it would take."

Boneboy burped. "Listen, Skunk," he said quietly. He twisted the cap off another Narragansett, its foaming hissing like a tiny snake. "What I'm telling you is that even if Lovecraft's spirit did think you were a human gateway back from the spirit world, he wouldn't use you 'cause you're black. And me, hell, what would he make of a 'bino?"

Weiner finished his grave-rubbing and dropped the remaining red nub of crayon in the grass. He turned around and sat down beside the ouija board, wet grass squishing under his faded jeans. "He didn't like Jews much either, did he?"

Skunk shrugged. "Did you ever read his story 'Pickman's Model'?"

Weiner smiled. "I have the Night Gallery episode on tape. Love that Rod Serling."

"You and your movies and videos," Skunk grumbled. "Don't you ever read any books? Or any magazines besides Penthouse and Fangoria?"

Weiner shrugged. "Just be cool, Skunk, and I'll try this with you. What do you want me to do?"

As the wind stirred again, they joined hands over the ouija board pointer. It was large and sculpted of wood, its surface worn smooth by decades of use. The tips of Skunk's ten black fingers settled on the indentation on the left side, and Weiner's ten white eased into the groove on the right. The pointer moved slightly as they took their positions, and then it stopped.

Skunk closed her eyes. "Lovecraft," she whispered quietly.

The wind stirred in the trees.

Boneboy stifled a burp.

"Howard Phillips Lovecraft," Skunk continued. "I summon thee, H.P. Lovecraft. I call on thee, the creator of Great Cthulhu. I call on thee, the father of Yog-Sothoth. I call on thee, the progenitor of Nyarlathotep. I call on thee, the sire of Shub-Niggurath—the Black Goat of the Woods with a Thousand Young...."

Despite the evening chill, Weiner felt his hands becoming sweaty.

The pointer seemed to move.

Very slightly.

Then again.

Weiner cleared his throat nervously, as if he doubted that the pointer was being pushed from the spirit world, as if he suspected it was just slipping in the sweat on his fingers.

The ouija board was old and brown-surfaced, with its letters, numerals, and symbols printed in yellowed gothic script and outlined in black. There was a YES in the upper corner guarded by the Night-Gaunt and a NO in the opposite corner shadowed by Great Cthulhu. The letters of the alphabet arched across the board below them.

The pointer moved slowly, at last seeming to come to rest with its tip on the letter F.

"Lovecraft," Skunk whispered.

The pointer slid again.

Skunk licked her lips with anticipation, for the pointer truly acted as if it was alive. Now it almost tugged itself from under their fingers, seemingly propelled by its own mysterious power.

Slowly the tip of the pointer drifted to a stop on the letter H.

First F, then H, Skunk thought. A double consonant. Whatever could that mean? "Lovecraft," she repeated aloud, low and quietly. The sound was almost lost in the stirring of the wind and the rustling of the leaves on the oak branches overhead.

The ouija pointer slid over to the letter T.

Boneboy was interested now. He propped up his half-empty brown bottle in the grass and shuffled closer, bending over the board.

The pointer eased slowly over to the letter A.

There it stopped, showing no inclination to move again.

"F-H-T-A," said Boneboy with open disgust. "Fhta, fhta, fhta. It's just gibberish. It doesn't mean anything."

Weiner started to lift his fingers from the pointer but Skunk shook her head and told him to wait and keep concentrating. She snapped at Boneboy, "Shut up, Bone. Keep that negative energy down."

"Do you think it's maybe a code or something?" asked Weiner in a whisper, apparently trying to sound optimistic.

"In a lot of his stories," answered Skunk quietly, "Lovecraft mentions a chant used by the disciples of the Old Ones. It goes, Cthulhu fhtagn. The spelling's not all the way complete here, though. There's an G and an N missing."

Boneboy shook his head. "Just say No to Cthulhu."

"Bone," said Skunk angrily, "will you just sh—"

She stopped in mid-word as the ouija pointer moved under her hand. It swooped up to the corner of the board, its tip coming to rest on the word NO printed there.

From his corner of the board just above this word, the tiny metal figure of Great Cthulhu stared motionlessly at the pointer. Wind stirred the oak leaves above and picked at the edges of the sketch paper Weiner had taped over Lovecraft's gravestone. The tree branches swayed and creaked.

Weiner and Skunk removed their fingers from the sides of the pointer. The boys were silent as Skunk picked up the little Cthulhu role-playing game figure, closed her eyes, and pressed it to her forehead.

The two boys waited patiently as she concentrated.

After several minutes she opened her eyes and set the gaming piece back down. "Nothing," she said. "I'm not getting a thing. Just like with Houdini."

"With Houdini?" repeated Boneboy, tilting his head back for another slug of beer. "You mean the famous escape artist?"

"Tony Curtis played him in the movie," said Weiner, "with Janet Leigh. Hey, did you know they were Jamie Lee Curtis' parents?"

"Shut up, Weiner," said Skunk. She nodded at Boneboy. "About two years ago I roadtripped to Houdini's grave with some other psychics and readers. We tried everything we knew, but we couldn't reach him."

Boneboy slugged back a swallow of beer and wiped his lips. "Houdini could escape from anything, except he couldn't escape from death."

"Right," said Skunk quietly. "And Houdini had told the whole world that if there was any way to come back from the afterlife, he was going to do it. But in all the years since he's been dead, nobody's ever made contact with his spirit." She gestured at Lovecraft's gravestone. "Just like him. There are no Houdini ghosts, and no Lovecraft ghosts either."

Boneboy offered her his beer. She took it silently and chugged down a long swallow.

"Hey, Skunk," said Weiner, "I thought you didn't drink that stuff when you were working. You told us it took away your edge."

She shrugged. "Might as well get wasted. I'm through trying anything here for tonight. Anyway, we'd probably better get outta this place before the security goons circle by and catch us."

Weiner got up and ripped the tape off Lovecraft's headstone. He pulled the rubbing paper free, and then took the trouble to scrape off every last stubborn little gunky bit of tape residue from the edges of the marble.

Meanwhile Boneboy made himself useful by gathering the metal figures and folding up the ouija board, putting them into the backpack along with what was left of the beer. "Gimme that," he said to Weiner, reaching for the grave-rubbing.

Weiner rattled the paper and whisked it away from Boneboy's grasp. "No way am I gonna let this get all rumpled up in the backpack with those bottles," he said. "I'll carry it loose."

Skunk finished off the bottle of beer and got a fresh one out of the backpack before they started out across the cemetery again. "You know," she said, "Lovecraft and Houdini knew each other, and they wrote a story together that I've never been able to figure out. It's called 'Imprisoned with the Pharaohs.'"

The three of them moved between the graves, Skunk's leather gear creaking as she walked. Weiner's flipflops slapped against his feet, and the remaining beer bottles clinked together in the backpack as Boneboy jostled it.

"What do you mean about figuring out that story, Skunk?" asked Weiner.

"Well," she said. "Houdini devoted his life to debunking psychics and exposing phoney mediums, yet the one short story he wrote with H.P. Lovecraft is chock full of monsters that meander around in the afterlife. And when Houdini died, he said he'd come back—but he never did. I wonder what he really believed, and what happened to his spirit after he died."

"Maybe," said Weiner, "maybe he's, like, being punished or something."

"Hey, there's an idea," said Boneboy. "And maybe Lovecraft's being punished, too—for writing the truth about the Old Ones!"

Weiner smiled. "Yeah, Lovecraft should've said No to Cthulhu!"

"Shut up, both of you" said Skunk, lowering the beer bottle from her lips, "and help me over this wall."

The three of them got over to the streetside again and had almost made it back to the van before the Barracudas circled around again.

A sudden gust of fierce wind snatched the grave-rubbing from Weiner's hands, and he darted into the street to catch it. Skunk lunged after him, but the flat bottoms of her black leather harness boots slipped on the dew-slick pavement. They both hit the street hard, the stiff paper grave-rubbing clenched in their hands.

The 'Cuda at the front of column locked its brakes. A banshee scream cut the air as layers peeled off its skidding Firestones for over 20 feet. And then the chromed steel of its bumper smacked hard into the two figures sprawled in the road.

The hot-rod Plymouth behind it swerved to avoid a collision, jumped the curb, and smeared Boneboy across the cemetery wall.

In the hospital emergency room later that night, it took the doctors more than half an hour to pick all the pieces of Cthulhu, the Night-Gaunt, and the other gaming figures out of what was left of Boneboy's heart and lungs. By then, however, it was too late. He was as dead as Weiner, and he looked even worse than Skunk.

"Where am I?"

"Hey, Skunk, is that you?"

"Yeah, it's me. Is Bone here too?"

"Right beside me."

As they drifted down the long corridor of pulsating greenish light, the mad piping of eerie flutes sounded from all sides. The air stank of burning rubber, of fish and salt brine, of fire and putrefaction.

Ahead of them swarmed a titanic mass of tongues and tentacles, of webbed wings and unblinking yellow eyes. Acres in size, it changed shape and hue in endless, horrible combinations which defied any known spectrum of color. What seemed to be human faces bobbed up from the amorphous mass; they opened their mouths, but were sucked back into the seething, wriggling horror before they had the chance to scream.

However, for a brief moment two human heads successfully struggled up from the writhing, stinking confusion. Skunk recognized one of them immediately from the photo in her precious copy of *The Dunwich Horror and Others*. Thin and lantern-jawed, it was the face of H.P. Lovecraft. The other, wider face, she realized, must belong to Harry Houdini. It was wrapped with coils of tentacles.

"I tried!" Lovecraft shrieked. His voice was high, nasal, and desperate. "I tried to warn you!"

Houdini started to say something, but was wrenched back into the confusion of drooling tongues and foul, oozing liquids. The great noxious mass surged as it consumed him, foul gasses spraying from a thousand unseen orifices. Its oceans of obscene tentacles thrashed.

Lovecraft's face contorted. His eyes squeezed shut and his forehead creased as his soul was torn by lightning bolts of undreamable pain. "Cthulhu!" he shouted. "Cthulhu lives and dreams! Cthulhu Fthagn! CTHULHU FTHAGN!"

It was Skunk who shouted it first, but Weiner and Boneboy joined in immediately. The cry was possibly the last human word they would hear for eons. For as their essences disintegrated in the acid grip of the soul-hungry Old Ones, the three of them opened their mouths and screamed:

"No!"

"NO!"

"NOOO!"

Then the swirling shapes of the two boys dissolved in the wriggling, bubbling chaos. Skunk felt herself lifted up and away, sensed her body being drawn backward as if by some gigantic hand.

She traveled in reverse, leaving the scene of monstrous evil and returning down the long corridor, past the throbbing green light, past the evil piping of strange flutes. The stink of burning rubber and the rancid, renewed stench of moldering fish made her choke and cough.

Then everything went dark.

* * *

She awoke slowly, her eyes burning from the bright light reflected off the white tiles. The piercing odor of medicinal alcohol stung her nostrils.

"Just stay still, honey," came a stern old woman's voice. "The doctor says you're gonna be in a lot of pain—and if you move around, that'll only make it worse."

Gradually Skunk realized that she lay in a hospital bed. Her legs were splinted, swathed in bandages, and suspended in traction. Tight gauze wraps encircled her left forearm, and a partial headcast obscured her vision. She ached—a deep, burning, below-the-muscle ache—through every centimeter of her body.

"That was quite an accident you had, honey," said the nurse, a fat white woman with gray hair and thick glasses. "You're really lucky to be alive. The doctor thought he'd lost you for a few minutes, but, well.... Listen, is there someone we can call for you? Your parents, maybe? We didn't find find much I.D. on either you or your two friends, so we—"

"Where are they? My friends, where—?"

The nurse shook her head sadly. "The doctors did everything they could, but I'm afraid they...."

Skunk nodded. She knew the rest without being told. "Uh, m'am," she said quietly, "whoever brought me here—did they find anything that belonged to me out in that street?"

The nurse shrugged. She leaned over in the big reclining chair in the corner, its worn cushion emitting a low hiss as she moved. From the little closet behind the chair she produced a leather jacket that was caked with dried blood and a large clear pastic bag which contained the bent-up ouija board, the pointer, and several small gaming pieces wrapped in their own individual plastic bags. "Just this stuff," said the old woman.

"Uh, bring me that bag, please," said Skunk. "And if you don't mind, I'd like to be alone for a few minutes."

The nurse placed the bag on a small imitation-wood serving table beside the bed. She stared at Skunk over the crystal rims of her thick glasses. "I'll give you 15 minutes," she said. "By then you'll be ready for another dose of codeine. And I'd better tell the doctor you're awake—I'm certain he'll want to see you."

As soon as the nurse left the room, Skunk eased the ouija board and the pointer out of the bag and placed them on the serving table.

Was it real? she wondered. What I saw—was it real or just something I dreamed? I've got to know....

She straightened the board carefully, straining to bend it back smooth. Placing the pointer in its center, she put a hand on each of its sides and slowly lowered her fingertips to its worn wooden surfaces.

"Weiner," she whispered. "Boneboy. Are you out there? Do you sense me? Do you hear me?"

The pointer moved slightly, then stopped.

Her pulse quickened. "Give me a sign, and tell if it was real. Tell if what I saw with you was real."

The pointer did not move.

"Do you hear me, Weiner? Do you hear me, Boneboy?"

Very slowly, the pointer drifted up to the corner of the board. Its tip came to rest on the word NO.

Skunk laughed, quietly at first but more shrilly as her tears began to flow. Her laughter raged like a great fire, echoing madly down the long white sterile corridors, until at last the nurse returned with two orderlies to hold her still and apply an exceptionally strong sedative.

Skunk drifted to sleep.

And then, the dreams began.

The Scourge

by

CHARLES M. SAPLAK

"YOU WERE WRONG about one thing, young man," said someone in the crowd around Reginald Lanier. Reginald searched the faces around him and felt his heart sink a little as he found the speaker and noted his odd face and figure. Reginald was quite uncomfortable around handicapped people, old people, and people who argued over meaningless points. The man who approached him now was a combination of all three.

He was short, but appeared to be powerfully built in the chest and shoulders. His legs were noticeably misproportioned, and he wore forearm crutches. He wore wire-framed glasses and the lens over the right eye was dark to the point of opaqueness.

His unique features notwithstanding, the man appeared to be well-groomed, and he was the only man in the crowd with tie and jacket. People didn't often dress up to come to the quarterly poetry and fiction readings held at the Radford Public Library.

Reginald smiled and hoped it wouldn't look fake. "Well, what was I wrong about, Mister...?"

"Tobias. Doctor M. Tobias. You were wrong in saying that there are thirty-six dramatic situations in classical literature. There is a thirty-seventh situation, dealt with in a short story written in 723 A.D., but I can count on the fingers of one hand the people in the world who have encountered it."

Reginald nodded. A lady beside him was saying that she often considered becoming a writer, but could never find time to actually sit down and write. A man with a moustache and an intense stare thrust forward a ream of single-spaced sheets of autobiography which he wanted Reginald to look at. One young woman was loudly telling another that the sort of thing Reginald writes was "the sort of thing people are buying these days."

"Well, the thirty-six situations are really kind of an artificial concept anyway..." Reginald said.

But Doctor Tobias was already walking away. Before he got out of sight he did something which struck Reginald as enormously impolite, if not disgusting.

"On the fingers of one hand," he repeated, then extended his own right hand which was missing the index and middle fingers.

* * *

Later that week Reginald sat in his office and stared at the screen of his word processor. He'd been granted tenure eight months previous, and the tenure board had looked favorably on a forthcoming fiction collection (Dead Leaves) which didn't exist. He was a failed writer who was now secure in his position as a failed writer, and he had a lifetime of leading sophomore creative writing classes and freshman composition classes ahead of him. Of course, all that would change if he could put one more good story onto paper, or if he could even string together what Hemingway had called the "one true sentence."

But the blue screen wouldn't allow itself to be touched, wouldn't even accept a single syllable.

Reginald welcomed the interruption of the Chaucerian scholar from next door, Waldheim, who wanted to bum a cigarette.

While they burned two Marlboros Lanier asked the older man a few questions.

"Was there ever a Doctor Tobias on staff here?"

Waldheim shook his head. "Not that I've heard of."

"Or over at Tech? Or at one of the community colleges?" Reginald made a great show of pushing his paperclip holder, cellophane tape dispenser, sticky back notes, and paper scissors around his desk.

"No. Why do you ask?"

"Well, the other night at the public reading I mentioned the theory of the thirty-six dramatic situations, and an old man who looked like a retired professor came up and said that there was one story done of a thirty-seventh situation, done in Medieval times."

Waldheim shrugged. "Probably just a variation on one of the others. The thirty-six situations are so broad, because they're designed to cover the whole of human culture. Speaking of culture, how's your writing going anyway?"

Reginald shifted to block Waldheim's view of the blank screen. "Fair. Working on some new ideas."

"To hell with new ideas," Waldheim said, grinding out his cigarette. "Shakespeare and Chaucer stole everything they did and they did all right."

Over the next several days, three different things happened, all related.

Reginald's writing capability gradually disappeared.

He also became obssessed with the idea of the thirty-six dramatic situations, and therefore also with the mysterious thirty-seventh situation to which Doctor Tobias had alluded.

And he began receiving at his campus address notes on brittle, thin paper from Doctor Tobias with no return address, all of the notes offering teasing tidbits regarding the "original" story.

Note: "The story, by Abdul Alhazred, has exactly 2100 words. (The mystic three times the mystic seven times the mystic ten-squared.)"

Everytime he sat at his keyboard and tried to start a story, he thought of the thousands of previous stories which had used that dramatic situation and had done it better.

Reginald looked over all the situations, and found those which applied to his own life—situation #22 (all sacrificed for passion); #25 (adultery); #27 (discovery of the dishonor of a loved one); #28 (obstacles to love); #32 (mistaken jealousy); #33 (faulty judgment); #34 (remorse).

He hoped that he could find some inspiration there, but the situations were oppressive. He couldn't help but consider how his own life stories paled beside the great treatments of the past.

Note: "The story, titled 'Al Jeldah'—'The Scourge' in English—is traditionally printed in six hundred and sixty-six lines with seventy-seven sentences."

Sometimes he looked over the stories he had written only a few years before, and marveled that he had once possessed such clarity of thought, such powers of concentration.

He tried to break his block by shutting down the computer and writing first drafts longhand, but he wound up doodling thirty-six pointed stars with jagged, barbed spiders lurking at their centers.

Note: "The story contains seven characters, the plot has three movements, and there are ten separate events."

In a comparative literature class he mentioned the theory of the thirty-seven dramatic situations, then spoke this unbidden thought: "There is a thirty-seventh situation which is a key, a mental key. It's something which no human culture so far has been able to divine, or to accept. It's been repressed with the same vehemence and terror with which the Old Gods themselves have been repressed."

He looked up and saw twenty-six young faces staring at him, wide-eyed. "Well—what is it?" one boy asked.

"What is what?" Reginald said.

When he sat down to write—to write anything, not just fiction, but also letters, memos, even syllabi or lesson plans—he had trouble concentrating enough to construct sentences longer than seven words.

Note: "Abdul Alhazred only wrote one story in his life, and it was a story based on this dramatic situation. Scholars argue whether the experience precipitated Alhazred's later occult researches."

All of Reginald's dreams became lucid dreams, and he often asked his dream-self if the dream situation was similar to the thirty-seventh situation. The dream-self refused to answer.

He tried to break his block by copying passages by writers he admired, but he found the passages from Gass and Brodkey and Hammett and Hemingway utterly flat and incomprehensible.

Note: "The story, in some thematic concerns, anticipates the sonnet 'Ozymandias' by Shelly, and in other concerns anticipates Crowley's Book of the Law."

He sat down one day to read a book by S. E. Hinton and found that he couldn't string the sentences together into paragraphs. Even as he sat there he lost his ability to understand the construction of sentences.

A young student came to him during his office hours to discuss taking an incomplete in his American Literature class. She tearfully explained that her father had been killed in an auto accident and her mother was distraught and needed emotional support. Reginald made a raspberry sound and waved her away, saying, "Loss of a Loved One—situation number thirty-six."

Note: "Legend says that Nizam ul Mulk once discussed the existence of this thirty-seventh dramatic situation with Omar Khayyam, and that the experience so unnerved Khayyam that he developed his obsessive concepts of fatalism and predestination as a defensivereaction."

So when the phone rang in his office one day and it was Doctor Tobias, Reginald was much too eager to speak to him.

"As a matter of fact, Doctor, I've been thinking about that Arabic story you'd mentioned. Do you have any idea where I could get a copy? No, my speciality is more Contemporary American...there are very few Orientalists around today...sure I'd be glad to meet you...there's a decent place called Nickleby's on Grove Avenue...six-thirty then."

After he hung up he realized that he was breathing heavily. Although Tobias hadn't committed to finding a copy of "The Scourge," Reginald hoped that he would, just as he also hoped that if he could see and read the damned thing, he could crack this obsession and recommence his life.

Nickleby's was uncrowded and sedate in the middle of the week. Classical was being piped in through well-balanced speakers— Reginald recognized the piece as part of Wagner's Tannhauser. He took a table amidst some ferns and eucalyptus branches, and had the waiter bring him a carafe of Zinfandel.

Three glasses into the carafe Doctor Tobias showed up and hobbled to the table. Neither the wine nor the dim light of the restaurant diminished Tobias' oddness in Reginald's eyes; the old man simply looked out of place, out of time, as if he should belong to some other era. Reginald noted that not only was the right hand missing fingers, but that three were gone from the left hand. Thankfully, Tobias wore gloves of beige linen to cover what were probably extensive and ugly scars.

"And what is your philosophy of writing?" Doctor Tobias said by way of greeting.

"And hello to you, too, sir. My philosophy? To tell a good story. Interest people. To examine the human heart and the world, and to illuminate." The wine had helped Reginald answer, so he poured himself another full glass in gratitude.

"'To illuminate,'" Tobias repeated. "An interesting usage. It conjures an image of a solitary explorer, wandering the chambers of a cave or a castle, his light revealing horrid drawings on the walls, or skeletal evidence of crimes and atrocities, or perhaps monsters."

"Hardly," Reginald said. "More like unhappiness, and its roots. The 'quiet desperation' Thoreau wrote of."

"In fact I've read many of your works," Tobias said, rubbing the remnants of his hands together. "You have an interesting perspective. Many of your works have the unusual combination of unflinching honesty and life-affirmation. But then, many of those I've read have dated from five or more years ago. Are you finishing up a long-term project? You could be described as having potential."

Reginald shrugged. "I'm currently marshalling my creative forces. I feel that I'm on the verge of something new. Is your interest in literature professional? You haven't told me much about yourself."

Tobias smiled slightly. "My name is Manssah Tobias, and by profession I've studied Oriental languages—specialist in Classical Arabic, Farsi, Ordu, and other Iranian branches of the Indo-Iranian tree. I worked with Burton, then later with Edward Fitzgerald, translator of the Rubaiyat. I saw many things in the Eastern World, things even more fascinating than the translation of Alhazred's 'Scourge,' though few more dangerous."

Tobias took off his glasses with the opaque right lens and stared at Reginald for ten solid seconds. His right eyeball was a milky sphere, devoid of iris or pupil. Reginald started to feel nauseous when Tobias returned the glasses to his face.

"This eye dates from the night I tried to read 'The Scourge' and made it through one sentence and a half. Although I can't directly prove it, the shriveling of my legs also started at that point."

Reginald had had quite a bit of wine. "Are you speaking metaphorically?" he asked.

Tobias smiled and shrugged.

Reginald pressed on. "To be honest, Doctor, I'm interested in that story."

"I tell you not to read it. 'The Scourge' is fascinating to be sure, with its acrostics, its numerous allusions, its density of metaphor, its roman a clef structure, its descriptions of torturous worlds coexisting with ours, its multiple interpretations...but I tell you not to read it."

"After you've made it sound so intriguing? How could I resist?"

"You must resist. If you resist, you'll survive—but you'll probably never write again, and you may never read again, but you will survive."

Reginald managed a nervous laugh. "Well, the question's academic, since I'll never find a copy. You see, I've made some inquiries, and Alhazred didn't exist. 'The Scourge' isn't the only chimerical work attributed to him."

Doctor Tobias leaned forward. "Could there be a better disguise than supposed nonexistence? There's a copy of the story in your box in the departmental mailroom. Twenty-one translators, working independently, suffered great harm to create the version to which you now have access. I had it placed there after you left work. It's in a red envelope sealed with medical tape. It's written on the same brittle, self-destroying paper as my notes were. Throw it away, crumble it, burn it, don't look at it."

He's mad, Reginald thought. A mad trickster. He inflicts himself on people. If there's any "Scourge" it's him. But even as he thought this he realized that his only hope was to see and read whatever Tobias was passing off as the until-now-unknown dramatic situation, to lay all this nonsense to rest once and for all.

"I have to leave," Reginald said.

"Of course you do."

Doctor Tobias, ever gracious, paid the check.

* * *

Days later, in a hotel room outside of town, Doctor Manassah Tobias read a newspaper report concerning the suicide of a young professor on the Radford University campus. The account stated that no note had been found, and that it may have been an impulsive act. The professor had been reading what authorities assumed had been work-related material in his office after hours. Sometime during the evening he'd plunged a pair of long-bladed paper scissors through his own eyes.

Doctor Tobias nodded and set the newspaper aside. Alhazred—and the Old Gods who had dictated "The Scourge" to Alhazred—would be pleased. Reginald Lanier had shown promise, and his sacrifice would help complete Tobias' own penance for his failure to finish Alhazred's story. One detail remained for Tobias before moving on to that young poet in Chicago whose career he'd been following.

Tobias carried a briefcase to the suite's bathroom and took out a sandwhich-sized plastic bag for disposal, a vial of disinfectant, and

a tourniquet. He ran some water and made sure it was body temperature. He arranged all the towels he would need. Then he went back
into his briefcase and took out the Craftsman pruning shears.

He stood for a short while before the sink, examining his left hand
and deciding which finger would represent Reginald Lanier.

Pickman's Legacy

by

GORDON LINZNER

"**D**ISGUSTING!**"** Miriam exclaimed when I showed her my unexpected find. "How can you even bear to look at it?"

I sighed, expecting that reaction. Only another art dealer could understand my thrill at discovering a genuine Pickman painting in an otherwise undistinguished lot purchased sight unseen from the estate sale of one of Boston's grand old families.

"Of course it's repulsive," I agreed. "That's what makes it so powerful. Art should be emotionally as well as intellectually moving. Most young artists don't understand that. You must admit, you had a strong reaction."

"I'll say! You owe me dinner, to make up for the lunch I nearly lost."

I carried the painting to the sunlit front room of my gallery. Pickman's art thrives on gloom, but I wanted to examine it closely. It was one of Pickman's ghoul paintings, titled, per a faded note on the back, *Guest of Honor.* The sinister face peering out from the left foreground had yellowish skin with dark green scar lines at the mouth and eyes. The ears rose to a point; the head was completely bald. The right hand beckoned the viewer, while the left indicated the painting's main focus. A half-dozen similar yet distinct individuals crouched by an open grave, from which two of them dragged a decaying corpse. The rest looked on hungrily.

"Pickman's bizarre subject matter," I explained, "and his eccentric insistence that he drew from life, earned severe criticism in his time. Loathsome as critics found his content, though, they agreed he'd executed it brilliantly. Look at these carefully wrought black and gray tones; his muted reds convey more horror where they don't appear than where they do. With a few strokes of white, he unnervingly conveys the corpse's cold radiance, the damp of a gold-leafed Autumn night."

"Sounds like you've got your catalogue copy already written," Miriam teased. "Should I type it up now?"

Prolonged exposure to the sunlight seemed to pain the painting's foreground figure, another tribute to the artist's skill. I hastened back to cooler lighting. "No need," I said, setting the painting on an easel in the middle of the main room.

Miriam balked. "You're going to leave it there, where everyone can see it the minute they walk in?"

"Of course. It's the star of my gallery." I glanced at the lot's other eight paintings, scattered face up on the floor.

"Now, what to do with these mediocre New England pastorals? *Ice Fishing* is as far from *Guest of Honor* as you can get, in both quality and content. How do people accumulate such jumbles?"

Miriam knelt beside *The Hay Barn*. "Hardly inspired," she agreed, "but I can look at it on a full stomach."

"I'm not sure I can."

"You're being facetious, David. I'm not. I'd almost rather take a chance on finding another off-the-books job than look at that thing every day."

I laughed. "Miriam, you may be the best undiscovered acting talent in New York, but you still know nothing about art. In under a month I'll get an offer for that Pickman I can't refuse. Mama Gail's Tuesday night lobster special okay for dinner?"

Two days later I was offered twenty times the cost of the entire lot, just for the Pickman by Jerome St. John, a wealthy and cautious collector who made Thursday rounds of Soho galleries. Every business instinct told me to take the check he was writing. Instead, I grasped his hand, pulling the pen from the green bank paper.

"One minute, Mister Saint John," I heard myself say. "I haven't accepted your offer."

His complexion, ruddy beneath a thick white beard, grew more florid. St. John towered over me, and was in excellent physical condition. A blow from either fist could fracture my skull.

"You dare...!" Cold blue eyes glowered under bushy brows. "I offered a fair price, not a penny less than it's worth!"

"That's true," I conceded. "Your offer is generous. I'd like a few days to think it over."

"I don't barter, Rostock. If this is a ploy to up my price...."

"I assure you, it isn't. But, well, I haven't had this piece long. It's a fascinating work," I ended lamely.

"Yes, Yes. What of it?"

"I want to look at it a few more days. *You* can understand that."

"You want to...!" St. John stuttered. He opened his checkbook again. "Very well. One week, no more. Here's a thousand on deposit. So help me, Rostock, if you sell that painting to anyone else I'll break you in two!"

"There's no need for threats." I put his check in my cashbox. "This guarantees good faith on both our parts."

"See that it does!" He turned on his heels and marched out.

Weekends brought lots of foot traffic, with sales generally in the lower range; little top-flight stuff went on those two days. The Pickman repulsed most tourists, but garnered reluctant praise from locals who hadn't seen it earlier. That Saturday afternoon, I'd just sold one of the Boston lot at a modest mark-up to a young tourist couple from Rhode Island. While I wrapped *The Hay Barn*, diverted by the intricacies of knotting string, the madman struck.

Later I realized his yellow raincoat was odd for the mild October day, but I'd developed a mental blindness to weird clothing, to avoid insulting potential customers. No one saw him draw the six-inch hunting knife from his pocket; no one saw the blade flash until too late.

"Death to the Foul Fiend!" he cried, slashing Pickman's masterpiece. "Destroy the devil's work! End this heathen worship!" Again and again the knife bit heavy canvas.

I dropped the package and leapt at the madman. Arms around his emaciated frame, I dragged him from the painting. The knife flew beyond my reach, luckily for him. I threw him to the floor, knee on his breastbone, hands about his shriveled neck.

"No, no!" he cried. "I must save you from yourself! 'Tis the devil who controls you. Fight him!"

"I'll fight *you*, you old devil." My fingers dug into his windpipe, ending his babble. I squeezed harder. He breathed in rattling gasps. His face turned violent purple.

"Stop it! Stop it, you're killing him!"

I recognized Miriam's voice, but the sense of her words could not penetrate my rage. Three athletic young men pulled us apart. I spat in the old man's face as they did.

After a minute, I said, "I'm all right now." My captors, though reluctant to accept my word, loosened their grips. I shrugged free. "It's all right," I repeated. "I'm okay now. Let me be."

The three joined the crowd around the man. I went to the Pickman, to try to survey the damage despite my anguish.

I saw several long, deep scratches. A triangular flap dangled from center left. The foreground figure now seemed to plead for help rather than beckon. I covered tear-blurred eyes.

Fingers touched my elbow. I looked up. Miriam's face looked thinner than usual, her look of concern mixed with fear.

"It's all right, Dave. He's only unconscious. You didn't kill him."

"Would to God I had," I snarled.

"Don't say that. Don't even think it. The poor man's sick. He needs sympathy, not bitterness."

"Doesn't the Bible say an eye for an eye? That's the kind of crap he was spouting. He wanted to kill this painting. Why should he live?"

"That's oil on canvas, Dave. You almost took a human life!"

"Oil on canvas! That's what you know! Go on, get back to that precious human life, while I try saving something more vital."

"What are you planning, David?"

"To restore this painting."

"You?"

"It was damaged in my care. It's my responsibility. No other hand can touch it."

"Think clearly, Dave. You've never repaired more than minor shipping damage in that basement studio."

"Your support is noted. Now go away! I have to tape the cuts flat before the edges sag and stretch."

Someone called the police, who took the old man away. They wanted me to swear out a complaint. I barely heard them. I had the painting out of its frame, flat on my desk, which I'd cleared with a sweep of my arm, and was carefully applying transparent tape to its back. My first shock had passed, replaced by a need to restore *Guest of Honor* urgently. Unfortunately, no decent reproduction had been made in the short interval of its discovery; only a set of Polaroid photographs I'd taken for my files. I'd be working mostly from memory.

I chased off everyone, especially Miriam, closed the gallery, and took the Pickman down to my workroom. High-intensity lights hung from the ceiling. Underground coolness kept the temperature down; a dehumidifier kept it dry. Buried below street level, I was insulated from the noise of New York traffic and street people. I hated to abandon the painting there, even for an hour, but I needed a file from my private room at the gallery's rear to map out a work plan.

A Rembrandt in the Rijksmuseum in the Netherlands, more extensively damaged, had been restored to near-perfect condition in months with a Belgian method. I'd saved the details out of curiosity, never imagining I'd have a practical use for them.

Sunday morning I cadged extra art materials from local artists I'd exhibited, unable to wait until the supply houses opened on Monday.

The cuts had to be repaired from the back, so the painting lay face down on the workroom floor, its surface protected by a coat of Japanese rice paper and cellulose glue. Miriam's footsteps clattered on the steep, narrow stairs.

"Here you are! I've been trying to reach you all day."

I didn't look up. "Close that door. The climate!"

"We're due at Gunther's opening at eight, Dave. It's seven thirty. Look at you!" She stepped inside.

I stomped past her, slammed the door shut. "Go without me."

"A couple hours won't kill you. You've probably been down here all day. You need a break."

"Watch where you walk!" I yanked her away from *Guest of Honor*.

"You hurt me, David!" she protested, sulking by the utility sink. "I won't step on you damned painting!"

"Sorry, Miriam. I'm just tense."

"All right. Forget the opening. I'll make your excuses." She paused. Then: "I have news about the man who did that."

"In jail, isn't he?"

"They couldn't hold him. You never filed a complaint. He was sent to Bellevue for observation. Somehow he slipped out."

"Damn his soul! Is there no justice?"

Miriam bit her lip, then left quietly. I bolted the door, relieved; she'd only have interfered with my work.

I began gluing many small linen fibers across the back of the canvas to bridge the cuts. Hours later, the last thread in place, fumes from the gluepot burning my eyes, I fell asleep, exhausted, on the concrete floor beside the new-found, almost lost art of Richard Pickman.

I woke Monday afternoon, stiff-jointed and ravenous, having fasted since lunch Saturday; devoured three hamburgers at the nearest bar, picked up a dozen candy bars, and dragged a cot downstairs.

By then the glue had set. I shaved away surplus fiber to leave a thin, unobtrusive patch, put down a new lining, and poured on a beeswax and resin mixture. A heavy, old-fashioned flat iron smoothed the lining into place. Finally, I turned the painting face up.

The seven men who'd restored the Rembrandt took six weeks to reach this point; but *Guest of Honor* was smaller than *The Night Watch* and the damage, though serious, was less extensive. The knife had gone through only four times. The front looked more scarred because layers of paint had been scraped away. Besides, the Rijksmuseum men worked only a few hours a day. I would forego food (excepting candy) and sleep (beyond naps) indefinitely for the Pickman's sake.

Removing the protective layer left a thick creamy residue of glue and rice paper. The ghouls were a cluster of vague shadows, their provender almost invisible. The foreground figure squinted through the haze. Had the sludge been gray instead of white, the atmosphere would have been too oppressive to bear.

I wiped a small patch of glue from the beckoner's hand with alcohol. Dead yellow skin shone through.

Suddenly I dropped my cleaning cloth and stepped back. My wrist felt as if it had been grasped by something cold.

I rubbed the spot. The fumes, combined with poor eating and lack of sleep, must have made me hallucinate. I stumbled to the cot for a few minutes' rest.

Those minutes grew to hours. Waking with a terrible thirst, I put my mouth to the spigot of the utility sink, then washed sticky chocolate from my hands. I didn't remember eating my hoard, but the wrappers circled the cot.

Suddenly I was certain the eerie grip had *not* been an illusion. The surer I felt the painting had reached out to me, the easier I was with the phenomena. We shared empathy.

Removing Pickman's original varnish over the next two days, I heard soft murmurs, muffled creaks, padding footsteps on freshly turned earth. None of this alarmed me. A patient is naturally anxious; talking to his doctor relieves his fears. Could Pickman's painting be otherwise with me?

When the varnish, yellow from age and poor storage, was gone, it was time to replace the trough of ground and paint that had been scooped out. "Be right back," I said, and climbed upstairs. More supplies were needed.

I'd relocked the cash box when a pounding on the gallery door, violent enough to splinter the wood, startled me. Opening the door brought me face to face with Jerome St. John.

"I've come for my painting." He glared at the spot the Pickman had been displayed. "Where is it?"

"There's been an accident, Mister Saint John." I started to explain, then shrugged. "Hell with it. I'll show you."

The narrow steps shuddered under his tread. I unlocked the restoration room. He shoved past me. His face crimsoned when he saw the unframed canvas.

"*What* have you done to my painting?"

"Not yours yet," I countered. "A madman did that. I'm working day and night to restore it. Had you seen it five days ago, your heart would have bled."

"You should have let me take it last Thursday."

"Your check's in my cashbox. I haven't deposited it. I'll give it back."

"No. I want this painting. At my original price, if I take it now. I have access to facilities and restorers who'll make your crude efforts look like patchwork." He reached for the canvas.

I flung myself in his way. "You can't have it! It's mine! I'll destroy your check! Just get the hell out of my studio!"

Growling, St. John shoved me into my cot, grasped the painting and strode from the workroom. I ran after him, leapt up those steep steps, and caught his right foot.

"It's mine! I found it!"

"Miserable ant!" St. John kicked at me. "You can't appreciate this work. It would drive you insane."

St. John's jibe angered me more than his abduction of *Guest of Honor*. As he started to kick again, I tugged on his leg with both hands. Off balance, his huge frame tumbled down the stairs. As he flew past, I snatched the Pickman.

Jerome St. John could have snapped me in two, yet a simple fall down a flight of stairs, landing at the wrong angle, snuffed out that suprahealthy life.

I couldn't report his death, even if it was accidental. That would mean police, and questions, and lose of time which could adversely affect the repair of *Guest of Honor*.

Nor could I dispose of the body. St. John weighed over two hundred and fifty pounds. Dragging him up those stairs would likely get my own neck broken, even if I could expend precious energy on him.

I finally dragged him back into the restoration room. The controlled climate would keep the stench of decay from attracting attention until I had time for a permanent solution.

I locked the room and went out. The sun was low and bright. I flinched from it, keeping to shadows, shaded alleys, any respite from that burning sphere. I bought powdered chalk, more glue, and a variety of tints with which to experiment, to match Pickman's original ground as near as possible with glue and chalk putty, then hurried back to my sanctuary, cursing whenever forced into the sun's glare.

I worked until my eyes grew blurred, puttying in most of the missing ground, then slept. When I woke, something had changed. The *Guest of Honor*? No. I scanned the room.

Jerome St. John's corpse had shrunk. That wasn't possible. I moved closer, knelt beside it, and gasped.

The right leg and arm were gone, torn off at the joints.

My spine chilled. I turned to the Pickman. The ghouls' eyes seemed to meet mine. Was there the slightest gleam in the eye of the beckoner, the faintest sardonic upturning of the lip?

The bones were wedged behind the utility sink's pipes.

A great painting lives and breathes, and Pickman's ghouls made up a great painting. They'd been injured, needed doctoring, which I gave. They also needed nourishment. Unwittingly, I'd provided dinner. I felt gratified, so much so that the pangs of my own fast abated.

I finished the ground, laid down a new, permanent coat of varnish, and set the painting on an easel for the delicate job of repainting the gouged parts. My hands trembled a long time before I calmed enough to start mixing paint.

Retouching was a greater strain than the previous phases. It shouldn't have been; painting over varnish, I could fix mistakes without harming the original. Yet I felt constrained to make each brushstroke count, avoiding the least slip. I wanted nothing to hinder my patient's convalescence.

I dared not work long stretches now; my eyes burned under bright lights and heavy fumes of glue, varnish, and paint. I found respite by turning off the lights, sitting quietly in gloom, sometimes falling asleep and coming to with a start.

In consequence, I'd only half finished retouching late Sunday afternoon when I woke to find only a few shreds of flesh clung to St. John's gnawed bones.

Good manners bid me clean-up after my guests. I filled a plastic garbage bag with the osseous remains and, after dark, carried it down deserted side streets to the Hudson River. Chunks of broken paving insured St. John stayed put when I dropped him off the abandoned pier.

A familiar yellow raincoat blocked the door of my gallery on my return. The madman was back.

His head swung around, birdlike, at my approach. "Know you the Lord?" he asked. "This is the Lord's Day. Have you asked Him to forgive you your sins?"

His scrawny neck was livid with bruises. I met his glazed eyes, shaking with the effort not to lay hands on him. Not here, where passersby might see.

I unlocked the gallery doors and motioned him inside.

"Bless you, lad!" he cried, seeing that the Pickman was gone. "You have seen the light! My work was not in vain! Have you cast the devil from your soul as well?"

I opened a desk drawer full of artist's tools. A dull, paint-spattered palette knife ended his chatter.

I caught and wrapped him in a dropcloth, to avoid bloodying the floor. He was less than half St. John's weight, and gravity was on my side on the stairs.

The work went rapidly now; inspiration sped my brush. I'd fulfilled my trust, revenged the painting with satisfying irony. My lethargy sloughed off. I worked through the night, napping only once, during which time Pickman's ghouls gorged.

By Monday afternoon I'd almost finished repairing *Guest of Honor*. Flushed with enthusiasm, I flattered myself that my work was as good or better than Pickman's original. I stopped to admire it before adding the final brushstrokes.

Someone gasped behind me. I turned. Miriam stood in the open doorway.

In my elation at killing the madman, I'd forgotten to bolt the door.

"Oh my God...." Her widening eyes went from me to the painting to what remained of the man in the gore-stained yellow raincoat.

I shook my head in pity, knowing what had to be done. "You never understood, Miriam. Sometimes a man's got to be alone with his work."

She screamed and turned to flee upstairs. Too late.

The painting is complete. Now I have time to think about other problems.

St. John's disappearance wasn't connected to me; he rarely confided his movements, would be even more secretive acquiring a valuable painting. And no one cared about the crazy man.

But Miriam's roommate undoubtedly knew of her visit to me. Somebody'll come looking for her. Already I think I hear footsteps overhead.

They won't find me, though. Who'd notice an extra ghoul lurking in the background of a painting that has never been catalogued or described?

No, we have only one real difficulty, my new colleagues and I. We can get water from the utility sink, but sometime soon I'll have to leave to get us something to eat. The others are grumbling, and I feel fresh hunger pangs myself.

Miriam was such a thin girl.

Of Dark Things
And Midnight Planes

by

DAVID NIALL WILSON

I LOOKED BLANKLY DOWN at the pages in front of me, nearly mesmerized by the sheer mechanical perfection of the script. Line upon line, stretching on for a seemingly interminable eight pages, the letters ran, never once deviating a millimeter from the pattern. If it hadn't been for the signature at the end of the last page, flowing and heavily sloped, but with the same eerie precision as the smaller calligraphy of the text, I'd have thought it was some sort of computer font or typeset manuscript.

The envelope had no return address, only a faded, barely discernible postmark canceling a stamp so old that my quick calculations put it out of circulation for a good twenty years. Kingsport Massachusetts. I knew nobody in Massachusetts, let alone some place called Kingsport, and I certainly hadn't ever met anyone with handwriting like what sat before me.

Sitting back, I began to read, and then I really became confused. It began with a short, terse commentary on my latest book, "The Thing from Within," almost a fan letter, but worded more like it had come from a co-conspirator than a fan.

"I am particularly pleased," it said cryptically, "with the way you handled the portal scene in chapter fifteen. We both know the delicate nature of such things, and I note that you have given nothing of importance away, yet have kept the main pieces of that very intricate phenomenon together in a remarkably coherent pattern."

"What the hell is this nut talking about?" I muttered to myself, reading on. I knew nothing more of portals than that they made an interesting device in tales of the supernatural. It got stranger.

"I wonder," he wrote, "whether it was wise to describe the creature in the final chapter so vividly? After all, knowing as we do the nature of that other realm and the thin barriers that actually shield us, it may be the better course to steer clear of such acknowledgement, lest we

attract those kinds of unwanted attention that men like yourself and
I can imagine but others are ignorant of. Perhaps you have, with the
few discrepancies you've integrated into your manuscript, rendered it
a safe practice, but I would advise against such passages in the future."

After this, and this was only the first page or so of the letter, the
coherency of the text became lost altogether. There were references to all
sorts of strange places and grimoires I'd never heard of, let alone researched. There were cryptic anecdotes about creatures beyond the scope
of my own imagination's ability to construct in any viable, three-dimen-
sional fashion. And all the while that I read there was something about
the words that itched at the back of my mind, something I was sure I
should remember, but couldn't quite put my finger on.

In any case, it was obviously the work of a very strange, or very sick
man, depending on one's outlook, and I was strangely relieved by his
ending, which reinforced the lack of a return address in its quest to forestall
a personal answer.

"I know that your work is important and consumes most of your
time in these later days, and I will not expect a reply. Suffice it to say
that I am tracking your efforts and your progress with anticipation and
great satisfaction, looking forward to the ultimate goal toward which
we are both, in our own manners, working. Keep yourself diligent and
precise, as always, and you will hear from me again."

It was signed with a single name, *Olafson.* I sat there for a while,
staring at the paper in perplexed silence, then I set it aside and moved
on to my other mail. I had received strange things before, though none
quite so obviously deranged, and I would most likely do so again. In
a profession like writing, how was it to be avoided?

There were a few bills, a letter from my mother, and one from my
friend and fellow author, Hubert B. Pitt. Pitt was a veteran writer of
the pulp era who'd befriended me early on in my career. His guidance
and advice had steered me away from more than one mistake along the
way, and I smiled in anticipation of reading the letter. He was
irreparably cheerful.

The nagging itch in my brain returned suddenly, and a few memories snapped into place. "Damn," I muttered, rising quickly and
heading for the extra bedroom that served as my office. I went straight
to the bookshelves that covered the wall beside my desk and began
searching. Organization is not my strong point, so it took a few
moments to locate the volume I sought.

"Mr. Pulp, a biography of Hubert B. Pitt," by Adrian Perrot. It had
been this book that had led me to write Hugh and initiate the
friendship we now shared. I took the volume to the leather chair at my

desk and began to flip through the pages. I wasn't exactly sure of what I was looking for, but something told me I'd find it in that book.

I did. In the third chapter, between notes on how Hugh's contemporaries in the Pulps had all kept in close contact with one another, was the passage I'd remembered.

"I remember," he said, "receiving an enormous volume of letters from a man named Olafson. They were the longest, most strangely conceived ramblings I'd ever set eyes upon. I got them through my agent, always without a return address, over a period of nearly ten years.

"There were others who received the same letters...writers, artists— even a few politicians, if Olafson himself were to be believed. He wrote as if there were a grand, mystic plan unfolding around us, and only he and I were privy to its secrets. He mentioned all manner of odd names and places, referenced books I'd never heard of, all the time assuming some knowledge on my own part that did not exist.

"I stole more than one mystic name or setting from those letters, and I recognized some in the works of others I knew. It always gave me a laugh when it happened. The man finally stopped writing, but the legacy of those letters lives on...."

My hands began to shake and I put the book down quickly. My friend was over ninety years old. The man who'd written him, Olafson, would be nearly that old too. How long had he been living in...Kingsport? How long had he been writing these letters?

Reaching for the phone beside my computer, I dialed Hugh's number as quickly as my trembling fingers could be forced into submission. After two rings, his cheerful voice filled my ear, and I breathed a sigh of relief.

"Hello?"

"Hugh, this is Nigel. You're not going to believe what just happened to me. I got a letter from an old friend of yours."

"Oh? Who?"

"Olafson." I didn't go on, I wanted to try and gage his reaction before I continued. If I'd expected something earth-shattering, I was disappointed.

"Who?"

I quickly explained about the letter and then reminded him of the reference in his own biography. After a moment's silence, he let out a slow whistle. "You're kidding, right?" he said finally. "I mean, Christ, Nigel, that man would be as old as I am, and I don't know anyone who's heard from him in almost twenty years. Are you sure it isn't some sort of joke? What's the return address say?"

"There is none," I told him. "There's only a faded postmark, Kingsport Massachusetts. You wouldn't happen to recall where *your* letters came from, would you?"

"It's been a long time, Nigel, and as I said in that book, I got them through my agent. All my fan mail came that way. I never saw the envelopes."

Now I was really intrigued. "You mentioned other writers who'd heard from this guy," I went on finally. "You wouldn't remember some of them, by any chance, would you?"

"Well," he said, and I could picture his brow furrowing as he thought it over, "there were a lot of us, and it was as often another name we wrote under as our own. The most obvious examples of names and places from the letters I received would have been Lovecraft. He and I weren't terribly close, as I've mentioned, but quite a few of his stories included names and places that this Olafson fellow seemed familiar with. There was Dunsany, as well, though I'm afraid I'm even less familiar with his work."

I spent a couple of seconds in silent thought, then asked, "what do you suppose it means, Hugh?"

"Means?" he replied. "I suppose it means I'm neither the oldest man interested in horror fiction, nor the strangest. What else could it mean?"

"I don't know," I said, my mind whirling. "It just seems so strange that after all these years he would start this writing habit again. And why me?"

"Maybe he's attuned to talent, my boy," Hugh chuckled. "I really don't see what else there could be to it, do you?"

I laughed with him for a moment, asked about his wife and what he was working on, and then hung up. I was anything but convinced that the letter was as harmless as he seemed to believe. Passages of nonsensical words ran through my mind, somehow memorized after only the first reading, odd chants and strange names. I went back to the kitchen and started up a pot of coffee, calming myself with the normal, every-day acts of grinding the beans and rinsing the pot. I usually avoided caffeine that late in the day, but something told me sleep was a long way off.

Once the coffee was brewing and the strong, mellow aroma of the beans was wafting through the house, I returned to my desk and flipped on my computer. A plot had begun to niggle at the back of my brain, something new. I wanted to get it down before the inspiration passed.

"A Wreath of Clouds"
By Nigel Waters

The old house looked down over the cliffs with empty eyes, shuttered against the odd, endless storm that seethed about its ramparts. From below, none could make out any details of the place, nor did they know the name or manner of the occupant. It was a mystery to be whispered at twilight, a story to frighten the children into their beds at an early hour. It was a mystery, and that is a rare thing in these later days.

I stared down at the words that glowed across my monitor, shaking my head slowly. Where had they come from? I remembered sitting down, and I remembered having some sort of great idea for a story. I did not remember typing these words, and they gleamed back at me eerily. They could not have seemed stranger had they been in some alien tongue.

"These later days?" I muttered, reading the paragraph over slowly. Where had I heard those words, or something similar, before?

The smell of the coffee had permeated the air of the house, and I rose to get myself a cup, still wondering just what the hell was going on. First that crazy letter, now this. I took the coffee and, after saving the short passage onto my hard drive, I turned the computer off and headed for my living room.

I grabbed the book I'd been reading, a contemporary anthology of horror stories that had printed one of my own efforts, and kicked back in my recliner to read. Several of my friends had stories in the book as well and it was littered with autographs. I smiled as I read each one. It was a surprisingly strong collection, and I found myself lost in its pages in a very short time.

I reached the final story in the volume at nearly midnight. *What the hell,* I thought. *I might as well finish the damned thing.*

It was a very short little piece by a young woman I'd never heard of titled "Smiling Eyes & Mourning Face." It was an intriguing title. The protagonist was a young man who met a woman on summer vacation. She was a melancholy, mysterious woman, and nearly every word that passed her lips seemed morbid—a prophecy of doom to come. He'd have left her almost immediately, but he was trapped within her eyes.

"Deep, laughing eyes. Eyes that whispered eloquent dreams into his eager mind. Eyes that spoke of Armageddon with glee."

As I said, a very strange story. Then I read the woman's name, and I started nearly out of my chair, flinging the book from me as if I'd been shocked. I knew that name, or, rather I'd read it. In that damned letter. I hurried to the other room and retrieved the thing, scanning it quickly to verify my fears.

It was there all right, third page center. Even the odd spelling and punctuation was the same. *Keziah Mason*. There was more to the story, but I couldn't bring myself to read it. I made a mental note to try and contact the editor of the book the next day and see if I could get an address or phone number for the author. Her name was Rhonda Tanyan.

Leaving on more lights than I was accustomed to, I headed for my bedroom. I wasn't certain I'd be able to sleep, but more reading or writing was out of the question. All I really wanted was for the night to end and for the morning sunlight to flash in through the windows to usher the touch of reality back into my home. Surprisingly, I drifted off almost immediately. I did not dream.

* * *

When I awoke it was to a headache such as I've seldom known. I felt as though I'd hardly slept at all. I stumbled to the bathroom and into the shower as quickly as possible, turning on the cold water and forcing my shivering frame to withstand it. Moments later I was toweling myself off and brushing my teeth, feeling no better, but looking a bit more presentable.

Coffee, I thought. *That's what this tired brain needs.* I filled a large mug with the remnants of the pot I'd made the night before and slipped it into the microwave, seating myself at the kitchen table to wait. The letter lay strewn across the table, but I paid it no mind. I had little enough strength for my own thoughts, let alone the ravings of some lunatic. He could wait until I was awake and feeling a little less hellish.

One of the things I've always prided myself on in my career has been my discipline. I set a schedule the first day I quit my job to write full time, and with small modifications, it is still the same. Get up at 8:00 AM, make coffee, read for half an hour to clear my head, and then write for about three hours. I rarely varied this schedule, with the exception of extra hours spent writing in the evenings, but for some reason this morning was different.

My last memory of the previous evening was the disturbing reference in the anthology I'd been reading, and somehow I couldn't bring myself to sit down and start something new. I decided to give work a try, after downing a small handful of aspirin, and coffee in hand I made my way to my office.

Something was wrong, though I couldn't immediately place what. Then I saw it. My computer was on, screen filled with text. Beside it, on top of the laser printer, a small pile of pages sat. I barely stilled the sudden shaking in my hand before the coffee spilled down my shirt. I set the cup aside quickly and went to the screen, scanning the print as rapidly as I could.

It was a continuation of the story I'd begun the night before—the *entire* story, in fact, all 10,000 words of it. I quickly saved the document and turned off the computer, then flipped it back on and watched the screen. I have a scheduling program that makes a log entry each time I turn off or on the machine. It flashed up with its message, "Logged on at 08:45, last logon 0315."

"03:15?" I read out loud. "Shit." I distinctly remembered what time I'd gone to my bedroom the night before, at least two hours before the time that now flashed before me. A wave of nausea washed through me, and I sat down quickly. What the hell was going on? Had I gotten up in my sleep to finish this damned thing? And just what the hell had I written, anyway?

I grabbed the manuscript from the printer and moved into the front room, pulling the blinds up and throwing the curtains open to let in the bright morning sun. It helped, but only a little. My perspective was tainted by fear; even the light streaming in the window was overly bright, too intense.

Settling into my chair, I took a gulp of coffee and began to read. I was trapped from the first sentence. It flowed with a lyrical style that oozed from one line to the next, slipping from page to page so easily that I was sitting, staring at the window with sun-blinded eyes for a good three or four minutes before I realized that I'd finished. It was stunning, powerful, and so totally alien to my own style that it sent shivers rippling up and down my arms.

There were more of the mystic references running through it, names I was starting to develop a morbid affinity for. It was obvious fantasy, and yet there was an aura of detailed reality about it that was chilling. I could see those bleak landscapes, those towers of arcane knowledge and occult power. I set the story aside and got a second cup of coffee. Now what.

I went to my office and flipped through my Rolodex until I found the number of the editor of the anthology I'd been reading, Tony Monticelli. He was bound to have the girl's phone number. The phone rang about five times before it was picked up, and I heard a crash, an eloquent, mumbled string of curses, then my friend's voice.

"Yeah?"

"Tony, this is Nigel—Nigel Waters. Did I wake you?"

"No, I always toss the phone across the fucking room when I wake up, and I've been chewing gravel. Christ, Nigel, it's only, what, about 6:00?"

Oh shit, I thought, though the image of him laying there with his hair askew and a scowl etched across his face nearly made me laugh out loud. I'd forgotten he was on the West Coast.

"Sorry, Tony, but this is important. You remember a girl named Rhonda Tanyan? You printed her story, "Smiling Eyes and Mourning smile" in...."

"I know who the hell she is, Nigel, what do you want?"

"Her phone number, if you've got it. There's something strange going on, and I think she may be able to help."

"I've got a number," he hesitated, then continued. "I don't know, though, Nigel. I wouldn't get mixed up with her for any amount of money. I can't explain it, but we talked on the phone once. It was a—strange experience."

"I'd still like to call." I told him. "I'd rather not go into it just now, but I promise you I'll have a good story to tell you when it's all over."

"Suit yourself." The line was silent for a moment or two, then he returned. He gave me the number, and I jotted it down quickly. "518 area code," I asked, "where is that?"

"Massachusetts," he replied. "Some place called Kingsport."

The phone fell from my limp fingers and I gripped the table for balance. *Jesus,* I thought. *Jesus.*

I dropped the phone into it's cradle, ignoring the insistent squawking that emanated from the speaker. Without thought I picked it up again, before Tony could call back and dialed the number he'd given me. It rang once, twice, then there was a mechanical click, and an operator's voice came on the line.

"I'm sorry, but your call cannot be completed as dialed. Please check the number and try again, or call your operator for assistance...thank you for using MCI....FF"

I tried it again with the same result. Damn, had he given me the wrong number? I dialed 0 quickly and a nasal but cheerful voice answered almost immediately. "Yes, I said, I need to know the area code for Kingsport, Massachusetts."

"Please hold...I'm sorry, sir, I show no listing for a Kingsport Massachusetts."

"That's impossible," I said angrily, "I just got mail from there yesterday. My friend just gave me the area code 518, but when I dialed it, it didn't work."

"I'm sorry, sir, I'm double checking...no listing for a Kingsport, and the area code 518 is not currently in service. Will that be all?"

"No, uh...yes, I suppose it will."

I hung the phone up slowly. *To hell with it,* I thought, *If I can't call this place, I'll go there.* I headed back to my bedroom, grabbed my suitcase from the closet, and began to pack away enough clothing and necessities for a two or three day trip. It was obvious that I wasn't going to get any work done until this was cleared up, and it was equally obvious that I was getting nowhere on the phone.

I called Hugh before I left and told him my plan.

"I wish I could join you," he said, his voice a bit far away. "These old bones don't travel as well as they used to, but I'll be damned if this isn't the most intriguing mystery I've encountered in several years. Good luck."

I thanked him and headed for the door. It was going to be a long drive up the coast, and I wanted my wits about me. With my bag in the back seat and my mind a whirl of conflicting fears and emotions, I hit the freeway.

* * *

It was nearly midnight, and discouragement was very close to driving me into a hotel for the night when I spotted the sign. It wasn't a standard road sign. I would have missed it altogether if I hadn't been shaking my head back and forth in an attempt to clear it and remain awake. It was a weathered, streaked wooden sign with the single word "KINGSPORT" emblazoned across it in faded black calligraphy. I exited onto the twisting, two-lane road and moved off into the unknown darkness, my heart beginning to pound for no reason I could ascertain.

It seemed an extremely long time before lights became visible. There was a heavy mist clinging to the ground and the old, rustic buildings I passed. With relief, I spotted another sign that announced the "Seahaven Inn— VACANCY." Pulling into the lot, I stood for a moment and looked off toward the sea. There were mountains there with stark, ominous cliffs that overlooked both the village—for that's all it was not a city—and the roaring ocean below. It was an awe-inspiring view.

Suddenly, a passage from the story I'd read (written?) popped into my mind.

"The portal peaked a cliff on the highest of the craggy peaks, barely visible from the dwellings below, and yet it's presence was strong. One could stand outside the door to the Inn on a stormy night and feel the rush or arcane winds and energies through its open maw...."

Was that the frame of a house I saw silhouetted in the flashing of the lightning, or was it a trick of the poor light and my own lack of sleep? I wasn't going to dwell on it there in the dark, in any case. I knocked and the door was opened a few moments later by an old woman with staring, suspicious eyes. Her skin was mottled—an odd shade—and her neck seemed to rise past a few small wrinkles straight to her mouth, as if she had no chin. I managed not to stare, barely, and she ushered me inside.

Without a word she got me signed in, key in hand and on my way up a curving stair to the old place's upper story. Room 23. I found it with no trouble, tossed my suitcase in a corner, and without further thought stripped out of my damp, mist-soaked clothes and slid between the sheets. It was a large, comfortable old bed, and sleep came quickly. As on the previous night, I did not dream.

* * *

My dreams were vivid, swirling symbols and twining tentacles reaching out to clasp me in cold, unfeeling embrace, windows through which stared huge, opalescent eyes, vertiginous whorls of energy that drew at my soul. I awoke with a start, eyes wide and staring, an image planted firmly in my mind. The other things, the nightmares, faded slowly, but this one mental picture would not fade. It was a cliff, wreathed in clouds and bleak against a storm-ridden sky. On the very edge of the cliff stood a house, or a similar structure, encased in a an aura of eerie, glowing light. And there was a pounding, loud and insistent, unceasing...my heart?

I shook my head, feeling the cold, clammy sweat that coated my skin, and swung my feet off the bed. Sitting up, I repressed a shudder and reached over to spin the clock to where I could see it. It was 6:00 AM. I rose, moving to the room's small bathroom, where I ran cold water on one of the washrags and held it to my face, letting the water run down the sides of my neck.

No sense wasting time, I thought. I moved to the shower, stripping out of my shorts and stepping in to the spray, feeling the heat of the water soaking the odd chill from my bones. Something about the whole scene, something just beyond my conscious thought, lent an air of unreality to my surroundings. I couldn't have explained it, but there was just a feeling of impending—*something.*

I dressed as quickly as I could, retrieving Olafson's letter from my bag, and I headed down the stairs. First food, then some answers. Nobody was at the front desk, so I headed out into the street and spotted a sign just up the road proclaiming "CAFE" in faded, flickering neon. The sign in the window said "Open," so I went inside, shaking off the slight chill of the morning air and looking around the deserted diner.

A small, squat woman stood behind the counter, staring at me with expressionless eyes. I slid onto the stool at the end of the counter and gave her my best attempt at a smile. "I'll have some coffee for starters,"

I said cheerfully. Without a word, or even a nod of acknowledgement, she moved to a dingy coffee maker on the back wall and returned with a steaming cup.

The menu consisted of standard fare, and I settled for eggs, toast, and orange juice, washed down with more of the coffee. All the while the woman hovered nearby, not close enough to encourage conversation, but within range if I required anything further with my meal. I could feel the faint, ghost-touch of her deadened eyes peering at me obliquely, and it began to get on my nerves. Reaching into my pocket, I pulled free the letter and called out to her. *Might as well get this over with,* I thought.

"Ma'am?" I said, "I'm just in town for a few days, and I was wondering if I could get you to take a look at something for me."

She spun toward me, coming slightly nearer, but her expression never changed. "I got this letter a few days ago," I went on doggedly, holding up the envelope so that the faded postmark and the odd, unvarying script of the address showed plainly. "It has no return address, as you can see, but it was postmarked here in Kingsport. I was wondering, do you have any idea how I might find this person?"

No answer. No expression. She walked to the coffee maker, grabbed the old stainless steel pot, and returned to stand before me stolidly, pot in hand. I started to say more, to continue with my questions, but there was something in the motionlessness of her stance, the lifeless turn of her lips, that stayed me. Shaking my head, I waved off the coffee, motioning for my bill. She brought it, and I left a five on the counter with another one for a tip and rose.

As I left, the oddness of the place seemed to crash down on my senses, and I moved more rapidly, nearly running by the time I reached the door. I did not look back as I slipped through and into the morning sunlight, but I was certain of what I'd have seen had I done so; those slack, staring eyes, following me, watching.

The village, for it was more that than a city or a town, was just beginning to awaken to the new day. A few shuffling forms moved about among the streets, and the sounds of automobile engines coughing into life rose from all sides. Lights flickered, then went out, bowing to the greater light of the sun. I walked down the street, glancing in shop windows and trying to get my bearings. At the end of the main street was a small office, set back from the street, with two shiny red white and blue mailboxes out front. "United States Post Office," the sign in the door read. Finding it open, I went inside.

There was nobody in the service window, so I went up and tapped firmly on the bell. I felt as if I were finally getting somewhere, and there was an odd, expectant fluttering in my chest. There was a clatter of footsteps from the back, and a small, wispish man popped into view, eyes bright and staring.

"Yes?" he said quickly. "May I help you?"

I was amazed at how good it was just to hear another human voice. I pulled out the letter again, plopping it onto the counter, and said, "I was hoping that you could help me locate the man who sent this. It arrived at my home a few days ago with no return address, and I would very much like to meet him."

At first he just stared at the envelope, turning his head one way, then the other, and squinting. Looking up at me at last, he nodded quickly. "I've seen the likes of this before." he answered sagely. "Seen it many a time, though not so often these days. Not so often at all. Seen a hundred of 'em if I've seen a one. Always the same."

I stared at him in confusion. "What do you mean?" I stuttered. "Are you saying you know who wrote these?"

"No, not at all," he said, his grin widening. "I only said I'd *seen* letters like it. Lots of them. They come through here all the time, always the same handwriting, always fat and just the right weight for the postage paid."

"But," I went on, "surely you've seen who left them?"

"Nope." he shook his head. "They come in the night, dropped in that box out front. I've asked about them plenty of times, but all I get is riddles and blank stares. Even the crazy old coot that lives on the next street over won't answer me, not really. Just laughs that weird laugh of his and points at the cliffs. I'm sorry, but I'm afraid that's all the help I can be."

Numbly, I turned from the window and left post office, the letter still clutched in my hand. I wandered aimlessly down the first side street I came to, not really aware of my surroundings, my mind a blank. It couldn't end like this. The sun was beginning to filter through the morning haze, beating down on my already pounding head. I stopped to lean on a fence post in front of one of the most run-down houses I'd ever seen.

At first I was certain that the place must be abandoned, but just as I moved to turn back to the hotel a face appeared in one of the dust coated windows. It was a leering, maniacal face, fissured with deep wrinkles that ran out from the corners of the eyes and the edges of the gaping, nearly toothless mouth. A white wisp of hair danced softly in a breeze that should not have existed inside the house.

Startled, I straightened and backed away. I'd thought at first that the man was staring at me, but as I moved, I saw that his eyes were locked on my right hand, the hand that held the envelope. Gathering my courage, I lifted the catch on the fence and walked toward the house. The face had disappeared from the window, and strange, bubbling laughter was rising from within.

I knocked, but there was no answer, only the laughter. At first it angered me, but then the sound began to get on my nerves, and I backed away slightly. The man had a crazed look in his eyes, after all. I spun to the right, glancing up at the mist-shrouded mountains above the village, and was nearly struck to my knees by a sudden sense of deja vu. It was as if the world had momentarily keeled over on its side, sending a wave of nausea through me as if I teetered on the edge of a great chasm.

It was just as I'd pictured it in my dream, silhouetted against warring clouds and silver mist, lone and ominous. The house on the cliff. The image from my nightmares. The other images, whirling vortices of emptiness and darkness, lurked in the corners of my consciousness, ready to pounce.

I turned back, but the door was still closed. There was a clammy, damp stench—like rotted vegetation, and I noted that the wood of the structure was eaten through with worm holes and decay. I backed away, stepping so rapidly that I nearly tripped over my own feet, slamming my elbow painfully into the gate as I stumbled through and back into the street. I could still hear the old man's echoing laughter floating out to mock me.

I don't know exactly when the decision to climb to the cliff was final, nor does it really matter. By the time my thoughts were calm enough to truly be called my own, I was well above the village and still rising. I passed a stagnant, ill-smelling pond and several outlying farmhouses, but I saw no sign of life along that way.

It was a difficult climb. There seemed no way up, at first, three sides of that stone spire being sheer drops of hundreds of feet. I was half-inclined to give it up when I stumbled, nearly falling into a small gorge, the other side of which, while still steep, seemed a passable route upward.

My memories of that climb are not clear. I am not one given to much physical exertion, having taken most of my adventures in front of my word processor, or in the armchair in my living room. I was certain that I would never make it, that I would fall to the ground in exhaustion and lay there until I rotted. It was that thought, I believe, that forced me onward—the thought of being alone in the dark on that mountain. At just after noon I crested the final peak and saw the structure looming from the mist ahead of me.

It was an ominous sight, though I cannot explain exactly why. There was no door in sight, only several gabled windows of antiquated style, shuttered tightly. I walked up to the building, moving along the closest side and cowering down beneath the windows in the grip of an inexplicable fear. I followed the wall to the cliff's edge, back around the rear of the building, and on to the cliff again on the far side, but there was no door. I leaned out slightly over the edge of the precipice, but there was no way humanly possible to pass along that fourth wall.

Leaning back against the cold stone, I let myself slip down to a sitting position, pulling my knees up and resting my head on them in exhaustion. Nothing. The trip, the crazy old man, the cliff, and still I had found nothing. I felt a great emptiness inside, a void.

Then I heard the footsteps. They grated, scraping over stone and sending small cascades of gravel down behind them. Someone was climbing up from the ravine. I pushed my spine back into the stone wall, trying to make myself as inconspicuous as possible. There was nowhere to hide, nothing but the mist, the stone ledge, and the house.

Who could it be? Suddenly, I was certain that I *did not* want to know who lived in this house, nor did I want anything ever again except to be gone from that mountain, back in my car, and out of that place. My questions seemed foolish, and a desperate feeling of "wrongness" dropped over my senses.

The steps grew louder and closer, and I began shivering uncontrollably. From inside the building at my back, I felt a vibration growing, a pulsing, rhythmic pounding that echoed through the mountain itself. It grew louder and I could no longer hear the footsteps, but it did not matter. A figure rounded the building and stopped, staring at me as I stared back. She let out a sharp gasp and a small cry, taking a step backward and raising her hands, as if to ward me off.

"What are you doing here?" she asked. Her attire was strange, archaic. She stood taller than most women, thin and willowy. Her eyes were black and riveting, her nose was and pointed. Long tresses of raven hair danced in the mist-laden wind, trailing back over the shoulders of the full-length black gown she wore. It was cinched in the center by a silver chord, and strange designs rippled across the surface of the material, then disappeared.

"I..." my voice cracked from the chill of the air and a sudden dryness in my throat, "I came from Kingsport...I received a strange letter, and...."

"Nigel?" she asked, trembling as sudden recognition flooded her features. "Nigel Waters?"

Before I could even begin to reply, she rushed forward, grabbing my arm and yanking me back toward the mountainside. Her eyes were wide with a mixture of terror and confusion. "You must leave." she said quickly. "There is little time. go to the village, pack your things, and go! It is not yet time!"

"Not yet time for what?" I asked, growing slightly more bold. "Who are you, how do you know me, and what the hell is going on?"

Very suddenly the pounding from the building behind me grew louder, enough so that the entire mountain seemed to resonate to the beat of a huge, primitive drum. Her eyes grew wider, and she slipped a quick frightened glance at the shuttered window, then a second at the mist beyond the cliff. "You must go!" She cried.

"Your name," I screamed, fighting to make myself heard above the crashing, pounding din, "your name and I will go."

"I am Tanyan, Rhonda Tanyan. Now go. You will hear from me when it is time."

I have no idea, to this day, why I accepted this, but I did as she bid. I turned, moving as rapidly as possible over the loose gravel and sliding dirt, down toward the valley below and reality.

Just as I crested the small rise that led to the gorge, something white and flapping in the growing breeze caught my eye. Leaning down to pick it up, I almost tripped and fell headlong in shock. It was an envelope, sealed and ready to mail, addressed to a man I know, another author. It was in the same eerily perfect script as the one I'd received, and there was no return address.

Tucking it into my shirt pocket, I continued my flight, unable to concentrate at the moment on anything but keeping my balance and making my escape.

It was nearly dusk before I reached the bottom, my feet blistered and sore from the trek and my clothing matted to my skin by sweat and grime. Everything seemed hazy, as though I were feverish. I probably was.

I staggered to the Seahaven Inn and inside. The clerk was not at her desk—in fact, I'd seen nobody since returning to the village, but I gave it no thought. I went straight to my room, found the door unlocked, and staggered inside.

Although I was exhausted, I didn't hesitate. I threw what belongings I'd brought into my bag, tossed a twenty on the bed for the room, and headed back into the night. As I moved into the misty twilight I remembered the letter. Pulling it free from my pocket, I stared at it for a moment, wondering just what the hell I should do. On the corner, just before I reached the parking lot, there was a mailbox. With a shrug, I dropped the letter inside and walked on.

Far above, shrouded in mist and silence, haloed by the moisture in the air and light of the morning sun, I could just make out the frame of the house, and I shuddered.

"When it is time," I repeated softly. I drove away then, a bit faster than I'd driven in, and I did not look back.

I have received no further letters from Olafson, nor have I seen the woman, Tanyan, or read any further stories she has written. Upon these two facts, precariously, rest my sanity.

The references from the letter have grown more common in the writings of others, though, and my story, "Wreathed in Clouds," has won an award. There have been others. Sometimes *I* write, sometimes I know nothing of where the words come from. The other that writes through me is more talented, somehow, and I fear him. Do I fear myself? The critics say I am "heavily influenced by the early pulp writers, but with a modern lyrical style." I don't know who is my influence, but in one thing they are close to the mark, I am certain I share that influence with others, many others.

I know the time is nearing, I write of it often enough that it is ingrained in my psyche. I do not know what comes, but that something *does* I have no doubt. I am scared, and I am curious, and I am not sorry; may God, or the gods, or whatever power prevails, forgive me.

The Likeness

by

DAN PEREZ

A SHIVER OF EXCITEMENT flickered down Mindy's spine as Jake throttled down and braked the Harley in front of the tattoo parlor. As Mindy slid out from behind him, Jake lit a Marlboro. "Well, here we are. So what are you going to get?" he asked.

She leaned close, laughing. He cocked his head to hear. Her lips brushed the skin of his ear. "I told you, shithead," she whispered, "it's a secret." She licked his earlobe, tasting the silver of his earrings. "But it's gonna be *radical*."

He nodded, blowing out smoke as she drew back. "Radical, huh? How long you gonna be in there?"

Mindy glanced at the glowing neon letters. *Tattoo You*, same as the title of the Rolling Stones album. She had scrimped and worked overtime for the last six months to get the biggest, most beautiful, most exotic tattoo she could afford. "I dunno, Jake," she said, barely aware of him. "As long as it takes."

"Well, I'm going to ride down to Galveston tonight. Randy got busted down there, and I want to go see him."

"I'll find my own way home," she said. Then, smiling, she gripped the black leather of his jacket and pulled him close. She kissed him hard, exploring the smoky recesses of his mouth with her tongue. Out of the corner of her eye, she saw a middle-aged man staring from the sidewalk several paces away. She started to moan out loud, writhing up and down as she kissed Jake. The man hurried off.

Jake broke away, laughing. "You're crazy, girl."

"He got his jollies, I guess. Say hi to Randy for me."

"The dumb-ass. Okay. Bye, babe."

The Harley roared, coughing exhaust as Jake pulled away. Mindy turned and strode up to the glass door of *Tattoo You*. This is it, she thought, opening the door. Music throbbed through the brightly lit front room. Mindy recognized it: the soundtrack from the movie *A Clockwork Orange*. Mindy took a deep breath: the smoky cinnamon smell of incense filled the air. Sample tattoos drawn on sheets of paper covered every square inch of the walls and the counter. Mindy glanced at them, frowning. Everybody gets those, she thought.

A figure appeared in the dim red light behind the string-beads covering the doorway in back of the counter. Graceful hands, stained blue, green and black, parted the beads, and Mindy saw that the man's spindly forearms were completely covered with tattoos of overlapping blue scales. He stepped through: a tall, thin man with long iron gray hair gathered into a ponytail and a thick beard like a gray storm cloud. His blue eyes sat high on his long face, and he surveyed Mindy for a long moment, his weathered lips pursed, silent except for the soft nasal rasp of his breathing.

She smiled at him, and stood up straight, letting herself be appraised. I'm his canvas, she thought.

He nodded appreciatively. "You want more than just a tattoo," he said, his voice low and husky. He waved a hand at all the illustrations on the counter and walls. "This shit won't do."

"That's right." she said.

His eyes narrowed. "Just how serious are you?"

Mindy shifted on her feet. "What do you mean?"

He frowned. "I mean, *how serious are you*? I know you're not here to play around: to get some stupid little cherry or flower or hummingbird like those hausfraus who think they're living dangerously. You're more serious than that. But are you serious enough to go out to the limit?"

Mindy tried to match his hard blue stare. "Just what are we talking about here?"

"We're talking about a serious commitment. We're talking you eventually walk away from this place with about 75 percent of your body covered with something incredible. Something *permanent*."

"I've thought about it a lot," Mindy said, feeling a little breathless. "I mean, I know I want something big, something radical, something unique. I don't know if I was thinking quite that extreme. Besides, it'd probably cost a lot more than I've got."

He nodded toward the other tattoos. "I charge for that shit because that's what pays the bills. What I'll do to you takes us both—the artist and his medium—to an extreme, to the frontier of expression. You can't set a price on that."

An inexplicable thrill tingled inside her. Her heart fluttered in her chest. "It sounds erotic."

"It can be. How do you handle pain?"

She smiled again. "Sometimes my boyfriend and I play pretty rough." She paused for a moment. "Really rough."

The corners of his mouth curled slightly. "An adventurer."

She nodded, feeling bolder now. "So what's it going to be?"

"Do you shave?"

"What, like my legs?"

"Like everything."

She felt herself blushing. *"Everything?"*

"I don't want any of my work hidden beneath hair. Any hair. Keep your eyebrows and the hair on your head—the tattoo won't reach that high."

She fidgeted. "But all the rest—"

"*All* the rest. I think your boyfriend will like that, too."

She giggled, glanced off to the side. "Yeah, I guess he might."

"Do you need some time to think this over? I don't want you freaking out halfway through and disappearing on me."

Mindy took a deep breath. "No. But I would like to get an idea of what you're going to put on me."

"First, introductions," he said. "I'm Cal."

She reached out and shook his hand. His slender, tapered fingers concealed a strong grip. "Mindy."

He smiled at her, then tilted his head toward the bead curtain. "C'mon back."

Mindy followed him through a short hallway to a small room, at the center of which sat a chair much like a barber's chair. Next to it was a table with a rack of tattoo guns and needles, plastic bottles of pigment, rubbing alcohol, a large tube of Vaseline, Jergens skin lotion and packets of sterile blotting pads. More supplies, including a gleaming autoclave, sat on side counters around the room. Beneath the mask of incense, Mindy smelled sweat and antiseptic. Cal went to a shelf and pulled down a thick book bound in peeling leather. He set it next to the autoclave and Mindy joined him as he unbuckled the straps holding it shut.

"What's this?" she asked.

"It's a modern Portuguese translation of a very old book written, or more precisely, compiled by an Arab named Abdul Alhazred."

"Is it an art book?" Mindy asked.

Cal's laughter was a deep, throaty, chortling sound. "Let's just say that it has art in it—based on descriptions in the text." His stained fingers turned the brittle, yellowed pages until he came upon a lithograph. Mindy gasped at the full-page illustration.

"Joachim Mendoza did this in 1911. He based it on one of the original woodcuts in the Arabic version," Cal said. He ran his finger along the swirling lines, past festoons of glittering stars. "I want to put this on your body."

Mindy stared, feeling as though she were being drawn into the illustration. Cal's voice sounded distant and faint.

"Yes," she said slowly, her mouth suddenly dry, her pulse pounding sluggishly in her ears. "I want that on me."

* * *

Warm steam surrounded Mindy as she toweled herself off. Her body dry, she wiped condensation from the full-length mirror mounted on the bathroom door and pirouetted, looking at herself. She had shaved her entire body from the neck down—only her short-cropped black hair and her delicate eyebrows remained. Aside from a few nicks and scrapes, her pale skin was unblemished. That's why Cal chose me, she thought. He knew.

She heard a tapping at the door. "Hey, babe," Jake said, "I'm home."

Mindy opened the door and stood before him, watching his eyes as they surveyed the curves of her body.

"Well, this is a surprise," he said, a vague smile on his face.

She sidled up to him, pressing her smooth skin against the leather and denim he wore, working her fingers up under his shirt. "Wanna go for a spin, big fella?"

* * *

Sweat drying on her skin, Mindy snuggled against Jake in bed as he took a drag on his cigarette and blew delicate smoke rings into the air above them. "Now I'm gonna have to take another shower," she said.

"Yeah," he said with a satisfied sigh. "I'm just the king of bad timing." He turned to her. "So how big is this tattoo you're going to get?"

She ran her fingers through the moist hair on his chest. "Big," she said. "Seventy-five percent of my body."

"I don't know if I'm crazy about that," he said quietly.

She leaned up on one arm. "Like it's your business in the first place?"

"That's not what I meant. I just figured—"

"Look, Jake—you know how long I've wanted this. I've had plenty of time to think it over."

"A tattoo that big is going to change your life," he said.

"I know that. I expect it. If *you* can't handle it—"

"Hey, I think I'll be able to handle it, okay? Don't get all bent out of shape. How long will it take?"

"He said probably about five or six eight-hour sessions."

"*Jesus.*"

Mindy slipped out of bed and walked back toward the bathroom. "I'm taking a week off work," she said. "But I still have to go in today. I'm going for the first session tonight after I get off. He wants me to come in after he closes the tattoo parlor at midnight."

Jake frowned. "Tell that guy to keep his hands to himself."

She glared at him from the door. "He has to touch me to do it, Jake. I'm not your fucking property, okay?"

He sighed and slumped back down in bed. "Whatever."

* * *

Cal leaned against the counter, sipping a canned Coke when Mindy walked into *Tattoo You*. She had worn her black tube top to show off her smooth arms and shoulders. Cal smiled slightly as he walked past her, locked the door and flipped the *Closed* side of the sign to face the glass.

"No interruptions," he said. "Are you ready?"

Mindy took a deep breath. "Yeah."

"Did you bring music to listen to?"

She nodded, jangling her bag. "Ramones, Sex Pistols, and Joy Division."

"The classics," he said, nodding. "Well, let's get started."

Mindy followed him back to the studio. She handed him a CD and he slid it into the player. As the grinding guitar music poured forth from the speakers, Mindy sat on the chair. On the table next to it, the book lay, opened to the page with the illustration. Cal pulled up a stool and settled on it. He reached across the book and took up a tattoo gun, then attached a needle to it.

"How does that thing work?" she asked.

He squeezed a drop of dark pigment onto the needle. "It's like a little miniature sewing machine," he said. "The needle goes in and out of the skin really fast."

Mindy felt skittish. "I bet I know where you want to start," she said.

Cal's bushy eyebrows arched. "Oh yeah? Tell me then."

"Somewhere kinky, right?"

"Actually," he said, taking her left arm and gently lifting it, "I was thinking about here." He squeezed out a dab of Vaseline and spread it on the skin of her armpit. "Are you ready?"

She nodded. Cal squeezed the trigger and the needle buzzed against her flesh. She felt a hot, prickling sensation.

"You're marked for life," Cal said above the buzzing of the needle. Mindy didn't laugh.

* * *

The hours passed to the rhythm of the bass beat from the CD player and the wasplike buzzing of the tattoo gun. In its wake, it left the sensation of a carpet burn. Mindy wanted to touch the tattoo—to see it as it took shape on her body, but Cal refused, saying that there would be time enough to admire it when the session was ended. The design spread to cover her armpit, her left shoulder and became a band which migrated down her arm to the elbow. That's when Mindy got her first glimpse of the design. Across the deep, purplish-black of space, glinting with tiny diamond-like stars, coiled a ribbed, gray-green tentacle, its dorsal surface flecked with what might have been blood blisters or glistening scarlet eyes. The underside of the tentacle was studded with pale gray suction cups, each of which contained a ring of tiny teeth.

Cal continued down to her wrist, and the tentacle slowly furcated into a web of whiplike tendrils, each terminating in a serrated blue claw. The claws gathered around her wrist like a bracelet.

Cal blotted a droplet of blood from Mindy's wrist, then laid the tattoo gun aside. He shook out his hand, flexed his fingers and stood, stretching.

Mindy admired her left arm. It felt sunburned. The tattoo was a skintight sleeve of color. "It's beautiful," she said. "Even more than in the book."

"Yeah," said Cal. "And we're making good time. It's only two-thirty in the morning. Do you have to work tomorrow?"

"No," she said. "I've got a whole week."

He returned to the table and sat. "Good," he said, dipping the needle into the ultrasound bath to remove the pigment. "I'd like to do your collarbone, breast and ribs next."

Mindy nodded. "Why not do the other arm?"

"So you can sleep on the untattooed side tonight. It's more comfortable and it'll give this side time to heal a bit. You'll have to take off your top."

Mindy took a deep breath and pulled off the tube top. Even though she considered herself an exhibitionist at heart she felt vulnerable as she sat half-naked in front of Cal. He watched her, expressionless.

"I'm a little nervous about this part," she said.

He reached out and dabbed Vaseline along the ridge of her collarbone. "Don't be. I see only a blank canvas wanting paint." The buzzing needle stung her skin, injecting color instead of venom. Mindy closed her eyes and listened as the Ramones sang "Needles and Pins." No relief there, she thought, grinning.

* * *

Mindy straddled Jake, bobbing up and down, her breath coming in shallow gasps. Her hands clutched his shoulders, fingernails biting into his skin. She moaned, feeling the wave gathering inside her, building strength and speed as it never had before. As it swirled up, massive, unstoppable, her skin tingled and burned. The half-completed tattoo made her skin feel alive, every nerve in her breasts, her arms and her ribs exploding at once. Mindy cried out as the wave crashed, filling her with its roiling intensity: a throbbing, unceasing orgasm like spasms of electricity inside her. Finally it ebbed, and she slumped onto Jake's heaving chest, her breath rapid and hoarse in her throat.

"Goddamn," he gasped. "I thought you were gonna have a heart attack on me, there."

Mindy couldn't speak. She panted, trying to catch her breath.

"You gotta go a little easier next time, babe," Jake said, his voice strained.

"Huh?" she gasped out. Her skin tingled.

"You scratched the shit out of me," he said. "You know I don't mind a little rough stuff, but this *really* hurt."

She leaned up, saw the blood covering his chest, smeared all over her, all over the tattoo. "Oh my god!" she said. She stumbled out of bed and ran to the bathroom to get a towel.

Jake followed her in. "Christ," he said with a shudder.

Mindy sat him down on the toilet and dabbed at his chest with the towel. "Sorry," she said, feeling dizzy. "I got carried away."

As she blotted up the blood, a network of ragged-edged lacerations appeared on Jake's chest and abdomen. "Jeez," he said breathlessly. "How'd you do that?"

A chill rippled across her skin. "I don't know."

Later, Mindy knelt next to the bed. Jake lay there, drinking a beer, his chest and stomach bandaged with gauze.

"You okay?" she asked.

He looked at her and smiled. "I'll live. You must have really gotten off, huh?"

She nodded, giggling. "Like never before. You wouldn't believe it. It just wouldn't stop."

"Well, maybe I'll tie you up next time so you don't pull the slice and dice routine on me."

She made a purring sound deep in her throat. "*That* could be fun."

* * *

Early in the morning after her fourth session, Mindy stood in front of the bathroom mirror and let her silk robe slip to the floor. Her skin felt swollen and hot. The nearly completed tattoo resembled a full bodysuit now—dominated by the image of Joachim Mendoza's creature. Its basic shape was a huge figure eight: the two connected lobes each resembled starfish of the type called sun stars, fringed with a multitude of short stubby rays.

But this creature was kin to the octopus as well, with great looping tentacles the color of muddy seawater that wound around Mindy's torso, arms and neck. The creature's pebbled skin was pocked with luminescent nodules and irregular clusters of blue eyes that gleamed at the end of translucent stalks. The starfish god, as Mindy had begun to refer to it, was still incomplete, with blank areas where Cal had yet to place detailing, but it was a magnificent thing already, suspended against a tableau of stars and space.

Mindy ran her fingers over her skin, over the surface of the starfish god, imagining that it had floated in space like that for millions of years, dreaming ponderous, incomprehensible dreams in the webbed, gelatinous cells of its alien mind.

Mindy blinked, then shook her head and laughed nervously. "Man, this thing really gets you going," she giggled as she bent, snatched up the robe and slipped it back on. "I didn't even know I could think like that."

She walked into the bedroom, yawning. Jake had gone on a three-day ride with friends; he'd be back tomorrow. She crawled into bed and as sleep overtook her, she hoped that the tattoo would be finished before Jake got home.

* * *

As Mindy walked into *Tattoo You*, Cal nodded at her. His long face seemed paler than normal, and the dark around his eyes gave the impression that they were sinking into his skull.

"You look tired," she said.

"It won't matter after tonight," he replied.

"Does that mean we're almost done?"

He smiled as he walked past her and locked the door. "Yeah. Let's go on back."

In the studio, Mindy quickly stripped off her clothing, now completely at ease in front of Cal. He watched her, hands on his hips. "It's magnificent," he said quietly.

"I dreamed of outer space today," said Mindy as she padded across the cool concrete floor to the chair. "The starfish god moved across the face of the void."

"Awaiting consummation," Cal murmured as he took up his position on the stool next to the chair and assembled a tattoo gun.

Mindy reclined on the chair, closing her eyes as the needle buzzed against the skin near her navel.

As the hours passed, Mindy saw that Cal was drawing mouths on the starfish god: small spherical ones ringed with rows of thorn-like teeth—Cal drew one of those around her navel. There were slit-shaped ones, too, studded with triangular teeth like those in a shark's mouth. She felt a tingle of anticipation, remembering the blank area on her labia. As Cal worked, he had begun to rock rhythmically, humming to himself, chanting under his breath. She had heard him speak of the magical chants the Maori sang during their tattoo rituals, and she didn't want to interfere. She made a game of trying to pick out recognizable words, but she never heard any.

As he continued, his chant rose in volume and pitch, and she listened to the strange language, making out what sounded like distinct words and phrases: *Iä! Vthyarilops! Ut ftaghu wk'hmr Vthyarilops! Iä! Iä!*

Mindy wanted to stop him and ask him what the words meant, but she felt sluggish, her mind fuzzy from the droning chant. The needle buzzed along her labia like a hot, rasping tongue and she gripped the arms of the chair, pain commingling with pleasure. She clutched the chair hard, spreading her legs for Cal, fighting the urge to rock against the sweet stinging tongue, jagged breath catching in her throat. *Finish it*, she thought. *Finish it.*

A tidal wave gathered inside her, its mountainous mass looming up, filling her with its unrelenting power. Underneath the rumbling roar of its breaking, the hot thundering rush of its waters inside her, she heard shouting. And an unearthly, bubbling roar.

* * *

Mindy opened her eyes. The dim light of the studio stung them, and she blinked rapidly. Panting, she lay still, trying to remember. *I blacked out*, she thought. *For how long, though?* She smelled acrid smoke and beneath it, a stench like seaweed drying in the sun. Shifting in the chair, she felt dizzy and her stomach twisted. She glanced around, looking for Cal, but he was nowhere to be seen. She took a deep breath, fighting back the nausea. She felt a hot prickling sensation all over, like the early stage of a fever.

"Cal?" she said, levering herself up on one elbow, her head throbbing. His stool was empty. On the table, she saw that the book was gone. A tattoo gun lay on the floor next to the stool, blackened and smoldering. Mindy's stomach lurched again. She jumped out of the chair, ran to the stainless steel sink in the corner and vomited.

Mindy rinsed her mouth with water from the tap, then splashed the cold water on her face. She dried her face with a paper towel and glanced down at her body. Her tattoo was—finished! Her fear gave way to amazement. She smiled as she ran her fingertips over the tender, aching skin. "Cal!" she cried out. "It's perfect!"

"Don't you want to see it?" she called out again. She went to the hall and peeked out, but didn't see him. She felt a chill and walked back to get her clothes. She had her panties and jeans on when she looked at the empty stool again. Panic swirled inside her. *He's really gone.* She hurriedly put on her blouse and shoes. Cal's keys were missing from their peg in the hall, and Mindy found that the front door was unlocked. Her skin rippled with heat and the dizziness swelled and ebbed as she pushed open the door and stumbled off into the darkness of predawn.

Mindy stretched luxuriantly beneath the covers. The fever had broken hours ago, and with it had gone the shivering, the weakness, the confusion. She licked her lips as she heard the front door slam. Jake was home.

He strode into the bedroom and tossed his jacket on a chair. "Hey, babe," he said, leaning over her.

Mindy pulled him down and kissed him.

"Are you naked under there?" he asked.

"Iä!" she said. "Vthyarilops awaits."

His eyebrows arched. "Huh?"

"I *am* naked," she said quickly, caressing his unshaven face. "Why don't *you* get naked and join me?"

He stood, smiling, and took off his jacket.

* * *

Afterward, Mindy lay on the torn, blood-drenched sheets, listening to the sucking, smacking sounds of dozens of mouths, a blissful, satiated grin on her face. Jake had been *good*. But now she'd have to find a new boyfriend.

An Early Frost

by

SCOTT DAVID ANIOLOWSKI

"Warmth, warmth, more warmth! For we are dying of cold and not of darkness. It is not the night that kills, but the frost."

— Miguel de Unamuno

GOLDEN RAYS of the rising sun filtered through wafting curtains, dancing across the bungalow floor. Beyond, waves ceaselessly rolled up the warm sands, their sound melodic and comforting. Palms rustled in the salty morning breeze. A lone woman, bronzed by the tropical sun, bent to scoop a trinket from the foamy surf, her silver hair playing about her face like silky ribbons.

Frolicking beams of sunlight sparkled on a glass-topped table, and played over a shirt of brilliant silk hanging over the back of a chair. Another wrinkled shirt lay in a heap on the floor, not far from a pair of sand-encrusted sneakers.

Alex Cirillo yawned and rolled onto his back; he felt the dark sandpaper stubble along his jaw, and stretched sleep-numbed arms over his head. He licked his lips, swallowing. The remnants of toothpaste, and sleep, and passion mingled in his mouth, leaving it sticky and dry. He lay there for a long time, just listening to the surf and the gentle flapping of the curtains. Everything was so fresh. So crystalline-clear.

The room, decorated in a vibrant tropical motif, bedazzled him with an orgy of color and life. It was alive and vital, and a welcomed change from the sterile white he'd grown so accustomed to.

The young man took a deep breath. The air was warm and clean and soothing. Too long had he settled for the toxic air of the city. And too long had he been obliged to breathe sickening, antiseptic air. That smell—the stench of medicine and disease and human suffering—he would never forget that smell. Just the thought made his stomach churn.

A flood of unwelcome images forced their way out of shadowy recesses of his memory. Images of uncomfortable beds with side rails, and of people clad in face masks and rubber gloves. Of yellow plastic water pitchers, and of wheelchairs. The images of disease and decay and death. Uncomfortable memories of sights and sounds and smells deluged his mind.

He rolled onto his side, bundling the corner of the silky sheet beneath his head. He closed his eyes, trying to shut out the painful images. Alex no longer heard the soothing crashing of waves—he could hear only the din of the city. He squeezed his eyes tighter, but the blackness only beckoned more visions. Streets poisoned by shrouds of exhaust fumes. Cold, grey towers of glass and steel.

Alex sat up, sheets falling away from his tanned body. The specters fled from his mind. Tranquility returned.

He rubbed the sleep from mahogany eyes and raked fingers through his jet-black hair. His companion, warm beside him, stirred briefly but did not wake.

It was so strange to Alex—this peaceful moment—like still he slept, dreaming of a paradise where each day was a beginning. Instead, he anticipated each to be the end.

This was the first moment of serenity he had known in months. He felt guilty for it.

Silently, he slid out of the bed, padding across to the bathroom. He glanced back once toward his mate. He had grown so thin and frail. Each day the wasting progressed, and the years accumulated.

In the mirror Alex performed the daily ritual of poking and prodding and peering: of searching for anomalies on an otherwise unblemished body. And Alex sighed, as he did every day, when the mirror was mercifully kind.

Today the mirror was surprisingly compassionate. Gone were the shadowy rings that regularly encircled his eyes: dark, uncaring bands that had haunted him from the looking-glass for too many months to remember. His body was taut and healthy with sun. Even the perpetual fluttering in his gut had subsided to a mere ripple. The young man felt for the first time a glimmer of hope since the nightmare had begun.

Alex pushed back the filmy drapes in the small bathroom window. The gentle breeze wafted warm through his hair. Beyond was a world that was so perfect as to seem almost artificial—like being on the big screen, an actor in a movie. Any minute someone would turn up the lights and the fantasy would fade. Gone would be the Hawaiian surf and sun, only to be replaced with the bleak streets of New York. The Big Apple. A hive of humanity, teeming with social victims and work-ethic drones mechanically repeating drudgery of their every-day lives.

The young man opened a small black satchel, taking out a dozen and a half amber-hued medicine bottles. Methodically, he counted out pills from each bottle, laying them on a tray. He returned the plastic bottles to the black bag. So accustomed had he become to counting and dispensing drugs, that Alex was able to do it without a thought. He filled a glass with tap water and returned to the bedroom. There, Alex discovered his companion sitting at the small table staring out at the ocean, absently fondling the clear crystal that hung around his neck.

"Good morning," Alex said, padding over to his friend and placing the tray and glass on the table.

"It binds and builds," mumbled the other without looking at Alex.

"What?" asked Alex.

"It binds and builds."

"Oh," replied Alex, not understanding his friend's cryptic words.

"I don't know. It keeps going through my head—it binds and builds. I must have heard it somewhere...or maybe it was in my dreams," Alex's lover responded, picking up several of the pills and swallowing them with a mouthful of water.

"Did you have bad dreams?" asked Alex.

"No. I don't think so. I actually slept quite well."

"Good."

"Yeah, its about time. Maybe this trip was worth it, after all," Tim said, absently pushing the remaining drugs around the tray.

Alex put his hands on his companion's shoulders. The pair stared out at the ocean in silence. For the first time in months Tim Ridgeway seemed relaxed—more like his old self. His pallid flesh was even beginning to get some color.

"Come on, take the rest," Alex instructed his lover.

Tim swallowed the remaining capsules. "We'd better get ready. Breakfast is promptly at 8:00, you know," he said.

The Center for Holistic Healing operated from a small compound on the north shore of Oahu. The select few who were chosen as guests lodged in a dozen private beach-front bungalows. Meals were taken in a dining hall, and classes and workshops were presented in intimate rooms or on the beach. The financially well-healed came from around the world to take part in the center's workshops: to learn how to meditate, and to channel the healing powers of crystals. In an era of religious disillusionment, the desperate and the optimistic came to the center hoping to heal their bodies, their minds, or their souls.

The brochures for the center were illustrated with pictures of beautiful people in a paradisic setting. Curvaceous bikini-clad women, and tanned shirtless young men frolicked in clear, blue waters. The pamphlet was filled with the "unsolicited" testaments of past clients who proclaimed to have been healed of life-threatening ailments, or overcome drug and alcohol problems. The center vowed to teach guests how to channel their energies and put their wretched lives back in order. On the back of the brochure was a photograph of the center's staff. A black woman in white robes was flanked by a large Samoan gentleman, a beautiful woman with long blonde hair, and a young man shirtless to show off his athletic build.

Space at the center was limited to a dozen guests at a time, and despite the well-publicized scrutiny of the skeptical who proclaimed the center a fraud, there was a two-year waiting list. Workshops began at each full moon, and lasted for two weeks. The cost for the fourteen days was enough to make it prohibitive to all but the wealthiest and most desperate.

The center employed a small staff to run the business and instruct guests in the holistic arts. A large Samoan named Mr. Charlie lead clients in meditation and visualization exercises, while a woman guests knew only as Lana instructed them in the holistic workings of crystals and gemstones. Randy Shaw, a former champion gymnast, acted as personal trainer, attending to the patrons in the center's state-of-the-art fitness center. And the facility's founder and director, the Reverend Katrina Williams, counseled the spiritual needs of her guests. Another half-dozen people were employed by the center to clean guest rooms, prepare food, and attend to office business.

"Close your eyes," said the woman. "Take a deep, deep breath and open your mind."

Nine people sat in a circle, each holding a clear quartz crystal. Eight of the people sat with their eyes closed. The ninth, a striking woman with long blonde hair and green eyes, lead the others through a relaxation exercise.

The eight participants had all come a long way. Tim Ridgeway and Alex Cirillo had come from New York City; Judy McQuillan and her son Danny were from Los Angeles; Albert and Rose Gray had come from London; and Gustav and Ella Pfohl resided in Toronto. Danny McQuillan was suffering from a malignant cancer; the Grays were on a course of spiritual cleansing and awakening; and Ella Pfohl was suffering from acute depression. They had all come to the center from different places, and for different reasons, yet ultimately they each sought the same thing. Salvation.

"Open your mind. Let all of your worries slip away," the woman said in a low, soothing voice. "Now, concentrate on the crystal. Let it fill your mind. You are one with the crystal. It is one with you. See its beauty. Feel its strength. Your mind is clear and strong. Your spirit is filled with the vibrancy of the crystal."

Alex felt silly. He peeked out of one eye. Everyone was intently concentrating on the exercise. His companion was beside him looking more at peace than he had been in a very long time, his drawn face awash with color.

When the exercise was over Lana asked each of the participants to relate their experiences to the group. Some claimed to have experienced a floating sensation, while others saw vibrant colors and beautiful images.

When it was Tim's turn to speak he looked at his peers and said softly that he had seen God. An awed silence fell over the group.

Alex hadn't seen or experienced anything. Just blackness. He had felt foolish, but he couldn't tell the others. They all believed in this holistic mumbo-jumbo. So he told them that he had seen bright flashes of color. He was met with a chorus of sincere sighs when he related his made-up experiences. This only made him feel even more ridiculous, and he wondered how intelligent people could take all of this so seriously.

Later, as they walked in the breaking waves, Alex asked Tim about what he had said. About seeing God.

"It was like I said—I saw God," Tim explained, kicking a bit of wet sand at Alex playfully.

"How do you know it was God? I mean, what was it like?" asked Alex.

"There was this brilliant light that sparkled," Tim explained. "And there was a shape. It was beautiful. The dancing light embraced me and I was filled with peace. And there was a voice," he said.

"God spoke to you?" Alex asked hesitantly.

"A voice came out of the light. It was sweet and soothing, and it knew me. It called me by name," Tim explained.

"What did it say to you, this voice?" Alex asked.

"It invited me to peace and to knowledge," Tim responded.

"Peace and knowledge?" queried Alex.

"Yeah. It was the voice from my dreams. I remember it now. It binds and builds—that's what the voice said. It was the voice of God!" he insisted to Alex.

"That's what you were mumbling this morning in the bungalow."

"Yeah, I know. Don't you see—it's a sign. It binds and builds. I'm going to be cured."

"Listen, Tim," Alex said, gazing softly into his companion's blue eyes, "that's the reason we came here—went through the long wait and the expense—to find help. But I don't think either of us should get too excited yet."

"No. These people here, they know some secret. They have some power. Why else would I have visions of God? Why now, after everything else?" Tim argued.

"I'm just thinking of all the other times," Alex said.

"Yeah, I know," Tim mumbled.

"Remember that faith healer? How about those doctors in Mexico?" Alex reminded Tim.

"That was different," Tim insisted.

"And that southern minister who danced with the poisonous snakes?"

Tim turned and gazed at the breaking surface, watching the sunlight dance across the blue water.

"Oh, and then there were those copper bracelets—they were supposed to cleanse your body, remember?"

Tim said nothing.

"Those horrible herbal teas? The coven of witches in Wisconsin? That woman in California who claimed to have been given the cure by a UFO?" Alex said.

"This is different," Tim insisted, finally.

"There are too many fakes and frauds in the world. I don't want us to be disappointed again. I just don't want you to get too worked up yet. Let's wait and see what happens."

"Look, Alex, I've had to live with this for a long time. The weight loss. The pneumonia. The bruises. Don't you think I'm skeptical? But I know what I experienced. And I know deep inside that this is it this time. This time we're going to beat this."

Alex didn't respond. He felt guilty for not having the conviction of his lover. There was so much still unknown. And the medical community just wasn't making any significant progress. Alex had heard of people surviving with the AIDS virus for many more years than expected. People who claimed holistic living had prolonged their life and kept the virus in check. Perhaps there was something to this. It just seemed so unlikely.

Alex smiled at his companion and they continued down the beach in silence.

Alex was awakened by the sound of Tim's voice. He turned toward his lover. He was bathed in pale moonlight. Tim's breathing was fast and he was shaking. His flesh was cold and pale. Worst of all were his eyes: although he was asleep, Tim's eyes stared wide toward the ceiling.

"Are you God?" Tim said, still asleep.

"Tim," Alex said, shaking his companion.

"No!" Tim screamed.

Alex shook his friend vigorously. "Tim! Wake up," he yelled. With a start, Tim bolted up in the bed, his eyes still staring wide. Beads of sweat sprang to his forehead and chest and he gasped for air, coughing.

"You were having a nightmare," Alex comforted him.

"No. Yeah. I mean, yeah, I must have been dreaming," Tim mumbled, the sound of his own heart still exploding in his ears. "It began so beautifully. So peacefully," Tim said softly.

"Its all right, now," Alex said soothingly.

"I heard a voice calling to me. It was beautiful. I'd heard it before. It was the voice of God. It was amazing. I could hear the blood racing through your body...taste pollen in the air...see the tiny atoms that hold everything together," Tim explained excitedly.

Tim went on to relate his dream to his lover. Of how he floated up, out of the bungalow. He drifted out, over the roofs of the compound, and into the night sky. Above, the black ether was alive and tempting him to truth. Lightning dashed through the heavens—streaks and cracks of scintillating color tearing through the darkness of space. Stars and planets danced by, rotating through ageless orbits.

At one point, he said he dreamt of soaring past a flock of crustaceous things that silently slid through the void. At first he was afraid of them, but they seemed to Tim to be very intelligent and very old.

He dreamt of a planet. Mars, he thought. There was an enormous scarlet blossom there, and it was a beautiful, sentient being with a sonorous voice. The strange spoke to Tim—told him secrets of the universe, and of life. It told him of the others—those ancient beings who strode among the stars before man walked the earth. The timeless ones. The true gods. They dwelled among the stars, these ancient ones, and some slept in hidden tombs, awaiting the time of their rebirth. The botanic intelligence was one of these gods, but not the god of light—not the god of Tim's vision.

"So I floated back into space," Tim explained.

"This was quite a vivid dream," interrupted Alex.

"Yes. I've never dreamt anything like it before. It was so real."

Tim went on to explain to Alex how he had dreamt of floating past the farthest planet, where he saw more of those pink crustaceous things winging their way through space. Stars and galaxies passed by him, but on he glided, the voice of God still calling him. Surrounding him.

In the blackest depths of space he saw something horrible. It was a planet, but it cracked open and looked at Tim with an enormous, unblinking eye. He shivered as he related this part of the unusual dream. This being—this colossal, sentient entity spawned from nightmare—must be one of Them. He thought that this must be another of the ancient gods. The planet-god sang to the planets and stars it passed. It sang songs that made the stars shift in their orbits.

The planet-thing was nothing like the beautiful plant-god he saw on Mars. It was horrible. Tim thought that he had screamed, but the coldness of space absorbed the sound.

Finally, he dreamt that he was on a lightless world. A world that the voice of God had called Mthura. God had directed Tim to this place. The surface of the planet was barren except for exquisite mineral formations of unthinkable proportions. Tim related to Alex how he had seen spires of crystal that soared into the dark sky, and of forests of mineral growths that dotted the landscape. And the place had been alive with sound—queer vibrations and high-pitched crackling sounds.

"I saw something move. Right before my eyes, these sparkling crystals grew and spread out like frost, decorating the ground with intricate patterns. Tentacles of this delicate crystal spread toward me, reaching for me. Then a figure began to rise up above the crystal landscape. That's all I remember. That must have been when you woke me up," Tim mused.

Alex grasped his companion and held him tight. As he glanced over toward the table, Alex noticed how the cool white moonlight sparkled off the crystal that sat there, near the window. Strangely, it no longer fell on his companion, or even near the bed.

"Today," explained Lana, "we're going deeper. Today we're going into the crystals."

The same group had assembled—Lana, Tim and Alex, and the six others.

"Close your eyes," said Lana. "Take a deep, deep breath and open your mind."

Alex began to squirm. He felt foolish and uncomfortable.

"Open your mind. Let all of your worries slip away," Lana instructed in her whispering, soothing voice. "Now, concentrate on the crystal. Let it fill your mind. You are one with the crystal. It is one with you. See its beauty. Feel its strength. Your mind is clear and strong. Your spirit is filled with the vibrancy of the crystal."

As happened each time, the Grays appeared to drift immediately into a deep trance, their wrinkled faces frozen in insincere smiles. The sound of Ella Pfohl sigh was unmistakable: her husband squeezed her hand.

"Let the energy of your crystal fill your mind. Let it fill your soul," instructed Lana.

When Alex peeked out of one eye, as he always did, he noticed Judy McQuillan gazing at her son, her eyes wet with tears. Alex turned his glance toward Mrs. McQuillan. Their eyes met and in that moment Alex knew what she felt...what she was thinking. He smiled sadly at her, and then he closed his eyes again.

"You are one with the crystal. Feel it in you. Feel yourself in it. You are in your crystal. Look out at yourself...at the world," Lana continued.

A tear ran down the side of Alex's face.

"You have the power to change yourself...change the world," said Lana.

Alex's mind was filled with images of hospitals and of death. Black hopelessness washed over him. He gasped and his heart fluttered. He felt as though he was drowning. The sounds of Lana's voice droned in his ears and became muffled, distorted noise. He felt trapped in a hell of shadows and memories. He tried to open his eyes, but couldn't. Numbness had captured his body.

"It binds and builds," Alex heard. His eyes snapped open in search of the source of the voice. His sight was at first blurry. He felt disoriented. Slowly, the faces came into focus. The eight familiar faces.

"It binds and builds," came the voice again that had jerked Alex back to reality. It came from Tim's mouth, yet the voice was not Tim's voice. It was a crisp, sweet, almost crystalline voice.

Tim sat rigidly in his place, his eyes wide and staring. He gripped the quartz crystal in one hand. Alex noticed how, strangely, he appeared to be bathed in a pale light.

The rest of the group stopped the exercise and were staring silently at Tim. Alex moved to grab his companion's arm but stopped when something dug into his shoulder.

"You mustn't," croaked withered Rose Gray, one of her claw-like hands clutching Alex's shoulder.

"Your friend is experiencing a higher state of consciousness," Albert Gray uttered through his fat lips.

"No. He's been having these nightmares," Alex insisted, shaking Mrs. Gray's hand from his shoulder.

"He isn't dreaming, Alex. He's deep in trance," explained Lana.

Tim began to gasp, his eyes still wide and unblinking. Again, Tim spoke in the dulcet voice, although what came out was more nonsensical sounds than words. "Iä! Iä! Q'yth-az fhtagn," he gurgled.

"He's speaking in tongues!" cried Mrs. Gray.

"Tim!" shouted Alex, pushing away the Grays. "Wake up," Alex ordered, grasping his companion and shaking him firmly.

Tim's eyes were faded and glassy as he stared blankly past Alex. His skin was cold, and yet perspiration trickled down Tim's forehead in glistening rivulets.

"Yes, God," Tim spoke again, this time sounding like his own voice. "Bring them to the light," he said, his eyes focusing on Alex's face.

There was something alien in Tim's eyes. Something inhuman. Madness and contempt filled his trembling, gaunt face.

"Tim, snap out of it," yelled Alex as he shook his partner again.

Tim's eyes finally blinked, and he went limp in Alex's arms.

"Looks like he'll be okay," said the handsome young man.

"Thank you, Randy," said the black woman. "Mr. Cirillo, I assure you that this is nothing unusual. Many people enter a trance state in which they experience visions or speak in foreign languages. It is just the spirit communing with the Higher Forces," explained the center's director, the Reverend Katrina Williams.

"Don't give me that communing with spirits crap. I don't buy any of this new age mumbo-jumbo. Something very strange is happening here," Alex argued.

"Nonsense, Mr. Cirillo, there is nothing unusual going on here," Reverend Williams tried to reassure her guest.

"Ever since we got here, he's been having these weird dreams. And he says that he sees God...that he talks to him. That's not unusual?" Alex pushed.

"Listen, Alex, I understand your concern, but there's really no reason to get upset," cooed Lana.

"Look, I've had it. All I want is to get the hell out of here. This place is obviously doing him more harm than good," Alex declared.

"But Mr. Cirillo," Williams began.

"I want all of you people out of my bungalow. Now," demanded Alex. "And you'll be hearing from my lawyer," he called as the center staff reluctantly filed out of the small building.

"Alex," Tim called weakly.

"I'm here," Alex answered.

"I don't want to leave," Tim explained.

"Tim," began Alex, "can't you see what this is doing to you?"

"The voice...God spoke to me," Tim mumbled as he began to drift back to sleep.

"Sh," Alex soothed, cradling his companion's head. "Just get some rest."

Tim slept through the rest of the afternoon and evening while Alex made preparations for their departure. The earliest available flight back to New York City was for the following afternoon. He booked two seats and reluctantly consigned to spend one more night at the center.

Exhaustion overcame Alex. He was asleep within moments of crawling into the bed. His sleep was restless and haunted with dreams of death. He tossed and turned for hours, his mind racing and populating his dreams with fragmented images. He dreamt of the hospitals, and of sickness. He saw the faces of the friends who had died...and those that were dying.

Alex stood next to the bed, dressed in sterile green robes and a face-mask. The room was grey and fuzzy, and filled with faceless, mumbling people in doctor's garb. The figure in the bed was nothing more than a shell of a man, skeletal and frail, trapped in a spider's web of tubes and wires and needles.

An alarm sounded, and the fragile man began to gasp and cough. The dancing blue line became erratic.

Alex grabbed one of the doctor-figures, screaming for him to help. The figure ignored him. The bed-ridden man looked at Alex, his eyes pleading.

A chorus of screams and moans sounded from beyond the door.

The doctor-figures backed away from the frail figure, and as they did one accidentally pricked himself with a needle.

The wailing neared.

Alex's heart pounded madly in his chest, sweat beaded on his forehead and soaked his sterile green cap.

Suddenly, the door exploded open, and a shapeless horror of blood and pestilence poured through the door. A vision from a nightmare, the beast was a churning red mass of glistening, pulsating gelatinous flesh. Wet mouth-like rents tore across the undulating form, and from out of these poured the screams and moans of the dying.

The thing surged forward, dripping blue viral puss, and filling the air with the stench of decay and death.

A flood of hopelessness and despair washed over Alex. He felt hot and nauseous. His stomach began to burn. Bile rose in his constricting throat.

The dancing blue line began to slow.

The thing spread toward the bed, coating everything with sticky, coagulated blood. The beast lashed out, striking one of the doctor-figures—the figure Alex had seen pierce himself with the needle.

Alex moved to block the thing, but it parted and swept around him like hot, melted wax. In the surging, pulsating mass, Alex saw faces. The faces of dead friends.

The wailing, dripping thing reached out for the man in the bed, oozing up his legs.

The skeletal man moaned once before he was engulfed by the lumpy, crimson tide. Dragged into the churning folds of blood, he was gone.

The dancing blue line became rigid.

The formless lump of dripping flesh oozed toward Alex. Long, glistening tendrils reached for him. A face formed on the beast. A familiar face. Tim's face. "Come to me," its gurgling voice demanded softly, "you are mine."

Alex's soul was gripped in terror. Somehow, he found the strength to squeeze past the grasping apparition and out of the room.

He fled into the street, running madly. The shapeless, faceless horror swept through the city behind him, devouring the population. He raced through dark, empty streets, but it followed him—hunted him. Decimation surrounded Alex. The thing's influence was everywhere.

Alex raced blindly around a corner and found himself trapped in a dark alley.

The beast surged forward.

Alex was surrounded by moans and the noxious stench of death. It closed on him, the festering mass of blood-choked folds enveloping him. He was suffocating...drowning.

He tried to scream, but his mouth filled with the sickening viral puss. The groans and wails of the dead screamed in his ears....

Alex bolted up in bed, his face and body soaked with sweat. He buried his face in his trembling hands, trying to shut out the images from his sleep. His ears buzzed with sound and his head was spinning. He choked and gaged, and felt as though he was going to be sick.

Yet there was still a sound in his ears—a strange, yet somehow familiar sound.

"Iä! Iä! Q'yth-az fhtagn," came the sound on the night air.

Alex slid out of bed and hurried to the window, still shaking from his nightmare. In the moonlight he could see a lone frail figure on the beach, its face turned toward the sky.

The figure was Tim. He was radiant with pale light.

"Iä! Iä! Q'yth-az fhtagn, Q'yth-az fhtagn. Yhrii ng'lah nogg-yron. Q'yth-az Mthura wgah'nagl fhtagn," came the sweet voice out of Tim's mouth. "Come to the light. Come to truth," he beckoned.

The wind began to howl, and waves dashed against the beach, throwing foam and sand into the air. In the dark sky above, clouds parted. Light from countless stars shone down upon the figure on the beach.

Alex noticed the queer crackling sound in the air as he stepped off the bungalow deck and onto the sand. From out of the corner of his eye he spotted movement. Others hand been drawn to the commotion on the beach.

"Come to the light. Come to Q'yth-az," said the voice from Tim's mouth. The voice that was at once Tim's and yet was not Tim's. It was crisp and hollow and sounded somehow far-off.

Tim was rigid, and his eyes stared wide into the heavens. Something glowed in his hand. A crystal. The stiff, gaunt form held the mineral in a death-grip, his hand white and trembling.

"Tim!" shouted Alex as he ran toward his companion.

The others neared. Albert and Rose Gray fell to their knees, their arms outstretched to Tim. The warm wind blew sand into their faces and between the folds of their nightgowns. "He has made contact!" screamed Mrs. Gray.

The surf frothed, churning up foam and spray.

The radiance from the crystal intensified and spread, bathing Tim in a brilliant, scintillating light. The sand around him began to steam. Sharp crystalline growths sprouted around his feet, sparkling weirdly in the moonlight.

"The way from Mthura is clear. Come to the light," came the odd voice from Tim's mouth. Crystallizing sand began creeping snake-like up his legs, encasing him in a sparkling shell.

"Tim!" screamed Alex, blowing sand stinging his eyes.

Randy Shaw, dressed only in shorts, approached from behind a bungalow. His normally-neat hair was tousled and his eyes were blurry with sleep. Reverend Williams appeared from behind the young gymnast.

"The mineral binds and builds. It is one with me—I with it," the voice came again. Tim's flesh began to take on a transparent, glassy look. He was rigid, his skin hard like glass. Jagged shards of faceted crystal sprouted from his body. "Tim Ridgeway is no more. Now there is only Q'yth-az," the melodious voice was now in Alex's mind.

A scream forced its way from Alex's throat. Sand and salty spray blew around him as the howling wind continued to churn the sea.

The alien, luminescent form grew rapidly, stretching into the dark night sky.

The air was electrified with an intense crackling.

"Since time immemorial, Q'yth-az has been. Before life sprouted on this world, Q'yth-az walked among the stars with His brethren," the voice sounded in the minds of everyone on the beach, becoming louder and more alien as the thing grew and spread.

Within moments, nothing remained of Tim Ridgeway.

The alien mineral formation towered above the assembled group, a cluster of colossal crystals, glinting with an unnatural inner-light. Shifting and growing—expanding and shrinking. Enormous faceted crystals sprouted like blossoms from the towering mass. An insane display of color and light sparkled and flashed through the looming, translucent entity. Colors that had never been seen by man—light that seared the eyes with alien brilliance.

From out of the formation swept long tendrils of sharp crystal, spreading frost-like across the ground. The thing grew and spread. Wherever a tendril touched a living thing, it caused the minerals to change—to take over. Every living thing touched was frozen into hard, glassy rock, preserved forever in mineral formations.

"Come to the light," resonated a sharp voice within their minds, "know truth." Frost-like tendrils spread toward the Grays.

The old couple prostrated themselves before the entity, eager to make contact with the crystalline intelligence.

The crackling formations swept over them, encasing them in an icy shimmer. Rose Gray moaned once as the living cells in her body were petrified. Instantly, the Gray's wrinkled flesh hardened. All color and life drained away.

Gustav Pfohl pulled his wife close to his body, shielding her face with a strong arm. A snaking tendril struck them, uniting them in a silent eternity.

Jagged shards of lightning flashed around the gleaming entity. Sharp spikes of weirdly-colored crystal erupted from the thing while others shrank away. A maelstrom of color and light bathed the beach, and delicate-looking tentacles continued to shoot forth and shrink back into the cluster of mineral spires.

Randy Shaw glanced over his shoulder. He saw only large lumps of crystalline rock where he had seen Reverend Williams and Danny and Judy McQuillan moments before. He had heard no screams, no pleas for assistance. Now there was only the sound of the wind and the surf and the crackling of the air. And there was the voice in his head. The sweet, shrill voice that beckoned him forward. Urged him to go to the light.

A tendril of frost slithered past Randy's feet. A half-dozen shards of rock sprang from the smoldering sand. The young man heard the voice boom in his mind again. He squeezed his eyes tight, clamped sinewy hands over his ears. The voice just echoed, and weird shadows danced across the blackness.

There was a churning in his gut; searing bile rose in his throat. The sand smelled hot, and he could feel the ground beneath his feet tremble.

The young man took a few blind steps. He felt something against his legs just as he lost his balance and toppled to the sand.

Randy found himself staring into the craggy, mineral-etched features of Rose Gray. Her mouth and eyes were frozen into a grimace. He touched her with a trembling hand. She was icy and hard like a great chunk of glass.

Cold perspiration beaded on the young man's body. Sand ground into his knees and stomach, sticking to his damp, clammy flesh.

Another tentacle whipped by Randy. He smelled the sand melt—felt the blast of cold air as the thing darted past him.

He staggered to his feet, his eyes trained on the looming colossus of crystal and light. He couldn't look away...wouldn't look away. He felt free—like he was floating. A psychedelic field of color and light played past his vision, and in his head Randy heard the musical voice. The soothing voice. The voice of God.

"Yes, God," Randy Shaw mumbled as he took a step toward the entity.

"Run!" shrieked Alex.

The young gymnast responded by taking another step toward the glowing obelisk.

The ground began to smoke and bubble. A line of glimmering shards sprang up.

Alex dove at Randy, knocking him to his back as another tentacle cut shark-like through the sand.

Randy Shaw felt as though the wind has been knocked out of him. His mind cleared and he felt the coarseness of the sand grinding into his bare back. He bolted to his feet.

"Get out of here!" bellowed Alex. He gave the young man a shove, sending him almost off balance.

Randy caught himself, and turned to run.

A crackling tendril whipped across the sand, a forest of mineral shards sprouting in its wake.

Randy caught his foot on a sharp rocky spike. He staggered and fell, the sand darkening with the small trickle of his blood.

The tendril swept over the young man. Spiny crystals stabbed into his back and the back of his legs, cutting into the soft flesh.

A wail of pain poured from Randy's throat.

The killer frost spread up his legs.

"My god, help me!" he pleaded. The alien growth spread up his muscled form like a blanket. Organs and tissues began hardening. He felt the blood painfully congeal in his veins—his flesh turning to stone.

Randy Shaw sobbed once, and then he was silent.

The crystalline tendril shrank back to the towering rocky column where it was absorbed into the glittering mass. Other frost-like appendages spread out and were absorbed back in, like some great marine creature feeling out its surroundings, groping for food.

The brilliant, scintillating light blinded Alex. The crackling sound deafened him.

More ropes of frost shot across the ground.

In his mind, Alex heard the voice, "Come to the light. Come to Q'yth-az. Come to God."

He backed away from the crystal colossus.

Something exploded.

Gunfire.

The large Samoan appeared from behind Alex, a small pistol in hand. Two more shots rang out, striking home. Shards of the thing fell away. More crystalline appendages flowed across the beach.

The sky began to cloud.

The Samoan was knocked to the ground by a mass of sharp mineral-formations that sprang from beneath him. He was grasped by an icy tentacle. Within seconds he knew peace.

"The mineral binds and builds. It is in everything. Q'yth-az is in everything," came the voice in Alex's head again. "Come to the light," it repeated.

Alex stood alone on the beach, facing the giant scintillating formation. He was alone with the entity.

Thunder rumbled through the heavens.

He watched as the frost-like appendages shrank back to the craggy bulk of the towering thing. For several seconds the two beings were motionless. Alex was numb. He stood gazing up at the alien obelisk, his mind cold and blank.

A large tendril formed. It raced toward him. Mineral formations exploded from the ground.

It came nearer and nearer.

A veil grew thicker over the moon and stars.

The sand at Alex's feet began to smoke and melt. He felt an odd vibration begin to resonate through his body.

Lightning flashed.

It was upon him.

Rain began to fall. Lightning cut through the storm-darkened sky. Thick, black clouds rolled over. The stars in the heavens were obscured, their ageless light shut out.

When authorities arrived at the Center for Holistic Healing, they found no signs of the guests or the staff of the center. The buildings showed obvious signs of recent use—clothing and luggage of guests were found in bungalows—yet there was no trace of human life. Most of the beds for the staff and guests appeared to have been slept in. It looked as though everyone had left abruptly in the middle of the night, yet all vehicles were accounted for.

A dazed figure was discovered wandering absently on the beach. He was unresponsive to questioning, mumbling incoherently. He held a small crystal tightly in one hand, and became violent when police attempted to remove it. Paramedics sedated the dark-haired young man, and as he slipped into unconsciousness his mumbling became coherent enough to understand. He was responding to a voice which only he heard. Brown eyes wide and staring, he gazed into the heavens. "Yes God," he sobbed as he fell limp.

Oahu police found a gun lying near a large rock formation. It had been fired, but at what? The incoherent man was the only living thing found on the beach, and there were no traces of blood to be found.

Several unusual rock formations littered the beach. Authorities traced tracks up to the formations but there they strangely ceased. There was something disturbing about the mysterious rocks. They did not originate on the beach, and had obviously been deposited there. But for what purpose? And stranger still, why were they formed into human-like shapes?

SCENE: A Room

by

CRAIG ANTHONY
(With thanks to Sam J. Hare.)

"Let it be known that there are two doors in: the mind and the body. And then that feast, where there are only but closed doors."

—The Pnakotic Manuscripts

SCENE: (*A room. The walls are bare but for cracks and thumbtack holes and stains and streaks of dirt. The floor is bare but for dust and crumbs and furrows along the floor boards from furniture previously present and conspicuously absent. The ceiling is bare but for its own stucco and a hanging lamp, lit. A window gapes upon.... A door is closed. A clock (a clock?) is ticking. A man is upon the floor sleeping. As the scene opens, he stirs, rolls, stirs, blinks, opens eyes, stares, moves arm, moves hand, rolls, sits up, shakes head, runs hand along stubbled cheek, turns his head to look around the bare room.*)

—What?...(*Moans, presses fingers into eyes. Groggy thoughts: Is I dazed? Am he been drinking? Are mental faculties functioning at a satisfactory level given the nature of the state of his recent my recent recumbent umbent—*)

> (ENTER: *The* EMPEROR. *The* EMPEROR *has not so much entered as come into focus as a thing to be apprehended as something apart from the already visible setting yet upon awareness of entrant not necessarily having already been present despite the sensation as a thing ing that has not ot already eady entered—*)

> > EMPEROR: Tall, pale as driftwood, a hoary beard flecked with yellow {stains,} in regal robes {purple and red and ermine and white leopard's fur,} some armour {greaves, gauntlets, of light mail.} and a crown {gold,} A sphere with cross is in his left hand {drops} and a scepter is in his right hand {drops.}

> > (EMPEROR *reels, cavorts, steadies himself, stands. Man stands, backs off in horror, stares at the newcomer.*)

—Who....

EMPEROR: (*Aside*) The melancholy hour approaches, and nothing
     may withstand that which necessitates you truculent desires. For each
     beginning there is an anointing; a cleansing. (*Implores ceiling.*) Even for
     you, your unholy majesty.

     (*Audience: Laughter. The* EMPEROR *grins* {teeth: blackened
     stubs.} *He turns to face the man.*)

EMPEROR: (*To man*) There is much, lamb, which exceeds your
     knowledge, much which defies the blackest of hearts. Sanity is fleeting;
     pluck the fruit—unrind me as you will—and soon taste the nectar that
     false essence betrays by virtue of creation.

     (*Pause. Man is still.* EMPEROR *clears his throat.*)

EMPEROR: I said taste the nectar that false essence betrays—

—Who are you? What is this? Who—where am I?

     (*Audience: Startled.*)

EMPEROR: (*Shocked, then quizzical*) In medias res? ...Ah, surely. There
     would be a gap for a non-adept of course. Hmm.... This requires....
     (*Gesticulating, motioning up and at. Audience: Observant.*) Foreshadow
     flashback! Background up front.

     (*Audience: Grudging accordance.*)

EMPEROR: (*To man*) Attend and learn, though this may appear to
     have little to do with you, insect....

     (EMPEROR *moves forward as man, confused, steps back.*)

EMPEROR: (*Obsequious at center stage*) There was a king who wore a
     mask and when that mask fell the subjects fell after. But masks must
     fall so ever more subjects must gather. Did I add the necessity of meat?
     Yes. When a certain book is opened it will not be closed. So a reader
     must be ushered in. Through any access. Footnote: physical likeness.
     Lastly, curtains up. (*Simpering smile.*) In a nut's hell. (*Audience: Reserved
     chortling.*) Now then: Ushers forward!

     (*Clock's hands swing counterclockwise. Door swings open.*
     POLICEMAN, *clad in blue, stands in doorway.*)

POLICEMAN: Mister Mitchell? Sir, there's been a...circumstance
     upstairs. We want to make sure you're all right. All right then.

(*Door swings shut. Clock hands whirls counterclockwise. Door swings open. LANDLORD, stout and repulsive, chomping cigar, wears a dirty tank-top.*)

LANDLORD: (*Dialogue, rent and irascibility. Evokes nature of the establishment: A run-down hovel for losers all, dreamers doped, drug fiends, welfare whores, fly-by-nights, one night fucks, end of the liners, secret strangers. He holds a paper of legal lease in his hand.*)

PAPER: Signed: Jacob Earwick.

(*Door swings shut. Clock hands whirl clockwise. EMPEROR steps forward and hands man a newspaper.*)

NEWSPAPER: ACID LAB DESTROYED! Lysergic Diethylamide, no less! One Man Found Dead (Murdered!) Shambles! Debris! Room Alone Is Damaged(!)! Chemicals Commingled! Please Bring A Gasmask.

EMPEROR: (*Wiping a tear*) Ah, Memories.

Tap, tap, tap.

(*Clock hands return to their places. EMPEROR steps forward and hands man a key.*)

EMPEROR: Now then. Come. We mustn't dally.

(*Audience: Murmuring.*)

"Michael?"

—What is going on here? I—I don't understand all this. Who are you?

EMPEROR: The book. We will need the book. The book.

Tap, tap. "Michael? Michael say you're awake. The Landlord's out and we need to—"

—What book? What are you talking about?

EMPEROR: The book! The book! The book!

—What book you fucking—what the fuck is all this?

Tap, tap! "Michael? What's going on? Michael, it's Jess!"

EMPEROR: (*Points*) The book in the floor.

(*Man turns to look where indicated by the direction of the pointing of the finger of the— A floorboard among floorboards bears a tiny brass lock. This floorboard is no floorboard! Man looks again to EMPEROR, then slowly shuts his eyes and slowly bows his head.*)

—I don't understand...I don't know what is....

EMPEROR: Yes, you are beginning to. I can tell. Now go get the
     book again.

Tap, tap! "Michael, let me in! Michael, it's Jess and I'm here, now let
me in!"

     (*Audience: Angry shifting.*)

EMPEROR: (*Nervous*) Quickly. The book.

—(*Slowly*) I...I just don't....

EMPEROR: (*To grumbling Audience*) Patience! Please! (*Pause*) It is
     evident that we require the Chorus.

     (*Audience: Settling.*)

EMPEROR: Chorus!

     (*The clock spins crazily. Enter* CHORUS. *Two figures of a
     cadaverous nature, shriven, glassy-eyed, staggering, in robes of white
     splashed with gore, approach. Figure one bears a placard around the
     neck that bears the inscription: One Man Found Dead; figure two
     a small panel that reads: Ditto. They caper past, opening their
     mouths to speak, yet with the Man's voice.*)

FIGURE ONE— Jess, you're into the occult, tell me. You know
     something about a French play, late nineteenth century, author
     unknown? It's been linked to various obscure occult sects, some even
     earlier than the date it was supposedly written. I've encountered five
     separate references to it in researching my thesis—even one in this, God,
     this sickly-sweet Celtic Twilight poem.

FIGURE TWO— No it's on Victorian age drama on the continent.
     Here let me have a hit. Will you sleep with me?

     (*Audience: Boos.* CHORUS *continues to shuffle across the room.*)

FIGURE ONE— Jess, come on, you don't believe all that. Look, if I
     get a hold of this it will be a neat little addition to my paper. Bill, you
     know, Bill's Books? Anyway, says he has a lead for me, "snare" he called
     it. A collector name of Earwick. Oh, now you *may* know an Earwick
     yourself, huh? Really.

FIGURE TWO— A little apartment way over on the east end, told
     me to meet him there. If I pretend I'm interested in the occult, will
     you drive out and let me feel your breasts?

     (*Audience: Hisses.* CHORUS *staggers.*)

FIGURE ONE— Yeah, it's me, I—I don't feel so well. No he wasn't
     here, I'm here alone. It was unlocked, so I looked around. Empty and

all so I thought I'd been had but there was this key on the floor and, well, I found it! I just read a page and of course now this headache. Yeah I know you told me to wait but come on it's just—what? What's wrong? What do you mean they'll need access now? Who? Are you all right—

FIGURE TWO— No there's no pictures in here. *No,* I'm not planning on getting stoned—what is wrong with you? More information on the play? Okay, okay, just— please hurry over. I'm not feeling so well and I do so need your wet flesh your wet raw flesh—

—(*Aghast*) No!

> (*Audience: Boos and hisses.* CHORUS *"exits."*)

EMPEROR: Thank you Bill, Thank you One Man. Fine exposition there. (*Clicking his tongue at man.*) Pathetic. Still, we're so happy you've arrived.

> (*The man, nonplused, begins to tremble, staring off into space, pace, ace, ace, ace—*)

EMPEROR: The book.
"Michael!"

> (*Man goes to the floorboard that is not a floorboard that is a floorboard that is not a floorboard that— He kneels, unlocks it, pauses, pulls it open. A small recess holds the book. Man pulls it out, then winces at the sight and touch of it.*)

—Oh no....

Tap! Tap! Tap! "Michael who are you talking to—oh Christ. Michael! Open the door!"

> (EMPEROR *gazes at the man, eyes resting upon him softly as, thinks the man, a beast to its meat.*)

EMPEROR: Ah. Now then. We will continue. You know the page.
—This can't be happening....

> (*Audience: Further angry shifting.* EMPEROR *is fearful, then angry himself at the man.*)

EMPEROR: (*To man*) Up, insect! Ready your meat! (*Continuing*) When the king takes the knife, the sheep will be carved and the blood will spill down his mad climax—
—No! Wait! (*Aware and terrified*) I took the precautions! This can't be!

Bang! Bang! "Dammit, let me in! Listen to me! A tenant told me there was an acid lab—Jesus Christ, I can smell it in the wood...."

(*Audience: Grumbles, groans.*)

"Michael! You've got to get away from here!"

EMPEROR: (*Pointing at the ceiling, smiling*) The doors of perception, my friend. There is always a way in.

(*Man looks up at the stuccoed, tuccoed, shuccoed, succoed, uccoed, uccoed, code, ode, ode, ode— He grabs his head, book to temple, and winces, as if to squeeze the drug free.*)

(*Audience: Grumbling, and amused grumbling.*)

—(*Fearful*) Only a page! Only one page! (*He throws book.*)

EMPEROR: A single word is all you need to read.

"Goddammit!" Bang! Bang! "Michael, don't pick up that book again! Listen to me. This was all a trap. Earwick is a sorcerer! Now unlock the door!"

—(*Frightened*) There is no access! I did what Jess said and there's no access!

"Oh my god...Michael! Whoever it is don't listen to it! Just walk away and open the door slowly. Just a bad contact high. That's all it is. It's nothing—don't...Do you hear me?"

(EMPEROR *smiles wide*)

"Michael! Listen! No physical likeness means no physical access—it's okay, just open the door! I'm here!"

—No access!

EMPEROR: Ah, but there is.

(EMPEROR *kneels, stretches hand to floorboards. A finger digs, and an object is pulled from the space between the floorboards. A single card is held up. The reverse is blue vines; the painted side bears a picture of a seated figure, pale as driftwood, a hoary beard, in armour and regal robes, holding a scepter and globe.*)

—(*Despairful*) The Emperor....

EMPEROR: (*Shaking his head*) Alas no. Only meat for the one true emperor.

"Michael! Don't listen to it! Open the door! Please!" Bang! Bang!

EMPEROR: There are many masks, but only one may wear the pallid
    one. He who shuffles from the shore in his tattered mantle.

—(*Inquiring of speaker*) Earwick?

EMPEROR: (*Smiling acquiescence*) Of this form, now, your guide
    and...play mate. (*He smiles.*) Now all doors may close.

—....

EMPEROR: Serendipity. You see you were, as was I, ready just in time
    for this present performance. You'll do well for a matinee. (*Smirks.*)
    Meat is meat. For here the plot is actually secondary to the reaction. To
    the climax. (*Waves hand around.*) *And don't you admire the staging, the*
    props, the background. (*Points.*) Absolutely authentic.

"Michael!" Bang! Bang! "Please!" Bang!

> (*Man turns gaze to window, newly aware, then turns away, newly,*
> *awfully aware. His features are aghast, his eyes wide and white*
> *with horror. EMPEROR turns his head towards window, calmly,*
> *then back to rest upon the reeling, cowering, kneeling, huffing,*
> *mind-blasted man.*)

—Hali...Hali....

EMPEROR: Hmm. Well then. (*Kneeling to retrieve book, then extending it*
    towards the stricken, recumbent form) You know the page.

EMPEROR: (*Turning away, continuing.*) And so this melancholy hour
    approaches....

    (*Audience: Laughter.*)

"What is all this shit anyways?" He jingled his keys. "Dragging me
from Charley's middle of a game and all will ya turn you lousy little—"
He turned the key, and Jess slammed open the door the moment it
clicked. The door banged against the wall. Jess pushed the hair from
her eyes.

    The room was empty.

    "Dumb bitch—What's I tell you! No one's here! The next time you
go off your freakin' head, do it somewhere else, hah? Murders and
jerk-offs...." The stout landlord, muttering, threw his cigar down and
walked away, waving off the other tenants who goggled and peered
down the hall.

    Jess entered the room slowly and stood at its center. She heaved a
sigh of remorse. The room was empty. A dusty window gaped upon a
brackish morning sky. The room was empty.

    Oh, Michael. She walked over and knelt beside a floorboard that was
erect upon a hinge. The niche beneath it was vacant. Seventy-five miles
too late, she thought. She shook her head, then paused. Her hand

reached out towards the only other object within the room. She held up a faded, battered tarot card. She stared at the seated figure, a glassey-eyed king, and closed her eyes.

Oh Michael.

> SCENE: *A room. There is an open book.* MICHAEL *and* EM-PEROR *stand. looking about, up, down, around. The clock is silent. All is still. {Beyond the window, the lake of Hali, newly vacant, is now still.} Their visages are locked in twin rictuses of terror. They are now themselves still. All is as quiet as dead space.)*

Audience:
EMPEROR: Here it comes.

> (*Enter the* KING IN YELLOW.)

The Seven Cities of Gold

by

CRISPIN BURNHAM

There are those who believe that humanity was not the first intelligence upon this planet, and that it will not be the last. These groups believe that those who once ruled here will return one day and wipe humanity away. Some of these cults wish to speed up that very day.

— *The Book of Strange Cults*, Dr. Edmund Samuel
(University of Kansas Press, 1991)

THE EVENTS OF March 26 thru June 21, 1993, really did happen. The disappearance of Dr. Edmund Samuel and Louise, his wife, was not the work of some madman. The deaths in the Dunwich excavations were not, as the newspapers reported, merely an accidental cave-in. They were the direct result of attacks by beings who had lived here in America long before humanity entered the trees. They were murdered by beings whose civilization was old when dinosaurs had yet to fully evolve.

I also have a very good idea about the June 21st disappearance of Professor William Atkins in the Flint Hills. I know these things because I had worked with the Samuels on their final research into the missing inhabitants of the small Kansas settlement of Dunwich. Dunwich was a ghost town that had been founded by settlers from the Miskatonic valley region of Massachusetts. It originally interested us when we came across some old tales and gossip that said the settlers had been driven west because of some curse, but no evidence has ever been uncovered to verify that claim.

It was reported that the settlers of Dunwich would have little to do with the other communities in that section of Kansas; except some reports of their selling of commerce to the shunned town of Harkness in the Dwayne Valley about twenty miles South of Lawrence. Dunwich took a neutral stand during the battle between the Free Staters and the Slave Staters; though again there were ominous rumors. And finally the entire population mysteriously vanished in 1893.

The legends and tall tales surrounding their disappearances are indeed strange. One claim is that a freak tornado sucked them all up, another speaks of an old Indian curse; or that the Indians wiped them out. The latter legend was dismissed due to the fact that the town itself was relatively untouched by the departure of the inhabitants; Indian attack tend to leave obvious clues. Although the damage reportedly suffered by some of the homes was similar to a tornado, it was much less than would be caused by a wind strong enough to suck up all the people. The Indian curse idea can be dismissed, because the townsfolk had no contact with the local tribes.

So it was decided that I would look at the original settlement of Dunwich, Massachusetts, to see if I could find any solid clues into the disappearance of the Kansas settlers.

I flew to Boston on January 12th and rode the bus to Arkham. At Miskatonic University I searched through their library for any records concerning the era of the migration. After several hours of fruitless search I found a related reference in a book titled *Devils and Demons in Miskatonic Valley*, by Henry Armitage. The important section reads:

> In the year Eighteen Hundred and Thirty-Three the Reverend Eezekial O'Sullivan led his followers into the Western Territories. Property was purchased from Mr. Amos Lawrence; the man who had started the settlements of Lawrence and Amoston. The reasons for O'Sullivan's extreme eagerness to move westward have only recently been uncovered by the Author. First, Rev. O'Sullivan claimed a "vision" of a perfect land in that area which he said was the legendary seven cities of gold. Secondly, while at Innsmouth, Rev. O'Sullivan had some dealings with an esoteric order and later spoke of having received, from them, knowledge and some "thing" which would allow him to work with the inhabitants of those fabled cities. From the experience I received in the Whateley incident, I know of these beings. For further information I refer the reader to page 1816 of the Wormius edition of the *Necronomicon*.

I stopped reading and went to the head librarian to request access to their fabled *Necronomicon*. As an academic in good standing I was granted permission and ushered into one of the private reading rooms. There I watched as the large, old book was taken out of a wall vault; where it was stored with other rare occult tomes, like *The Book of Eibon, Unausprechlichan Kulten, Cultes des Goules*, and *The Black Book of the Skull*.

I was more than a little unnerved when the library insisted on having two armed guards in the room while I read the elder text, but, thankfully my stay was not to be very long. My Latin is excellent and I quickly had the following translation of page 1816:

> In the times when The Old Ones ruled, Othuyeg gave to its servitors the seven golden cities. These cities were as magnificent as they were terrible. Blood sacrifices were made to many Old Ones and it is said that Nyarlathotep ruled there in the form of the Dark Man. Contact was made with Black Zathog, the master of the Zarrians. Their intention was to open the gate and allow the Zarrians to destroy the Pain Lords, *even at the cost of all time and space*. In the time when The Old Ones fell, the seven golden cities were cut off from the surface world and remanded to deep fissures.

I sat there and shuddered to think that the Rev. O'Sullivan might have known the location of those cities and felt he had the power to return the Great Old Ones to the Earth. Just thinking about it gave me great dread, for I had heard rumors about the town of Harkness, where they say such monsters as Jack the Ripper lived. I had heard it said that many, if not all the residents of that town worshipped a dark god called Othuyeg, which lurked deep beneath the Kansas limestone caverns. I had also heard reports of a similar creature in Germany and had read many of the myths surrounding the Old Ones. The sheer number of coincidences bothered me.

I returned to the Armitage book and found this reference to his assessment of the events leading up to the Kansas disappearances:

> The end began on April 29th 1893, when the farm of Ezra Wallace was destroyed by something unknown. The house had been blown apart from the inside. The entire Wallace family was missing along with all of their livestock. Not a single spot of blood was found anywhere on the farm.
>
> After several weeks of fruitless searching, the sheriff asked a Circuit Judge James Mayo to declare the Wallace family dead.
>
> Three days later a sink hole appeared in the center of the main town road, swallowing the Abel Zelick family and their wagon. The sheriff had his deputies put up a fence around the pit and keep people back, but that evening, and for several more nights, strange sounds issued from deep in the pit. Some townsfolk claimed to hear human screams.
>
> Four days later, Jeb Wilson was seen staggering very near the pit's edge when something described as white tentacles seized him and pulled him into the pit. There was not any mistaking the screams of Jeb Wilson that evening. People kept far back from the pit.
>
> It did not matter.

On June 21st, 1893, Circuit Judge Mayo came to Dunwich on his route and found it empty of human life or any activity; even the strange pit was gone. Judge Mayo went into several of the buildings and found some of them to be damaged like the Wallace farm. He remembered the screams he had heard from the pit and left town quickly before nightfall.

The next day he had returned with a posse from Lawrence and a thorough search was conducted. The only piece of evidence that the posse uncovered was a cryptic note that had been left at the office of the town paper. It read: *"There are everywhere. We are doomed! Out of the pit. Like in the third warning of The Black Book of the Skull."*

The note was dated July 3rd, 1893.

I returned to the rare book room and got access to their edition of *The Black Book of the Skull*. The third warning begins on the 140th page and reads:

Beware of that which lives under thy feet for one night it will rise up to take thee. For it is known that beneath central Cakatomia, lurks Great Othuyeg and his spawn. Trapped for eons, they wait for when they can reclaim the land above their sunken cities.

* * *

I flew back to Kansas City the next day and brought my notes, and my concerns, to the Samuels.

"This is exactly what we have been looking for. All that remains is for us to go and see the site ourselves."

"When?"

"Spring Break starts in two weeks. We will try to get it organized for that whole week."

It was Friday when they called. I was listening to Pavarotti singing "Nessum Dorma" and sipping a glass of Beaujolais when the call came.

"This is Professor Samuel, the trip to the Dunwich site is on. Will you be ready to go next Sunday."

"I'll be ready."

"Excellent. I knew you wouldn't let us down. Wilson is sending his best graduate student, from the Geology department to take seismic readings, Dr. Brandon is going along to help us identify and anthropological discoveries and I called Dwayne University and got permission to borrow their copy of *The Black Book of the Skull*."

That last comment reawakened the deep concerns I was having about this whole mystery and sent chills up my spine. "What do we need with that book, sir?" I asked.

"Well, Frank, Louise and I had done some research on that book and there are some passages I think we might need at the site...to help solve the mystery of the disappearances. You do understand this, don't you, Frank?"

"Not completely, but I'll defer to you judgment."

"Excellent. I'll see you early Sunday morning."

* * *

That Sunday saw us all gathered together outside of Lindley Hall. The group included the Samuels, Marie Ingelman, a graduate student and an old girlfriend, My good friend Dr. Earl Brandon of the Anthropology department, Suzanne Comb of the Geology department with tons of seismic equipment, seven more assorted students and myself. We were organized and loaded into the bus by Eight-Thirty and off to our first destination; Dwayne University.

It was a half hour drive from Lawrence to Amoston where Dwayne University is located. It is not as large a school as KU, but their library boasts the largest collection of arcane lore this far west of Miskatonic.

A point Dwayne has over Miskatonic is their edition of *The Black Book of the Skull*. Dwayne's copy is an earlier and more accurate, Greek edition. It is said that the Latin scribes had refused, even on pain of death, to translate several sections. Academics can be pretty stubborn, as we discovered when Dr. Atkins got into a heated discussion with Prof. Samuel about the actual loaning of the book.

"Edmund! This is the one copy of the Greek edition known to have survived the Inquisition's burnings. If something were to happen to it...."

"Nothing will happen to it, William. It will be under my direct care."

"You can't guarantee that an accident won't happen."

This went on until a compromise was finally reached. The passages that Prof. Samuel thought would be of value were photocopied. Dr. Atkins *still* seemed to have his misgivings when it came to the book for he continued to voice his concerns.

"What about that investor from Arkham that tried to buy this very book and his horrible death. Then there was the case of Arthur Gillings, who went mad while trying to translate it, and what about that fire which burnt every book near *The Black Book of the Skull* but left it untouched. Explain those away with promises to be careful."

"William, you of all people should know that I am always careful with such arcane lore. You were present when I solved that case of the Yig cult in Oklahoma."

"It was a miracle we got out of there with our lives. Edmund, I have a bad feeling about this, *a fatal fear about this....*"

"Don't worry, we'll take every precaution. Think of it William, the Seven Cities of Gold. We could find what Coronado and his Spaniards couldn't. Think of the notoriety, the book rights alone...."

"Stop. Okay, you've got your copies. Let me get my bags."

"How long do you need to pack?"

"Edmund, you know me. I'm always packed."

* * *

We reached the ruins of Dunwich around sundown, pitched our tents, ate dinner and turned in of the night.

On the first day of the dig we set up the volunteer students to mark off the area surrounding the site of the town's refuse dump. Marie supervised the students while the rest of us checked out what remained of the town's buildings. A century of neglect had not been kind. There wasn't enough material left to judge the validity of the stories about the buildings being torn out from within. We returned to the campsite just as Marie had gotten the site ready for digging. But by evening, nothing had been dug out of the area to give us any clues as to either the disappearances or Professor Samuel's cities of gold.

We all turned in early that night to get a fresh start in the morning, but Dr. Brandon and I shared a tent and we talked for several hours about nothing important until we both dozed off to sleep.

Late Sunday morning, Marie made the first discovery at the site. She was working near the center of what we determined was the town's refuse area when she recovered a small statuette. Dr. Atkins studied it for only a moment before he sent a student to retrieve the Samuels and myself from where we were helping Suzanne set up the seismic equipment. The gray stone statuette was as large as my palm and looked like a mass of tentacles surrounding a single cyclopean eye.

"Othuyeg," remarked Professor Samuel.

"Or one of his spawn," added Louise.

"But, why would anyone buried here?" I asked.

"Who knows," said Dr. Brandon. "Maybe someone threw it away, or they put it here on purpose as a ward of some kind."

Prof. Samuel smiled, "This confirms our suspicions about the towns belief in the Seven Cities."

Just then another student, working beside Marie, called out in surprise as he frantically worked something else loose from the soil. "I've found something else here."

We looked into the pit as the student handed Marie a gold colored cylinder about a foot long and four inches thick.

"It has some strange carvings all the way around the base." Marie said as she passed it up to Dr. Atkins. "Some sort of Hieroglyphics, I think."

"Yes but not Egyptian," said Dr. Atkins.

"It's not Sumerian or Mayan either," added Louise as she looked the case over.

In the center of each end was a depiction of the same creature as the statuette, with several smaller versions surrounding it in an intertwined mosaic of bas-relief curves.

"Definitely Othuyeg." Remarked Dr. Atkins.

"We had better leave it closed until we get under better controlled conditions back in Lawrence." Professor Samuel said. This was quickly agreed to and I returned to the tents to clean and catalog our finds.

We dug around the area, but found nothing else before darkness fell and we quit for the night. I had turned in for the evening and was sound asleep when Prof. Samuel came tugging on my tent around midnight.

"We've found something that you should see."

I rose and dressed quietly, so as not to awaken Dr. Brandon and crossed or small camp to the Samuels' tent. He, Louis and Dr. Atkins were gathered around the photocopied passages from *The Black Book of the Skull*. "We've found a reference that *definitely* points to the Seven Cities," Professor Samuel explained excitedly.

"Yes, read the translation I've made," chimed in Dr. Atkins.

I did, and this is what it said:

It is said that within the Seven Cities of Gold, much wealth exists but is guarded by the Spawns of Othuyeg. It is also said that none could enter the cities, not even Yog-Sothoth, except on the day of the longest sun. Only lord Azathoth can enter it at will, even those blessed by Othuyeg with the knowledge of the spells and the seal must only attempt to enter on that one day.

Very few have entered The Seven Cities. I, J'Cak Igguratian, the scribe of Quy, once made that journey. I had sailed with the adventurer Rogos to the land of Cakatomia and traveled by foot northwestward across the great wide plains, to reach the outposts of Harkn'ss. There we waited for the day of the longest sun, when the very earth opened and we were allowed into the first of the seven cities.

It was a fabulous place where the streets and the buildings themselves were covered in gold. The center of the first city was decorated with statues to Cthulhu, Azathoth and Quyagen; which was a welcome sign for me, although Rogos claimed that it didn't look a thing like him.

It was a day's journey in the underground darkness to the second city which had its center graced by large statues of Nyarlathotep, Yig and Yog-Sothoth. Thus we journeyed to the third, and fourth cities; which were separated by a great river. There we were given strange fruits to eat and glorious wines, so we halted for several days.

Too soon though, we proceeded through the remaining cities until we arrived in the seventh city where the Spawns of Othuyeg reside. Here only one statue filled the central plaza, that of Othuyeg himself. It was a terrifying sight and the people of the seventh city were quick to attack us. Only Rogos and I escaped from a horrible fate and it was with great gratitude that I beheld the sun again. If you must travel to the Seven Cities, travel not to the seventh city or you shall suffer the same fate as those with me.

I looked up at the three of them; doctors and professors in their fields and respected authorities in the scientific community. "You're not seriously thinking of looking for the Seven Cities of Gold, after reading this?"

"Why not?"

"Are you mad? What about those disappearances nearly one hundred years ago? What about this translation?"

"We'll avoid the seventh city."

"Fine, chase after your treasure hordes, but you can't do anything until June Twenty-First."

They exchanged glances. "You're right, the summer solstice, the longest day of the year," said Dr. Atkins.

"So I think a second expedition would be in order." Added Prof. Samuel.

"Then, let us concentrate on the Dunwich disappearances." Louise said. "We only have a few more days of Spring Break."

We spoke for several more minutes then I excused myself and headed back to bed. When I was just outside my tent, Suzanne waved me over to the tent she was sharing with Marie.

"What's the scoop?" she asked as she nodded her head back toward the Samuels' tent.

"Talk of underground cities and mythic creatures," I said rather off-handedly.

"Really? I have noticed some quite peculiar contours in the land around this area, as if someone had been strip mining here centuries ago. Of course that's impossible for the Indians of this region didn't use limestone for building purposes. I wonder what their could have been digging for?" I shuddered, remembering what I had read about the mysterious limestone mines found in Vermont in the Nineteen-Twenties and the coincidence with other legends.

I excused myself and spent the rest of the night lying in bed and thinking thoughts that ensured a sleepless evening.

The next day they attacked. Their first ambush occurred just after Suzanne had called my attention to some readings she was picking up on her equipment. "We have some very localized seismic disturbances of point two with migrating epicenters," she explained, "and they appear to be centering on the dig site."

Several screams cut the mid-morning air from the direction of the dig. I was the first to arrive at the site, so I was the only one to witness the last student being pulled into the dirt by a mass of dark white tentacles.

The second attack occurred less than an hour later, as I frantically tried to convince Brandon, Atkins and the Samuels of what I saw. Suzanne had stated emphatically that she wanted off the dig and had headed off to gather her equipment when the ground shook rather violently.

We all rushed to where Suzanne's equipment was working, only to see her being pulled under. There was nothing we could do but watch. Then she was gone and the expedition was ended with Prof. Samuel's words. "Grab what we've found, I'll start the bus."

Within minutes we were boarding the bus, but the Spawns were not finished with us yet. The ground shook violently and a sink hole quickly opened up in front of our escape vehicle. Hoards of creatures, each looking like the statue, swarmed towards the bus. One wrapped its tentacles around Marie and threw her to the ground. I grabbed our wood axe and chopped it free of her. But by then they were scrambling all around us. She was grabbed by several more and drug towards the pit in the road. I fought off several from around myself but could not get to Marie before they had her to the pit. Then the Spawns retreated.

"Frank!" screamed Professor Samuel, "Get on the bus! We've got to get out of here!"

I hesitated between safety and plunging to Marie's rescue. "Get on the bus now or we're leaving you here!"

I jumped into the bus and we raced out of that accursed town. That night we stopped at a motel outside of Emporia and got rooms. I wasn't able to get any sleep, for every time I closed my eyes, all I could see was Marie being dragged down, being devoured before my eyes.

I decided to take a walk after that and it was fortunate that I did for several minutes later the wall of the room I was sharing with Dr. Brandon, exploded *from inside*. I was the last of our group to arrive back at the room. The Samuels, Atkins and myself watched in horror as several of those things devour Brandon. Then they scurried out the window, one of them carried the odd gray statuette of Othuyeg.

"The idiot!" cried Professor Samuel, "I told him to leave that in the bus. Now we've lost him as well."

Louise broke into tears and wailed, "I wish we had never started this. No more Edmund, no more expeditions."

"But what about the Seven Cities of Gold?"

She looked at him as if he were some kind of a monster and stalked off to their room.

I considered punching him in the jaw, but settled for storming off to the front desk where I hired a cab to drive me the rest of the way back to my house in Lawrence.

* * *

It wasn't until June 15th that I next heard from Professor Samuel; I had quit my position at the university and was finishing my Doctorate papers when I received his phone call.

"Frank, this is Edmund, I have found out some amazing things from the cylinder we found in Dunwich. It contained some copper scrolls, I really need your assistance at once. Please say you'll come over right away."

I should have slammed the phone in his ear. The memory of Marie's horrible death still lingered in my mind and I blame Samuel for all those deaths in Dunwich. He is guilty, even though the investigation accused no one of any crime, there were many things which no one wished to include in their statements.

But, I was soon in my car, driving over there not really knowing why. I guess it was to finish this once and for all.

When I approached the front door to the Samuels' house I saw it was open and heard the heated argument inside.

"No, no, no!" Louise yelled. "You promised me, no more expeditions!"

"I will not pass up this opportunity...."

"To die! Is that what you're searching for? Those creature killed a lot of good people...."

"But I know more now. That won't happen this time."

"If you go back down to Dunwich on this gold hunt, I'll divorce you. Do you hear me?"

There were slamming doors and Louise passed me as I entered the house. Her face was streaked with tears as rushed into another room and slammed that door. I walked quietly into Professor Samuel's den. He stood behind his desk studying the glyphs on a brownish-green colored scroll. Near him was the scroll case Marie had found. I could not look at it and turned to face the wall.

"Oh, Frank, don't go." Professor Samuel called. "Thank God you're here. I found something that you ought to read."

"I don't want anything to do with those things," I said as I turned to face him.

Samuel nodded his head and I knew what was coming before he opened his mouth. "I need you on this expedition with me. After you read these you'll understand, as I do, the importance of this discovery. Why I'll...."

The house shook with a violent explosion and I could hear Louise scream. Samuel pushed passed me and bolted down the hallway. I turned and exited the den in time to see him turn around as the hallway was enveloped by a horde of Othuyeg's Spawn. They scrambled forward on their mass of white tentacles, their single eyes staring directly at us as we ducked back into the den.

Samuel darted over to his gun case and pulled out a rifle. He quickly got off a shot, blinding the lead creature. It was no use, it was on top of him in the next instant and the room was quickly filling with more of those hideous things. I leaped out the nearest window and ran to my car. I drove like a madman until the police pulled me over. I told them the whole story, had to take a drunk test, then had to tell my story twice more at the police station.

It was about two hours later when the police accompanied me back to the Samuels' house. Many of the walls were torn out from the inside and the furniture was destroyed. During the ensuing search there was no trace of the Samuels or the scroll case I had mentioned.

It was by chance that I found the translations while no police were near. I wrapped them up and later, mailed them to Dr. Atkins. He called me three days ago. He had organized an expedition into the Flint Hills and he wanted me to accompany him. I had no trouble at all turning him down.

It still haunts my sleep, but at least I can sleep.

Shadows of Her Dreams

by

CARY G. OSBORNE

WORDS SPLATTERED across the computer screen. They came faster and faster. Fingers could not keep up with the speed with which they came to mind. Most were at least misspelled, at worst unrecognizable. She would correct them when the story was finished.

Meg had worked this way for five days, one story after the other. The spurt would last until tomorrow morning when she would collapse. Sleep would last two whole days. On the third day came the polishing, printing, mailing. Several publishers eagerly awaited promised work, mostly pro journals paying high rates.

Her tale "Crimson" had won numerous awards from many of the major horror publishers and groups. Every publication was enamored with her work these days. Less than a year ago she could hardly give stories away. But, the stories had changed and so had everyone's appreciation of her talent.

Rightly so. Her work was damn good. Now. However, even she admitted that the earlier fiction had lacked the intensity of the current work.

God, how she loved the way words, thoughts, whole scenes rolled off her fingertips. Rarely was any serious content editing needed. Stories appeared intact in her dreams; every word, every line whole and in its proper place.

Publishers and editors practically begged to publish Meg Garrard's stories. A whole anthology would be out in three months. Three anthologies including her work were scheduled in the next four months.

Not only the professionals, but also the public, loved her. They bought every scrap of paper with her name on it. Critics damned her work but they were the sort who always hated genre fiction, particularly horror. To them it wasn't serious literature; just entertainment material of questionable value. Not all critics viewed her work in the same way they viewed other horror writers but even she had not been able to get even half of them to favor her in a review.

The keys clicked, the cursor sped left to right, line after line.

Arthur raced into the swamp following Emma's screams. The night was ill-lit by the half moon. The path barely discernible. A turn and, as he planted his right foot to adjust, he slipped on the wet moss. His arms flailed but he couldn't regain his balance. With a cry, he tumbled into the mud. Like silk, the ooze enveloped him, folding to the curves of his body. Emma's screams were drowned out as his head disappeared.

Bubbles broke the surface....

The doorbell rang, breaking her concentration. Meg reread the last sentence.

The unwanted visitor beat on the door.

"Meg, open this door or I'll break it down," Greer shouted.

Greer, go away, she prayed silently.

A muffled thud indicated that he meant what he'd said.

"Wait!"

Meg ran through the hall hoping to prevent any unnecessary damage to her house. She threw the door open.

"Dammit, Greer! What do you think you're doing?"

"You're doing it again, aren't you," he accused as he stalked into the living room. "How long have you been at the computer this time?"

"It's none of your business."

"Yes, it is. Someone has to protect you from yourself."

He ran short, rough fingers through wavy brown hair. It was one of the little masculine habits he had that appealed to her and, for a moment, she almost forgave him the intrusion. He turned to her, taking hold of her shoulders, firmly but gently.

"You can't keep doing this. The doctor said...."

"I know what the doctor said, Greer. He doesn't understand any better than you do. When a writer has to write, nothing can stop the...the...."

"The Muse?"

"Call it what you like. Someone who's never experienced it can't appreciate it. It's a force from inside—it drives you. It won't let you rest until the work is done. You can't even sleep because it invades your dreams."

"Dreams? Are you having dreams again, too?"

His right hand brushed back a stray bit of her red hair and came to rest on her chin, lifting it slightly so that she had to looked him directly in his green eyes. She was tall and thin to the point of emaciation, he was only of medium height and barrel-chested.

Everything about them was opposites. No two people could be worse suited to each other. Yet, they loved each other. His love was written on his face at that moment by concern. She loved him, too, appreciated his concern, but the words kept scrabbling around in her head, demanding release.

His hand dropped from her chin; the other released her shoulder.

At least eat something," he said, his voice edged with defeat. "I can run out and get you a burger or a pizza."

"No, Greer. I've eaten. Right now, I must get back to the computer."

She turned away quickly, unable to bear the defeated expression in his eyes. Every time they saw each other it ended the same way. Perhaps it was time to admit they'd made a mistake. Maybe....

With a cry, she turned back to him, wrapped her arms around him, burying her face in his broad chest.

"I *do* love you," she whispered.

"I know."

His body radiated warmth, suddenly making her aware of a chill deep within her body.

She pushed away gently.

"I'll call you when it's finished," she said.

Greer sighed. "Okay. Make sure you do."

She smiled, blew him a kiss, and started down the hall to the study. As the door closed behind him, she paused in front of the hall mirror. There were black circles under her eyes and her hair was flying in all directions. She looked a sight.

Bubbles broke the surface as the last breath was forced from his lungs by the pressure of the mud.

She ran the rest of the way back to the computer.

* * *

Meg slid six brown envelopes to the postal clerk.

"Six this time," the woman said.

"Yeah. All first class, please."

The clerk nodded. As she figured up the postage on each envelope she kept glancing sideways at Meg. In turn, Meg shifted from foot to foot not quite sure she wasn't imagining the surreptitious looks.

"That'll be fourteen forty. And I guess you'll need a receipt."

"Yes, please."

If only the woman would hurry. Meg wanted to get back home, back to bed. She was so tired, even after twenty-six hours of uninterrupted sleep.

Except the dreams. Crowding into her head, demanding she give them life. Showing her the monster and his followers. This time she'd changed them in two of the stories. People would get tired of them if they were always the same. Of course, the opposite could happen—the editors, readers, everyone, might feel cheated if they didn't get what they expected.

The clerk finished and Meg slid the receipt into her jacket pocket. Too late to change her mind. With a thanks and a wave of the hand she left the post office, jumped into her car, and dashed for home. A few more hours sleep and then she'd call Greer this evening. If she didn't keep her promise he'd come looking for her.

A slavering beast peered in through the window.

A traffic light turned red and she stomped on the brake.

"Not yet," she murmured.

The car behind honked. The light had turned green. Concentrating carefully, she made it home, pulled into the driveway, slipped out of the car.

Foggy depths...crimson stars...slimy...cold...golden....

Meg staggered to the door. There were too many...too demanding....

The key wouldn't go into the lock. Tears fogging her vision made it more difficult. At last, the front door crashed open. She slammed it behind her.

Terror...doom...maiden...monster....

Too soon. She was still so tired.

She collapsed to the living room floor, began beating her head against the bare wood.

* * *

The panel was going rather well, so far. No one in the audience had asked any of the usual silly questions and Meg's answers had made sense. Another fifteen minutes and all would be finished.

She hadn't wanted to come to the convention but the publisher thought it a good idea for the forthcoming anthology. Such events had actually been more fun when she was a struggling writer still trying to make a name for herself.

A man in his fifties and wearing glasses stood, three rows back. His white hair was combed straight back. Overall, he looked like a professor.

"Yes, sir," she said, acknowledging him.

"Miss Garrard," he said, "where do you get the ideas for you stories?"

A moan rose from the crowd. Of all the stupid questions to ask!

"Sir," she began once the general noise of disapproval died down. "As you may be able to tell, that is a question few writers and fans take seriously anymore. But...."

"They come to you in dreams, don't they?" he interrupted.

"I beg your pardon?" she said.

"They come to you in dreams, night after night. They give you no rest. They are dangerous dreams, Miss Garrard."

Irene Donaldson, the moderator, took the microphone as the man rambled. "I think that's it for this afternoon. Miss Garrard will be down in the lobby at the autograph table for those of you who would like any of her numerous stories signed. Thank you for coming."

The man remained standing, silent, throngs of people moving all around him, watching Meg leave the meeting room. She couldn't help wishing there was a back door. Although she kept her eyes straight ahead as she exited, his eyes followed her all the way out. The touch of his gaze was cold. If only she could go straight back to her room. Maybe there wouldn't be a whole lot of people wanting her autograph this time.

Forty-five minutes later she closed the door behind her, blessing the quiet. She hadn't finished signing all the proffered books when the words began filling her head. She opened the laptop, switched it on and, in a few minutes, words spilled onto the screen.

The monster rose once more, the foul thing that appeared more and more in her stories. It was unstoppable. Sometimes the good guys at least survived. Sometimes they didn't. While Meg had slept the night before, the good guys battled and lost and now they demanded that their struggle be noted. And the monster wouldn't let her change him this time.

A knock came at the door and she ignored it. She must have release from the pressures of the scenes, the terror....

"Miss Garrard?"

With a cry she jumped from the chair, half expecting to see the monster standing in the middle of the room. Instead, it was the man from the meeting room.

"Miss Garrard. You didn't answer the door when I knocked," he said. "I must speak with you."

The monster never spoke. It was his thoughts that communicated his desire, his hatred.

"Miss Garrard?"

This man wasn't the monster. He was just trying to keep her from the peace she so desperately needed. She sat back down, fingers finding the home keys then moving rapidly.

"Your work could destroy you and so many others," he said gently. "I'll leave my card here on the dresser. "My name is Samuel Gates, by the way." He paused, the keys clicked. "My room number is written on the back. Call or come by as soon as you can. It's desperately important."

She sensed it was very late when she at last stopped. The story was finished. Thank goodness. She couldn't have typed one more word. Peeling off her clothes and dropping them heedlessly on the floor, she headed for the shower.

Steam clouded the mirror and she stepped into the tub. The heat and steam soothed the stiff neck and shoulders. Water splashed and flowed, rinsing lather down the drain.

Relax. Sleep. Dream.

Suddenly she was on her knees, coughing, choking, trying to catch a breath. The spray of water beat on her back and shoulders, running into her face. Desperately fighting to control her coughing, she crawled under the water and slid along the tub until she could reach the faucets. Struggling against her shaking body she fumbled with the handles.

At last, the water stopped. Silence descended, broken only by her sporadic coughing.

Shakily, she stood and stepped onto the bath mat. The heavy terry robe felt comforting as she wrapped it around her. Trembling hands could not make a knot in the robe's tie so she held it closed as she stumbled into the bedroom.

In a few minutes, her breathing came easier and the coughing lessened, although she couldn't quite stop shaking. What had happened was too frightening.... She was losing her mind. Working too hard; everyone told her that, especially Greer.

But, the whole thing had occurred before. In her dreams last night. For some reason, the scene had not appeared in the story as she wrote it, sort of tossed aside as unnecessary, and not remembered until now.

Meg forced herself to remember exactly what happened, to anchor the events in her mind. Even though it was hardly credible.

She had stood under the shower, her mouth open, inhaling as if she intended to breath in the water. Dear God, how many people tried to drown themselves in the shower?

But it wasn't a conscious act. She saw it in her mind as if the whole thing happened to someone else. As if it happened to a character in a story. Or to a character in a dream.

She searched the top of the dresser until she found the strange man's card. On the front, under the name "Samuel Gates," it read "Editor, Weekly Sentinel." In the bottom left corner was an address in Afton, Virginia. On the back, he had written, "Room 1033."

Meg picked up the phone to call, thought better of it, and began dressing. A short time later she stood before his door, hesitating to knock.

What if he was a crackpot, hoping to somehow cash in on her fame as a writer? She had to take that chance in case he knew what the hell was going on.

The door opened almost instantly when she knocked. Gates' expression changed from hope to relief in an instant.

"Come in, Miss Garrard."

He opened the door wider and stepped aside. The room was brightly lit, papers and books strewn over bed and floor.

"Excuse the mess," he said as he hurriedly cleared a path to the table and chairs on the far side.

Meg sat down, accepted the offer of a Pepsi, and waited impatiently for the man to settle down. When he did, it was to sit silently across the table from her for several minutes.

"I first read your work," he said, breaking the tense silence, "when your publisher sent me a pre-publication copy of your anthology for review. Ours is a rather small newspaper but the outside world does find us occasionally."

He looked down at the piece of paper his fingers kept turning on the table top.

"I read the first story and I can't describe the horror, amazement.... Well, you can imagine. No, I guess you can't. You have no idea what's happening."

"What is happening, Mister Gates?"

"Let me show you something."

He went to the dresser and took something wrapped in white tissue paper from the top drawer. As he brought it to her, he unwrapped it, careful to keep it hidden from her by his hand.

As he studied it he said. "Does this look familiar?"

He then reached out to hand it to her but she shrank back. Lying there in his hand was a small carving of the monster, the nameless thing which caused her characters so much terror. Scales and wings and octopus-like head rendered in stone, in great detail, so terribly accurate to her dreams.

"You carved that? From the description in my stories?" Her voice quavered and she cleared her throat.

"I have read every story you have written. Even if you put them all together, you would not have this creature. You have never described it that completely. No one could construct this likeness from your stories."

"Then how...."

"Your creature isn't new and it isn't of your making. Cthulhu has existed for centuries."

"Cthulhu?" Her tongue stumbled over the unfamiliar word.

"Its name is carved here," he pointed to the base "in these glyphs. This little figure is several hundred years old." He turned it in his hands. "And it's carved in a stone that no one can identify."

"Wait a minute," Meg protested. "I know my stories are strange and they do come to me in dreams but.... A real monster? Where the hell is he? Why don't more people know about him? How...."

"I've been studying him for two decades. All of these papers and books..." Gates waved his arm toward the rest of the room, "... document his existence in one way or another. He is telepathic and when he's awakened...."

"Awakened?"

"Yes. He apparently sleeps for decades. Huge natural disasters waken him. Or that seems to be the case. I first discovered his existence after Mount St. Helens erupted. A friend of mine had gone to Florida on vacation. He disappeared in the Everglades. When the police found Earl—or his body—he had been killed by members of some strange cult.

"I had to go down and identify the body and arrange to have it sent back to Virginia. His parents were old and just wouldn't have survived the trip.

"It was the members of the cult who had this figure. Between what they told the police and what came out in court, it was discovered that the thing's called Cthulhu. They had a larger figure—an idol, if you will—that they worshipped; I'm not sure they know why. Most of the cultists were nearly illiterate, almost bestial at times. Except for their leader."

Gates shivered. He went to the small refrigerator on the low end of the dresser, took out a Pepsi. Meg refused his offer of another; her first one was still half full. He sat back down, opened the can, then continued.

"Darryl Ryder was the leader's name. College graduate. Smooth talker. Except when he got fired up. He was like one of these new 'born-again' preachers, the ones with so much charisma their followers would die for them. Sometimes they do. Except, the preachers are burning up inside with energy and hate. Darryl Ryder was cold inside and out.

"Anyway," he said and sighed, "after I got back home I started researching this Cthulhu cult. As a newspaper editor, I at least know where to find information: newspaper morgues, news magazine stories, obscure books, TV news. Any story that seemed even remotely connected, I followed up with more research. Interviewing witnesses, visiting sites. Cthulhu is everywhere. He intends to take this world and he has demonstrated infinite patience over the centuries."

He told her stories of other murders, of ceremonies, and Meg's revulsion grew. The things the cultists did, to themselves and to others, were unbelievable. If only Gates would stop, but she couldn't ask him to. The scenes of horror his words conjured up were mesmerizing.

"It's bad enough for the average folk," he said. "But it's creative people who really suffer." He looked her straight in the eye. "He comes to them in their dreams and manipulates them. Artists create likenesses of him, always represented like this, in clay or on canvases." He held up the figure. "You're the first fiction writer I've encountered under his spell."

He sat back in his chair, still watching her closely. She lowered her gaze to her hands on the table.

"Why?" she asked after a prolonged silence. "Why aren't there other writers?"

"I don't know. Oh, there have been a few in the past, like Lovecraft, Howard, and Poe. They wrote about Cthulhu and his followers. And, they all died young. In more recent times a few philosophers and essayists have appeared, but they never capture the essence, the nature of the being. People don't read them, at least not in large numbers. How many people have read your stories, do you think?"

She shrugged. "Hundreds. Maybe thousands. But, if it's because of the number of readers, why hasn't it been done before?"

"Do you remember what I said about his appearance in your stories? Your description is never complete. Even if someone put all your descriptions together from every story it would still lack certain elements. Perhaps a fiction writer can't be forced to bend the story to his will. Your muses, if you will, are more independent than that of a sculptor or a painter."

Meg thought back to the first story dealing with the monster. It was the first time a story had flowed so easily from her mind through her fingers.

"Are you afraid of him?" Gates asked suddenly.

She jerked her head up, her breath caught in her throat. Was she afraid of her monster? Did he represent a threat to her?

"Not until tonight," she answered. She described what had happened in the shower, then, thinking back, about beating her head against the floor.

"It's like the words are beating against the inside of my head and if I don't let them out, the pressure builds until I think I'll explode. But when I'm writing, when the words come out, they come so fast I can hardly keep up. Nor can I stop. I usually go five or six days straight without stopping except for drink and food. When it's over I've got five or six finished stories and I sleep for two days solid."

At first, these spells had come infrequently but, as she described the methods, she realized that after nearly a year, the occurrences were closer together. She told him as much, then how the dreams didn't come every night until it seemed that it was time to start writing again. Except lately, she was resting less and less.

"Maybe the way to make it stop is to stop writing down the dreams," Gates mused. "Maybe the pressure is so great because he is trying to force you to work. Or maybe there's no pressure when he's asleep or preoccupied with something else. But I think the thing to try is to stop writing and see what effect that has."

He spoke rapidly, excited about the prospect of doing something. Meg, on the other hand did not find the prospect of losing so much inviting.

"Quit writing?" she said. "For how long?"

"Until Cthulhu releases you." He looked at her sharply. "Don't you want to be rid of him?"

"I only have your word that he exists at all," she said. "It's because of the dreams that I'm a recognized pro writer. Do you have any idea how long it has taken me to get this far? Eight years. Eight long years of appearing in the small press, of practically begging editors and agents to look at my work.

"Now, you come along and you want to take it away from me. Just because you think it's a real monster sending me telepathic messages. What proof do I have that this Cthulhu exists?"

She hit the table with her fist and stood. No one could ask her to give up what she'd dreamed of for all her thirty-one years. Gates' story was not even as good as one of her own.

"You have what happened in the shower tonight," he reminded her softly.

The shower. Nearly drowning in the shower. Yes, she had that. But couldn't it have just been a moment of unconsciousness brought on by stress? One didn't have to believe in monsters.

Gates rose and stepped beside her, placed a hand on her shoulder and said. "I know how hard it is to believe. Look, it's one in the morning. Take one of my journals back to your room, and some cuttings. Read them over the next two days. Call me and let me know what you think before you go home on Sunday."

He picked up a thin ledger book and a small bundle of newspaper articles and held them out to her. She knew she could just walk around him and leave the room, forget this bizarre night ever happened. She took the material and started toward the door. Gates stepped back to let her pass then followed.

"I'll expect your call sometime Sunday," he said. "I promise I won't bother you until then."

Back in her own room she picked up the phone and dialed Greer's number. It might be nearly one-thirty but she needed to hear his voice.

* * *

Mid-morning on Sunday, Meg settled into a chair in the hotel dining room. She hadn't slept well for two nights. The dreams left her exhausted each morning; and confused.

Reading Gates' material hadn't helped a bit. The picture the journal and articles painted was bizarre and frightening, but she'd made herself read every word. She knew some of them by heart. Or nearly so, from her own stories, particularly those in the journal.

Gates made his way toward her looking boyishly eager. Clearly, he expected her to agree with his findings and to assist in his plans. After all, she'd agreed to have breakfast with him. He sat across from her, grinning from ear to ear.

"Well?" he said.

The waitress set a menu in front of him. "Are you ready to order," she asked Meg.

"I'm just going to have the breakfast buffet."

The woman nodded.

"And, you sir? Or would you like a moment?"

"Some coffee and the buffet," he said impatiently.

She wrote the orders on her pad, picked up the menus and departed.

Meg rose and started for the buffet. Gates jumped up after her.

"Miss Garrard, please." The smile had left his face.

"Let's get our breakfast, first," she said. "I'm still not quite sure...."

"After everything you read?"

She concentrated on piling her plate with food. Gates prattled on, giving chapter and verse of several more incidents. One moment berating her for her lack of insight, the next cajoling and flattering.

They returned to the table. Meg set her plate down, piled with more food than she would eat under normal circumstances. This morning she had no appetite at all.

Gates set his plate down, too, but showed even less inclination to eat than she did.

"How can you possibly ignore the evidence?" he began again.

"Mister Gates, I'll need to think about this more than a couple of days," she said. "You're telling me that what I and the rest of the world have seen as my God given talent is a product of an evil entity from some other world bent on the destruction of humankind." She took a deep breath. "I worked for eight years without any recognition at all. I've worked hard honing what I took to be my talent and garnering the recognition I craved for so long.

"Now you come along with news clippings of bizarre atrocities and a journal full of the stories I've already written."

"Exactly! It all matches...."

"Mister Gates. You said, yourself, that you've read every story I've written."

"But, you can't just ignore..."

"I still have your card. If you like, I'll take more of your documentation with me to study. That's my decision at this moment."

His lower lip quivered and tears glittered in his eyes.

"You can't mean that."

"I'm sorry. I do mean it."

He leapt to his feet, turning over his chair.

"I...I.... You can't...."

His jaw muscles quivered under his tight skin. His fists clenched at his sides. Without another word, he turned and stalked from the dining room. Meg hoped that the sight of his retreating back would be the last she would see of him.

There had been a long moment in which she had believed him. It would have been easy to accept his explanation, even his help. In the end, there were too many coincidences.

The food in front of her suddenly looked and smelled pretty good.

* * *

Meg followed the bellboy out of the elevator and through the lobby. She waved to several people she knew but her goodbyes had been said to all friends Sunday afternoon, some of whom had already left for home.

She was tired, eager to get home, mostly because of the dreams Sunday night. They'd never been about real people. This time, however, Mr. Gates was there—in his room—and the terrible things—the monster's minions— broke in and....

Only once before had she seen those particular creatures. She'd hoped to never see them again. Their features were unclear in the darkened room: crab-like figures with wings that carried them across the room toward the terrified man. Gates backed away. Soon he would be pinned against the curtain window. But, no. He disappeared, carrying the curtain with him into blackness. Without a cry or scream.

Meg shivered at the memory and laid the room key on the desk.

"Thank you, Miss Garrard," the clerk said.

Irene Donaldson hurried up, started walking toward the door with her.

"Uh, have you heard the news this morning about the odd man, Mister Gates?" Irene asked.

"What news?"

"He jumped from his window early this morning. Weren't you woke up by all the sirens and stuff? I thought you would know. Such a strange man. You had breakfast with him yesterday, didn't you?"

"He fell to the parking lot, all wrapped in one of the curtains." The words tumbled over one another.

"Are you all right?"

Meg gripped Irene's arm to steady herself. Gates was dead; just like in the dream.

The monster called his minions back to him for their job was done and he was safe.

And another story must be written.

The Herald

by

DANIEL M. BURRELLO

MUST, GET, THROUGH. There! My, but it's cramped in that one dimensional field. Let me s-t-r-e-t-c-h.... And What is this?

Ah! I am *here*, on this page, with you sharing my thoughts.

Don't turn the page! I-It would be rude. And besides, we haven't gotten to know each other yet.

I know you're there. I can feel you.

The same way I can feel the growing Chaos that follows me. I wonder how much of your 'time' will elapse before It senses that I have crossed to this two dimensional world of ink and whiteness.

I apologize, but you won't be able to see me, unfortunately your human eyes deal only with what you want to see, what you can believe; your four dimensions.

No, I don't mean to offend! Truly, that is the last thing I should wish to do. You are, after a fashion, my savior. Simply by reading along, you give me life. If you stop, I become as static as any dusty volume on your bookshelf; not dead, but worse.

Then with my stillness, 'It', that first Chaotic Intelligence, the coolest of the cold ones, will eventually find me, lose me in Its fractal bulk and with me, possess the key to your world of experience. So please, lets continue reading, and keep the amorphous unnamables on the other side of the looking glass. Shall we?

Oh! Let me correct myself, I said "amorphous", but you're familiar with Its subtle shapes and hues. You have seen more of Its nature than most. I see It has taken the shape of Death and Horror for you. Fed on your stresses. Well, to each his own.

Do you think this unusual? Unbelievable?

Ha! My friend, It influences you from out there and from *here* more often than you realize. Or did you believe Lovecraft was alone in the creation of his netherworlds, or Bloch, or even Stephen King? Naivete is a delicacy to It. You would be a prized and tender morsel.

Be more than careful. It has a thousand young, and as Poe or Goya will attest even now, It will squeeze every ounce of being from you, lay waste to your soul and take you to its putrid, timeless heart as Its own.

Your disbelief strikes a chord of humor in me. You have seen Its face and failed to recognize It. Can you not remember? Think back. On the cold nights, the lonely ones....

It is that secret, hoarding Nothing that sweeps through you midnight mind as you contemplate the waste in you life. Not recreation, not fiction, It is supreme emptiness, touching all, remaining untouched by but a few.

So, you begin to recall!

Perhaps a forgotten miner, in his naked struggle to take the last breath of trapped air, the hapless student who happens upon the texts of the Necronomicon and seals his doom upon the utterances therein, or the infants, tossed to freeze in wastebins of a hundred desolate alleys tonight will know of It briefly, but only Its effects. It cannot cross the bounds without help. Too much order...physics and all that nonsense.

Unless, of course, It were to follow me here. And then.... Oh but that's unlikely.

Still, I wonder if you wouldn't mind holding the page steady, and certainly more level, that smooth curve there, where you thumb is, makes the surface rather less straight than I would like. It may attract attention. Better safe than sorry.

There now, that's a bit better, but still quite curved. No matter, I have a better idea. Why don't I come out there with you; in fact, more or less, *in* you? It's painless, I assure you.

Really, it's been a while since I've ventured into your particular realm. Besides, being two layers away from It, will make me all the more difficult to trace. Don't worry, you would know quickly if It were approaching. Chaos is too obvious to mistake.

Just keep your eyes here on the page and your hand just there, don't move, steady...steady—

There now, that wasn't so awfully bad, was it? All comfy in here. I must say, after so much time in the first and second dimensions, this is a treat. And what wonderful senses, what depth of field in those eyes, the scents you retain, the texture of the page on your fingers. I have to admit to a special fondness for this place, it has been a long time...

But enough of this sentimentality. Relax now, and let me explore this body. Deep breath...come, come, you can do better than that.... Oh well, I guess we will have to make do. Anyway, I can feel you. Here I go, across the back, around the top of that magnificent spinal column. For something as lowly as meat, you are quite an achievement. Crude? Yes. But you hold a singularly sensual charm.

Come on, relax! ...What does your doctor say?...this won't hurt a bit? Well, you know that's a lie, don't you.

And what is this!? Here in you lymphatic system, just behind the lumbar region. And it seems to be spreading. What a surprise for you! But let the doctor tell you about it. It will be well enough along by then. And we won't have any of that biopsy nonsense will we? In fact, I—

h¿çFé

Th-that's odd.

Those symbols, I mean. But I'm sure it's nothing.

So, tell me about yourself, or better still, I'll find out for myself. After all, you are a consummate liar. Let me get closer to that skull, and the mass of nervous tissue within.... I'll just...crawl up here...and....

Hmmm. It's not as cramped as I'd thought. Plenty of room for improvements up here. The master will be pleased.

Damn!

No, no, I meant to say "You're the master of your destiny." Yes." Yes, that's it! "The master of your destiny. Keep a stiff upper lip," and all that sort of rubbish. Just reacquainting myself with your language. It's more difficult than you might believe. Why, In my—

5é&&xx@¿ç*ç*!hgdyszctri32gd!

Oh, pay no attention to that. A typo. I can't be expected to be in my best shape right out of such a tight squeeze, now can I?

Let's continue. Where were we? Ah, yes, in your head. Can you feel me up here, just behind you eyes?

Just watch the page. Let the words flow through your eyes, back there to you visual cortex and straight to me.

Such awful memories, dead pets, dead loved ones, dead love. These black shrouds here, around your thoughts of money, of sex, of Gods. Hmmm. And your mind, it flips from one thing to another so quickly. Have you lost your ability to savor things? Pleasures? Agonies? Perhaps I can help.

My yes, our attention span has suffered. Along with our intelligence. Too much television. Or, perhaps not enough.

Things are so much easier when simple. When others think for us. Let me do that for you. Just relax.

If you would, take another of those deeper breaths.

Yes! Better. See, isn't it easier when we work together. You feel better too! In fact. . .You feel much better—despite our little bundle of joy eating away at the surrounding cells in you lymph glands—you feel very good! It's just the sort of mutation that could grow, chaogenously speaking. With the help of a special someone, it could reshape you, make you all that you can be.

HW#@¢%¢*y(Twxsrt)$#%¢¢ç¿&é&**&é¿çé5gdtsBGEdjslaal
And here comes that special someone now!

Pay attention....

New energy is filling you even as you read this, and soon you will be at a state of comfortable rest. Another deep breath.... It's easier to do what you're told. It makes the whole world seem so very exciting and new.

No, you won't put this down. You will continue to read, even after the words are beyond comprehension by one such as you.

So, now that we've become friends, I'm sure you want to know more about me and perhaps even a few phrases of my language! We are friends. You want to do what I say, want to please me more than life itself.

Good.

Now, repeat after me....

Iä! Iä! Cthuluh Fhtagn! Ph'nglui mglw'nafh Cthuluh R'lyeh wgah-nagl fhtaga!

And again.

Iä! Iä! Cthuluh Fhtagn! Ph'nglui mglw'nafh Cthuluh R'lyeh wgah-nagl fhtaga!

ay, there's the rub.

¿ *7 fej$¢**lfedk
GSHGAJHGSKDHDJ(ELL@LDIUI@(**N X@&#(ççç*93H&¿é&
¿é**&ç¿&¿é&é¿é&*&&!{ééç%##@@ XXXXXXXXXXXXXXXXX
XXXXXXXXXXXXXXXXXXXXXXXXXXXXXXXXXXX XXX

Typo

by

MICHAEL D. WINKLE

133.427
H139b/1913
Hali. (Trans. E. S. Bayrolles)
Revelations of Hali. (New York: Golden Goblin Press, 1913)

THE AMBER-GREEN LETTERS popped up across the screen as Julie typed. She set the black book aside and picked up the big folio with the crimson cross stitched on the cover.

223.2
D39/1885
De Mauleon, Alberic, 1644 - 1701.
Canon Alberic's Scrap-Book. (Cambridge University
Press, 1885)

She hefted the *Scrap-Book* aside and rubbed her eyes before turning back to the CRT and the next volume. It had been something of a coup for her to be hired by the Armitage Library of Miskatonic University, because by all reports they didn't choose just anybody. And they did, for a fact, ask a lot of nosy questions. Any madness in the family back four generations? Jeezus! It took a week to find that out! Does my parents' house get its drinking water from Blasted Heath Reservoir? What were they afraid of—communist fluoridators?

133.42101
A102m/1900
Abraham du Paris, 1362 - 1460. (Trans. S. L.
  MacGregor Mathers)
**Book of the Sacred Magic of Abramelin
the Mage, the.** (London: John H. Watkins Press, 1900)

Linda believed they didn't hire her solely because her last name was
Whateley. Anne thought she was passed over just because she came
from Innsmouth. At least, that was what they said. Funny the preju-
dices you found in the nooks and crannies of New England. The old
fogies of M.U. took the cake, though.

The next book she picked up was called *Unaussprechlichen Kulten* by
Fvindvuf Von Junzt. Her eyes throbbed just looking at it. She set it
carefully behind the pile of books to be put on-line. Carol could do it later.

842.913
A61c/1919
Anonymous. (Trans. Hildred Castaigne)
King in Yellow, the. (Paris: Cassilda Press, 1919)

Miskatonic was so far behind the times. Only now were they getting
rid of the card catalogs and entering everything on the new
DRMQUST Library System. And she heard rumors that old Professor
Wilmarth was still railing against it. What was his problem?

398.16045
H676/1877
Hohman, John George.
Pow-wows; or the Long Lost Friend. (Chapel Hill:
University of North Carolina Press, 1877)

Frankly, Anne or Linda could have this job, for all Julie cared. Sitting
in front of the CRT, entering the unlikely titles and authors of these
crumbly old books, was all she'd done this week.

Oh, well, it paid $7.50 an hour—$8.50 if she'd work after sunset
(another kooky arrangement of Professor Wilmarth's, but that one she
didn't mind).

It was almost six-thirty by now, so she could take off an hour for
dinner. She'd probably go to The Spanish Cave for their shrimp and
fish special. But first she could slip in one more book.

813.08
B581f/1928
Blake, Robert Harrison, 1907 - 1935.
Feaster from the Stars and Others, the.
(Arkham: Miskatonic University Press, 1928)

*   *   *

The night was dark and moonless, but the sky was filled with stars like frost on the Burying Ground. Julie hurried past the Geology Department, across the square that seemed to have emergency phones on every lamp-post and phone pole, and finally she reached the seventeen marble steps of the Library.

She entered the main hall, showed her I.D. to the guards (of which there always seemed to be an inordinate number), then she started up the staircase to the second floor. She paused beneath the Rules of Conduct sign, briefly scanning Rule #8 again. It was so freaky:

8. Report all unusual lights, noises, smells, substances, and apparent movement of inanimate objects to the Security Office immediately. Do not approach areas where such phenomena have been observede until Security has investigated and deemed them non-hazardous.

The official reason for Rule #8 was that a fault line ran beneath the library, not detected until recent times, and that vibrations and static electricity from the earth's crust caused funny things to happen—even hallucinations and poltergeist-like disturbances. However, rumors had spread suggesting that the library was haunted. After all, didn't those two students commit suicide in the third floor men's room? Didn't Professor Abercrombie drop dead of heart failure in the closed section?

Certainly those were reasons enough for a haunting.

But even *that* didn't satisfy Carol, the other girl who worked in Acquisitions. Oh, no. She always had to go one better....

"I've heard the professors talking," she had commented the day after Abercrombie's funeral.

"Which ones?" Julie had asked.

"Travison and Wilmarth. Did you ever notice they talk in code?"

"Code? Maybe in Statistics for Business, but not usually."

"To each other," amended Carol. "Unless you know what a Nigh—Nigh-Arlotto—what a Zathoth is."

"Oh, that's a book. *Azathoth and Others*. I've seen it."

"Oh," said Carol, momentarily deflated. "Well, they were talking about a lot of things I couldn't catch, but I did hear them mention Abercrombie and the others. The gist of what they said was, the haunting wasn't a result of those deaths—the deaths were caused by the haunting!"

Julie entered the Acquisitions office on the second floor. Carol was sick today; Julie would be alone here the next four hours.

"Thanks a lot, Carol," she muttered.

"I thought Miss McArdle wasn't working tonight, Miss Dennis-toun," came a voice from the labeling table.

"Oh! Professor Travison! You startled me!"

The stout, grey-haired professor rose from the chair behind the table. He was usually a friendly sort, but this evening he looked like he'd lost a filling.

"I was just—talking to myself," Julie explained. "Is there something I can do for you?"

The professor indicated the old volumes stacked about.

"I was wondering if you were through with these books yet. I'm rather anxious to get them back under lock and key."

"I'd like to re-check the on-line entries first, Professor," said Julie, setting the paper cup from The Spanish Cave on the nearest desk. "We've had more than our share of typos on these items."

Travison cracked a smile at last.

"That's understandable. Well, just call me at x5171 when you're through. I'll be in my office 'til ten."

The grey-haired professor turned to leave, but he paused at the door.

"Oh, by the way, Miss Dennistoun. I believe Professor Peaslee told you girls that these volumes were not to be left unattended if at all possible. Some of them are very valuable, you know."

Julie shrugged.

"Carol and I usually alternate dinner hours, Professor Travison, but I'm alone here tonight."

Travison nodded.

"I suppose it will be all right this once. It's not May Eve, or anything.... You're almost through modernizing, I understand."

"Just a day or two more, for the fiction section."

"But you're nearly finished with the closed section?"

"Yes."

"Good. Well, carry on, Miss Dennistoun."

Travison left, shutting the door quietly behind him. Julie dropped into her chair and scooted up to the terminal.

May Eve? she wondered. What's so special about that? Oh, well. Who could figure out professors, anyway?

She snapped on the CRT and dragged the nearest book toward her. The first volume of the Chinese author Hsan's works.

$LOCATE SUBJECT = HSAN?

She pressed ENTER and awaited an answer.

DRMQUST SEARCH #42: HSAN

7 HITS FOUND
PRINT HIT #1?

Julie typed YES.

398.9917
H83d/1940
Hsan. (Trans. Etienne-Laurent de Marigny)
First Cryptical Book of Hsan, the. (Boston: Silver Key
Press, 1940)

. . . .
DRMQUST SEARCH #42: HSAN
7 HITS FOUND
PRINT HIT #2?

Well, that checked out okay. Julie pushed aside the *First Cryptical Book*
and picked up the second. And after ol' Hsan, only a few hundred other
authors to go....

* * *

It was almost ten o'clock. Julie yawned and stretched again. A couple
more items and she could call Professor Travison. None too soon, she
thought; she was developing myopia and terminal saddle-sores.

She drew the next to the last item near. *Fractal Geometry and the
Crawling Chaos*, by Emil Hadath.

$LOCATE SUBJECT = KADATH?

She ENTERed before catching her mistake. *I am getting tired*, she
thought muddily.

DRMQUST SEARCH #217: KADATH
2 HITS FOUND
PRINT HIT #1?

I might as well see what I have, she decided. She pressed Y.

The screen went blank. Overhead the fluorescent lights flickered,
darkened, and came back on, but only a dim, dull orange.

Now what? groaned Julie. It seemed like the electricity went out in
Arkham every time a bird squatted on the wires.

She blinked. Her screen was back on—sort of. It displayed no yellow-green lettering. Instead there was a scene, a desolate landscape, like pictures of Iceland in *National Geographic*. There was a rocky expanse in the foreground, empty of all life save a few scraggly clumps of grass. Flurries of snow skittered across the bare steppe, and on the horizon the jagged silhouette of a mountain range cut the sky.

In the center of the screen, from the midst of the distant mountains, a tower rose into the sky. It was shaped a little like a lighthouse or rook; it was coal-black, and though it looked like the work of men, it was vastly taller than the snow-capped peaks around it. There were cumulus clouds in front of the tower, and others partially eclipsed by it; judging by them, the black edifice must have been several *miles* high....

The phone rang. Julie nearly fell out of her chair. She groped blindly for the receiver, unable to tear her eyes from the screen.

"Hello?"

"Miss Dennistoun! This is Travison!"

"Uh—oh, hello, Professor Travison. I was just about to come over..."

"We've just experienced a power surge of some kind. I was wondering if you'd—er—seen anything unusual."

"My CRT's turned into a TV set. I'd call that unusual."

"What?"

Something seemed to be happening at the apex of the black tower. Julie bent low to watch the screen.

"It must be receiving TV signals from somewhere," she continued, half to herself. "I didn't know that was possible. It must be like receiving a radio station through a gold tooth."

A pin-point of light appeared at the top of the tower and slowly grew in size. It soon obscured the ebon pinnacle and began eating up more and more of the screen, as though rocketing nearer. Julie scooted her chair back and straightened uncomfortably.

"Miss Dennistoun, please tell me exactly what you see!"

Before Julie could open her mouth again, a bright ball of yellow light erupted from the screen and sailed within inches of her head.

"Eeyow!"

"What is it?"

"My terminal just fired a photon torpedo at me!"

"A what?"

Julie twisted to watch the light ball's trajectory. Then the receiver dropped from her hand and clattered to the floor. Travison's voice became a distant insect buzz.

In the dim orange light stood a man. He was tall and olive-skinned, and a long, thick, black goatee jutted like a solid knob from his chin. He wore a multicolored robe with voluminous folds, and on his head an Egyptian-looking crown was perched, like a gold keg with a cobra flaring out of the front.

"Julie Dennistoun," the apparition said, and its words seemed to echo out of the walls rather than issue from its mouth, "you have seen that which is unlawful for waking mortals to see. You have gazed upon unknown Kadath in the cold waste."

"Who—who are you? Where did you come from?" Julie squeaked.

"I have as many names as I have forms," said the Egyptian-looking man, "but in this place and time I am called Nyarlathotep."

"Nigh-arlot —?"

"Many are the dreamers who have entered the Gate of Deeper Slumber seeking Kadath. Most, such as Zenig of Aphorat, whose skull is set in a ring on the finger of one Unnameable, have failed utterly. A very few, such as your countryman, Randolph Carter, have succeeded, and looked upon the black tower of Kadath. But you, Julie Dennistoun, have by-passed the Gate; you have not opened a lawful window into Koth, or Leng, or Lomar; you have used no grimoire or appealed to any Outer God; yet your mortal eyes have looked upon the Onyx Castle."

Julie's jaw worked soundlessly up and down, and finally a few meek words emerged, as mouselike as she felt before this vision.

"But—but it was an accident! I didn't mean to see anything! You're not even supposed to see anything on DRMQUST—except words and diagrams!"

Before Nyarlathotep's reverberating voice could answer, Julie heard footsteps clop down the hall and an angry voice shout "Powell! Wait!"

The hall door burst open, and Powell, the newest security guard, jumped in. The bizarre garb of Nyarlathotep seemed to stun him momentarily, but he recovered and steadied his .38 in both hands.

"All right, King Tut, freeze!" The guard took in the fact that Nyarlathotep's arms were lost in his vast, rippling sleeves. "Hands where I can see 'em!"

Nyarlathotep complied. He raised one hand to shoulder height, and suddenly a bolt of blue lightning joined it with the crown of Powell's head like the arc between the poles of a Jacob's ladder. The guard's scream was short, and it was drowned out by Julie's own.

Powell crashed to the cold, tiled floor. Tongues of flame erupted from his shoulders, his elbows, and his knees, right through the material of his uniform.

"It is unwise to confront the Crawling Chaos with so inadequate a weapon," observed Nyarlathotep.

More faces appeared at the door; they belonged to the other guards. The voice that had ordered the first guard to wait started swearing.

By now, smoking pieces of Powell were breaking off and crumbling to the floor. Julie bit the back of her hand until it bled. Nyarlathotep turned to face the newcomers.

"Be warned, mortals," said the Crawling Chaos. "My patience is at an ebb. Leave, or suffer a fate far less desirable than clean death!"

Then Nyarlathotep lowered his hands, frowned, and even took a step or two backwards. The guards advanced slowly, spreading laterally from the door. There were six in all, not counting the pitiful remains on the floor, and one held out a strange object at Nyarlathotep like a crucifix at a vampire.

Nyarlathotep was recoiling like a vampire as well, but what the guard held was no cross. It looked like—a little grey-green starfish?

"It seems that anyone can rifle the temples of Mnar in these irreverent times," observed the Crawling Chaos. "Yet that Sign will not protect you all. You have goaded me, mortals, into revealing one of my less pleasant aspects."

Nyarlathotep's multicolored robes began bulging in the most unlikely places, as if he were growing new, malformed limbs beneath his clothing. His eyes flared like live coals. Then a third blazing orb opened in the center of his forehead.

Julie could take no more. She crawled under her desk and threw her arms over her head. She heard a voice she recognized as Professor Travison's shouting, "I've got it! I've got it!" from the hall. Then she heard a disgusting sucking noise, followed by Travison's voice again, speaking in a language she couldn't understand. Then a blast of wind filled the room, and there was a ghastly cry something like a pig squeal and something like metal tearing. Finally there was silence.

* * *

"Miss Dennistoun?"

Julie moaned.

"You can come out now, Miss Dennistoun. He's gone. Better than gone, in fact. Imprisoned again, after all these years!"

Julie looked up timidly. The lights were bright again. Professor Travison was bent over, peeking under the desk at her, his face scarcely less bright. She emerged slowly and allowed Travison to help her up.

"What—where is he?"

Travison looked over his shoulder at a large gurney, like one from a hospital, and she followed his gaze. Sitting on the gurney was a grey metal box with a hinged lid, which hung open. Within was a black, egg-shaped crystal striped with crimson. There appeared to be a cloudiness inside the crystal that writhed, like a caterpillar in a cocoon.

"You can't mean he's in *there*!"

"The Shining Trapezohedron was created to hold Nyarlathotep in check. He's not really *in* the crystal. It is not so much a prison as a doorway to a prison. We had to drag Narragansett Bay to find it, but find it we did—and tonight, when I heard that name over the phone, we had the chance to use it!"

Julie found a chair and sat down dizzily. Travison ordered the guards to take the gurney to Professor Peaslee's lab, then he turned back to the girl.

"Miss Dennistoun—do you happen to know how *he* came to be here?"

"I—" She raked one hand from her forehead to the back of her neck, as if brushing a long lock of hair out of her eyes. "I made a typo calling up something. . . but I got a hit anyway. . . and when I tried to see what it was, I got an image of something on the CRT—and he came out of it. He came right out—"

Her voice trailed off as she caught sight of her CRT again.

DRMQUST SEARCH #217: KADATH
2 HITS FOUND
PRINT HIT #2?

Travison reached out and clicked off the screen. The message collapsed to a yellow-green point at the center, which soon faded.

"What—what could *that* have been?" Julie asked.

"If we're lucky, we'll never know," said Travison darkly. "Meanwhile, Miss Dennistoun, you and I must have a long, long talk."

* * *

The handsome, cinnamon-haired Burt Haddon carefully wrote his name, address, phone number, and student number on the library card. He handed it back to Julie, who stamped it and an orange slip of paper with the due date. She placed the orange paper like a bookmark into the middle of *The People of the Monolith*, Volume I, and slid it around to Burt.

"Sorry you were sick all weekend," he said.

"Nothing serious," she replied. "Or catching."

"See you tonight?"

"You bet. No more working nights for me."

Burt stepped away from the check-out desk with a smile and headed for the main entrance. After the guard checked his student knapsack, he left, giving a final wave as the door closed.

Sick all weekend was the story she and the professor had cooked up to explain her absence from the world. It took that long for them to explain what Nyarlathotep and the starfish and the black crystal were. And even now Julie suspected they had barely skimmed the surface of the strange doings at M.U.

She wondered how they explained the dead guard's unauthorized cremation to his family....

"This is so ridiculous!" complained Carol, at Julie's side.

"What?"

"They spend I don't know how many hundreds of thousands of dollars to modernize the library, and after one week the system's down, maybe forever!"

"I think they found a few bugs in it," said Julie. A few seconds later, she shuddered.

"That's not the half of it!" Carol raved on. "I've heard the professors talking...."

"Again?"

Carol looked around carefully, as if someone might overhear. "They're talking about scrapping the computer system entirely and going back to the card catalogs!"

"Lucky we stored them in the basement, then, instead of just tossing them," Julie observed. "Good old backward M.U."

Star Bright, Star Byte

by

MARELLA SANDS

A FLOCK OF SHELL-PINK flamingos waded along the shore under a beautiful turquoise sky. A single white cloud scuttled by overhead. Warm tropical breezes caressed my suntanned skin while the gentle lapping of the blue-green waves lulled my senses into contentment.

I wiggled my toes. They were perfect, down to the nails—that detail, plus the dozens of others, like the hair on my chest and the white stuff on my nose, had taken up gobs of system memory I could well have used elsewhere. But I wanted this setting to be perfect. If I couldn't go to the Bahamas myself, at least I could come here, lie under a hot yellow sun, and never, *ever* have to worry about sunburn, sunsickness or heatstroke. If I'm out in the sun much—the real sun—I break out into blisters and get sick.

I had a feeling that, after this, I'd only be disappointed with the real Bahamas, anyway—even if I could enjoy them without worrying about blisters. No real beach could match the paradise I'd programmed here.

It could have been a private paradise, all my own, but it wasn't. I was proud of the programming I'd put into this beach—all the niggly details like the fiddler crabs and the lumps of driftwood washed up at the high tide line—and I wanted other people to see it. It was a showcase of sorts; for an extra fee, other users on the net could come here and enjoy. Most users paid the fee and came here regularly.

A woman popped into existence on the beach. She gazed around her as if deciding whether to stay or go. Apparently, the beach was to her liking. She waved and walked over to me.

Her VR construct was as detailed as mine, maybe more. Dark brown curly hair flowed down her shoulders to her waist. Bronze skin, stretched over taut muscles, glistened with oil. Her neon orange bikini covered only bare necessities, and as she walked, her breasts swayed in such a way, I wasn't at all sure she had programmed the suit to stay in place.

She sat down next to me and smiled. I caught the aroma of suntan lotion and a subtle, exotic perfume that made my heart beat faster.

She grinned. Perfect teeth, of course.

"Hi," she said. The voice flowed with honey and sunshine. It tickled all the hairs on my neck and sent a shiver down my spine. "You're Kent, right? The sysop?"

"Kent Taylor, Systems Operator. That's me." I couldn't help but gawk at her—God, she was gorgeous. Of course, she could be a balding corporate executive in real life. Or another all-American male computer jock like me. Not all people program constructs to match their gender on the Outside.

"Um, is there a problem?" I asked. The woman looked at her fingernails; each was painted the same color as the bikini. Toenails, too. Such attention to detail was impressive—and costly in terms of system memory.

I didn't remember allocating that much memory to any of the regular net users.

"No, no problem," she said. Her voice was somewhere between a sigh and a caress. "I just wanted to meet you and tell you that I've enjoyed using your bulletin board. I didn't used to be into all this virtual reality stuff—I'm really more into dream interpretation and dream therapy. But this is like a dream, isn't it? Only you've made it real."

She looked at me as if she expected an answer. I realized I'd been paying more attention to her voice than to what she was saying. That and the scent of her cologne. Whatever she'd programmed into it, it was fantastic.

"Oh, well, interpret away," I said with a shiver. "Just let me listen to your voice and I'll be your slave forever."

She giggled. "An interesting proposition. I just might take you up on it." She giggled again. The sound rippled pleasantly through my skull. "What was I saying? Oh, yes. It was the name of your network that hooked me, you see. *Star Byte*. It reminded me of that old children's song...."

"Star light, star bright."

"Yeah." She looked up at the cloudless blue sky. "I like to watch the stars. I live for the night."

She stopped speaking, just gazed up at the sky. Hair cascaded down her arm onto the beach. Her perfect chin, tilted up towards the virtual heavens, could have been carved by a sculptor. Her skin was flawless. I wanted to reach out and touch her....

With an effort, I restrained myself. If she were a real woman, I'd be on my knees, begging her for a date, for a kind word, for anything.

But she wasn't real. The woman next to me existed only inside this computer system. The person behind her could be anybody. Anybody at all.

"Um, what's your name?"

"On the bulletin board, I use Narla," she said.

Asking after her real name or gender would be the height of boorishness—even in VR, we have etiquette. I'd have to look through the user index to find out who she was. Shouldn't be too hard. She was obviously hogging up a great deal of system memory.

"Hey, Kent! Got a date, I see!" The skinny, athletic-looking construct that belonged to my friend Joe sat down on the sand next to me. He leaned over me and waved to Narla. "Hi." She merely nodded. Joe's construct's voice was harsh and low and the lips barely moved.

Joe's construct was simple compared to mine and Narla's. His hair was merely a block of color that was supposed to resemble blond. It looked more yellow than any real blond I'd ever seen on the Outside, though. His face was flat and some of the features—like the ears and nose—only hinted at.

He was wearing the standard on-line uniform of t-shirt and jeans. It was standard because it was so easy to program: solid colors, solid shapes, little detail. Joe had wasted as little storage space on this construct as possible. He wanted to use his share of the board's memory for games.

"What do you want?" I asked Joe.

"Hey, you don't have to get rude, you know," he said. He sounded annoyed. "It's not like I'm interrupting something."

I bit back a retort and swallowed my resentment. He was right. I turned to Narla. She was looking out at the ocean now.

"This is Joe," I said. She glanced at him briefly. "He's a friend of mine." I turned to Joe. "This is Narla."

Joe waved at her, then slapped me on the arm. "Hey, guess what. Those cultists are at it again. It's all over the current events board."

"What cultists?" I asked.

Joe leaned over to me. "Not that this beach doesn't have its attractions, but you should get around to the other boards sometime. Anyway, you know, the ritual slayings and all that."

"Ritual slayings?"

"Yeah, some group's slicing people up. Always on hilltops, always the same sorts of cuts. Police think it's a new cult. Victims seem to be anybody—old, young, fat, skinny... whatever."

Narla dug her toes in the sand. "I wonder what those people dream."

"The victims or the people with the knives?" asked Joe.

Narla turned her bright green eyes on him and flicked brown hair off her shoulder. "Does it matter?"

"Geez, sure it does, lady," said Joe, his voice rising in anger. "Are you saying any random American dreams the same things as those murdering scum? Taking over the world and all that?"

Narla shrugged and turned her attention back to the sky. "Maybe they are drawn together by the same dream. Many people are. Many more will be some day."

Joe looked at me and shook his head. He didn't have to say *she's a lunatic* out loud for me to know what he was thinking. I could read the thought even on his construct's face.

"Well, it's been pleasant meeting you, and taking in this incredible view," said Narla. "You've put a lot of yourself into this program, Kent."

"Uh, thanks," I said. Narla nodded once and blipped out.

"Christ, Kent, what possessed you to program a psychopath into your beach program?"

"What?" It took me a moment to realize Joe thought Narla was my idea. "I didn't—Narla's one of the board users."

"Oh, sure. With a construct like that? Who's got access to that much memory but you?"

"I don't know. I'll find out, though."

"I bet you will!" Joe hooted. "But I bet she doesn't look anything like that on the Outside—if she even *is* a she!" He rolled over on the sand, helpless with laughter. A passing flamingo eyed him gravely before moving on.

"Oh, hell," I said. "I'm going to check it out right now." Now that Narla was gone, our conversation rankled me. If one of the net users had managed to grab more than his or her share of memory, the system should have warned me. And if I were a user who'd done such a thing, would I drop in on the sysop and boast about it?

Narla was a boast, as much as this beach was. *See how well I can program.* She was a challenge of sorts. I just wished I understood the nature of the challenge.

* * *

After the paradise of the beach, the interior of my apartment seemed dull and drab. Dirty laundry was piled over every bit of furniture. Unwashed dishes lay in the sink, on the counters of the kitchen, on the table. Three dirty coffee mugs graced the TV tray next to my computer terminal. A rancid odor came from their direction.

I sighed. I spent too much time on the system and not enough cleaning my apartment. I'd get around to it one day. Just not now. Now I had to figure out what Narla was up to and who she might be.

I shook a lock of unruly red hair out of my face while I typed my access code into the Star Byte system with pale fingers.

ACCESS DENIED flashed across the screen. I stared at the message in shock. Access denied? Whose system was this, anyway? I'd programmed it, I ran it. I had all the access codes.

I tried again. Again I got the flashing message. Faint stirrings of fear nibbled at my mind, but I pushed them aside. There was a logical reason for this glitch. I'd just have to work it out.

I tried all my personal codes. They were keyed to every area in the system. No luck. I got sick of seeing the blinking *ACCESS DENIED* message every time. Anger warmed me from the inside and kept me going. Whoever Narla was, she was good. It was clear now that her arrival on the beach had been designed to get me off the board long enough to lock me out.

I was startled by a flash of lightning. I jumped and blinked in the sudden whiteness, momentarily blinded. I could feel my pulse in my throat. Slowly, vision returned and my heartbeat slowed to normal. I could hear the pattering of rain against the window.

No, not rain. Hail.

I got up and peeked through the blinds. Hail the size of marbles shot down out of the black sky, blown by gale force winds. Smaller trees bent over double before the tremendous gusts of wind, while larger ones leaned precariously. Lightning flashed again, and thunder rattled the teeth in my head. A lone pedestrian struggled to walk across the parking lot, purse held over her head for protection.

Suddenly, it was clear. The wind, the dark cloud cover, the hail—all gone. The sun shone down merrily on the street. Sunlight sparkled off the melting chunks of ice.

I turned back to my computer and realized I'd left it on. Damn—the lightning could have fried every circuit. But then, the storm had lasted barely half a minute, hardly enough time to power down the system. Crazy.

A feeling of unease settled around my shoulders, soft as a feather, as I sat back down at the terminal. Narla was my problem right now, not freak storms that swept through town in a matter of seconds. I had to get into Star Byte and find out what she was doing to my board.

It was safer to fix any glitches on Star Byte from outside the system, but I had the option to rewrite Star Byte's programming from within. I'd never used it before—if I made an error, I could overwrite myself and end up trapped inside Star Byte forever, or, worse, dead. Of course, the chances of making such a complete and utter blunder were remote. Still, in the interests of safety, I preferred to do any rewriting of Star Byte's operating system from my terminal.

It seemed this time I didn't have the option. I inserted the VR jack into the socket at the base of my skull.

And dropped into Hell.

* * *

I had been expecting to enter what users referred to as the "Front Door" from which pull-down menus could direct the user to any open pathway. Instead, I was in a swirling mass of color. Spikes of pain shot through my mind.

Screams resounded throughout the terrible kaleidoscopic chaos. Screams of fear. Screams of agony. I could feel a cold wind at the back of my neck. It reached into my skull and the spikes of pain jolted in intensity, constricting my thoughts. Freezing my mind.

Furiously, I entered the backdoor code I had come here to use. Instantly, the screams stopped and I found myself in my personal waiting room. Narla was already there.

She looked me up and down, green eyes blazing with an intensity I didn't understand. The orange bikini had disappeared, leaving her clothed only in her waist-length hair.

Narla walked over to me. I was still shaking with the memory of the pain. And the screams.

"What do you want?" I asked. She didn't answer, just kept coming closer. I couldn't help but stare at her. Genes could never produce a perfect body; everyone had flaws on the Outside. But Narla's programmer had not been saddled with such limitations. Narla stopped mere centimeters away from me. Once again, I caught the odor of that exotic perfume. My heart beat wildly and my knees felt weak.

Narla wrapped her arms around me and whispered in my ear. "You could never imagine what I want."

"Why are you doing this?" My voice cracked as a surge of desire washed over me. God, whoever had programmed Narla had even made her feel warm. I could hear her breathing. Her hair tickled my nose....

Narla laughed and let go of me. Detail by detail, she began disappearing. Fingers, toes, belly button, feet—Narla unraveled before me until only her eyes were left. Twin shimmering green and white globes hung in space a moment before they, too, were gone.

I pulled down the menu option that would allow me to enter the network's programming. I felt weak and disoriented. I imagined I could still smell Narla's perfume.

"Kent!" Joe popped into the waiting room. His construct was battered and broken.

"Joe! Shit, what's happened?" I rushed over to him, my heart pounding out my fear. What could have done this to Joe?

Joe dropped to his knees. "Kent, it's too late. Everything's already started." The voice was even more low-res than usual for Joe.

"Started? What are you talking about?"

Joe looked at me. His construct was missing nose and an eye. His fingers were gone. Someone must have stolen a chunk of his system memory.

"I thought it was just some cultists, maybe Satanists, but it's worse than that," he gasped.

"Satan doesn't really exist, Joe—come on, snap out of it!"

"Maybe he doesn't," Joe agreed. "But there are other gods."

A knot of panic bloomed in my chest. Joe sounded dazed. He wasn't making any sense. Maybe losing system memory while on-line had sent him into shock. I had to get to Star Byte's main program, kick everyone off-line, and find out what was going on.

"Other gods," mumbled Joe. "I remember reading it somewhere. Usually, they're dead. But when the stars are right, they can live and make the world their playground."

"Great story, Joe," I said, desperately trying to remember anything I'd heard about the symptoms of shock. Dammit—I didn't know what to do! I felt helpless watching Joe sit on the waiting room floor babbling about dead gods.

Joe giggled. "You can't stop it, Kent. The stars will be right soon. Star light, star bright!"

Quickly, I entered the special code that would take me from the system's regular user net to the operating system. I felt guilty leaving Joe behind, but I couldn't do anything for him while we were both on-line. I had to get him out—had to get everyone out. I couldn't shake the memory of the screams I'd heard when I'd logged on.

God, they must have been the screams of people being slowly drained of their system memory. I shuddered. What would happen to their minds? At this time of day, there were usually several hundred people on-line at Star Byte. Several hundred people in pain, in shock, maybe dying. The thought was terrifying.

I scanned the operating system. Someone was dumping information into it as fast as it could process. I reached for the override switch I'd programmed in, which would shut down the system and erase all active memory—after kicking out all users.

"No, Kent, don't."

I turned around. Joe was behind me. He had no arms now, and other details, like his hair and his remaining eye, were gone.

"I've got to shut it down," I said. "I've got to get all of us off-line so I can reboot the system from Outside."

"No," whispered Joe. His voice was so low I could barely understand him. "Don't. It's been booby-trapped."

"What?" I demanded. "That's impossible. Only I can get to this switch."

"Impossible?" asked Joe. His construct sank to its knees as its feet disappeared. "Like the way I'm being whittled away? The way the system didn't warn you when Narla grabbed the active memory? What's possible about any of that?"

I thought about it. Joe was right. Nothing that had happened was possible for anyone but the sysop.

"There's nothing else to try," I said. "I'm locked out of everything else."

"You'll kill me," said Joe. Slowly, his legs dissolved.

"So I should just let you disappear?" I watched him, gritting my teeth in anguish. He was suffering terribly and I couldn't do anything. If he were right, I'd kill him right here and now by throwing the switch.

It was one thing to watch your friend suffering, possibly dying, and another thing to pull the switch yourself. Frustration and grief washed all other emotions away.

"What can I do?" I screamed.

"Don't let her make you a killer, Kent," said Joe. "Don't throw the switch."

Anger bubbled up through the anguish. I couldn't do *nothing*. Right or wrong, I had to shut down the system and stop this madness. Besides, Joe didn't know the system like I did. He couldn't know this was his only chance to get off-line.

I turned my back on Joe and threw the switch.

"No..." whispered a low voice behind me. I didn't turn to look. I didn't want to see Joe fade away into madness or death. Of course, there was always the chance that he would be all right once off the system. I clung to that hope.

Someone chuckled behind me. The chuckle was low and rich, soft like velvet. I turned. Joe was gone. In his place stood Narla. Golden robes dripped off narrow shoulders, plunged to the floor and spread outwards in carefully arranged pleats. The intensity I had seen in her eyes before was back, but a thousand times as bright. I had to look away.

"Who are you?" I asked. "What are you doing to my board?"

I glanced towards Narla and saw her smile. It was a cold smile, without a hint of amusement. A chill rippled down my spine.

"It was necessary to distract you," she said, "while you still might have done something to thwart me."

"I've pulled the override switch—that ought to stop you, Narla," I said, realizing, even as I said it, that it hadn't worked. If it had, I would have been kicked off-line along with all the other users.

"The switch was reprogrammed. I'm afraid all your users are dead. Their minds have been...consumed." Narla favored me with a patronizing smile. "Don't blame me—I tried to warn you." She shimmered out of existence for a moment, to be replaced by the image of Joe's damaged construct. Then Narla was back again. She tugged at one of her sleeves idly.

"What about Joe?" God, let him be all right!

"Joe is hardly a concern of yours any longer," said Narla as she finished the inspection of her sleeve. "Or of anyone's."

"Damn you!" I screamed in grief and anger. "Damn you—who do you think you are? Why are you doing this?"

Narla made a slight bow. "My name is Nyarlathotep. Not that it means anything to you, Kent Taylor. And I am doing this so that the stars, after so many eons, will be right once more. Once more the Elder Gods will come forth to revel and destroy in their own mindless way!"

"The stars are right? What does that mean?" I screamed louder as Narla began to disappear. "Tell me!"

"The stars in the heavens are wrong," she said in that honeyed voice as she faded away. "But here they can be anywhere I want them to be for as long as I wish. Good-bye, Kent Taylor." I was alone.

* * *

I wandered around the innards of Star Byte, unable to escape, unable to alter anything around me. Terror had become my constant companion. I was almost used to the constriction in my chest, the rapid breathing, the shaky feeling in my knees and gut.

I was cold. Normally in VR, I don't feel temperature except, as on the beach, when I specifically program temperature into a setting. But now, my bones ached with cold. My teeth throbbed with it.

What was going on? I didn't understand. I wanted to scream and scream until someone answered me. But when I passed the user index file, I saw that, although three hundred and forty-five people besides myself were currently logged onto Star Byte, all three hundred and forty-five files were inactive. Dead.

You killed them said a voice in my head. My own voice. God, was I going crazy? I'd only wanted to help them, to get them off the system. Instead, everyone was gone. Their minds had been drained away, deleted. *Consumed.* I tried not to remember their screams.

Laughter rang throughout the board. I recognized the deep chuckle of Nyarlathotep. It was accompanied by another, more disturbing sound.

Starting softly, then growing slowing in intensity, a single voice shrieked a descant that could have come from no human throat. Other voices chanted along in tones so deep I heard them more in my skull than in my ears. My mind refused to make sense of it. It was inhumanly gleeful and mindless. Panic surged through me; I choked back sobs of horror.

I fled the chanting, but it was everywhere, in everything. It rang throughout the active memory, its horrible uncivilized tune echoing painfully in my bones.

"No!" I screamed over and over, but the chanting and the horrible descant grew louder until I could no longer hear my own voice.

I had to get out of the operating system. I grabbed at a desperate hope; I ran to the first active port I could find and dove into it.

Screams were torn from me as a confusing set of images and sounds impaled my thoughts and pounded on my mind. I was swept along in the chaos as stars and laughter swirled around me.

"Join us, Kent Taylor," said the laughter in Joe's voice. "Join us and feed the power of the Elder Gods. Feel them rising even now from dead and forgotten R'lyeh!"

Caught up in the maelstrom, I spun crazily through the terrible stars towards...towards something monstrous that was just now rising out of the ocean of Star Byte's active memory.

The thing betrayed any attempt of the eyes to focus on it, or of the mind to discern its shape. A long tentacle reached up from the thing towards me. I shrieked as it grabbed my foot and pulled me down, down, down towards its dreadful form.

A star no larger than a marble spun by and I grabbed it, praying I would be able to hold on. The star burned me, but I welcomed the pain, welcomed anything that would blur my memory of the thing that held me in its cold grip, that pulled me towards its gaping maw.

"Kent, you fool," shouted the velvet voice of Nyarlathotep. "You don't know what you're doing! The stars must be right—let go!"

The star burned unholy agony into my mind, but I held on. The terrible chanting stopped, only to be replaced by an awful moaning. The moaning rang painfully in my ears, rising in pitch until it became a shriek. The shriek became an ear-splitting keen. I thought my eardrums would surely burst. The sound rattled through my head, my teeth, down into my gut.

My foot felt as though it would be ripped off. Pain hammered through my leg, up my spine. The star squirmed in my grasp, but I squeezed it more tightly.

And then the pressure from the awful tentacle became too much. The star in my grip was wrenched from its place in the swirling sky. Together, the star and I plummeted, first slowly, then faster and faster, towards the repulsive open mouth of the creature below.

"No!" I couldn't tell if the scream was mine or Nyarlathotep's—everything crashed in on me; stars, nebulae, interstellar dust clouds. I screamed as they tore through my mind and ripped my thoughts from me, then sped away into infinity.

The tugging at my ankle grew fainter and fainter. Finally, it was gone. The star's fire died and I was left, cold and burned, in the memory of Star Byte.

I opened my eyes. Nyarlathotep stood over me. She knelt down. I flinched from the hard glint in her emerald eyes.

"This time, you win," she hissed. "But the stars *will* be right—I will make them so."

She reached down towards the back of my neck as if to pull out the VR jack.

That's impossible, I wanted to say. But I couldn't move, couldn't speak. Nyarlathotep yanked away the cord that bound me to Star Byte and I fell through the dark, formless void into the chair by my computer console.

I was trembling violently and soaked with sweat. I felt my neck for the VR jack, but it had been torn out of the socket and flung across the room.

I stumbled painfully into the bathroom and threw up. After a few minutes, I felt strong enough to splash some water on my face. Then I crawled back to the computer.

ALL FILES PURGED read the screen. I typed in a query, but it was true: everything in Star Byte was gone. The board no longer existed. Not the games, not the beach, not the constructs.

Not the people.

I sobbed, grief dragging me down into black misery. Joe gone. All those other users gone. And for what? So some dead gods could play with the Earth, with humanity?

I sobbed until the sobs turned into screams and the screams into deep, chaotic dreams that grabbed my thoughts and squeezed me down, down, down into the dark.

* * *

I woke up in a hospital. They told me I'd been there three months. Three months since the day a freak hailstorm had scrambled Star Byte's system and killed three hundred and forty-five net users.

The doctors shook their heads and said I was lucky; I was the only on-line user who'd escaped with my life. The police, the insurance people, and the power company had investigated the disaster, but had not found me to be at fault. It had been an accident, they said. One in a billion chance of ever happening again.

The doctors offered me the use of their hospital net. They wanted me to take advantage of their stress-reduction programs, get my mind off what happened.

But I refused. I'll never use VR again. That part of me is dead. As dead as Joe. As dead as the nameless Elder Gods trapped in R'lyeh.

Even so, I do not feel safe. I'll never feel safe again. Nyarlathotep may have failed this time, but there are other boards out there, other VR universes to corrupt. This time she picked mine.

Maybe next time, she'll pick yours.

INCLUDES RARE OUT-OF-PRINT TALES!

AVAILABLE NOW

All of the important tales from the Lovecraft Circle of writers about the terrible Mythos horror known as Hastur. Includes out-of-print rarities unavailable to most fans of horror fiction.
THE HASTUR CYCLE

Chaosium Fiction

TO ORDER CALL 1-510-547-7681
or write 950-A 56th Street
Oakland CA 94608

INCLUDES RARE OUT-OF-PRINT TALES!

AVAILABLE NOW

CALL OF CTHULHU FICTION

MYSTERIES of the WORM

CTHULHU CYCLE BOOK

New Second Edition, Revised & Expanded

By **Robert Bloch**

Early Tales of the Cthulhu Mythos
By the Author of PSYCHO

Robert M. Price SERIES EDITOR

Chaosium

A collection of early tales of the Cthulhu Mythos written by Robert Bloch, the author of PSYCHO.
MYSTERIES OF THE WORM
#6002, $9.95
ISBN 1-56882-012-7

Chaosium Fiction

TO ORDER CALL 1-510-547-7681
or write 950-A 56th Street
Oakland CA 94608

FANTASTIC FICTION

Allilile wakes from a long illness to find herself within a shadowy, enormous fortress in the company of strangers. Amidst decaying grandeur and still-powerful magics, she explores the world within the walls of the castle, and penetrates its secrets to he peril.

A collection of ancient Gloranthan manuscripts published for the first time. This book provides an anecdotal chronology for the history of Dragon Pass, from the extermination of all life in the Dragonkill war, its eventual resettlement by humankind, the Lunar Empire's invasion and conquest of the Pass,

Chaosium Fiction

TO ORDER CALL 1-510-547-7681
or write 950-A 56th Street
Oakland CA 94608

Chaosium Inc.
SELECTED TITLES
SINCE 1974

FICTION

THE HASTUR CYCLE
#6001, $9.95 - Cthulhu Mythos stories by the original authors including some rare, impossible-to-find tales.

●ISBN 1-56882-009-7

MYSTERIES OF THE WORM
#6002, $9.95 - A collection of Lovecraftian tales written by master storyteller Robert Bloch.

●ISBN 1-56882-012-7

CTHULHU'S HEIRS
#6003, $9.95 - New Cthulhu Mythos fiction! This trade paperback contains 19 original stories and 2 rare reprints focusing on the Cthulhu Mythos and the mosnters, denizens, worshipers, and victims thereof.

●ISBN 1-56882-013-5

CASTLE OF EYES
#6000, $14.95 - A woman wakes from pain-filled dreams to find herself trapped in the Castle of Eyes.

●ISBN 1-56882-005-4

KING OF SARTAR
#4500, $14.95 - The facts, history, and secrets of Prince Argrath's heroic struggle against the invading Lunar Empire.

●ISBN 0-933635-99-0

CARD GAME

CREDO!
The Game of Dueling Dogmas

#1011, $14.95 - A new card game combining hilarity with history for two or more players. Players represent factions of the early Christian church, competing for flock and striving to have your doctrines accepted as the belief of the one Church.

●ISBN 1-56882-008-9

ELRIC!

ELRIC! is a new heroic, swords & sorcery roleplaying game based on

Chaosium Inc.　　　　　1-510-547-7681

the fantasy novels of noted British author Michael Moorcock.

ELRIC!
#2900, $19.95 - Everything that you need to play including rules, character-creation instructions, hints, tips, and adventures.

• ISBN 0-933635-98-2

MELNIBONÉ
#2901, $20.95 - Background, new magic, and adventures.

• ISBN 1-56882-001-1

THE ELRIC GAMEMASTER SCREEN
#2902, $14.95 - Summaries of important rules, spells, tables, and special options for combat.

• ISBN 1-56882-011-9

ROGUE MISTRESS
#2111, $18.95 - A high-powered, dangerous campaign aboard a dimension-traveling ship.

• ISBN 0-933635-73-7

SORCERERS OF PAN TANG
#2112, $18.95 - Evil bad-guys and chief rivals of the Melnibonéans. This book includes background on Pan Tang, a map of the island, notes on their history and their magic.

• ISBN 0-933635-79-6

PERILS OF THE YOUNG KINGDOMS
#2113, $18.95 - Five adventures exploring marvelous, mysterious, and treacherous locales.

• ISBN 0-933635-82-6

SEA KINGS OF THE PURPLE TOWNS
#2114, $18.95 - The mercantile center of the Young Kingdoms and a haven for adventurers.

• ISBN 1-56882-000-3

CALL OF CTHULHU

A horror roleplaying game set in the world of the Cthulhu Mythos, as described by H. P. Lovecraft, the father of modern horror.

CALL OF CTHULHU

#2336, $21.95 - Contains everything that you need to play, except dice. Includes character generation, extensive background, notes on the Dreamland sand playing in the 1990s and 1890s.

•ISBN 0-933635-86-9

TERROR AUSTRALIS

#2319, $17.95 - A source book for the Land Down Under.

•ISBN 0-933635-40-0

THE GREAT OLD ONES

#2321, $17.95 - Six different looks at particular Great Old Ones or their influences.

•ISBN 0-933635-38-9

cover art for
ADVENTURES IN ARKHAM COUNTRY

cover art for
CALL OF CTHULHU

MANSIONS OF MADNESS

#2327, $17.95 - Five frightening adventures.

•ISBN 0-933635-63-X

FATAL EXPERIMENTS

#2328, $18.95 - Three adventures including an encounter with the King in Yellow.

•ISBN 0-933635-72-9

BLOOD BROTHERS

#2329, $18.95 - 13 one-night scenarios, all based on familiar themes typical of the kind found in B-movies.

•ISBN 0-933635-69-9

RETURN TO DUNWICH

#2330, $18.95 - An accursed backwoods town.

•ISBN 0-933635-71-0

Chaosium Inc.
1-510-547-7681

cover art for
ESCAPE FROM INNSMOUTH

HORROR ON THE ORIENT EXPRESS

#2331, $39.95 - Our largest adventure pack ever, set on and along the route of the Orient Express.

•ISBN 0-933635-76-1

TALES OF THE MISKATONIC VALLEY

#2334, $18.95 - Six adventures in settings along the Miskatonic River.

•ISBN 0-933635-83-4

FEARFUL PASSAGES

#2335, $18.95 - A collection of adventures focusing on transportation in the 1920s.

•ISBN 0-933635-87-7

ESCAPE FROM INNSMOUTH

#2338, $20.95 - A complete description of shadowy Innsmouth.

•ISBN 0-933635-65-6

THE THING AT THE

THRESHOLD

#2339, $16.95 - A campaign from Arkham to England to the Dead Sea.

•ISBN 0-933635-90-7

BLOOD BROTHERS II

#2340, $18.95 - They're B-movies, they're bad, and they're back.

•ISBN 0-933635-91-5

ADVENTURES IN ARKHAM COUNTRY

#2342, $18.95 - Adventures which take place in or around Arkham, Dunwich, Innsmouth, and Kingsport.

•ISBN 1-56882-004-6

INVESTIGATOR'S COMPANION VOLUME I

#2343, $10.95 - Are there flashlights in the 1920s? Flashbulbs? Discover the types of equipment, research facilities, and firearms available

•ISBN 1-56882-007-0

cover art for
H.P.L.'s DREAMLANDS

KEEPER'S COMPENDIUM

#2344, $12.95 - A supplement created especially for keepers. Expands upon Forbidden Books, Secret Cults, Alien Races, and Mysterious Places.

•ISBN 1-56882-010-0

INVESTIGATOR'S COMPANION VOLUME II

#2346, $10.95 - More exciting data on the 1920s, focusing on the Occupations and Skills from that era.

•ISBN 1-56882-018-6

YE BOOKE OF MONSTRES

#2349, $10.95 - A collection of new horrible and generally unfriendly creatures for use with CALL OF CTHULHU.

•ISBN 1-56882-019-4

CTHULHU CASEBOOK

#3305, $19.95 - Nine terrifying adventures.

•ISBN 0-933635-67-2

CURSE OF CTHULHU

#3306, $19.95 - Visit Egypt, Transylvania, the moon, and the alien library at Celaeno.

•ISBN 0-933635-74-5

CTHULHU NOW

#3307, $16.95 - A source book for the 1990s.

•ISBN 0-933635-51-6

H.P.L.'s DREAMLANDS

#3308, $16.95 - The lands beyond the wall of sleep.

•ISBN 0-933635-97-4

GASLIGHT ADVENTURES

DARK DESIGNS

#2332, $18.95 - Explore the occult in 1890s England.

•ISBN 0-933635-75-3

SACRAMENTS OF EVIL

#2345, $18.95 - Six adventures set in 1890s England, the green and pleasant land at the height of its glory.

●ISBN 1-56882-015-1

MODERN DAY

AT YOUR DOOR

#2326, $17.95 - Uncover the secret agenda of the Full Wilderness environmental organization.

●ISBN 0-933635-64-8

THE STARS ARE RIGHT!

#2337, $18.95 - Modern era. A radio telescope detects the presence of an alien body.

●ISBN 0-933635-88-5

GUIDES & SOURCEBOOKS

FIELD GUIDE TO CREATURES OF THE DREAMLANDS

#5107, $15.95 - 27 frightening creatures from beyond the wall of sleep.

●ISBN 0-933635-52-4

COC5 KEEPER'S KIT

#5110, $14.95 - A keeper's screen measuring 40" across, Lovecraft Country adventure, bookmark, condensed rules and tables, special character sheets, and scale model of the Strange High House In The Mist.

●ISBN 1-933635-96-6

INVESTIGATOR SHEETS

#5111, $8.95 - A pad of two-color forms useful to every Cthulhu player.

●ISBN 1-56882-002-X

DIRE DOCUMENTS

#5112, $8.95 - Letter heads, commitment papers, release papers, and other items.

●ISBN 1-56882-003-8

PENDRAGON

Based on the legends of King Arthur, Lancelot, Guenever, and the Knights of the Round Table.

PENDRAGON

#2716, $26.95 - The basic rules; includes everything that you need to play, except dice. New features include Celtic magic system.

●ISBN 1-56882-006-2

THE BOY KING

#2708, $18.95 - A complete cam-

cover art for
PAGAN SHORE

paign covering the entire reign of King Arthur.

●ISBN 0-933635-78-8

SAVAGE MOUNTAINS

#2710, $18.95 - Four adventures set in the wild mountains of legendary Wales.

●ISBN 0-933635-81-8

BLOOD LUST

#2711, $18.95 - A medium-length campaign set across Britain.

●ISBN 0-933635-84-2

PERILOUS FOREST

#2712, $18.95 - Extensive background for western Cumbria and the Perilous Forest.

●ISBN 0-933635-44-3

PAGAN SHORE

#2713, $18.95 - Extensive background information about the mysterious realm of Ireland, her people, and her hisotry. Complete with rules on creating Irish characters and Irish magic.

●ISBN 1-56882-016-X

THE SPECTRE KING

#2714, $18.95 - Six heroic adventures.

●ISBN 0-933635-94-X

ELFQUEST

ELFQUEST is a fantasy roleplaying game based on the best-selling graphic novels of the same name, published by Father Tree Press.

SEA ELVES

#2603, $7.95 - Background and details about a band of isolated elves living on an archipelago.

●ISBN 0-933635-24-9